SLAYING
the
SHIFTER
PRINCE

CLARE SAGER

For the women who are more sharp than sweet.
May we all find the ones who appreciate that.

CONTENT WARNINGS

Please note this is a revenge story featuring cruelty, violence and fantasies about violence and punishment. It contains themes of an adult nature, including the following:

- Sexual threat.
- Murder.
- References to sexual assault.
- Brief mentions of stillbirth and the death of a child.
- Primal play.
- Light blood play.
- This is a villain romance with bully elements. The MMC behaves in ways we'd never expect a hero to.

I

Ten years.

It was a long time to wait.

But revenge was a patient master, and I was its creature.

From up here in the fly loft, the stage looked so small... and yet the audience looked smaller. In the dimness, they stared at the performers who threw flame into the air. The jugglers caught it, tumbled with it, danced with it, like it was a beautiful partner and not a deadly one.

At my side, Eric shifted, worrying the cuff of his shirt. He wasn't usually this agitated, and we'd fucked twice today, so he'd had a chance to get out his pent up energy.

Then again, this wasn't any usual performance.

And this wasn't any usual audience, as a pair of horns jutting from the darkness reminded me.

These were fae.

Prince Sepher of the Dawn Court lived here outside the capital—exiled. (I might've had something to do with that.)

In his exile, he'd gathered the misfits and the monstrous—the fae who struggled to fit in at the capital and instead dwelled in the Court of Monsters.

And monsters they were.

At the back, I spotted one with leathery wings, another with feathered. Various horns, curled like a ram's or stubby and short like a young goat's, as well as branched antlers that caught the stage light.

My prince had no horns. But he was the most monstrous of them all.

From up here, he was only a shadow amongst his followers, but I knew what those shadows hid.

Claws. Fangs. Slitted pupils. A tail that had swept in agitation the one time I'd properly seen him.

More animal than fae.

I didn't bother to keep the sneer from my face—they couldn't see me up here in the theatre's labyrinthine catwalks.

Eric and I sat above the stage, legs dangling. The prince had quite a set-up in his partially ruined palace with its own theatre. The walkways up here were chaotic and jumbled, some repaired. Below, an impressive thrust stage extended into the seating, allowing the audience to sit on three sides.

It was my favourite stage set-up, giving me the opportunity to perform left and right, making eyes at my spectators, angling my poses to best excite them. Tonight, I'd have one focus, though. He sat right at the end of the stage, front and centre, in a large, gilded chair.

At my side, on the far more mundane seat of the catwalk's timber, Eric chewed a cuticle. His sovereign ring caught the light, the little flower engraved in its flat surface glinting.

"You'll ruin your hands." I gave him a sidelong look.

With a huff, he thrust his fingers into his lap. But a moment later, he was chewing his lip.

"I'll be fine." I squeezed his thigh, running my thumb along solid muscle. They were quite impressive muscles, too, thanks to hours rehearsing and performing on the trapeze.

He pressed his lips together. "Hmm."

My reassurance was a lie. And from his reaction, he knew it.

I didn't expect to survive the night. But as long as I was successful, as long as I ripped apart that bastard prince with my iron blade, it didn't matter.

"Are you sure about this, Zita?"

Not my real name, of course. Average women from Albion didn't have such exotic names. That was exactly why I'd chosen it for the stage.

The great and beautiful Zita will spin impossible feats before your very eyes. It had much more of a ring to it than *Marigold will dance in a suspended hoop and try not to fall and break her neck.*

In performance, it was all about the sell.

"Am I sure? Hmm, I don't know." I pulled a thoughtful face, touching my chin. "It's only been a decade in the making. Let me think... Of course I'm bloody sure. That bastard thinks he got away with it. It's about time his past caught up with him." My smile was stiff and sharp—it might've looked more like a snarl.

Eric's jaw flexed as he searched my eyes and finally inclined his head.

Below, the jugglers—a dozen brothers and sisters who lit up the stage with constant movement—took their marks, ready to form a pyramid for their frenetic finale.

That was my cue to get ready.

3

Heart keeping constant time despite the speeding music, I rose into a crouch. "Aren't you going to tell me to break a leg?"

"You don't need luck," he muttered, eyes still on the Lightning Siblings and their leaping flame.

With a scoff, I pecked his cheek. Then, on impulse, instead of heading to my mark, I cupped his jaw and pulled him to face me. His dark eyes widened, glinting in the light spilling from the stage.

I took my time kissing him—it might be my last, after all —and finished by nibbling his lower lip. His groan was soft, but the fact I'd drawn it from him made my resolve all the harder.

Before I could turn away and finally act upon that resolve, he gripped my arm. "I love you, Zita."

I blinked at him, replaying the words.

If I'd been another girl in another life, in another place and time, my heart might've skipped in my chest. My stomach might've fluttered like butterflies on a summer afternoon. My skin might've warmed with happiness or pleasure or the simple rightness of a handsome young man telling me he loved me.

But *ifs* were not reality.

I was me, and this was my life.

Once upon a time, I'd loved him, perhaps.

Before.

I couldn't really remember how that had felt, only the fleeting thoughts that went with it. The way I'd watched him practise on the trapeze. The way I'd look away when he caught me. The way I'd envied my sister when he watched her perform, while I skulked around helping backstage, unseen in the shadow cast by her brilliant light.

She might as well have been a different person for all I'd changed since then.

That girl would've giggled or smiled or sighed at his confession of love.

But me?

I felt nothing.

My chest was a cavern that could never be filled.

Only one thing would end that yawning emptiness.

And tonight, I'd have it.

2

A hush descended over the theatre as darkness filled the stage. My heart was a lead weight in my chest these days, but this anticipation was the closest I got to joy. The bated breath of a whole audience waiting for me.

With a deep inhale, I settled back against my hoop, thighs holding me as I curved along its inside edge like the crescent moon. It lowered into place, stopping smoothly, and the spotlight hit me.

The music hadn't yet begun, so I heard the collective intake of breath as my skin-tight costume sent motes of light scattering around the auditorium.

One of the reasons the Gilded Suns was the most successful performance troupe in Albion and the only one invited to Elfhame was our fae-worked lights. The manager had paid a pretty penny for them—an investment, she'd called it. And gods, had she been right.

Oil lamps were nothing compared to the pure white glow lighting me now.

I blinked and turned my gaze to my audience. They were just shadows from up here, but each person would swear I was looking right into *their* eyes. Performance was a seduction, one I was very good at.

Below, the musicians began. A lone cello at first, joined by violins, a double bass, drums, and more as the sound grew.

I kept my lashes low and hinted at a smile before tipping from the hoop. Another gasp, harder this time as I fell for a fleeting second.

One leg extended, back arched, I caught myself and held the pose as the hoop spun slowly.

The music rose and swept. I was part of it, a creature of rhythm and movement. My pulse was its tempo. The rush of my blood was its hymn.

Through the hoop, under it, over it, holding by hand, elbow, the crook of my knee, and for one move, just the nape of my neck. I pushed harder into every single move than I ever had before. I needed the prince to believe this performance, to be captivated by it—to be captivated by *me*.

I'd heard swallows spent their life on the wing. My performance was like that. Not once did my feet touch the floor as I spun, sometimes fast, sometimes achingly slow, letting my audience get a good view of my body posed for their pleasure.

My sister used to say it was the closest thing to flight. As she'd danced in the air like this, she'd worn a look of pure joy —eyes bright, teeth beaming in a wide smile.

I felt none of that. Not tonight, and not any other night.

But I held her face in my mind, or at least its fragile memory, as my gaze flicked back to the prince upon his throne.

The low light caught on the edge of a straight nose, the curve of a smirk, the glint of an eye.

I didn't believe in the gods anymore. If I did, I might've asked them to make sure that eye was on me.

But of course it was.

That was why I'd blistered and bled on this hoop, that was why my muscles sang through each move, a sweet burn as I pushed harder and harder. It was all for this.

For him.

For *her*.

Tonight, she would be avenged.

AT LAST, my performance reached its crescendo, and I spun with dizzying speed, held in the hoop by my legs spread in the splits.

Less inhibited than humans, fae loved that pose, and I always caught many of them staring openly between my thighs.

I didn't say performance was a *subtle* seduction.

I let my hoop slow as the music faded and the lads on the weights lowered me. With a flip, I landed and took a bow to rapturous applause.

Back arched, tits and arse sticking out, I turned to each side of the stage, keenly aware it was *him* I stood before.

He sat back, one ankle crossed over his knee, but I felt his attention. It was a weight, a subtle pressure in the air. If I'd been alone, it might've been a tickle at the back of my neck that said danger.

And this *was* dangerous—his claws or fangs could rip out my throat—but it was a danger I welcomed. One I sought.

At last, I turned my full attention to him and gave one final bow. Just on the edge of the light, his clawed fingers tightened on the arm of his throne.

Perfect.

The lights winked out.

In the darkness, I hurried to the wings. "You were mesmerising, Zita," the eldest of the Lightning Siblings said, her eyes round and glinting in the low light. "What's got into you? I think that was your best performance yet."

"Thanks. Gotta do something special for my swan song." I peeked out through a gap in the curtain, ignoring her confused sound.

The house lights went up. From this angle, I couldn't see the prince's face, only his body on its stupid throne. It was a large body, broad-shouldered, thick with muscle. His shirt hung open like he was proud of it.

I looked forward to seeing that body at my feet, blood emptying across the floor.

Eric edged along the aisle to him and bent in for the same quiet conversation he had with important folk at the end of every show. I didn't need to hear his words to know how it went.

"Would Your Highness like a private performance? The artist of your choice."

The prince leant forward, and I caught a glimpse of the edge of a square jaw. He touched his chin, thoughtful. He must've asked a question, because Eric nodded and gestured to the stage.

Was he asking for me, though?

For this to work, he had to. I'd saved a year's wages for this costume with crystals like sunlight. It was meant to be irresistible for him, a son of the Day King.

Eric held still, the lines of his body taut as though he hung on an answer.

I held my breath.

From the audience emerged a horned fae who strode down the aisle, grinning as he swept Eric aside.

"No, you bastard," I hissed, fingers knotting in the edge of the curtain. He was ruining everything. Ten years of work. All that planning. All that preparation.

The interrupting prick cocked his head, saying something as he leant against the throne.

I'd only ever wanted to kill the prince before this moment, but right now, I'd gladly add him to the list.

Gaze flicking this way, where he knew I'd be watching, Eric took a step back.

"No, stay," I hissed, staring like I could make him feel my will. "Try again. Wait for him to—"

The prince's hand shot out and closed around the horned fae's throat. The fae's head jerked back as he was dragged halfway across the throne. I could just see him in profile, eye wide, jaw slack as he had a very intense conversation with his prince.

He was thrust away, the collar of his shirt staining red. The prince didn't look armed, but he didn't need manufactured weapons when he had natural ones, did he?

I swallowed as he raised his hand and beckoned Eric close with a bloodied finger. He bent and spoke in my friend's ear, his mouth edging into view. Curved lips, as cruel as I remembered them, and those long, sharp canines.

Instead of smiling, Eric frowned and bowed his head like a man defeated.

Shit.

No.

It couldn't be.

I'd worked so hard.

This performance, this outfit, my hair—they were all just as hers had been that night. He'd found her so irresistible, he hadn't been able to keep himself from taking her life, and he was meant to find me just as irresistible tonight.

How had I failed?

My fingernails cut into my palms.

How could he not remember her? How could he not remember *killing* her? Day by day, even when Eric fucked me, it was all I could think of.

My sister's body on the floor. That fae bastard bent over her, taking a lock of hair like the sick fuck he was.

At last, Eric left the prince's side and looked up at me.

He nodded.

And *that* was the closest thing to joy.

I'd waited ten years for this. Ten years of blisters and rage. Ten years of this cold deadness inside. Ten years when no joy or pleasure had been able to reach me.

Tonight, it would end.

And I was going to savour every gods damned moment.

3

I had a whole sketchbook full of him. The angled planes of his cheeks. The proud line of his so very fucking regal jaw. The red hair streaked with creamy white. I'd drawn it a hundred times so I wouldn't forget. I'd nursed my obsession, my rage, my hurt, and my desire to destroy.

It still hadn't prepared me for the sight of him on his throne, now brought into a large, private room.

I waited in a curtained alcove, ready to make my entrance.

"An intimate performance"—that's what I'd told Eric to say. Those exact words. The advertisement was also a seduction. While "intimate" might *seem* innocent, merely referring to the fact it would only be him and me, we all knew what it really meant.

I'd been doing it for years. Private performances that became very intimate indeed.

Sometimes just nudity, but other times, I let them fuck me hard, fast, slow, however they wanted. I didn't take pleasure from it, but I took a healthy chunk of extra cash and pretty gifts. They all went into my costumes and gilding myself with jewellery and expensive treatments for my hair and skin.

My body was my work, my tool, and tonight, my weapon.

I waited until he shifted in his seat, signalling restlessness. My aerial silks had been secured to the rafters, ending a foot in front of him.

And above, next to their knots, sat an iron dagger.

The iron made my slumbering magic cringe into an even smaller ball, but it would do worse to a fae.

Another object I'd traded my body to get.

Such things couldn't be bought in any regular shop. Not when iron was banned in Albion. But there was a market for everything, if you only knew where to look.

I'd had ten years to search.

It hummed in my veins now. Something close to true feeling.

When he shifted a second time, nostrils flaring as he went to rise, I sauntered out from behind the curtain.

Under a sheer robe, this costume was black. Better to hide the inevitable blood. Where the white one had covered me from neck to ankle and wrist, this one was cut high over my hips and scooped low at the neck and back. Practice in front of a mirror had told me that when I hung upside down, it teetered tantalisingly close to exposing my tits. Only a thin strip of fabric covered my pussy.

Perfect for an *intimate performance*.

And perfect to distract him while I pulled my blade across his throat.

I let that thought curl my mouth as I approached, keeping my eyes on him.

He watched, sitting back in his throne now, chin lifted so he looked down upon me.

When I ended him, I would make him gaze *up* at me. I would make him see the look on my face as I did it. Let him witness my joy, at last.

Zinnia hadn't deserved to die like that. My sister—my dear, sweet sister. My only family.

But he deserved this.

I stopped in the space between his parted legs, not touching. Not yet.

Seduction didn't start with touching.

"Your Highness," I purred and bowed into his space, giving him an excellent view of my cleavage.

His feline eyes might've unnerved me if I hadn't spent ten years drawing them over and over and over. Thank the nonexistent gods for preparation.

I kept my gaze on his and was rewarded by the sight of those odd pupils expanding.

Success.

I slid the tie of my robe between my fingers, the well-practiced gesture snaring his attention. "Perhaps Your Highness would care to...?" I finished the sentence by canting my head, one eyebrow rising as I offered him the end of the tie.

He took the bait.

Oh, this was going to be so easy. So perfect. I would bathe in his blood and finally, *finally* feel something. I wouldn't even care when his guards came in and cut me down.

It would all be worth it.

Slowly, he wrapped the tie around his hand, once. Twice. Again and again. I couldn't tear my eyes away from his dark claws, currently retracted to small points that looked no more threatening than sharp fingernails.

Much as I wanted to make him pay by taking it slow, I would need to strike decisively. If those claws ripped out my

14

throat before I landed a killing blow, this would all be for nothing.

The bow pulled loose and he didn't stop. He didn't stop, in fact, until he'd pulled it off the robe entirely and had the full length wound around his knuckles.

I swallowed, something trickling down my spine.

Maybe he wouldn't be so easy to manipulate as I'd thought. Taking the tie—it was a possessive act, an arrogant one. One that said he didn't need my invitation and he wouldn't stop at its boundary. He would take what he wanted, when he wanted.

His golden eyes on me, hard and dark, said the same.

But I looked up at him from below my lashes, gave a coy smile, and shrugged the robe off my shoulders. It fluttered to the floor, pooling around my feet.

I held still, body tight as he took it in with one slow sweep of those odd eyes. If he decided to take me now, I wouldn't even get my hands on my dagger.

"I designed this choreography for Your Highness. When I heard you'd invited us to perform, I knew I had to create something truly special just for you."

None of it was a lie. Not technically.

I took a step back and mounted the silks, glad to be out of his reach.

Here, the nervy tightness left me. Here, there was only room for precise movement, for muscles to pull and bunch in the illusion of effortless grace.

I sank into the performance, not quite losing myself in it. Not when every nerve was aware of *him*. So close. So fucking close.

His hands rested on the arms of his throne, a tumbler of amber liquid in one. The tie from my robe lay discarded across his lap. He followed my movements with hooded eyes. Lazy and bored, half-drunk. I'd seen dozens like him. The bored and wealthy, only interested in entertainment and pleasure. It worked well for me.

When I stretched and danced low on the silks, their lengths wrapped around my ankles and wrists, his eyes fixed on those bindings. I'd had other patrons who liked to tie me in them and fuck me while suspended. No doubt, he was imagining doing just that. His pupils had blown wide, and every breath came as a deep rise and fall of his chest.

Distracted. This was my time.

I worked my way up the silks, posing as I wrapped them around me, noting the point that would have me stopping level with him. I would hold his gaze as I sliced his throat.

When the blood sprayed, I wouldn't blink.

Once I reached the top, I pointed my toes and spread my legs, doing the splits in mid air. While that sight kept him occupied, I reached up onto the beam. There was a moment's relief when my fingers closed on my dagger's leather-wrapped hilt. If someone had found it and removed it...

But they hadn't.

It was mine.

And in about ten seconds, so too would vengeance.

"For Zinnia," I whispered and let go.

I wheeled through the air as the silk unwrapped. On a stage, this move drew a gasp from the crowd as they feared I wouldn't stop. I always did, though, exactly where I intended to, and this was no different.

Jolting upright, I landed and straddled him. His hooded eyes drank up every motion, making my skin prickle. His body was as solid as it looked, powerful like the beast he was. This close, I could smell honeyed whisky on his breath, feel the

heat of his skin, taste the coppery victory of the blood I was about to spill.

I smiled as though this was the seduction he expected and let my gaze lower to his lips like I was going to kiss him.

They curled.

Heart pounding, its throb echoed in my temples and throat. I raised my dagger to one side, ready to slash.

Without dropping my gaze or his smirk, he closed his hand around my wrist.

My heart stuttered, but I didn't have time to worry or even think. I dropped the blade and caught it in my other hand.

A swift stab upwards and this would be over.

I thrust, biceps springing.

He grabbed that wrist.

No.

Tighter than his grip on me, something seized my heart. Something cold and dead. Something that squeezed. I couldn't breathe, couldn't shake him off, couldn't think straight.

I could only stare into those golden eyes with their slitted pupils and think how much they looked like a cat's staring down at its prey.

"Oh dear, little bird," he murmured. "What have you done?"

4

I should've been afraid. He was surely about to kill me. But all I could think about was how I'd let my sister down. And all I could feel was... nothing.

Just my heart thundering so fast, so hard, my ribs had to be close to shattering. Was I having a heart attack?

If that didn't kill me, he would. Which would be worse?

I tried to clutch my chest, but he held tight, the tips of his claws threatening my skin with ten pinpricks.

"Now, now, little bird. No fighting. You had your chance." His canines showed as he smiled.

"Guards." He didn't take his eyes off me when he called. The door opened much too quickly, like they'd been expecting this.

But that was impossible.

He jerked his chin at the dozen fae. "Bring my new friend."

With inhuman strength, he pulled me from the silks and yanked my arms together. He bound them behind my back with the tie from my robe and, one hand on my shoulder, forced me to the floor.

The floorboards bit into my knees, hard and smooth.

Everything was too bright, too loud, too much. I hadn't seen so much, felt so much for years. That had to be the pain in my chest—shock from a speeding pulse where it had plodded, deadened for so long.

How ironic that my body chose now to wake when I was surely about to die.

Ha-ha-fucking-ha.

But I'd expected to die tonight. I'd long made my peace with that.

What I hadn't expected or made peace with was failure.

I was supposed to die bathed in blood and victory, smiling viciously as his guards rushed in and cut me down. Although I was no fighter, I'd take as many as I could with me—I had my silks and speed. They would be enough to let me take down at least one. I'd do so knowing that in the next place I'd see my sister again, knowing I'd be able to tell her how I'd made him pay.

But this?

I twisted against my bindings, but a large hand closed over my shoulder, claws pricking my collarbone.

"I told you." His voice was a low purr of warning that made goosebumps rise on my arms.

I'd failed.

"What are you going to do with me?"

"Patience. You'll soon discover the price for your assassination attempt. I must say I'm surprised. I always expected it to come eventually, but I never thought they'd send a *human*."

Before I could work out what he meant, the door opened again, and the world tilted.

"Eric?" He was no friend of the prince's. They must've brought the wrong person. They must've misunderstood his instruction. Or else he'd come to beg for leniency. I glanced over my shoulder at the prince.

He bent close, took a handful of my hair, and angled my head so he could murmur in my ear. "Your uncertainty is delicious. Keep it up, treacherous little creature."

Straightening, he gestured towards me and smiled at Eric. "You were right. She did attack me."

My heart ticked slower and slower, each beat deafening. I'd misheard. Eric couldn't have—

"And with an iron dagger." The prince held the blade between finger and thumb like it was something scraped off the sole of his shoe.

"Eric?" I couldn't blink, but no matter how much I stared, he refused to so much as look at me.

He'd been there for it all. From the day Zinnia and I had joined the Gilded Suns, fleeing my arcane accident, through her murder, my training and planning, all the way to this now.

This betrayal.

The word was a fishbone in my throat. A spear in my chest. It mingled with the fear, cutting me open in a way I hadn't felt since finding my sister's lifeless body.

The prince gestured for Eric to approach. "I'll let you two enjoy a few final words."

With a ghoulish grin, he skulked off to my silks, which now hung empty. He gave a thoughtful frown, fingers running along their lengths.

The claws that had been retracted now lengthened. With slow purpose, he tore them down the fabric.

Eyes on the prince, Eric edged close as though he didn't

want "a few final words." He paused before me, staring somewhere over my head.

I managed to choke out, "Why?"

"I'm sorry," he whispered, words covered by the sound of ripping silk. He shook his head, lips pressed together until they went almost as pale as the rest of his face. "I had to think of the troupe. I couldn't let your vengeance destroy us all."

"It wouldn't have. It was mine—*mine* alone."

"No." His nostrils flared as the word echoed through the room, and his gaze snapped to mine. "It was never just yours. It would've got us all killed. You couldn't even see it." He huffed, shaking his head. "Your sister is gone. And it's awful and tragic, but you're still here—*I'm* still here. Yet all I ever got of you were pieces and moments... and I don't think you were even there for most of them."

Jealous. He was jealous of my sister and my planning—my need for revenge. That was why he'd stopped me.

I opened my mouth to tell him what a fool he was when the prince yawned.

Yawned.

I gritted my teeth as something hot rolled through me, like fire consuming spilt liquor.

"Yes, yes." He turned from the tattered silks and approached. "All *very* fascinating. But we have a punishment to be getting on with." He waved at Eric dismissively and nodded at his guards. "Pay the man."

"Pay?" I hadn't intended to speak, but the word fell from my lips on a breath.

"He did me a service. Never let it be said the Prince of Monsters is stingy." Again, that cruel and dazzling smile.

Had Eric told the truth? Was the sake of the troupe why he'd betrayed me? Or was it just for money?

One of the guards opened the door and waited, giving Eric an expectant look.

He glanced at me. At least he had the good fucking grace to appear contrite. "What will happen to her?"

"She was caught red-handed about to murder me. There are witnesses." The prince nodded at his guards. "They saw her with the blade in her hand, straddling me. And *you* told me exactly what she had planned."

Eric took a step towards the fae, but guards caught his arms. "What does that mean?"

"By our laws, it means I, a prince of this realm, may cast summary judgement, and I find her *guilty*." He lifted his chin.

"Bring my sword."

5

Goosebumps flooded my bare flesh as a guard left carrying my dagger, disappearing with the one weapon that could kill the prince.

I pulled against the bindings on my wrists. But he had tied them well.

His claws pricked my shoulder. "Now, now, human. Don't think you can come into *my* home with an iron blade, try to kill me, and then escape your punishment." He clicked his tongue as he circled in front of me.

From his great height, he peered down at me. My performance lights gleamed upon his perfect, smooth skin, highlighting the fact he was no human. He might've been the statue of a god—a cruel one, with the sneering smirk on his lips. An arrogant one, with the look he gave me.

I gritted my teeth and glared back, hands fisted uselessly. "You bastard."

But that only made him smile more. "No, murderous little beast, it's pronounced *master*."

The guard who'd left reappeared at his side, head bowing as he held up a large sword, emeralds set in its hilt.

"Good." A fierce smile showed his teeth as he took the blade. With a casual twist of his wrist, he spun it, as though re-familiarising himself with the weight and balance. It sang through the air—a deadly version of my own dance upon the silks.

As the lights caught its edge, realisation coalesced.

Hands tied, on my knees at his feet—this was my execution.

Something cold unfurled in me. It seized my breaths, making them shallow and fast.

I twisted at the bindings, not ready to give up. But for all that I was stubborn, they were stronger and didn't shift a hair's breadth.

"You have been found guilty, Zita of the Gilded Suns." He seemed to grow even taller, as though regality filled him. "By Elfhame's laws, your punishment is my choice. Since you were going to take my life, *your* life is forfeit."

I dug my nails into my palms as a choked sound came from my throat.

It couldn't end like this. Him alive and me dead at *his* feet. That wasn't how it was supposed to go.

If my hands had been free, I'd have pointed at Eric and cursed him for his betrayal. But I was tied, and he was gone—safe and free, enjoying his gold.

The prince's canines showed as his smile widened. "I may take your head or claim your life. Which would you prefer, little bird?"

I bared my teeth at him. I wasn't about to beg for my life.

Had my sister done that?

Hot tears filled my eyes at the injustice. The shame of failure. The sheer fucking unfairness of it all.

I hadn't cried for her in years, but here I was, kneeling at her killer's feet, tears about to spill right before my blood did.

I'd been numb for so long, this maelstrom of feelings was overwhelming, threatening to drag me under.

And yet it was also exquisite. Hate. Pain. Grief. Guilt. Fear. Anger—no, make that *rage* at the way Eric had betrayed me and the fact my revenge had been cut down before it had bloomed. It burned and froze me in turn, a reminder that I was, in fact, alive.

For the first time in a decade, I felt it.

"Hmm." He tossed his head. "No preference. Very well." He shrugged and brought down the terrible weight of that sword.

I braced myself.

It whistled past my ear, wafting my hair.

It stopped.

My held breath huffed out as, slowly, the blade's tip pressed into the point between my neck and shoulder. Pain bloomed there, and I couldn't help the soft sound I made as it shivered down my nerves.

Cold, then hot, my skin flushed as he pulled the point away and warm blood welled and trickled down my chest.

My pulse roared in my ears as though questioning why —*how* I was still alive.

He'd spared me.

And yet the cruel smile he gave as he bent down said mercy was a word he had no understanding of. His palm pressed into the cut, making the pain throb, before he dragged it up my throat to my chin, forcing me to meet his gaze.

His pupils had blown wide, like he enjoyed my fear and

pain—my punishment. "I claim you. Your life is mine. Every part of you is mine."

Unable to move, unable to so much as breathe, I stared as he pulled away and swiped his tongue over his bloodied palm. When he lowered his hand, my blood was smeared upon his cheeks. "Mm. I wonder if every part of you is as sweet."

My mind stuttered over his words. I was his? What did that mean?

With a quick sweep of his sword, he cut the tie from my wrists. It wasn't as though I was a threat now I had no iron blade.

"On your feet."

I clenched my jaw and remained kneeling. I wouldn't be ordered around by a fucking fae.

But instead of glowering at my disobedience, he smiled, a look of pure, feline pleasure. "Prideful little human, I don't need any more reasons to punish you, but I'll gladly take them. I'll make a catalogue of them and believe me when I say I'll make you pay for each and every one."

I stayed there, weighing my options. There weren't many. And I didn't want to give him any more pleasure by refusing to obey.

At last, knees shaking, I rose. "What are you going to do with me?"

His teeth flashed pale against his blood-stained skin as he bent close. I tried to back away, but he thrust a hand into my hair and gripped.

He brought his face an inch from mine. The smell of my own blood was a coppery accompaniment to his musky scent. He took his time, holding my gaze before tightening the fist in my hair and tilting my head back. "Don't you know, little bird? Cats like to play with the little creatures they catch."

6

His threat echoed in my ears as he marched me through the cracked marble halls of his palace. We crossed what I thought was a courtyard, with ferns and saplings growing amongst pale rock and a glittering fountain at the centre. But when I looked up, I found the roof was a broken glass dome. It had once been a room. Some pieces of glass remained, but most of the steel frame stood empty, open to the night sky above.

Stars winked back at me as if saying this was my fate written in them. Every action I'd taken over the past decade had led here.

Claws prickled my shoulder. "I didn't tell you to slow down."

I'd been gawping. Swallowing, I hurried on, the prince a constant presence just behind me. At least the walk gave me a chance to sort through and examine the jumbled emotions that chased through me. It had been so long, my body hummed with *so much* feeling like a battle raged inside.

Fear—that seemed to be the primary one. Anger bubbled beneath it, and frustration was a hard ball in my stomach.

Whatever the prince's punishment involved, however cruel, at least if I was alive, there was a chance I might still get my revenge.

I clung to that as he shoved me through a door into a room so bright I had to shield my eyes.

"Sepher? It's rather late, isn't it?" A woman's voice, sweet and soft and musical, like a distant songbird's call.

Behind me, the prince made a low sound that I might've called a growl.

When my eyes adjusted to the light, I found myself in a pretty parlour decorated in pale cerulean blue with white marble columns. Every item of furniture wasn't quite matched, but they shared a common theme that made them work together. Gold motifs of wings and suns, white or blue upholstery, glittering quartz tabletops.

At the centre of it all, curled up on an elegant settee, sat a fae woman. Even sitting, I could tell she was tall and willowy. A curtain of hair pooled around her, pale gold and platinum that glistened in the fae lights drifting through the room.

Her long, slender hands cupped a crystal wine glass as she looked from the prince to me. Her eyes were like a sunrise, pink and violet blurring into blue. She cocked her head. "What's this?" Her eyebrows rose slowly as she leant forward and examined me more closely.

"A would-be assassin."

The prince had referenced a cat when he'd threatened to play with me. Now I thought of his rumbling voice and his size, I suspected he meant a sabrecat like the ones we rode and used to pull carriages, not a house cat.

From the stories and our annual visits to Elfhame for

performances in their capital, I knew fae all had magic, but it took different forms for each of them.

I'd heard whispers that he was a shapechanger—a fae who could change forms to another species. With his tail and claws and that comment, his other shape had to be a sabrecat.

I swallowed as a shudder swept through me. To think I'd been afraid of his natural weapons. If I was right, he could shift into a huge feline with fangs longer than my hand and claws that could rip me apart like I was nothing more than a dandelion clock.

The fact he was behind me, out of sight, made the thought even worse. Any second, he could lash out and I'd have no warning before my life spilled over the lush white carpet.

At last, the woman finished her inspection of me and one corner of her mouth rose. "They deem you important enough for an assassin?"

The prince made a sound that was half grunt, half laugh. "Well, she's mine, now." He stepped into the periphery of my vision and bared his teeth in a feral grin. "I thought she'd make an amusing pet."

Deep beneath the chill of fear trickling through my veins, something bubbled, like a pot about to reach boiling point.

A *pet*? And speaking about me like I wasn't here... Was this how fae generally viewed humans, or was it part of my punishment?

I gritted my teeth against the desire to remind them that I was here and could speak.

A warm palm landed between my shoulder blades and I flinched. That only made the prince's grin widen. "There, there, little bird. Don't flinch from your master."

That word again. I shot him a glare, but pleasure flared in his eyes as he leant closer.

"Don't worry, I plan to take great care of you." Behind him, his striped tail curled slowly from side to side.

Tossing his head, he pushed me forward. "Clean it up and give it something to wear. See if you can make it pretty."

The skin around the woman's eyes tightened as she unfurled from the settee. "I believe the word you're looking for is *please*, Sepher."

He sucked in a breath, then crossed the floor in three long strides. He plucked the glass from her, discarded it on the table, and closed her hands under his. She was tall, yes, but he was a giant in comparison, and his hands completely covered hers. "*Please*, dearest Celestine." A playful twitch pulled on the edge of his mouth.

When he approached her, I'd expected a kiss. He'd barged in here without so much as a knock. In itself, that didn't mean they were intimate, but did mean he was every inch the arrogant, presumptuous prince I'd thought. The fact she called him by his name rather than *Your Highness* said their relationship was close.

Yet he only stood there, holding her hands.

Eventually, she rolled her eyes and nodded. "Fine, I'll look after your new pet." She threw me a curious glance as the prince stepped back. "What's her name?"

"Zita. She's from the Gilded Suns." He shrugged as he approached me. "Had an iron blade and everything." He huffed a breath through his nose and shook his head. "Now, little bird." He paused on his way to the door and leant closer. "You behave for Celestine or I will feed you to my hunting hounds while you're still alive. Understand?"

Even though the promise streaked a chill through me, I clenched my jaw and glared back.

"Another defiance to add to the catalogue?" He gave me a bright smile that I wanted to punch. "This is going to be fun."

I wouldn't give him pleasure or fun or whatever else he hoped to get out of me. Whatever he wanted, I would do the opposite. "I understand," I bit out.

With a soft sound, he nodded and continued to the door. "Bring it to me tomorrow, Celestine... *please*."

"Tomorrow?" She approached, her evaluative gaze on me. "And what will you be doing while I make her presentable?"

Arms spread, the prince turned. "Tonight, I need a good fuck." With that, he stalked out and left us.

Her dawn eyes unnerved me, roving over my face and down my body. "Make her pretty?" She shook her head. "The dear little thing already is." Smiling, she picked up a lock of my hair. "Hmm, though a little bloody, I see. Are you hurt?"

She circled, and I debated whether to answer. Admitting I was injured felt like admitting a weakness. Answering also felt like weakness.

"Ah, here." She pushed the hair from my shoulder, revealing the cut between shoulder and neck where the prince had pressed the tip of his sword into my flesh. "You know, Zita, I won't hurt you."

I bit the inside of my cheek. As a fae, she couldn't lie... and yet that didn't mean I should trust her. I kept quiet.

"I suppose you've had a fright." She gave me a gentle smile, lifting one shoulder. "Come along, then. Let's get you cleaned up."

In a room off the parlour, she ran me a bath and filled it with sweet-smelling bubbles. All the while, she chattered about inconsequential things like the coming snows and what colours would suit me best. I didn't answer.

She poked around the room while I bathed, pulling out

different toiletries for me to use. When I stared at a contraption sticking out of the wall in one corner, she followed my gaze. "It's a shower. I don't think they have them in Albion. Pity. They're divine, though not quite as relaxing as a bath."

The idea Elfhame could improve something as basic as a bathroom grated on my nerves. I scowled and turned away as she returned to her pottering.

At one point, she disappeared and called for a servant. I emerged from the steaming water and searched the room for a weapon. No luck. I tried the windows, but they wouldn't budge. Though, the cut on my shoulder didn't twinge too much as I tried to push them up.

When her voice grew louder as she spoke to a maid, I slipped back into the bath and tried to calm my breaths as though I hadn't been hurrying around.

But as soon as she entered, she eyed the telltale puddles of water.

Shit, I hadn't thought of that.

I held still, waiting for her to grab me as her prince had. She didn't. After a long while, I dared to glance up and found her watching me with a wry smile as she ran her nails over the teeth of a jade comb. The soft *click-click-click* was the only sound.

Eventually, she kneeled behind me. "Such lovely hair," she said as she combed conditioner through it. "Such a rich colour."

When I was younger, I'd thought it boring and brown. But after my sister had died and I'd taken her place on stage, I'd realised it was the same tone as hers. Using her treatments and oils had brought out the depth of colour, revealing tints of gold and red in its chestnut lengths.

"Thank you," I muttered. One thing I remembered from

the stories about fae that had turned out to be true was their love of good manners. Every year we came to Elfhame and performed in their capital, and the folk we dealt with were always polite.

So they were killers who had barely sniffed in the direction of my sister's dead body to investigate, but at least they were courteous.

Under the bubbles, I fisted my hands.

"You don't seem much like an assassin." She didn't say it in an accusing way, but a thoughtful one, and when I glanced over my shoulder, I found her head cocked.

"Maybe your prince isn't as clever as he thinks."

She guffawed behind her hand—the action at odds with her elegance... and definitely not what I'd expected when I'd made my comment with a vicious smile.

"There, you're probably correct, but only because Sepher thinks he's the cleverest person in the world. And the most handsome, strongest, funniest, best at... well, *everything*." She chuckled and shrugged, then smoothed my hair behind my ear.

Her gaze snagged on its rounded edge and her eyes narrowed. "Why *did* you try to kill him, then?"

The prince hadn't bothered to ask, but Celestine was clearly curious. If he was as arrogant as he sounded and she told him I wasn't an assassin, it would drive him insane to not know *why*.

He was used to having what he wanted, when he wanted.

Was that why he'd killed my sister? That night, I'd found him standing over her after her usual private performance. It had crossed my mind that they'd been lovers, but now another possibility opened up.

Maybe killing her wasn't a way of discarding a lover, but

an act of rage because she'd refused to become one. Spoilt princes weren't used to being denied.

I turned my back on Celestine and squared my shoulders.

The prince might have me at his mercy, but he wouldn't have my answers, and neither would his friend.

7

My heart pounded in time with the swift *clip-clip-clip* of my shoes on the cracked marble floor. Celestine led the way in silence—not even her footsteps made a sound.

It was the day after my arrival and I'd slept on a huge settee in her rooms. She'd received a message early this morning and had been tight-lipped ever since.

I wore a cream bodice with sheer skirts and a slit high up the thigh. Gold floral motifs glinted as I moved. My performance clothes weren't cheap, and I took great pride in designing them myself and working with the best garment-makers I could.

But even I had to admit, this was the most beautiful item I'd ever worn.

That only made my heart beat harder. What had I been so elaborately dressed up for?

She'd even placed a diadem on my head, weaving it into my hair so it looked like its gold leaves had grown there. I

35

touched the pale blue stone on my brow. Its facets were cold and hard but carried no hint of magic.

At last, we reached a huge set of double doors. Green and gold leaves covered their surface sprouting from twisting vines. I wasn't entirely sure if they were carved or real—some plant that didn't need soil to grow. In faerie, that might be possible.

We stopped and Celestine turned to me. Her dawn eyes gave me a once-over, and she adjusted my hair. Once she was satisfied with my appearance, she met my gaze and opened her mouth as if to say something, but she only exhaled and closed it again. A muscle in her brow twitched as she nodded, and the doors swept open.

We emerged behind a dais, my view obscured by the back of a gilded throne. But the ceiling arched high overhead, supported by columns as big as tree trunks, telling me how massive this room was—larger than any theatre I'd ever performed in. Fae worked at a completely different scale to humans.

A chill crept down my back and it took a second to realise why.

Beyond the sound of my own pulse was the rustle and heavy quiet of a room full of people waiting. It was a sound I knew well—the one that came right before a performance.

Except this wasn't one I'd prepared for.

I swallowed and pulled my shoulders back. Whatever the prince had in store for me, I would face.

Celestine led me up the dais and the room opened up before us.

Horns and wings. Skin of scales. Flesh of bark. Antlers and fangs.

These were the denizens of the Court of Monsters.

Morning light spilled through the massive windows that covered the walls to left and right and another cracked glass dome above. It highlighted every inhuman feature, rather than cloaking it in darkness as the theatre had last night.

Just as during my performance, every pair of eyes was on me.

My pulse rose to a dull roar in my ears as I took in these creatures. In the front row stood a huge man with stone-grey skin and backward-sweeping horns. The impressive muscles of his bare chest flexed as he leant forward. Black eyes seared into me.

"And here it is, my new pet."

My heart leapt, painful, as I sucked in a breath.

I'd been so absorbed in the grotesquely intriguing sight of the assembled court, I'd completely forgotten about their prince.

He unfolded from the throne at my side, towering above me. My form was small and compact, well-muscled from my work, but he was much bigger in all directions. Maybe I hadn't fully registered last night, so absorbed in my task and the shock of its failure.

But now?

Good gods, he was a giant. Tall and thick with muscle.

He wore another tight-fitting shirt that stood open halfway down his chest. Celestine had said he thought himself the most handsome. Showing off his body, which was admittedly something worthy of showing off, was clearly part of his arrogance.

Shoulders back, he commanded the room with a dazzling, spiked smile that matched the glinting crown atop his head. His audience leant in, eyes wide, flicking from him to me and back again. A hundred held breaths sucked the air from the room.

Anticipation scraped over my skin, raising the hair on my bare arms.

He touched my shoulder, making me flinch. He made a low sound alarmingly like a purr.

Jaw clenched, I held still as his hand slid up my neck and into my hair, where it fisted.

"Come now, little bird, say hello to my friends."

He liked my defiance, and I refused to do anything to please him. "Hello." My voice piped, lost in the cavernous room.

A ripple of laughter passed through the crowd.

"This is not a matter for laughter." The prince released my hair and smoothed it down. He turned to his audience. "Last night, this human took an iron blade and tried to kill me."

Eyes widened. Some returned to me, re-evaluating the tiny human before them.

"Naturally, she failed. But..." He raised his hand. "Her life is mine, in exchange for the one she tried to take. So let it be known, this treacherous creature is mine. You will treat her as my pet."

My stomach turned, sending bile to burn the back of my throat. The pet comments weren't just a nasty nickname or a threat. I swallowed, fighting nausea. What did this mean?

"And to ensure she doesn't forget what she is, she will wear this at all times." He returned to his throne and beckoned me closer. "Come to your master, pet."

Something inside screamed for me not to go.

I forced my legs to disobey that survival instinct.

"Good girl," he crooned when I reached him. He gripped

under my chin, the tips of his claws pressing into my cheeks. "You're learning."

Beneath my stiff fear, that bubbling sensation started again. I welcomed it, scooped it up, and brought it close. Hells, I even welcomed the icy fear and my earlier nervous anticipation. A catalogue of feelings I'd forgotten how to have.

The prince nodded to a servant, who approached carrying a green velvet cushion.

My stomach plummeted when I saw what glittered upon it.

A ruby-encrusted collar.

When I managed to drag my gaze from it, I found the prince's mouth curled in a smirk. I must've given some outer sign of my horror.

But rather than tightening his grip, ready to hold me still as he fastened the collar around my throat, he released me. A challenge flared in his golden eyes.

He was giving me the chance to pull away.

Daring me to.

He enjoyed my discomfort. My horrified stare at the collar had given him pleasure. He *wanted* me to refuse it—or try to.

That was when I realised.

For him, this was all a game.

And I didn't lose games.

I had only one way to win this one.

I wouldn't cry or ask for help. I wouldn't beg him to stop. Whatever he asked, I wouldn't back down.

And when he least expected it, I would fucking kill him.

So, I pulled my shoulders back like he was about to bestow on me a great honour. Holding his gaze, I smiled and raised my chin.

A flicker passed over his expression, but he took the collar from the cushion. He watched me as he brought it closer, gaze intent like I was a creature he stalked and he was ready for the instant I spotted the danger and ran.

Oh, I knew the danger.

And I would not run.

As he closed the last couple of inches, I lifted my chin a little higher. His gaze dipped. Did he see the pulse leaping in my throat?

The blood red leather of the collar reached my skin, soft and warm. His touch was surprisingly gentle as he lifted the hair from my neck and fastened the three small buckles. He ran the pad of his thumb over a particular spot in my neck. Yes, he'd seen my pulse and he enjoyed it.

His touch lingered, and it was another challenge—to cringe away.

So I leant in.

The way his brow and jaw tightened sent a thrill through me. It was pure delight, cutting through my deadened senses, as bright and addictive as an orgasm.

For the first time in I didn't know how long, I smiled in a way that wasn't ironic or stiff or a matter of politeness for someone else's sake. I smiled for *me*.

Nose wrinkling, teeth baring, the prince curled his fingers around the back of my neck and yanked me closer. It spiked through me, part fear, part more of that terrible glee at displeasing him.

"I could bend you over this throne and fuck you in front of all these people you know." He hissed the words, a dangerous whisper that I loved simply because it spelled out how damn annoyed he was. "None of them would help you. None would bat an eyelid." His chest heaved at the open neck of his white shirt.

"Get on with it then," I murmured back. "I have an appointment at three."

He laughed, a vicious thing that showed his fangs and all the hard cruelty of his handsome face. "Oh, I'm going to enjoy this."

I smiled and bit back the reply burning on my tongue: *Not as much as I will.*

He wanted a game. I would give him a fucking game.

8

With that on my mind, whatever he told me to do, I did.

Starting with "Come."

I followed him from the room. When we reached a cosy study, all warm-toned wood rather than white marble, he finally looked my way. His golden gaze trailed over me, so intense it might as well have been a caress.

"Turn."

I did, letting him survey me from every angle.

I let him stroke his fingers over my hair. His claws caught in the strands, sending a flutter of fear through my stomach— a reminder of what he was. He gripped my chin and turned my head left and right, bending close to inspect me.

"Hmm." At last, he nodded. "Celestine chose your outfit well." The claw of his thumb scraped up my chin, and his slitted pupils followed. The light touch crept over my skin, a trickling sensation that wasn't wholly unpleasant. He finished with that point resting on my lower lip.

Perhaps he wasn't going to fuck me in front of all those people, but here in private.

It was only a decade of disciplined training that allowed me to hold still at the thought.

I wouldn't back down. Even from that.

Maybe he thought me a typical human, easily scandalised. But travelling performers like us were a breed apart. I displayed myself night after night in skimpy outfits that would've got me kicked out of any other public place, but in a theatre, they were allowed.

Hells, they were *expected*.

And I'd pleased more patrons than I cared to remember in private performances.

Whatever this brute did, I wouldn't beg him to stop. I wouldn't give him that satisfaction.

Maybe the dare showed in my eyes, because he met and held them for a long while. His eyebrows squeezed together. "You're strangely compelling... for a human."

Such a compliment. I rolled my eyes.

Snorting, he jerked his chin towards the fireplace. "Sit."

I went to obey, but there was no chair, only a familiar chest. *My* chest. All my belongings from the Gilded Suns. My locket containing a drawing of me and Zinnia. Her mirror, her favourite hair clip, a love letter—little inconsequential things that were all that remained of her. I thought the troupe had taken it all with them or the prince had thrown it away.

I glanced back at him. A smirk threatened at the edge of his mouth as he held up the key and placed it in a drawer, then locked that, too. "I said, *sit.*"

Still, there was no seat. Had I misunderstood? But his smirk was my answer.

Of course. Pets didn't get chairs.

Flashing him a bright smile, I sank onto the rug in front of the fire.

He let out a breath, shoulders sinking a touch, before he sat behind the large desk at the other side of the room.

So began my first day as Prince Sepher's "pet."

He worked for a couple of hours, occasionally trying to engage me in conversation. I pretended I was asleep and entertained myself by fantasising about killing him. I could get my dagger back and murder him in his sleep, in the bathtub, while he ate a lavish meal. Or, best of all, as he sat upon his gilded throne.

"Come." His bark had me jolting upright, blinking away sleepiness.

The warmth from my fantasies combined with the fire and cosiness of the thick rug must've made me doze. The elegant clock on the mantlepiece said one o'clock. I had only eaten a little breakfast in Celestine's rooms before being taken to the throne room, and now my stomach felt like it was imploding.

He guided me through the corridors, hand on my shoulder sometimes, the back of my head other times.

This place was labyrinthine, with corridors that twisted and turned. Sometimes I glanced down an intersection and found the hall disappearing into darkness, even though this was the middle of the day. Other times, the offshoots ended in rubble or led suddenly outside. No door, just lush ferns and grass and the gardens beyond.

There was an odd beauty to this ruined palace. Little plants I didn't know the names of grew in cracks and crevices. Huge slabs of marble lay where they'd fallen, reminding me of the rugged landscape I loved watching when we travelled from performance to performance in the deep north of Albion.

And the light.

The light.

We'd turn a corner and find it beaming through a glassless window or shafting down from one of the cracked domes. It hazed through the air, highlighting drifting motes of dust. It caressed the edges of the invasive ferns and weeds, making them look like they belonged in a painting rather than being mere accidents of nature.

At my side, it caught in the impossible red of the prince's hair and the slashes of cream running through it, gilding its length. It lapped at the strong angle of his jaw and the regal lines of his nose. It did nothing to soften the cruel edges of his lips. Under it, his golden skin took on a new depth, like he was a statue cast from pure metal.

This was why fae were so dangerous. Even as they threatened your life, they did it so beautifully.

At last, we arrived at a set of double doors. He paused, hand on the back of my head. "Such a little thing. Let's see how well you serve your master."

The doors swept open, though no one held them, and I found myself in a large dining hall. Dozens of fae already sat at the long table, including Celestine and the horned man from the front row. His black eyes fixed on me before turning to the prince.

But it was Celestine who spoke. "Sepher, I was starting to wonder if you'd ever join us. I hope you're not working too hard."

I had to admit, working alone in a study was *not* something I'd expected from His Princely Prickishness—or *any* prince of Elfhame.

He scoffed and plopped into the seat next to hers. In here, every chair was large and well-upholstered, with curved arms —almost thrones. I wasn't offered one.

That left me standing awkwardly on one side, unsure what to do. A couple of servants stood against the wall. Should I wait with them or—?

"Little bird." He said it in a singsong voice and beckoned around the chair's high back. "Fetch me wine."

His tone prickled across my shoulders. Apparently, the fae's preoccupation with manners didn't stretch to their pets.

Dozens of pairs of eyes turned to me. Celestine held still, but her lips thinned the slightest fraction. The others leant in. A couple exchanged glances as though silently placing bets on whether I'd obey or defy their prince.

Who said I only had two options?

I smiled sweetly and went to the decanter of deep purple liquid I could only assume was some sort of fae wine. Taking my time, I approached the prince, swinging my hips, making each step a slow saunter.

Oh yes, I was absolutely playing up to my audience. And they drank me up, unblinking.

I took his glass and poured, lifting the decanter high above its rim to give a little theatre. With an unreadable curve to his lips, the prince watched from hooded eyes.

I held them as I deposited the decanter on the table with a little flourish.

Now for my *pièce de résistance*.

My third option.

Still smiling, still maintaining eye contact with the arrogant, murdering prick, I bent my head over the glass and spat.

Someone gasped. A few chuckled. A couple hissed.

The prince didn't move, not even when I held out his drink.

Silence reigned over the room, pregnant with the undivided attention of his followers.

The anticipation buzzed in me, bright and alive. What would he do? How was he going to react? Surely he wouldn't drink my spit, not in front of all these cronies. That would be shameful.

Or had I gambled wrong? Was this different for fae in a way I didn't understand? Would it not dent his pride as much as it would a human's?

Slowly, so slowly I didn't spot it at first, his mouth spread in a smile terrible and beautiful.

He took the glass, and before I could turn, he caught me by the waist. "Come here, little bird."

Like I had a choice. The threat of a laugh bubbled in my chest, but my throat was too tight to let it out.

His claws pricked through the light silk of my dress as he reeled me in until I stood pressed against the arm of his chair. The wood bit into my hipbones, but I refused to pull away.

He came close and it must've been the sheer size of him that set my heart pounding—a reminder of the danger he posed. And yet wasn't danger sometimes thrilling?

My sister and I had played a game as children, when the nights were dark and we were alone. One would wait for the other, tucked around a corner or behind a door, and jump out at the perfect, terrifying moment. There was no winning, no rules, just the surprise and the inevitable shriek. My heart would beat like thunder as I crept through the darkness, knowing she was waiting.

This was something like that, a spike of fear. But where I'd always been safe with Zinnia, now with this fae prince who'd murdered her, I was not.

Still, my body didn't seem to understand that, because the same thrill ran through me. And I must've been starved of feeling for so long that it had made me sick, because I threw myself upon it, like an offering on an altar.

The prince's hand trailed up my spine until he cupped the back of my head. "Drink." He pressed the glass to my lips and tipped it back.

I had no chance to pull away or even snatch a breath before it was spilling over my tongue. Sweet and sharp, heavy and thick with blackberries and something spiced like winter buns. I gulped it down and went to take a breath when the pressure of the glass on my lip eased.

But he didn't take it away.

His grip tightened on the back of my head, and he tilted the glass, sloshing more wine into my mouth.

It filled my throat, and I choked it down as best I could, but a trickle went the wrong way and I ended up coughing as much as swallowing.

Still, he didn't stop.

"Go on. Give her more." Out of the corner of my eye, I could see it was the horned, grey creature speaking. He bent over the table as though keen to get as close as possible to the spectacle.

Next to him, a more human-like fae with pointed ears and silver hair started to rise, but the prince stilled him with a twitch of his finger.

Tears stung at the corners of my eyes. I clung to his arm, not sure if it was to try to stop him or just to steady myself as the choking shook my body and the wine kept coming. I just had to swallow. *Keep swallowing and it'll be over soon.*

But the wine kept coming.

That wasn't possible. I'd drunk and spilled more than I'd poured. Must've.

A cold realisation seized my throat, making me cough up more of the sweet-sharp liquid.

He'd enchanted the glass to keep refilling.

Just when I thought it would never end, he righted the glass. Wine dripped down my chin as I sucked in air, greedy for it.

And when I met his gaze, I saw it was greedy for my suffering.

Clinging to the arm of his chair as my head spun, I gasped for breath, still half-coughing. "Why don't you just beat me and be done with it?"

His teeth flashed in a victorious smile and I instantly hated myself for speaking. But as soon as my head dipped, he caught my chin with a claw and raised it until I met his gaze. "Because I don't want to hurt you, my little pet. I want to *break* you."

The threat trickled down my shoulders, my arms, my back like winter rain leaching through clothing.

Beating me would be too simple—the kind of punishment a mere mortal might deliver. This man—this *creature* was something altogether different. He'd had years, maybe centuries, to study people, what made them... and unmade them.

He was a connoisseur.

And yet still a fool.

My sister's murder hadn't broken me.

He stood no chance.

9

I managed to keep my newly rediscovered feelings largely in check for the rest of the day, despite the fuzzy drunkenness from the wine. There were no more flares of defiance. I sat at his feet and fetched his food, like a good little pet. I even served drinks to his friends—spit-free—and ate from the little plate of food he handed over, despite the fact he gave me no cutlery.

All the while, I told myself I would get my hands on that iron dagger. And when I did, I would cut him from belly button to throat and show him his own insides.

That kept my smile sweet all afternoon.

As did the fact my refusal to answer his questions made a particular muscle in his jaw twitch.

It was a sight that made something warm unfurl inside me. At first, I touched my stomach, worried I was getting ill, perhaps because of the wine.

But... no... it wasn't unpleasant, it was...

Pleasure.

I'd forgotten what it felt like. All those times I'd fucked Eric and come on his cock, it had only ever been a fleeting, physical thing. Even before his betrayal, it had left me hollow in the sticky aftermath. But this? This was deeper, more sustaining.

The prince's irritation pleased me.

It felt... *good.*

I carried that thought from the dining room, which had devolved into the kind of debauched fae party my sister had enjoyed reading about in her favourite novels. The prince had kept me close, often touching my shoulder or hair as though checking I was still there. Maybe he didn't want anyone else playing with his pet.

The fae had no such qualms about playing with each other, though.

If he thought to shock me, it would take more than that. Performers were a horny breed.

Perhaps it was meant to prepare me. He'd announced he was retiring for the evening, and now guided me along more twisting corridors, one hand on the small of my back.

His chamber was everything I'd expected. Walls of pale marble shot through with dark blue-grey and gold. Wide doors that opened onto an east-facing balcony. Thick, soft carpet I buried my toes in. A huge bed that could've accommodated half a dozen people with ease. Gauzy curtains surrounded it, drifting on a breeze I couldn't feel.

But the thing I couldn't tear my attention from was the moving painting that covered the ceiling. Clouds of pink and violet edged with golden light drifted across a pale blue sky, like someone had captured the quintessential dawn.

Despite myself, despite him, it filled my heart. Something like hope, like possibility, like the promise of a new day.

A nice idea, but every day was the same for me. It was all in service of ending the man who'd killed my sister.

That helped me drag myself away from the painted clouds scudding overhead and loosened my tongue. "Aren't you going to ask why I did it?"

He turned from discarding his thorny crown on a dressing table. The absence of those spikes made him look the slightest bit more human, but then I caught sight of the striped tail curled around his calf and the effect vanished.

He raised an eyebrow. "Did what?"

I gritted my teeth. Had he forgotten already? Had he forgotten my sister, too? The furnace that opened in me stole my breath, keeping me still and silent for a long moment. I stamped it down. I needed to be in control. I didn't want to spill too soon.

Once I'd mastered myself, I lifted my chin. "Tried to kill you."

"Oh, that?" He shrugged. "Well, I worked out you're not a hired assassin. So I should imagine you have some terribly boring, inane human reason." With a gesture, he turned down the blankets on the bed without touching them.

Inside me, the fire broke free of the furnace and streaked through my veins. I shook, fists clenched against the near-overwhelming urge to march up to him and claw his eyes out.

I had to bide my time. My hands would be useless against him, even if I was quick enough to reach his skin.

No, I had to make him think I was tamed. With how fucking enraging he was, that wouldn't be easy. But I had patience. I could play the long game. What was a few weeks when I'd waited a decade?

When he turned back to me, I was under something like control. He gave a pleasant smile, unfastening the solitary button of his shirt. If he thought I'd be impressed by a muscle-clad torso, he didn't understand performing troupes—they were full of men who'd honed their bodies through hour upon hour of practice.

I met his gaze, giving him a bored look.

Unfazed, he unrolled his sleeves. "Did you enjoy your first day of pet life?"

I pressed my lips together. It wouldn't do to become too tame too quickly—he'd grow suspicious. Plus, I couldn't help myself when my silence made his jaw flicker.

He gave a faint grunt as he slid the shirt off. He was as well-muscled as I'd expected, large and strong.

But what I hadn't expected was his skin. The stripes from his tail, deep autumn brown, continued across the rest of his body, encircling his powerful arms, trailing around his sides. When he turned and tossed the shirt on a chair, I spotted that they covered his back, too.

One of the circuses we occasionally teamed up with had a pair of trained tigers from the east. His stripes reminded me of theirs, a broken, organic pattern that sometimes showed up in sabrecats.

When I met his gaze, he wore a smile that was part lazy, part preening. He'd mistaken my attention for interest. And yet, as he unbuckled his belt, there was a challenge in his gaze.

He expected me to turn away or show discomfort.

Fuck that.

And fuck him.

I was not the human he expected. A little nudity didn't bother me.

Not looking away, I unhooked my sheer skirt.

There was a flash of something in his eyes. Surprise, perhaps? Or excitement?

He didn't miss a beat, though, yanking his belt from its loops with a crack of leather.

No backing down.

I let my skirt fall, leaving only my undergarments and the boned bodice.

His eyes narrowed as he unbuttoned his fly. I wouldn't look at what he revealed—I wasn't interested in the contents of his trousers. But I wouldn't turn away or blush like he wanted me to.

Instead, I pulled loose the bows at my shoulders and reached back to unhook the bodice. It was a task easier said than done, and I bit my tongue against a curse.

That won a smirk as he stood there, trousers unfastened and clinging to his hips. Above the waistband, the hint of deep auburn hair and the base of a thick cock showed. "Do you need a hand, pet?" He didn't say it low and husky, like Eric might've when he was trying to seduce me, but with a teasing, playful lilt that said he was as unaffected as I was.

I wasn't sure if that pissed me off more.

I fiddled with the hooks a moment longer before clenching my jaw and turning my back to him. It felt less like defeat if I didn't say it out loud.

His feet were silent, like all fae, and it was only the fact his chuckle grew louder that told me he approached. With or without words, I'd invited him into my space, and now I waited, breath held. He hadn't hesitated in touching me all day. Was he now going to take this as the opportunity to escalate that?

My stomach knotted. I wouldn't back down, but that didn't mean I'd like it.

Something warm grazed my back, then the sound of tearing fabric ripped through the room.

I spun on my heel. "I only meant to unhook it, you—!"

His broad smile silenced me.

I wasn't supposed to be speaking to him. I wasn't giving him that pleasure. I bit my tongue and peeled away the tattered remains of the bodice. Should've known a monster like him would be incapable of treating the garment with the respect it deserved.

With a smirk, he followed my movements and let his gaze trail over my breasts. Like when he'd presented me with the collar—now the only thing I wore besides my underwear—I lifted my chin.

This was no show. I *was* proud of my body. I'd worked at it, honed it over a decade. It had earned me money. I looked after it and it looked after me.

No way was I going to cower under the bold gaze of some arsehole prince.

The corner of his mouth twitched, and he made a faint sound as he turned away, like I was only faintly interesting.

Damnation was he tedious. I suddenly found myself eager to sleep, even if just to escape him for several hours.

As he walked away, he let his trousers fall and stepped out of them, every move powered by feline grace. The stripes continued over his arse and thighs, fading down his calves. His tail swished side-to-side. "You'll sleep there." He tossed a cloud-grey blanket on the foot of his bed.

Not *in* his bed, but on its end, like a favourite lapdog.

I gritted my teeth. No backing down. No begging. I nodded to myself and slid under the fluffy blanket. The bed was as soft as a cloud, better than any I'd experienced, and I had to bite back a sigh as I sank into it.

He gave a huff, and I closed my eyes, refusing to even glance at him in a questioning manner. There was the scrape of pen on paper, followed by a faint ripple of magic that danced across the hairs at the back of my neck.

Despite the curiosity tugging on me, I kept my eyes screwed shut and pretended I was already asleep.

A few minutes later, the door clicked open and a soft female voice crept into the space. The tone he took as he welcomed her and her answering giggle told me all I needed to know—this was a lover. Perhaps the one he'd fucked last night.

There was a whisper of cloth, then her muffled moan suggested they were busy kissing, so I dared a peek. Tall and willowy, it was one of the women who'd been at the party. Her long, pale hair curled like a cascade of clouds over her bronze back as the prince's hand trailed down and squeezed her backside. She didn't seem the slightest bit bothered that I was in the room. It wasn't as though I was hidden, so she had to know.

Claws scraping over her skin, leaving pink lines in their wake, he pulled her thighs around him. He carried her closer.

He was going to fuck her on the bed.

As he teased her arsehole with one finger, his golden eyes landed on me. He didn't pause his kiss, but amusement glinted there.

Not just a murderer, but also a prize prick.

He'd failed to embarrass me with his undressing, so this was a fresh attempt.

Good luck with that.

You didn't live in canvas-walled wagons for most of your life without learning how to ignore the sound of others fucking.

I rolled my eyes before closing them.

The bed jostled as they landed on it. There was more

movement and a low groan from her that turned into a rising whimper. As I dozed off, I noted he made no sound.

Her cry of completion woke me. I tugged the blankets closer, trying to ignore the impression I'd been dreaming of one of my own lovers. At my core, my pulse throbbed. I pulled the blanket tighter, like that might shield my dreams from their sexual influence.

"Enough," he muttered, a growl edging the word.

"But you haven't even fucked—?"

"I said *enough*. Go back to your room."

"I don't understand. We normally—"

"Go. I'll speak to you in the morning."

There was a long pause with only their heavy breaths.

"Is it because—?"

"Anya." His voice carried a low note of warning.

"Fine," she huffed. The bed jiggled, the door opened, and before it closed, I sank back towards sleep, a single thread of thought following me.

Zinnia. I promise I'll get you justice. I'll taste his blood, just like he's tasted mine.

Except when I did it, he'd lie dead at my feet.

10

I woke with a foot digging into my ribs.

It was all real, then. I was the pet of a fae prince, sleeping at the end of his bed.

I lay in the dim room and listened to the soft sound of his breaths. Meanwhile, my wheeling thoughts went over and over the disaster that had led here and the first twenty-four hours of my punishment.

When I eased upright, the prince didn't stir. He lay on his back, spread out, like the whole world was his to take up space in. I gritted my teeth and crept closer to the red hair spilling over the pillows.

Sleep had erased the self-satisfied smirk he usually wore. The amused arrogance had gone, too. His dark lashes brushed his cheeks and a slight crease had formed between his eyebrows. Most people looked younger or more peaceful in sleep.

Not him. He looked more serious, like he was doing all his thinking now after a hard afternoon of partying.

My fingers ached for the cold iron of my dagger. I could ease it between his ribs right now. He even had the blankets pooled around his waist, leaving his chest bare. It was practically an invitation.

The want buzzed through my muscles, making my hands clench and unclench. But I had no weapon.

Something pressed on the back of my eyes. Something I hadn't felt in a long, long time. It licked the back of my throat with salt and flooded my tongue with the bitter taste of guilt.

I'd failed. Not just in my task, but worst of all, I'd failed my sister.

Maybe these reawakened feelings were my punishment. But that would require me to believe in the gods.

I dashed the tears from my eyes and slipped from the bed. I couldn't kill the prince—not yet—but I could work this quivering need from my muscles. I pulled on his shirt and tied it at the front—it was loose enough for exercise, unlike my ruined outfit.

Deep breaths, then I eased into my warm-up stretches. By the time I was halfway through the routine, the tears stopped. By the time I started the strength portion of my workout, I was smiling.

I used various items from around the room as my weights —a stack of books, a small chest, a surprisingly heavy candlestick—and squatted and lunged, lifting them in a variety of configurations.

My muscles hummed pleasantly. It wasn't the revenge they called for, but it was enough to keep them occupied for now.

I rose into a handstand, counted as I held it, each part of me involved in the micro-adjustments that balanced my body. After ten seconds, I lowered myself and slowly, slowly tilted, until my hands were level with my waist, my weight on them as I lay on my front in mid-air. My arms burned and trembled a little. But it was a good burn.

"What *are* you doing?"

Holding my balance, I looked up and found the prince sitting up in bed, watching. His hair pooled around his shoulders, sleep-mussed, and his eyebrows bunched together. I couldn't decide if it was in confusion or irritation that he'd been woken.

I hoped it was the latter.

With a long breath, I returned my attention to my exercises. Legs pulling apart, I pushed my torso upright, until I was in a sitting position, with only my hands in contact with the floor.

I could feel the prince's scrutiny. Maybe he really was confused. After all, I doubted hard work came into his vocabulary.

On the count of ten, I swung into a handstand, then flipped to my feet.

He huffed and rolled his eyes. "Trust you to ruin mornings with"—he waved his hand at me—"whatever that is."

I gritted my teeth and arched back into a bridge. I wouldn't give him the satisfaction of my attention. This was my morning routine, and I wasn't going to let him spoil it.

"I should've known you'd do something like this. You even ruin sex."

Then he'd sent his partner away early because he'd been unable to enjoy it without my discomfort. Kicking back into a handstand, I grinned. My day was rapidly improving.

I lifted one hand from the floor and spread it to the side in presentation. But when I flashed my triumphant grin at him, he wasn't wearing the irritated expression I'd expected. Head cocked, eyes narrowed, lips parted, he watched me, *fascinated.*

His gaze trailed over my body as I held my balance, arm trembling a little now. At last he met my eyes and sucked in a quick breath as he saw I'd caught him. A frown crashed into place like a door slamming shut.

Slowly, his mouth curled. "Very impressive. It would be a shame if you were to lose that hand, wouldn't it?"

My heart leapt to my throat at the reminder of the dangerous game I was playing.

I righted myself, graceful, but quicker than usual.

My life was his. Under the stupid rules of this country, I belonged to him. The stories said fae hated slavery, but apparently this didn't count.

Smirking, the prince strode past me and through a large door I hadn't noticed amongst the room's marble panels. I caught a glimpse of a bathroom before he closed it.

By the time he emerged, naked, I'd finished my exercise routine. I refused to look at what swung between his legs as he sauntered around the room. The way he walked made me wonder if he'd prefer to be naked all the time. I certainly didn't doubt he'd mind everyone seeing his cock. I didn't need to look directly at it to know it wasn't something to be ashamed of.

Neither was the rest of his body—perfect, like a book of anatomy studies I'd once seen.

Except for his tail. It wasn't that his body was marred by the fact it existed, but that the smooth perfection of his golden skin was interrupted by a jagged scar halfway up it. And now I looked more closely, I could see it was slightly crooked there, like it had been broken.

He rifled through a wardrobe. "I've set out toiletries for

you in the bathroom. Cleansers and lotions, shampoo and conditioner. Celestine mentioned your... *plumage*"—he flashed a grin as though he found his own joke terribly amusing—"requires some maintenance."

I was loath to admit anything fae was in any way good, but after Celestine's bath, my skin felt incredible and I'd never seen my hair so shiny. Even the cut in my shoulder had smoothed to a thin, red line. It had barely twinged during my exercises.

"You'll wear this today." He pulled a dress from the wardrobe, flipping it to show me the front and back. Dreamy dawn pink layered with gold and powder blue, its gauzy fabric created a complex interplay of colours that tugged on me.

I wanted it. The sleeveless cut would show off my toned arms, and the low back would hint at my muscled shoulders.

He hung the dress on the front of the wardrobe before turning to a dressing table. "This scent will complement your own." He indicated a bottle, then gave me a long look, eyes narrowed in calculation. "And, yes, these will be perfect." He pulled out a velvet jewellery case.

I couldn't help the steps I took, drawn closer, closer like a fish being reeled in.

Inside glittered a pair of pale gold bracelets, each shaped like a wing, with feathers picked out in perfect detail. I let out a little breath.

The prince smiled.

I'd never kept my vanity a secret or been ashamed of it. My work required it, yes. But after my sister's death, when I'd stepped out from the darkness of backstage and become a performer, it had saved me.

I'd once cared for her, helped her get ready, helped her practice and choreograph her sets.

With her gone, I'd had nothing.

Only grief. Only despair. And they were things that threatened to drown me.

Taking her place on stage had given me purpose. Learning the hoop and silks had given me something to do to earn a wage and keep myself from spiralling into the void. And looking after my body had given me a sense of worth.

My looks were valued, both by the Gilded Suns and by our clients. It flushed me with something close to pleasure to see the way people lifted their heads and watched as we rode into town on our wagons. The feeling of their eyes following me until I was out of sight said I mattered.

Once, my sister had said I mattered. After she was gone, strangers were all I had.

With a dress, a few bottles of chemicals, and a set of bracelets, the prince had triggered all that. And although I hated him and hated being his pet, I couldn't help standing taller in anticipation of how I would look today.

It had to be a trap.

The certainty of it pulled my face tight. I frowned up at him, searching for some sign of cruelty. What was he *really* up to?

His smiled flickered. "I don't normally have women's clothes lying around. That would be a bit small for me." He nodded towards the dress. "I had a selection of women's garments and jewellery sent here while you were with Celestine."

But the *how* wasn't my concern. I wanted to know *why*. I narrowed my eyes at him.

Head lifting, he held my gaze as though trying to work out what my problem was.

Useless man. And I refused to talk to him. Asking the question felt weak and withholding speech irritated him just enough, but didn't cross the line into disobedience territory.

I eyed the bracelets. But, honestly, they just looked like bracelets. Cursed jewellery was a thing, but I didn't want to give away that I was gifted. Who knew what he might do if he found out I had magic?

Like it was just a caress of something pretty, I brushed a fingertip over the gold feathers. No hint of power.

Then what was his game?

"Stars and Suns, they're not poisoned." He rolled his eyes before tossing the jewellery case on the side. "If I'm going to have you following me around, I want to at least enjoy the view." With that, he huffed and shoved me towards the bathroom. "Get on with it, little bird."

I hurried inside. Just before I closed the door, his voice reached me once more.

"I may be a patient man, but even I have a limit."

II

This particular twisting corridor seemed familiar, but the prince marched me along it so quickly, I didn't have time to check on the little details I thought I remembered.

Sure enough, a few turns later, it opened up into the ruined chamber with its fountain and broken glass dome.

Maybe I would eventually get used to the odd layout of this place.

I lifted the layered skirts of my gown to avoid catching them on the wild plants growing through the rubble.

Admittedly, the prince had chosen well. The ensemble suited me. And although he hadn't spoken a word since the comment about his patience, the way he'd looked at me before we left had said plenty. Even if he couldn't admit it, I looked incredible.

A few minutes later, we reached a familiar door. The prince reached for the handle, but stopped and clenched his hand. Sucking in a breath, he knocked, then opened. "Celestine?"

"Ah, so you remembered how to knock today." She sat in the same position as last time, one eyebrow arched, a steaming cup cradled in her hands.

"I was a little... preoccupied the other day." He slid a narrow-eyed look to me.

She scoffed and rose. A sheer, pale blue robe covered her body, its full hem trimmed in matching fur. "But, let me guess, you're here for a similar reason." She threw me a glance and smiled. "She looks delightful today, so it isn't for a spruce up."

"You know me too well." He gave what on anyone else I'd have called a rueful smile, but I didn't think him capable of rueful. "Look after it, would you? *Please?*" His expression soured. "I have things to do and her inability to speak is irritating."

I beamed, and I swore Celestine's eyes glimmered with amusement. Maybe it was just their odd dawn sky colouring.

"Very well. I can keep her occupied for the day. Some of the others are joining me shortly. I'm sure they'll find her entertaining." She stroked my hair like I really was a pet.

I clenched my jaw against a reaction. Though it seemed a fond gesture, rather than one that signalled ownership, as the prince's touches seemed to.

"You're the best." The prince flashed her a dazzling smile that seized my breath for a second, because it was warm and unguarded and gorgeous.

But only for a second.

Because then I remembered who and what it belonged to. The fae who'd murdered my sister. Whatever he may look like while he slept, and however gorgeous his smile, I had to remember that. Every single moment.

His gaze turned to me and the smile flattened. Eyebrows lowering, he leant close and gripped my arm. "Remember, you behave for Celestine, little bird."

With that delightful warning, he left.

She sighed and drained her coffee before tidying away the cup with a click of her fingers.

I didn't want to envy a fae, but that was a useful trick.

Tension clipping her movements, she set up a particularly plush rug in front of the fire. "He's... uh... Well, he's told us you're not allowed on the furniture, so..." With a wince, she met my gaze.

An apologetic fae. Wonders would never cease.

I nodded to show I understood. I even gave her a half smile to try to make her feel better. Still, I wasn't going to speak to her. My silence extended to all of them. They'd only run to their prince and tell him everything if I opened my mouth.

I settled by the fire while Celestine flitted between the rooms, readying for her guests. As she passed through the parlour, she mentioned little details about the treats she'd be serving and asked what I liked. Did I prefer tea or coffee? Did I take sugar or honey or prefer them plain? What did I think of fae food? Was it much different from what I was used to?

Innocuous questions, but it felt like they were designed that way—to lure me into talking. And if I started, who knew what other, more probing things she'd ask?

Still, I found myself tempted. She had such an easy manner, a welcoming warmth that reminded me of my sister.

I pulled my knees to my chest and stared into the pink-flamed fire. The stories said only iron or aconite's poison could kill fae, but that didn't stop me fantasising about burning the prickish prince.

Eventually, Celestine was ready and emerged from her

chamber in a silky gown that skimmed over her frame. There was something delicate to her. True, most fae women I'd seen were slender and willowy—that was why they liked human women so much. Our exotic curves excited them. But on top of that, Celestine's skin had a blueish tinge, like it was so thin it had grown transparent.

Even without the prince's warning, I wouldn't have given her any trouble.

When a knock sounded at the door, she bounced on the balls of her feet, eyes lighting up. "They're here, Zita." The smile she gave me was warm, save for the long canines it revealed. "I just know they're going to love you."

The door opened and admitted a dozen fae. Tall and short, but mostly tall. Pale and dark in colouring. Some wore smiles almost as warm as Celestine's, while others had a cooler, more knowing quality to their expressions, especially when their gazes landed on me and sharpened.

Anya, the woman with bronze skin and cloud-like hair, was amongst them. She threw me a glance and muttered something to the woman next to her. What I hadn't seen last night was that she had two short horns—they looked like twisted hazel branches sprouting from her forehead and sweeping back. When she took one of the offered cups, I saw that instead of fingernails, the tips of her long fingers were covered in bark.

As they served tea and coffee that appeared in a puff of steam, they filled the air with chatter and laughter. It wasn't so different from when the women from the troupe gathered. We'd all bring our mending or other little tasks and something tasty to share, and we'd chat and eat as we worked. Well, I'd listen and they'd chat, but it was a comforting sound as I focused.

I had little skill with needle and thread, so I'd usually take my sketchbook and draw the same faces I always did. The prince's and my sister's. Sometimes diagrams of new moves on the silks or hoop would find their way onto the page, forming odd little borders. But always my focus was on those two faces—ones I wanted to keep seared into my memory forever.

Celestine brought over a saucer of tea and another of coffee. "The prince said you're only—"

I cut her off with a nod. No prizes for guessing the rest of that sentence. I was a pet—no cups for me. I took both saucers and drained them.

"So that's the prince's new toy." A fae with eyes the startling green of spring foliage inspected me. Their pointed face and lithe figure seemed somewhere along a spectrum of male and female, beautifully androgynous, and heightened by the short-cropped hair in pale gold-green like aspen leaves.

"She slept at the foot of his bed last night," Anya said with a little toss of her head.

"But didn't you—?"

"Yes." She watched me over the rim of her cup. "He made me come, but then wouldn't fuck me." Her eyes narrowed as she took another sip.

"It sounds like her presence put him off." The aspen-haired fae smirked, then approached. "She's a sweet-looking thing—those large brown eyes. And such pretty hair." Crouching, they held out their hand like I was a cat or dog who'd sniff it.

I arched an eyebrow, fighting laughter and indignation in equal measure.

"She *can* talk, Essa." Celestine's expression was unreadable, and I couldn't tell from her tone if she was amused or pissed off. "And she understands everything you're saying."

Anya frowned, flicking a glance at me. "Sepher said she was incapable of speaking."

Essa leant closer. "I'm going to stroke you now." They said it slow and loud, like I had a problem with my hearing, then stroked my hair. "Look at these rounded ears."

A couple of the others approached, craning to see.

I caught Celestine's gaze. She shrugged and shook her head. The amusement glinting in her eyes was contagious and I found myself grinning.

"How cute!"

"Oh, and her teeth are so blunt!"

"Where? Let me see!"

Trying not to laugh, I bared my teeth at them. Their eyes went wide at my canines, which were a little shorter and flatter than a normal human's.

After my accident, Zinnia had filed them down. But once, they'd been sharp and long, like Celestine's. The only outward sign of my magic. Every gifted human had a fae mark. Sharp teeth or an unnatural hair colour. Eyes that changed from green to blue or an oddly specific birthmark. In some towns they were a source of pride—amongst aristocrats, especially. They valued the power and prestige magic represented.

However, in some parts of Albion, they were a liability—a marker of otherness. A sign of danger and a person not to be trusted.

On me, after my accident, they had been a danger—a distinguishing feature that would lead mobs straight to us. So, crying, I'd endured the rasp of the file in my mouth as Zinna had taken them away.

It made the fae's wonder all the more amusing.

They examined my hands and ears and fed me treats from their plates—pretty cakes and rich pastries, delicate sandwiches filled with a bewildering complexity of flavours. One thing fae knew was food. I'd never tasted anything so good and that dulled the humiliation of being fed scraps off little saucers.

Eventually, they settled into their chairs and chatter. Essa had made great progress in their music and was excited to debut some new pieces at a forthcoming ball. Celestine clapped with delight and the others leant in, eyes bright and keen as Essa dropped a few hints of what to expect.

Anya had recently been to the capital, Luminis, but there was some tension in her shoulders as she spoke of seeing her siblings and visiting the shops. As the conversation drew on, the reason became clear. Barky fingers tapping on her coffee cup, she told the group that a few people had made cruel comments about her horns.

Several of the folk made sounds of disapproval.

"That city needs to wake up." Celestine's expression darkened, and despite the delicacy of her appearance, a low fury edged her voice. "We are fae. We come from Nature. We *are* Nature, and She contains multitudes and infinities."

With a sharp click, she returned her cup to the table and swept to Anya. Kneeling before her, she took the woman's cheeks. "*She* understands there is beauty in variety—it sweetens life—even if those fools in the capital have forgotten."

Anya held still, but her eyes gleamed over bright.

Celestine nodded, fingers trailing up Anya's temples to the base of her horns. "We are animals and there's no shame in that. We are no better or worse than the wolf or the squirrel."

"Speak for yourself," someone muttered, followed by a brief chuckle that flitted through the group.

A slight smile edging into her intensity, Celestine continued. "The trees are our cousins—markers of our sacred bargains." She followed the curves of Anya's branch-like horns with her fingertips, making the woman shudder. "To be kissed by that is a blessing."

Pressing her lips to Anya's brow, Celestine rocked back on her heels. "The city-dwellers have lost touch with their roots, and I pity them for it. It is their failing, not yours." Jaw set, she nodded at Anya and waited for her to nod in return before she rose.

Tears trailed down Anya's cheeks, glistening in the bright fae lights. They tugged on me, making the back of my throat raw.

As Celestine returned to her seat, a number of the others expressed their agreement and sympathies. Essa squeezed Anya in a hug.

I pulled my knees close to my chest, a strange feeling twisting in my gut.

These were fae, and I'd expected yesterday's debauched party. I'd expected the prince's cruelty. I was even expecting to hear them plotting ways to toy with humans using brutality and pleasure in equal measure.

But I absolutely had not expected this.

These were friends. Just normal friends. They shared their hurts and their triumphs. They cheered each other up and lent support whether it was needed to pull another from the depths or to lift them to even greater heights.

I stared at the fire because I didn't want them to see the tears in my eyes.

After a decade of emptiness, they came from the hollow

place in my chest. They called out for Zinnia, for the one who'd shared my hurts and triumphs, who'd hugged me, who'd protected and loved me. Who'd been my sister and my friend.

How long had it been since I'd really thought about anything other than avenging her? How long since I'd acknowledged how much I fucking missed her? There was no one in the world who'd lived our shared experiences. Who could tell me little details of what she remembered of Mama and Papa before they'd died. Who made me feel like less of an orphan. No one else knew the story of the time we'd found guards bathing in a river and had watched, giggling, from the bushes. No one else had been there when my gift had awoken. No one else had filed down my teeth.

Without her, I was truly alone.

12

I curled up in front of the fire and dozed away the tears, letting the friendly chatter lull me. I woke with a soft blanket being draped over me and a steaming cup of honeyed tea on the hearth.

"I'm just going to leave this here," Celestine announced. "I might forget about it. It would be a shame if some little creature were to drink it while I wasn't looking." There was a ripple of laughter before the conversation continued.

"Such an adorable little thing," someone else said.

I wiped my eyes on the blanket, dried tears scratching my skin, and sat up enough to take a good long gulp of tea.

A cup. A proper cup. I never thought I'd be so glad to hold one. Honey and lemon coated my tongue, sweet-sharp and glorious.

The afternoon wore on and they swapped tea and coffee for alcohol, although they still poured it from teapots. Celestine left me a little in the bottom of the cup but mentioned it might be a little strong for human constitutions.

Deepest purple-black with flecks of gold shimmering in its depths. It tasted of late summer, like a first kiss with sticky fingers and blackberry-stained lips. Another drink was pale gold, like a white wine, but flavoured with delicate elderflowers, springtime, and a hint of vanilla.

With the alcohol, their chatter turned to lovers and failed lovers and funny stories of truly disastrous couplings. Interestingly, it emerged that fae men took a monthly tincture to prevent unwanted pregnancy. No need for the preventative tea I'd taken all my adult life.

Which seemed to make fae much freer with sex than humans were... and bolder. How refreshing.

I found myself chuckling, and more than once, I leant forward, about to add to the conversation before I remembered where I was.

An idea crept through me, stronger each time I went to join in. Maybe I had it wrong. Maybe it would piss off the prince more if I spoke to everyone *but* him.

So when Anya gave me a sidelong look and wondered out loud whether I was a virgin, I answered. Celestine sat up as I laughed and said, "Absolutely not."

And that was how I ended up getting my cup topped up again and again as I told a room full of fae about the men and women I'd had. The room was spinning by the time I got to the duke who liked to watch me fuck his wife but wouldn't let me touch him.

"I had no idea humans were so *interesting*." Essa stared at me, bright green eyes wide. They hadn't touched the cup in their hands for the past half hour. "I always thought Albion was terribly... *proper*."

"It is." I shrugged, sloshing blackberry wine on my dress.

"But when you're in a performing troupe, the usual rules don't apply."

Anya sat up, a sly smile on her lips. "That reminds me of the time I had twins."

Essa cocked their head. "I didn't know you had children."

"Not like *that*." And she told us how a theatre group had visited her parents' estate when she'd still lived with them, and amongst their number had been a pair of gorgeous twins. I'd never had two men at once, and I think my eyes almost fell out of my head when she told us how they'd fucked her at the same time.

As the sun faded outside, the guests drifted away and I curled up on my rug, half listening to the conversation of those left.

"Little bird, here. Come." The deep voice cut through the warm cocoon I'd lost myself in.

Groggy, I blinked and pushed myself upright. Only Celestine remained, and the cups had been tidied away.

The prince stood in the doorway, pointing at the floor in front of his feet. His eyes bored into me, the glint of challenge sending a thrill down my spine.

He was calling me like a dog. And he knew I understood that.

I was supposed to refuse to come, maybe say something like "I'm not a dog, you know." Then he'd march over here and haul me out by my arm.

I want to break you.

But I wouldn't break. I would beat him at his own game.

So I smiled and pushed myself to my feet and started towards him, ignoring the way the room spun.

His mouth flattened. His brows lowered.

I'd spoiled his fun. My smile widened, and I missed my

sharp canines at that moment. They would've painted a perfectly vicious picture to match my perfectly vicious pleasure.

He raised his chin. "On your hands and knees."

Celestine huffed out a short breath. "Is that really ne—?"

"Hands and knees." He ground the words out like he took delight in breaking them where he could not break me.

I sank to my knees and took my time crawling to him, as though I enjoyed every minute. And when I saw the way it made his nostrils flare, I *did*.

When I reached his feet, I looked up at him, wide-eyed and innocent, like I didn't understand exactly how much I'd pissed him off.

His irritation hummed in the tight set of his muscles, the flat line of his mouth, his fisted hands. "Thank you, Celestine." He inclined his head at her before throwing the door open. "Get up—I'm not going to wait for you to crawl all the way back to my chambers."

Oh, no. He wanted me on my hands and knees, and that's where I'd stay. Call it malicious obedience.

I crawled out after him and threw a grin over my shoulder at Celestine. She waved and smothered a smirk behind her hand.

The prince went on a few steps, then stopped and spun. "What the fuck are you...?" He huffed. "I said *get up*."

I kept crawling.

In silence, his shiny black boots stepped into my space and before I had a chance to look up, an arm banded around my waist and hoisted me up. I couldn't help squealing and hated myself for it.

Especially when I landed over his shoulder and found him glancing back at me with a smirk. That tiny, pathetic sound had been enough of a protest to please him. It wasn't a sound of me breaking, but for him, it was the sound of a crack forming.

I clenched my jaw against any other noises I might make as he strode down the corridor, hand fastened around my thigh.

"You stink of blackberry wine. What else did she feed you?"

Cheek leaning on my hand, I stared back the way we'd come and refused to answer.

His harsh exhale made me feel a little better.

He asked me a few more questions on the way to his chambers, and I maintained my silence. When we arrived, he undressed with his back to me as though he couldn't stand to look at me.

That suited me perfectly.

I tugged off my dress, noting the lack of purple stains even though I'd definitely spilled my drink. Celestine must've used her magic to clean it. Despite snoozing, my limbs still felt heavy and fuzzy, and I was glad to crawl under my blanket at the end of the bed.

"No. Not tonight." He had his back to me still. Its muscles were taut, his shoulders square. "You've displeased me, so you'll sleep on the floor. The bed is a privilege for when you've been good."

Sharing his bed was a *privilege*? I snorted. Let him wonder what I was laughing at—that would torture him more than any words. I grabbed my blanket and nestled in front of the fire.

Instead of images of his death waiting behind my eyelids, I found Zinnia. Long, chestnut brown hair. Matching eyes. The slight bump to her nose where she'd fallen while learning the silks. A faint scar on her chin from the same accident. It was the clearest I'd seen her in a long, long while.

I'll kill him for you. I'll make him suffer.

But she shook her head and faded into the darkness, leaving me alone.

THE BEST PART of two weeks went on in a similar cycle. I'd trail him for the day, serving and obeying with malicious enthusiasm. He'd get pissed off and leave me with Celestine the next day. I'd trail him for the day...

On and on until the morning of the ball Celestine's friends had mentioned, when he woke up in an excellent mood, despite how much I'd irritated him the previous day.

It set my nerves on edge, and I almost fell from my handstand.

Sitting up in bed, watching me wobble through my exercises, he smiled. It showed far too many teeth, bright against his golden skin. "You might want to skip your routine today, little bird. You're going to need your strength." With that, he leapt from bed and disappeared into the bathroom.

I thought I heard him *singing* from the shower.

He didn't say anything more about *why* I needed to save my strength, and I refused to ask. I cut my exercises short, though, just to be on the safe side.

He chose my outfit, just like every other morning. Pale green today, but no perfume. That was odd. I eyed the selection of bottles on the dressing table, trying to remind him. He glanced at them but didn't pick one. For jewellery, he chose my collar and a pair of matching anklets that, for some reason, made me think of manacles. They looked nothing like restraints. It was just that I'd let the bastard in my head.

I cursed myself and followed when he beckoned, a tight feeling in my stomach.

What the hells did he have planned?

13

We met a dozen of his hangers-on at the edge of the forest that formed part of the palace grounds. Amongst them was the grey-skinned, horned one, who I'd learned was called Roark, together with Cadan, the silver-haired man who'd stood as the prince had forced wine down my throat. They were in high spirits, and the prince laughed and clapped them on the shoulders as we arrived, a spring in his step.

It made the tightness in my stomach clench into a ball.

The golden sun necklace he wore today swung as he swaggered to the centre of the group. He didn't have to speak to gather their attention. He just stood there, shoulders back, smile dazzling. He would've made a great performer.

Once all eyes were on him, he gave an expansive gesture. "Today, gentlemen"—his yellow eyes flicked to me—"we hunt."

The whoops and cries that broke out around me faded as my pulse roared in my ears. I could pretend the sound was an adoring crowd, but the cold trickle running through my veins and the tingling of my face knew the truth. I was afraid, and rightly so.

Because the way he looked at me, eyes hooded but glinting, almost lazy but not *quite*, there was no doubt.

In this hunt, I would be the prey.

This had to be not just punishment for trying to kill him, but also for my refusal to back down. I hadn't just irritated him—it had moved into anger. I might've crowed about the fact if not for the question of what was about to happen.

Roark watched me, black eyes glinting with predatory interest. I jerked my attention away.

At his side, but a step back, Cadan wore a faint frown that almost looked like concern. Maybe it was just that I found his expressions more familiar. With his smooth skin and handsome, almost human features, he didn't fit in at the Court of Monsters. Over meals, I'd learned he spent most of his time at the capital, only visiting the prince a couple of times a year.

I tried to focus on his nearly human face, since it was the only one that didn't watch me with such vicious intensity.

Unlike his prince, whose attention seared into me like a brand. "Whoever catches our quarry may do with it as they wish, short of killing it. The creature's life is mine."

His words tightened around my throat, like the grip of an overeager lover. And yet, like I really was in bed with a lover, a sick, starved part of me liked the thrill. It vibrated through me, horrible and lively.

The gathered fae leered and laughed. Several made outrageous claims about what they'd do when they caught me. I let my pulse drown them out.

I couldn't just sit down and refuse to play. It would irritate the prince, but his friends... I had no doubt they'd follow through on their claims.

My muscles reverberated with gathering energy, ready to run. Despite the chill air, I was glad of my lightweight dress as heat blossomed along my limbs.

If I could keep ahead of them, maybe I could even escape the prince's lands. Not that being free and alone in Elfhame would be much better than this. But at least I'd survive to make another plan for vengeance.

Thinking about vengeance will kill you. It was a voice of certainty in the back of my mind. One that didn't speak often, but that always reminded me of Zinnia.

It spoke the truth—right now, I needed to focus on this "hunt."

Jaw clenched, I took a deep breath and tried to keep my fear hidden.

"Such exquisite prey doesn't come around very often." The prince stalked closer, and I had to plant my feet on the ground to keep from backing away.

My heart pounded in an urgent rhythm, telling me to *get out, get out, get out.*

He towered over me and bent closer until his nose was an inch from mine. If he tried to kiss me, I wouldn't stop him. I would lean into it and give him the kiss of his life before biting his lip until I drew blood.

That thought kept me steady as he smoothed the hair from my face and trailed a claw across my cheek.

"You wear fear so beautifully, little bird." His voice was a low purr, like it was only for me. His claw traced down my throat—a pinprick of sensation, a tickle that could turn deadly in a mere fraction of an inch. Eyelids flickering shut, he inhaled deeply. "The smell of it is quite intoxicating."

That was why he'd given me no perfume today. He wanted to smell *me*.

My mouth went dry, and I had to clench my hands into tight fists to keep from obeying the call in my muscles to *run*.

"Don't worry." He gave a soft smile, golden eyes snapping open. He cupped my chin and lifted it, the claw of his thumb pressing into my lower lip. "I'll be the one to catch you. And I won't be gentle." The soft smile broke into a vicious grin. "Now, little bird, *run*."

I stumbled as he shoved me back.

The fae's laughter and cheer had faded, and now they stood in a semicircle, leaning forward like they were on the starting line of a race, focus intent on me.

That image burned in my brain, I turned and I obeyed the prince.

I ran.

My dainty slippers slapped as I crossed the grass and entered the forest's shade. Pine needles carpeted the ground, making it springy, muffling the noise of my footfalls. Their fresh scent clung to the air, sappy and green. To my dismay, little grew beneath the soaring pines, save for moss and the occasional scrawny sapling, giving me precious little cover.

There was no sound of the prince or his friends counting like in hide and sneak. How long did I have before they followed?

Pulse speeding in my throat, tingling at the point where the prince had pressed his claw into my lip, I leapt over a fallen log and lengthened my strides. I needed to put as much distance between myself and them before they set off. That was the only thing that mattered right now.

The breaths heaved through me, hard and urgent. Every part of my body buzzed with energy.

I'd never known anything like it. How had I lived so long deadened and now felt like *this*? It was as though my body had roared into life.

I had no idea how long I ran before howls cut through the forest's quiet.

A deep and primal part of me responded to that ancient sound, and raw, obliterating fear flooded me. My heart rate spiked. My lungs heaved. One slipper had fallen off, but I couldn't afford to give a shit about the pine needles digging into my feet.

Other than the howls, there was no other sound. Not birds. Not the shouts of my hunters. Not the slightest scrape of any footsteps other than my own. Even when I ducked behind a tree and paused, holding my breath to listen...

Quiet.

I peered out from my hiding place. Nothing but the forest —trunk after trunk, moss-covered ground, and scant glimmers of light that broke through the dense canopy.

Were they really chasing me? Or was this a joke on the prince's part, and he'd find it hilarious that he'd made me run headlong into the forest?

My eyes burned as I scanned for movement.

Nothing.

He would love the fact he'd made me so afraid and uncertain. But in case they really were pursuing me, I'd keep going.

I turned and jerked to a stop.

A dozen feet away, red hair gleamed in the green shade. Slitted yellow eyes watched me, unblinking. A long tail twitched. His form seemed bigger than usual, and he was already huge.

With a soft sound, I darted right. He didn't move, just watched.

My muscles burned as I pushed them harder, faster. Step after step after step.

There was no sound behind. Maybe he just wanted to scare me into running again and wasn't even chasing.

When I glanced back, though, he was very much chasing.

A gasp sawed through me. Fear exploded, lending my muscles more speed.

But his long legs ate up the ground, and his wicked teeth came closer with every step.

My lungs were a pair of bellows now, each breath consuming. Tears gathered at the corners of my eyes.

Whoever catches our quarry may do with it as they wish.

What did he plan to do with me?

He gave a low growl that raised every hair on my body.

Fuck compliance. This wasn't just play anymore. He was half animal and on my heels.

I zigged and zagged between a dense clump of trees. It stopped him gaining on me, but it didn't open up the distance between us.

They didn't offer me any escape, either. A different species might've given me low branches to climb, but these pines were tall and straight, their lowest limbs far overhead. I had no chance.

Zero.

Just like Zinnia.

Then something slammed into me. Huge and hard. Hot and grasping. It bowled me over, setting the world spinning. The ground smacked my knees and elbows hard enough to bruise.

We came to a stop, the ground at my back, and the prince grinned down at me. My head was still whirling as I twisted.

Then I was free.

SLAYING THE SHIFTER PRINCE

It took me a second to register the fact, but my feet didn't delay. I was running across a clearing, dappled sun bright, flecking warmth across my shoulders.

But my blood pumped cold.

Because that grin he'd given me.

That grin.

It was every wicked beast and every cruel villain in every fairy tale I'd ever heard. It was a promise of brutality. A promise of destruction. A promise to consume and crush.

And I suddenly understood the princesses in the stories hesitating before they ran. Because for a second... the briefest, brightest spark of an instant, part of me had been engulfed by that promise. It had swooned in the face of such over-whelming force of feeling all directed at me.

Fucking idiot.

That promise would be my end.

I whimpered with each breath, heart seized by horrible certainty.

This was no game.

14

An instant later, something crashed between my shoulder blades. The air whooshed from my lungs, then the ground rushed up to greet me. It slammed into flesh and bone.

Someone crushed my face into the dirt, and red hair streaked with off-white fell around me like a curtain. The prince.

"Naughty little pet, trying to escape your master."

The pressure on my head disappeared, but that thing between my shoulder blades stayed there, weighted. Through my light gown, I felt the prick of claws. He had me pinned with just one hand.

But... not entirely helpless. I lashed out with my feet, connected with something hard. There was a sound from him, but I didn't stop to check. I kicked again, and the pressure on my back eased enough for me to drag myself out.

On hands and knees, I scrambled away.

Fuck him. I wasn't dying here.

I wasn't dying without taking him with me.

A few feet ahead sat a thick branch. Not iron. Not aconite. But I had nothing else.

I staggered to my feet, reaching out. My fingertips brushed coarse bark.

A grip closed around my legs. He yanked, and the ground flew from under me. Face-first into the dirt. Pine needles prickled my skin. Breaths panted above.

I wriggled, but his grip only tightened as he dragged me closer. Gods forbid the prince would deign to come to me.

Teeth gritted, I managed to twist onto my back before he used his massive body to pin me.

That grin again. It stayed in place as I clawed at him. My fingers snagged on something—his necklace—and it snapped, tinkling to the ground. An instant later, he caught my hands.

"So much fight for such a little creature." I hesitated to call the soft sound he made a chuckle—it was too low, too dark a sound. But that was the closest word I knew for his humour-less laugh. "And here I was starting to worry you'd never fight back."

"If you want a fight, give me back my dagger."

Another low chuckle. "I want to toy with death, but *yours*, not mine." He released my wrists.

At once, I groped for the branch, but he'd dragged me out of reach.

Amusement glinted in his eyes, and I realised. He'd released me deliberately. He wanted me to keep fighting back.

I wasn't going to give him any more amusement by trying to hit him. No.

Instead, I smiled and closed my hands into pathetic little fists.

His eyes lit up, the slitted pupils going wide and round.

But my fists weren't empty.

I turned away and threw two handfuls of pine needles and dirt.

With a grunt, his perfect, princely face screwed up, and he shielded his eyes.

Too late.

It was enough for me, though. His flinch opened up space for me to escape. Two steps, and I had the branch.

He was still rubbing his eyes and staggering to his feet when I smacked it around his head. The contact jolted up my arms, sharp and vital, beautiful and brutal.

I cranked my arms for another swing, breaths fast and full, veins alight.

I swung.

He caught.

He smiled, and the thick hunk of wood crumbled to splinters in his grip.

His breaths heaved, only...

It wasn't only his breaths.

His shoulders and arms strained against his shirt. His thighs bulged, renting the fabric of his trousers.

Holding shards of branch, I could only gape as he *grew*. Seven feet tall... eight. His clothes couldn't keep up and fell around his feet in tatters.

Except they weren't feet anymore, but something between feet and paws, clawed and covered in fur. His legs, too, they weren't... entirely human... entirely fae... Their joints were in the wrong places, pointing the wrong way, like an animal's. Sleek fur covered them, doing nothing to hide the solid muscle beneath. The stripes I'd seen on his skin continued in his fur— gold and russet—fading to a cream belly and chest, the same colour as the streaks in his hair. Not a style choice, but part of his true nature.

His narrow hips gave the impression of speed before his torso widened to a broad chest and wide shoulders. Where before he'd been large and well-built, now he was massive. A solid wall of muscle and sinew.

And his face?

The gold eyes watching me were familiar, but the rest...

Not quite fae, not quite feline. His nose had grown broad, and a slit ran down to his mouth where two long canines dimpled his lips, too long to remain hidden. Large cat's ears pricked, alert to every sound.

Somewhere between man and beast, he stood there, like a werewolf from stories I'd read as a child, only feline rather than lupine.

I didn't run. Couldn't.

Couldn't blink, either.

But my bones screamed at my muscles to move—*move*. It was only when my shoulders hit a tree I realised they'd backed me away.

Those long fangs bared fully as his upper lip curled.

Slowly, slowly, he stalked closer. His tail, now furry and thick, swished side to side.

Fear had hold of my lungs. Grey nothingness formed blotches on the edge of my vision.

Some corner of me was still sane and registered my throbbing scrapes and bruises. I'd lost my other slipper in the struggle. Half my skirt was missing. Twigs and needles clung to my hair and coated my cheek where he'd pressed my face into the ground.

But that part of me didn't have the power to make my body move.

At last, the prince reached me. His claws, now even bigger, traced the edge of my cheekbone, my jaw. He used his thumb to tilt my head to one side, then dipped his face close. "You ran so well, little bird." Each word blew into my ear, the heat a sharp contrast with the fear flooding my veins. A purr rumbled through his voice in this beast-man form. "I like your fight. I'm going to like it even more when I break it."

I was ashamed he didn't have to hold my wrists or wrestle me into stillness. What was the point in trying to hit him when he was this huge, this strong? Even my malicious compliance seemed foolish now—a drop in the ocean compared to his power.

How had I ever thought I could win against a fae? A prince? A creature who could change its shape to something so monstrous?

His hand—something between a hand and paw—slid down to my throat and closed.

This was it. He was going to strangle me.

With any luck, it would be quick.

I'm sorry, Zinnia. Tears welled in my eyes as his grip tightened—just enough pressure to make me aware of it, but not so much that I couldn't breathe.

He nuzzled below my ear. His fur tickled, drawing my muscles tight.

Maybe he wouldn't strangle me but sink those elongated teeth into my flesh instead.

"I could rip your throat out," he said, as though understanding where my thoughts had wandered. "These teeth were made for just that. I already know your blood is delicious."

I hated myself for guessing right.

"Your fear smells so sweet," he murmured against my throat.

The shudder rippled through me, despite how hard I tried to hold still. Heat flooded my stupid body, which didn't understand the difference between a man about to kill me and one about to fuck me. I'd always loved dirty talk, and his tone matched that, low and deep. The brush of his lips against my skin was just like a lover's, light and teasing.

"I wonder how it tastes."

Yes. He was going to bite me. Rip my throat out, exactly as he'd threatened.

His hot breath fanned my skin as his thumb pressed my head over further. Just below my collar, a rasping lap of his tongue over my fluttering pulse left my face tingling. Its roughness was like a cat's, made for cleaning. But also for stripping the meat from bones, as a sabrecat breeder had once told me while fucking me over the table. He'd been a little too obsessed with his cats. What would he have made of the prince?

"Yes, I like that." He laved my throat again. "Delicious. I might have to sample every part of you."

I froze as a point that felt different from his claws—larger, less sharp—trailed from my jaw down to my collarbone, clicking over my collar. One of those huge canine teeth. The light touch had me pressing into the tree, all too aware that if he applied a little more pressure, I'd learn they were still sharp enough to pierce flesh.

I tried to ignore the size of his body, its firmness. I tried not to think about the large dick I'd seen between his legs as he'd stalked closer. Or the way his balls in this form were covered in short fur that gleamed like velvet. And I tried so, so hard not to think about the times Eric had made me come while gripping my throat as the prince held mine now.

But my body was a traitor. It remembered all those things. Focused on them, like it could cling to those as he killed me, and it would make my end a little less bad. My pulse throbbed in my throat, between my thighs, low in my belly. I didn't feel the chill of the shaded forest as my skin burned.

I wasn't sure I wanted feelings anymore. Not when they could skip from guilt for my sister to this breathless place between want and fear.

Being dead inside was better than the storm buffeting me from one extreme to another.

"When you performed for me, you seemed to want death, and yet..." He nipped the point between my neck and shoulder, near where he'd cut me with his sword.

Breath seizing, I flinched.

"Yet today you run from death, cower from its promise." He pulled back, teeth bared in what must've been a sneer in this beast man form. "Even you have something to lose. I'll remember that."

Then his heat, the tickle of his fur, the rumble of his words were gone. He strode away, tossing over his shoulder, "Hunt's over."

It was only as I sucked in fresh air and released the terrible tension in my body, I looked up and saw his friends amongst the trees.

Was it their turn now?

I gripped the rough tree trunk, but instead of coming closer, they melted into the forest, all but one. Cadan watched me, lips pulling in what looked like an apologetic smile.

"Cadan," the prince's voice drifted back, "fetch my necklace. That vicious little creature must've torn it off."

I mastered myself enough to retreat as he approached. His gaze alternated between skimming the ground and glancing up at me. Eyebrows pinched together, he surveyed my tattered state.

I refused to cower or be ashamed about how I looked. I'd survived this hunt—that was a thing for pride.

The fact I'd been affected by the prince's proximity and threat was a different matter. It squirmed in my stomach and just the memory made my cheeks burn. Still, I gritted my teeth and watched the fae doing his prince's bidding.

I couldn't decide whether Cadan was a friend or servant to the prince. He seemed more friend, with the familiar way they spoke to each other and the fact he'd been included in the hunt. Yet most times I saw him, he was running around after the prince, serving him.

He ducked and snatched up the necklace. When he rose, he paused and took a step closer.

I backed off, keeping the same distance between us. The prince had said the hunt was over, but he wasn't here to make sure his friends kept to that.

Cadan stopped, exhaled, then inclined his head. The dim light glimmered on his silvery hair. I could understand why the old stories thought fae otherworldly—he didn't look like a creature of flesh and blood at this moment.

One hand raised, palm out, he ducked again and placed something on the ground before taking a few steps away and retreating into the forest.

Only when he was out of sight did I go and look at what he'd left. A jar of cobalt blue glass. The handwritten label read *Wound Salve – heals cuts and bruises.*

Frowning, I glanced the way he'd gone, but could see no

sign of him. His Prickishness had only ordered him to fetch the necklace. He'd said nothing about helping me.

I started back towards the stables, following the sound of the men's voices as I cradled the salve. If it was anything like whatever Celestine had put in my bath that first night, it would heal my injuries with astonishing speed.

Cadan had helped me... but fae never helped someone just for the sake of it.

Yet he hadn't forced a bargain from me in exchange for the salve. And hadn't Celestine been friendly and warm towards me?

Maybe I'd been wrong about fae... except for the prince.

He was exactly the monster I'd always known, and today he'd shown me his true colours.

15

The salve worked a charm, and a bath soon had my body regulated against troubling temperature changes and reactions. When I emerged, the prince was pacing his bedroom.

"You took your damn time." He scowled at my wet hair wound in a towel on top of my head. "And you needn't bother to dress up. The ball is cancelled." He strode for the door. "Come."

"But I'm not—"

"I said *come*." A growl laced his words, silencing me, and I hurried after him into the corridor, even though I was only wearing a dressing gown. I hadn't even replaced my collar.

His steps were clipped. His movements when we reached a door and he pulled it open were jerky and staccato rather than smooth with a hunter's grace.

I knew the route to Celestine's rooms by now, but it had never filled me with such trepidation before. In the space of a week I'd grown used to a routine and, apparently, the prince's manner. This switch in him was as stark a contrast as charcoal scrawled on a white page. What had him so on edge?

He didn't knock before he opened the door, and Celestine wasn't on her settee. The fae lights in the sitting room drifted, little brighter than match flames. Without hesitation, he swept into her bedroom. I trailed, footsteps slowing as I entered the dimly lit chamber.

"Celestine?" His voice... I'd never heard it this soft—this *gentle*. Where he'd murmured to me earlier, against the tree, it had been quiet but edged with the threat of teeth and claws, the promise of suffering and death. None of that laced his voice now.

"Seph?"

As a couple of servants scattered from the room, he strode to the bed and knelt at its side. Without him blocking my view, I could see Celestine lying upon it.

If I'd thought her pale before, I was mistaken. Her skin was beyond pale now, edging into grey. Sweat beaded her brow, plastering her hair. Her eyes gleamed, glassy and bright.

Stomach plummeting, I crossed the room and stopped at the foot of the bed. I gripped the bedpost, like that could settle the ill-feeling rocking through me.

She'd seemed fine yesterday. A little tired, perhaps. Now, her hand cradled in Sepher's looked small and frail, like a songbird, her skin papery and thin.

He stroked her knuckles. "I got here as soon as I could." He gave her a tight smile and didn't even throw me a glare for unwittingly holding him up. "They said you were unwell, but I didn't realise..." His brows lowered and he shook his head as he felt her brow. "Shit. You're burning up. You should've sent for me sooner."

"Sent for you?" She huffed out a breath. "Even I don't send

for a prince. Besides, I didn't want to interrupt your ball preparation."

"The ball's cancelled."

"But it was meant to..." The sentence dissolved into coughing.

"Water," he muttered, starting to rise.

"I've got it." I grabbed a jug and glass from a side table.

Exhaling, he sank back to his knees and helped Celestine to sit up. One arm around her shoulders, he propped her up while I held the glass to her lips. She took a few sips before pulling away and catching her breath.

She gave me a white-lipped smile. "You brought Zita. Lovely thing."

He made a low sound, like he wasn't happy about it. Expression hard and tight, he busied himself dipping a cloth into a bowl on the nightstand and wringing it out before mopping her brow and cheeks.

"Oh, that's nice," she sighed, eyelids easing shut. "But," she went on as he helped her lie back down, "I really think you should go and have your party."

"Well I don't." The words came out clipped and gravelly, like he said them between gritted teeth.

She opened one eye. "And I suppose it'll be a waste of time arguing with you, won't it?"

"I *am* a prince." The edge of a grin threatened on his lips, but it was a grim thing rather than his usual smirk.

"An insufferable one, at that." She sank into the pillows, but a small crease remained between her eyebrows.

"Well, you're going to have to suffer me, aren't you? I've sent for a healer from Luminis, and I'm not leaving your side until they have you fixed."

"I'm sure you have better things to..." Her voice faded as she drifted into sleep.

We waited at her side for a long while, but she didn't wake. Eventually, I realised kneeling couldn't be comfortable for Sepher, and since he wasn't being a prick for once, I took pity on him and fetched a chair. He blinked when I brought it through.

"It's for sitting on."

He gave me a flat look. "I know what chairs are for."

"You looked so blank, I had to wonder. Or is the problem that it's not a throne?"

"The problem..." He sucked in a breath, probably realising his voice was rising. "The problem," he went on, more quietly, "is that *you're* bringing it to me. And yet I can't see how it could be a trap." He watched me with narrowed eyes, still not rising from his knees.

A trap? Then he still thought I might be a danger to him, however small. He hadn't seemed the slightest bit frightened as he'd hunted me this morning.

"Temporary ceasefire." I nodded at Celestine to indicate she was its reason.

His eyebrows rose, and he inclined his head as he stood. "Thank you."

"For the chair or the ceasefire?"

He shrugged as he sank into the seat, still holding her hand. "Can't it be for both?" His attention returned to her, as though I'd been dismissed.

I watched him fuss over her a long while, wiping away sweat, giving her a little to drink, calling for fresh water to cool her brow.

If I hadn't known better, I'd have said he really cared. But

His Prickishness? What did he care about except for how good his body looked in those open shirts?

There didn't seem to be anything romantic between him and Celestine, and he hadn't called her to his bed since I'd been staying. In fact, he hadn't brought anyone back to his room since Anya and the night I'd ruined sex for him.

But even the thought of that wasn't enough to bring a smile to my lips. Not when Celestine looked so sickly and there was still no sign of the healer. My stomach knotted as I topped up her glass. Even Sepher, who usually seemed so carefree, watched her with fierce intensity, like his will alone could make her better.

She woke when a fae woman with cream-coloured braids and a calm demeanour arrived.

Sepher ran through Celestine's symptoms and the medicines she'd already taken with surprising efficiency.

"And I took white willow tea before you arrived," she added as he helped her sit.

The healer inclined her head. "Thank you, Your Highness." But her nose wrinkled as she glanced at his tail, which hadn't stopped swishing with agitation. "You've been a great help." She nodded towards the door.

He snorted, though sudden tension cut through his body, squaring his shoulders. "I'm not going anywhere."

"Sepher, darling," Celestine said with a sigh as the healer felt her hands, "yes, you are. Let the woman do her job."

His tail swished faster as he stood there, looking from the healer to Celestine.

Celestine widened her eyes at him, then at the exit.

"Fine," he growled, and strode out. I followed, shutting the door behind me.

Tension carved the lines of his back and arms as he poured

two drinks from a decanter. He handed me one before slumping on the settee. It looked comically small for his frame, but I found myself unable to laugh in the face of his tight expression.

I swirled my glass, watching the golden liquid flecked with shimmering silver particles. Celestine had called it *aurgwyn*. I edged closer to the armchair opposite him, watching for a reaction as his "pet" threatened to sit on the furniture.

Nothing. He just sat there, knuckles white on his glass, brows in a tight line, shadowing his eyes.

He really was worried about Celestine.

I eased into the chair and took a sip of *aurgwyn*. Its spiced flavour warmed my throat and did a little to soften the knot in my stomach.

"I have to admit..." I finally said into the dim quiet. Maybe the fact I couldn't see his slitted pupils let me pretend it wasn't him I was speaking to. Or perhaps it was because he wasn't wearing one of his usual arrogant or cruel expressions... or his crown. "I'm surprised to see you so concerned about Celestine."

He glanced up. The low light softened his features, caressing the square jaw and strong chin, rather than cutting them so harshly. He gave a slight grunt before taking a gulp from his glass.

I supposed I hadn't exactly asked a question for him to answer.

"This isn't the first time you've had to call a healer for her, is it?"

His eyebrows scrunched together in a glower when he looked up at me again, as though I'd interrupted some terribly important work. "No." The way he said it with such an air of finality made me think he was going to stop, but a soft exhale followed and he continued, "She's prone to illness."

"And you cancelled the ball *because* she's ill. Didn't you?"

"Obviously." He drained his glass and swept to his feet. Back to me, he poured more *aurgwyn* from the decanter. "Celestine was a sickly child." His voice drifted across the room, its softness at odds with the hard angles of his shoulders. "Thankfully, she tends to be better now than she was then, but still..."

He turned and brought the decanter over, his lips pressed together in a thin line. When he placed it on the table before me, he nodded towards it as though inviting me to help myself.

It seemed tonight I'd offered a ceasefire and in return, I was not a pet. I rubbed my throat where the absence of my collar was... strange. A lightness. A lack. A place air touched but shouldn't.

Still, I liked being able to sit on the armchair, feet tucked under me. And I liked being able to pour myself another drink without having to sip from a saucer or sneak a cup Celestine had "absentmindedly" left unattended.

"So, you've known her since you were children?"

"Mmm." He jerked his chin at the fireplace and orange-pink flames burst into life. They glinted on the *aurgwyn*, making it shimmer a coppery colour. "She is..." He paused, frowning at the fire as though searching there for the words. "The closest thing I have left to a sister. We were born on the same day—her, me, and my twin."

A twin? He had an elder brother—the crown prince of the Dawn Court. But I'd never heard of another sibling. I pressed the rim of my glass to my lower lip to keep myself quiet. If I prodded him too much, he might realise who he was talking to and stop. But my curiosity hungered for more.

"That day, as I took my first breath, my twin sister... didn't." His nostrils flared as his brow lowered.

Something in my chest clenched, like a tight scribble in my sketchbook when I just didn't know what to draw.

"It's a strange thing, to share such a small space with another being—the first being you ever meet. To grow intertwined. To have a primal understanding of 'us' and 'them' before you have any concept of 'me' or 'her.' And then to come out into the world and... it's gone."

Maybe I'd been wrong and the gods did exist. And right now they were taking great delight in playing with me, because there was the slightest hint of pressure at the back of my eyes. How could I be even remotely upset for this monster?

No. It wasn't him I was upset for—it was his twin sister who'd never had a chance to *be*. The idea of her being born and never taking breath—that *was* sad. And, of course, it tugged on my heart and my own loss.

Maybe I'd also had too much to drink. Fae alcohol was hard to predict—it seemed to interact with my emotions more than regular spirits. One day, it had little effect; today, it had my heart sore for a fae. Tricksy stuff, indeed.

Sepher—no, *the prince* sucked in a long breath and shrugged. "So... I grew up with Celestine instead of my sister, and she... well, I suppose she stepped into that void." The corner of his mouth rose, its usually cruel lines softened by the rosy fire. "I still wonder what it would've been like had it been the three of us. But maybe Luminis couldn't have handled that."

Despite myself, I gave a soft laugh. I caught myself before I apologised for his sister. I wouldn't do that. Not when he'd taken mine.

I might've called a ceasefire for tonight, and I might've felt something for his sister, who never had a chance to live, but that didn't mean anything. Seeing Celestine so ill was getting to me, together with the *aurgwyn*. It didn't change anything. It didn't change my plans.

It just meant that when the prince lay dead at my feet, I'd know all the facets of his monstrousness.

And, it turned out, even monsters had feelings.

16

That night, we didn't go to bed until late. Sepher wouldn't leave until after the healer had finished and said Celestine would be well come morning. Not until after we'd sat with her a few hours more, and she finally woke. Smiling, she told us to "fuck off and let me get some proper sleep without the pair of you fussing over me."

It seemed being ill allowed you to get away with telling a prince to fuck off. Noted.

In the morning, I woke late and had to drag myself out of bed to my workout routine. My scrapes had almost disappeared, thanks to Cadan's salve, but my legs were sore from my desperate run through the forest.

"I suppose with all these workouts, you're going to want to perform, aren't you?" Sepher sat up in bed, watching.

But last night's ceasefire was over. I wouldn't answer. And I needed to stop thinking of him by his name. He was "the prince" and nothing more.

Belly on the floor, I reached back and gripped my ankles, forming a loop.

"I asked you a question."

I shot him a look and smirked to say I'd heard him perfectly.

His jaw worked side to side, that muscle twitching.

As I did press-ups, he asked me a couple more questions. I didn't answer.

At last, he came to the one I'd been waiting for. "Why did you try to kill me?"

I glanced up, one eyebrow raised, as I pushed my arms straight. I would give him a little something this time. A reward for asking the question I most wanted to hear. "I thought you didn't care."

"I'm curious."

I leapt to my feet and, just as I'd hoped, his eyes widened and he leant forward, keen attention on me. He thought I was going to answer.

Instead, I shrugged and stretched, then slunk into the bathroom to wash.

When I emerged, he was fuming, muscles practically vibrating with barely suppressed anger. He stomped into the bathroom, tail swishing. He'd left my outfit, jewellery, and perfume tossed on the bed.

I took my time dressing, smiling to myself. It wasn't quite the same as sinking an iron dagger between his ribs, but it was as close as I could get right now.

Every day when he bathed, I searched a different part of the room for my blade. I'd been methodical, laying out sectors in my mind, checking one each day. Yesterday, I'd completed the sweep and found no sign. Not that I could blame him for hiding it somewhere else. He was arrogant, not stupid.

My victories would have to remain petty ones for now. I plotted ways to get alone time in other parts of the palace and extend my search.

He swept out of the bathroom, completely naked, dick swinging with each step. It was so sudden, I found myself watching its breathtaking length for a moment before I remembered and tore my eyes away. He must've been mightily pissed off, because he didn't even smirk or make a suggestive joke when he found me staring.

That was my first warning.

My second was his choice of clothing—all black. The prince never wore such sombre tones unless they were paired with a colour. He favoured greens and blues—colours of growth and clear skies. I'd put it down to his affinity with the Dawn Court, but perhaps it was more a reflection of his bright personality.

He was cruel, yes, and arrogant, absolutely. But he laughed a lot and made the others around him laugh even more. He sometimes even smiled with simple pleasure, rather than wickedness. Playful and spontaneous, I could understand how he'd amassed his own court.

But today...

Today he wore black and ordered me to follow.

Wearing unease like a cloak, I hurried after.

We arrived in the bustling dining room for lunch. Celestine took one look at the prince and her eyebrows rose.

Another warning.

Roark greeted him, smile wide, black eyes glinting. Cadan pulled out a chair and went to pour him a drink.

"No." The prince's voice echoed through the room with a buzzing quality I hadn't heard before. It reverberated in every glass and plate, in the tiled floor, and even in the chandeliers overhead. They rang in a discordant chime that set my teeth on edge.

Everyone fell silent.

"My pet is going to serve us today." With a flick of his tail, he dismissed the servants.

Cadan returned to his seat, brow creased.

Serving them. Fine. That wouldn't be so bad. Maybe the prince didn't have much taste for punishment after worrying about Celestine all night.

With an overly sweet smile, I grabbed his plate and piled on potatoes that had been roasted with rosemary and garlic. Their scent made my mouth water.

"Closer, pet." His large hand slid around my waist and tugged me in, so I was pressed against his leg as I spooned more vegetables onto his plate.

I didn't pull away. Not because his warmth was welcome. Only because he wanted me to resist.

He grinned at his friends, canines showing. "This is how I expect her to serve you." His hand slid up, playing with my hair before lowering to the small of my back. "Be sure to show her your appreciation however you see fit." As I leant over the table, reaching for a platter of bloody roast beef, he patted my backside. "Good girl."

I froze. Just for a second. Just with a momentary flare of mingled surprise and irritation.

But it was enough to make him chuckle, low and dark, and tug me closer. "Such a good girl," he crooned.

Laughter rippled along the table. Celestine broke its wave, frowning instead of joining in.

He'd half-mauled me yesterday, but he hadn't touched me quite like this before. Certainly not in front of his friends.

Teeth gritted, I slapped two slabs of meat onto his plate

and presented it to him. My flourish wouldn't have looked out of place at one of my performances.

Celestine was next. She picked up her plate and reached for a spoon to serve herself.

The prince's hand splayed over her plate and pushed it onto the table with a warning look.

Lips pursed, she frowned at him for long seconds before finally sitting back.

That muscle twitched in the prince's jaw, and he jerked his chin at the table, indicating for me to get on with it. I served her.

The next person touched my back and exclaimed about how small I was, but otherwise left me alone. Anya stroked my hair and murmured a thank you I suspected was too quiet for the prince to hear. I worked my way around the table with nothing worse than lingering touches of my waist or back and leering looks. Maybe they didn't entirely trust the prince's permission to play with his toy.

Maybe it was the way he watched as he ate, gaze gripped by me.

A chair stood empty, so I started towards the next, Roark's. He sat back, legs spread, grin spreading even wider. Since he had no pupils, it was often hard to tell where his black eyes were pointing. But not now.

They burned into me.

Then a broad chest blocked my way, and when I looked up, I found Cadan smiling down at me. "I'm next." He slid into the empty chair and gestured to his plate, placing himself between me and Roark.

From the look he'd given me, I had no doubt the horned fae planned to take full advantage of his prince's permission, but Cadan had stepped in, literally. He hadn't saved me, but he'd bought me a short reprieve.

My smile as I served him was genuine.

Under the prince's gaze, he held my shoulder. "Thank you, Zita."

"You call her 'pet.'" The prince's voice rumbled across the table, chiming in the chandeliers again.

Cadan cleared his throat and inclined his head. "Of course, Sepher." His hand trailed to the back of my neck, tickling the soft hairs there.

As I placed the full plate before him, his touch remained, holding me in place as his gaze lingered on mine. His chest rose and fell deeply, and a slow smile lifted the corners of his mouth. "Thank you, Zi... *pet.*" Something in his deep blue eyes was soft, reminding me of the moment in the forest when he'd given me the salve.

I nodded acknowledgement. I would've thanked him for the salve—I wanted to—but I doubted the prince knew and it certainly would've got Cadan in trouble.

Bracing, I moved on to Roark. He sat back, positioned so I'd have to step between his legs to reach his plate.

How delightful.

I'd encountered men like him before, though, and I'd earned good money out of them. I wasn't about to let him cow me like I was a trembling human, afraid of touching *such a big strong man.* I let myself smile at the simpering, sarcastic tone in my head, and he must've wondered at the expression, because a frown flickered between his eyebrows.

As I bent over the table to reach the first platter, his hand landed between my shoulder blades.

"Thank you, Sepher," he said as his touch trailed down my spine, "for so generously sharing such a great view."

Goosebumps flooded my skin. I wasn't sure if it was at his words or his touch, but it was definitely at *him*.

Amid the sounds of eating, I caught the faint noise of fabric tearing. The pinprick of claws traced over my skin. He'd torn my dress, and his hand showed no sign of slowing in its descent.

With a deep breath, I continued spooning food onto his plate. The temptation to spit on it bubbled in my veins, but the prince watched me, unblinking, his meal forgotten, knife and fork still in his hands.

Roark reached my arse and squeezed, fingers cupping right under the cheek. I gasped at the five points of pain shooting through me where his claws broke my skin. A second later, I mastered myself and plastered a smile back in place, but it was too late. He was already laughing.

It spread through the group, skipping Celestine and only lightly touching Cadan.

The prince held very still. That muscle in his jaw twitched, and for a moment I thought he was going to reach across the table and kill me, but his lips curved slowly.

No one had told his eyes that he was smiling, though. They remained blank as he straightened and put down his cutlery.

Roark's laugh faded to a chuckle, and he squeezed my flesh again. "And here I was thinking she wouldn't react to *anything*. Shame, I was going to try somewhere else next. Maybe I still should." He turned his hand, fingers straying between my legs, his target unmistakable.

Teeth creaking together, I placed a slice of beef on his plate and waited.

The prince huffed and slammed his palm onto the table. Every plate and platter leapt. A glass toppled over, sending

SLAYING THE SHIFTER PRINCE

crimson wine seeping across the white tablecloth. Roark stilled a hair's breadth from my pussy.

"This is taking too long." The prince flicked a finger at Cadan, but his yellow eyes remained on me. "Bring back the servants. Little bird, come here."

I tried not to let my relief show as I straightened and stepped out of Roark's space.

But my relief was short-lived, because the prince gave a slow, slow smile, and this time it did reach his eyes, glittering and wicked. "I should've been more specific." He leant forward, fingers steepled over the table. "Crawl to me on your hands and knees."

This again? As if it would bother me.

"Of course, *Your Highness*," I said with a theatrical bow.

A couple of fae jerked upright. Other than at my "collaring," this was probably the first time they'd heard me speak.

Like this was a stage rather than just a dining room, I sank to my knees with a dancer's grace and crawled the length of the table. Head up, I batted my eyelashes at my audience until I rounded the corner and could see the prince. Then I kept my focus on him with a rigid smile.

Break me? Impossible.

I was going to crush him into pieces and fucking devour him.

17

The prince's smirk didn't waver as he held my gaze, but there was something brittle about it.

On my knees at his feet, I spread my hands and presented myself.

"Such a good pet." But there was a gritted edge to his voice that told me he wasn't happy. Perhaps he didn't think I'd do this in front of so many people.

He watched me a long while, calculation in his predatory eyes.

"What are you going to do, Sepher?" Roark leant forward, and although I didn't break from the prince's gaze, I could feel those black eyes boring into me. "I have a few suggestions."

The prince lifted his chin as though preening under the attention. "I know you hate me. You tried to kill me, after all. But..." He held my throat and slid his hand up until I was forced to tilt my head back. "I've seen how you look at me, little bird." He came close, breath hot in my ear as he murmured, "And I scented your arousal during our hunt yesterday. How deliciously twisted."

He sat back with a grin, and I fought to master myself. But with his hand there, he must've felt my thick, slow swallow. Maybe even the burning flush of my skin.

"So, I think it will be best for you to admit the truth. Nice and loud for everyone to hear. A cleansing, if you will. Tell me I'm the most handsome man you've ever seen." He sat back, one eyebrow arching in challenge.

My teeth fused together.

Prick.

And even more of a prick, because it was true. He *was*. But fae were all beautiful. It was like they'd been made with superiority in mind. Stronger. Faster. More handsome. Apex predators with us poor mortals as their prey. They didn't even need to stalk us and leap from the shadows—they could simply fascinate us with their stunning, not-quite-human looks.

Most had fae charm, too. A powerful magic that rolled off them and could compel a human to obey their every command or throw themselves upon the fae. If the human had no magic, that was.

My gift made me immune to fae charm and gave me a watered-down version of its power. It had served me well on the stage.

But here, kneeling before this Day Prince and his smug smirk, I felt no relief at the fact, only hate.

I hated the look on his face.

I hated him for killing my sister.

I hated that he was right. He was horribly handsome. The most attractive person I'd ever met—even more than the other fae.

And, most of all, I hated myself for thinking that.

One side of his mouth twitched as though he sensed he was winning this dare.

Fuck him.

I rose on my knees, placing myself between his spread legs. "You are the most unutterably handsome, the most gorgeous, the most beautiful man I have ever seen." I lifted my chin and gave him a sweet smile before adding in a low tone meant only for him, "It's simply a shame you just can't win. Poor prince."

His smile remained in place. But his eyes twitched narrower for an instant, and he gripped the arms of his chair a little tighter, claws digging into the lacquered wood with a splintering sound.

Finally, the tension faded, and his gaze trailed down me. "You look hungry, little bird. I think you need feeding." He pointed to his lap. "Here."

Inviting contact and forcing me to initiate it. That was another step.

But another one that didn't bother me. Foolish man, did he still not understand what he was dealing with? I had draped myself over all sorts of wealthy folk in the name of performance. Sitting on his knee was nothing.

Not dropping eye contact, I slid into his lap. There were leftovers on his plate. I eyed them, wondering which he'd order me to start with.

"Good girl. So obedient today." His smile lacked the earlier tension, and that sent unease trickling down my spine, like a drop of cold water had found its way under my clothes. "Now, place your hands behind your back."

I shot him a frown. I must've misheard or misunderstood. How could I eat with my hands behind my back?

But he only raised his eyebrows, prompting me to obey or give in.

And giving in wasn't an option.

So I obeyed, trying to ignore the way my pulse went that little bit faster.

Something warm slid around my wrists. My breath caught, because both his hands were still on the arms of the chair.

His tail. I'd never touched it before. It was surprisingly muscular. Years ago, I'd held another performer's snake, curious to see what it felt like. Pure muscle that undulated and wrapped, strong and hard. The prince's tail was the same, but covered with smooth skin rather than scales.

Its grip tightened and pulled my arms back until I couldn't do much more than move my head, helpless.

And that was when the prince's smile widened. "Perfect." He took one of those delicious-smelling potatoes from his plate and held it an inch before my mouth.

He was going to feed me.

I couldn't say why, but this edged closer to some line I'd drawn in the sand many years ago. On one side were the things I would do with clients: fucking, sucking, dancing, and laughing. And on the other were things I wouldn't.

I'd always thought there was nothing on the other side of that line, just a wasteland.

But this?

Its closeness to the edge lifted goosebumps across my flesh.

Perhaps it was the fact I had to lean forward and accept the food from him, making me complicit in my own helplessness. Maybe it was that being fed was... intimate somehow. I was sure my parents must've fed me when I was very small, though I didn't remember them. But no one had ever placed food in my mouth.

The rest of the table had gone back to eating, with knives and forks scraping across plates and the low murmur of conversation. But I could feel the periphery of their attention upon us.

I could practically hear them wonder, *Will this be the thing that breaks her?*

Lips pressed together, I eyed the prince.

He watched my mouth, the corner of his rising. "You know, my sweet human rebel, I could use charm to make you do this."

I was glad for my tight jaw right now, because it stopped me smiling in triumph at the fact he still hadn't realised I was gifted.

"Or anything, in fact," he went on, voice a low purr. "I could make you fuck me if I wanted. I could make you bend over this table and beg me. But I don't want to resort to such obvious tactics. Besides..." His canines flashed in a wicked grin. "I think you might enjoy that too much. No, the beauty of this is that you're totally in control while you do as I command."

The unease that had trickled through me was now a gushing waterfall. I twitched, brow pulling into a tight frown.

Fuck.

I'd thought I was winning by obeying so thoroughly. Before, my disobedience had pleased him, and he seemed to want me to fight against his orders, so I'd done the opposite.

What I hadn't counted on was that my compliance *also* pleased him.

Fuck.

But... no. I'd seen him irritated by my vicious obedience. That twitch of his jaw.

I searched his glittering gaze, trying to find some hint of truth in its golden depths.

There was no truth. Only challenge.

He wafted the herb-flecked potato before me, one eyebrow arching.

Oh shit. He wasn't just *not* stupid: he was cunning. He'd created a situation where, whatever I did, he could enjoy it. Either I was disobedient and he got to punish me more harshly. Or I was obedient and therefore a creature under his control.

If I hadn't been so full of roiling rage, blasting through me like storm winds, I might've admired the way he'd played this game.

"Eat." His tail squeezed around my wrists. "You'll do it anyway. If I have to charm you, I'll make you do it with a smile on your face. You do it yourself, and you can scowl all you like."

Fine. I snapped the potato from his fingers. My lower lip ran along the pad of his thumb as I took it, and his eyebrows shot up.

Not a studied expression. Not triumph or smugness. Not cruelty or a dare.

Surprise. Maybe even a hint of something close to unease.

Perhaps there still was a way I could win. Challenging and daring him right back.

I tested my theory and licked his finger as though eager to get every scrap of flavour.

His breath stilled. His pupils grew round and wide.

You even ruin sex.

Oh dear. My poor prickish prince.

Because, yes, he was the most handsome man I'd ever seen, and my body responded to him in ways it shouldn't.

But his body was responding to me, too.

I closed my lips around his thumb and sucked, flicking my tongue over the tip before I pulled away. He snatched a sharp breath.

I gave a low chuckle, twin to the one he gave so often. "You think I'll back down," I whispered against his skin. "Oh, my poor prince, do you understand now who you're dealing with?"

Still bound by his tail, I managed to slide up his thigh far enough to make him tense. With a roll of my hips, I ground my arse against him and was rewarded with the twitch of his cock.

The achievement flooded me, hot and bright and pulsing.

I smirked, letting the claw of his thumb press into my lip. "Does this look like backing down to you?"

"Leave us." His husky voice boomed across the room, chiming in the chandeliers.

The room emptied.

18

He didn't break from me, eyes locked with mine in a battle whose only sound was the mingled one of our deep breaths.

The door closed, and that was when he erupted.

One hand around my throat, he slammed me into the table. I wasn't even entirely aware of it happening—I just blinked and then I was there, plates smashing to the floor, the hard surface biting into my back.

The prince bent over me, breaths harsh and hot against my face, teeth bared. "You're speaking, little bird." His voice shook with vicious intensity. "Sounds a lot like backing down to me." He pressed into the space between my legs, which only added to the sweet sensation of triumph chasing through me.

My hands were free now, but I left them splayed on the table. Let him see I didn't need to lift a finger to win. Instead, I cocked my head at him. "It's a sad position you're in that getting me to speak is such a great victory."

My body throbbed with the heady pleasure of winning. I blamed that for my legs looping around his hips and pulling me flush against him. He was already semi-hard, and hot wetness flooded my centre.

He made a low sound but did nothing to pull away or bring me closer.

"You're the one *beneath* in this position, pet. You're the one wearing a collar." There was a series of soft clicks as his claws scraped across the jewels at my throat.

Danger, my speeding pulse warned. But also, it whispered, *pleasure*. And that was something I'd been starved of for too long.

So, too, was this bright and beautiful rage surging through me. The heat of all these emotions merged, their borders lost, until I didn't know where fear ended and anger began, nor how desire fit with them.

I ground against him. It only took a moment before he was hard, the tip digging into my belly through our clothing.

Another victory. It pulled a soft moan from me. I definitely didn't make the sound because of the feel of his hardness against my softness, the sweet friction against my clit.

No. This was all about the elation of winning.

Maybe it was the sound I made, but at last, the prince shifted from a still participant to movement. His grip around my throat tightened, like he could catch my moan, and he pressed into me, hips snapping like we really were fucking.

His breathless weight on my body was delicious. Real and vibrant.

I tried to pretend it was the weight of his death. But the way he rolled against me snatched my attention, honing it to a fine beam of light that centred on my pussy.

Snarling, he held my gaze. I grinned right back, high on his ensnared attention.

Making my enemy want me. It was a dangerous game. A thrilling one. One that made me feel far more alive than a decade of plotting to kill him ever had.

It roared in my ears like rapturous applause. A standing ovation.

Maybe murder had been shortsighted. This could be a much sweeter revenge.

Because he'd called me his little bird and his pet, and yet I was a bird freed.

I soared on the glory of feeling. On the glory of *living*.

On the bone-fracturing brilliance of victory.

It was an intoxicating brew, stronger than fae spirits. And I gulped it down. Greedy. Wanting. Half-starved.

I writhed and rocked beneath him, now, chasing pleasure he both wanted and hated, taking sustenance from that fact. He crushed me into the table, spiking sensation through my nipples as he rubbed against me. One hand gripped my hip, the other my throat, bracing me for each drive of his body.

"Tell me to stop," he growled. It rumbled through his chest into mine, reverberating at the point where we'd be joined if not for our clothing.

"Never," I spat.

He thrust once more, fingers flexing so they cut off my breath.

He was going to kill me.

I lifted my chin, some part of me welcoming it as what I deserved. Some part that saw what I was doing and was disgusted that I could spread my legs for the fae who'd killed my sister. Some part that hated me for feeling alive as I did it.

His nose wrinkled, then his grip was gone. He turned with a roar that shook the room.

Gulping in air, I watched his square shoulders as he stormed out. He didn't even bother to slam the door behind him.

The chandeliers were still tinkling when I laughed.

I'd won. A battle, if not the war. But I'd *won*.

19

I didn't see the prince for the rest of the afternoon. It was like he'd forgotten about me, which suited me well. I explored the dining room and nearby parts of the palace, searching for my dagger and learning the layout. There was a whole library, but I wasn't here to read, only to find the weapon that would allow me to win this war.

I had no luck.

And even less when I found the door to his study locked. Maybe I could swipe the key from him one day. The dagger had to be in there.

Eventually, Cadan came and fetched me for His Royal Prickishness. I took the opportunity to thank him for the salve. Glancing along the corridor, he only acknowledged my thanks with a nod, then mouth in a tight line, he delivered me to the prince's room.

I was not allowed to sleep on the bed that night.

The prince spelled out his displeasure in various other ways over the following couple of weeks. I served him at every meal. I wasn't allowed to wear shoes or jewellery other than my collar. Most days he left me with Celestine as though he couldn't stand the sight of me.

But I knew better.

He couldn't stand *liking* the sight of me.

One morning dawned bright and crisp. Snow had fallen overnight, leaving the palace under its heavy blanket. It softened the broken lines of ruined outbuildings. It erased the cracks in the garden's statues and crept through the broken domes.

I was allowed silk slippers that day, but they offered scant protection as the prince led me out to the eastern side of the gardens. Cold nipped my toes through the thin fabric, which was soon soaked with snowmelt.

He moved silently and swiftly over the fluffy inches of white, while my steps creaked. Our breaths streamed mist through the frigid air. His came out in great plumes, perhaps because of how hot he always was.

He wore his crown and the usual shirt and trousers. His only concession to the snow was a light jacket. Meanwhile, I wore one of the many silky dresses. No coat or cloak. Not even a scarf.

We passed a ruined building that might've once been a small temple. Its roof stood open to the sky, and ivy crept over its crumbling walls, battling with the snow to reclaim the stone remains.

It only took a few minutes to reach the lake that dominated this side of the gardens, but my feet burned with the cold. Unfazed, he took coffee and breakfast under a dome overlooking the lake's frozen surface, leaving me to stand in the snow.

It looked like something from a painting or a dream.

Perfect white columns with subtle gold decoration at their bases. Snow encrusting the dome. The splash of colour that was the prince sitting upon a marble throne as he contemplated his domain.

He took his time eating, only pausing to call, "Are you hungry, little bird?"

I stood to attention, eyes on the lake and the moorhens scuttling across its surface, their black feathers stark against the frosted landscape.

"I'll take that as a yes. Here you go." Grinning, he threw a pastry in my direction. It landed in the snow three feet away.

I'd eaten from his hands. I'd sipped from a saucer. But I wasn't going to eat off the floor.

Arms at my sides, I kept still and tried to ignore the biting cold. It tugged on my muscles, whispering at them to shiver for warmth. I wouldn't give him the satisfaction of seeing my discomfort.

With a grunt, he shrugged and returned to his food. "Suit yourself."

As the minutes ticked by, I kept my arms clamped to my sides, but eventually I couldn't help shivering. Icy cold stabbed my toes in wave upon wave of shooting pain. At least my teeth weren't chattering.

Subtly, I lifted one foot, giving it a brief respite from contact with the snow before replacing it on the floor and lifting the other. I wasn't sure if the chilly air against the wet slippers was better or worse, but I was stuck for ideas about how else to alleviate my suffering.

The prince was on his second cup of coffee when Cadan came out with a handful of letters. He wore leather boots and a thick coat with a fox fur trim. I couldn't help but stare at it longingly.

I'd been forced to cross my arms by this point, trying desperately to tuck my hands into my armpits for some measure of warmth. At least my toes were numb rather than painful now. My nose and cheeks had lost all feeling, too.

Cadan eyed me as he passed and flashed a quick smile while the prince wasn't looking. I wasn't sure what to make of him. Was he trying to become an ally? A friend?

"These arrived this morning, Sepher." He handed over the letters. "I think they're all from Luminis."

"Oh, joy."

I could only see the prince in profile, but his lowered eyelids and flat mouth still spelled out his sarcasm. Being unable to hide his beastly side had made his relationship with the capital strained.

The first time I'd seen the prince in the audience for one of our performances, he hadn't looked so different from Cadan. Pointed ears and sharp canines, but otherwise human-like, albeit taller and more attractive than any human I'd seen.

His shapechanger magic had allowed him to hide the claws and tail, and there'd been no sign of stripes on his arms, either. It had helped him blend in, make himself acceptable for the capital.

But a curse had taken that all away. Now, he couldn't hide the beast within.

Good.

It was a tiny candle flame of comfort amongst the gnawing cold and my shaky breaths.

The prince rifled through the letters, though Cadan hovered at his side. "Was there something else?"

"Your... pet." Cadan threw me a glance. "She looks very pale. I think her lips are turning blue."

"She's fine." The prince's tail twitched in the same way

someone might flick their hand dismissively. "If she needs mercy, she'll ask for it..." He looked up from his letters and gave me a wide smile. "Or beg."

That wasn't going to happen.

I squeezed myself, holding back my shivers for a moment as I tried to give him a bored look. He was so fucking tedious.

"Perhaps she'd like my coat?" Cadan undid the top button.

The look the prince gave him was colder than the snow. "You will *not* give her your clothing."

The knot of Cadan's throat rose and fell as his hands fell away from the fastenings of his coat. "Of course." He inclined his head and left, a crease between his eyebrows as he passed.

Again, he'd tried to help me. He must disagree with my punishment. Celestine had made it clear with her disapproving frowns that she did, too. I wasn't sure if I could use that to my advantage, though.

It wouldn't matter if I could find my dagger. Hugging myself, I mapped out the palace in my head and marked off the sections I'd been able to search. Not many.

But the longer I stood in the cold, the harder it became to keep hold of all the threads of my thoughts. The image grew fuzzy. Had I searched the library or had I only thought about it? Was there a lock on that door or was I misremembering?

The plumes of my breath came slower and slower as my mind grew sluggish. At least my shivering had stopped.

I just needed to stand here and wait for the prince to grow bored and head indoors. He rarely stayed away from others for long. He'd go inside for company soon.

Soon.

I placed one foot on top of the other. But I couldn't feel it. That fact scraped the back of my throat with wrongness, nauseating.

Eyelids drifting, I swayed.

Just wait. Just a little longer. Just...

A dark night. The silhouette of a man with tail swishing. And at his feet, light pooling on the still and silent body of my sister. Her chestnut hair pooled around her head, gleaming and gorgeous. The man crouched over her, and that was when the light hit his face. A square jaw. Straight nose. Strong chin. Beautiful and brutal.

From my hiding place, I cowered. I had no weapon. Certainly not one that would affect a fae. And how could I explain a dead prince in his own capital city?

I blinked away the image in time to stop myself from staggering forward. Curling up in the snow was an appealing option right now. It would be quiet and it couldn't be any colder than I was right now.

It would be peaceful.

That was something I wasn't sure I'd ever known.

I caught my knees as they bent. I locked them.

No. Stay standing. No matter how tired. No matter how tempting.

I had no idea how much time slipped away, only that I blinked and the prince was striding away from the columned dome, passing me without a glance. "Come along."

I told my leg to move. It might've obeyed, albeit slowly.

Then the world tipped, the snowy ground flying right up at my—

Everything went white.

20

"Little bird?" His voice came from far away, somewhere beyond the white. "Pet?"

Something burning touched my waist, and I whimpered but couldn't pull away.

There was the crunch of an object dropping into crisp snow. "Shit. You're freezing."

I tried to lift my head and tell him to fuck off, but only a slurred mumble came from my mouth.

Then I wasn't on the ground anymore, but that burning sensation seared the whole of my right side and around my legs and back. I couldn't cry out, as pain snatched my shallow breaths. But for some reason, I curled against that brutal fire —better that than the ice I was encased in.

It hurt and yet I craved it.

I tried to ride its pain down into oblivion. It seemed a good escape, and I was so tired.

But something jostled me and gently—so gently—stroked my cheek. "Zita? Zita!"

My eyelids fluttered, giving me snatches of an image that made no sense. The prince's face crowded my field of view. A frown was etched so deeply between his brows, it looked like someone had drawn it there with thick, black charcoal. Flame surrounded that pretty face. That explained the burning.

No. Not flame, just his impossibly red hair, falling in a curtain, the crown gone. Understanding crept through my sluggish mind: his face was above mine as he held me.

The heat I leant into was him, his body. His arms around me. He carried me somewhere, tension thrumming through his muscles where he held me so tight. He'd even wrapped his light jacket around me, blocking a little of the chill air.

As I blinked up at him, the corner of his mouth flickered. "There," he breathed with something that sounded like relief. But even with that threat of a smile, his eyebrows pulled tighter together. "Don't die, little pet." The sense of movement sped.

I dipped into brightness and darkness, squirming at the pain of his heat.

"I ordered you not to die." His voice rumbled through me, pulling me back. "Stay awake."

Malicious compliance, I reminded myself.

That forced my eyes open, and I anchored my awareness to the spill of red hair and the streams of soft, creamy white running through it. Like blood and snow. Or blood and bone. Pretty. So pretty. The cool, snowy light glistened along its lengths.

I wanted to draw it. To paint it. Though I'd never even bought paints. I only needed my sketches—they were simply to keep hold of the memories. To keep focus. To remind myself of Zinnia's face. And of his.

Why had I wanted to keep that? Why was it so...?

The line of thought skittered away off the page.

"Zita," he growled, and I blinked awake. "I swear to the gods, if you die, I'm going to march into the Underworld and drag you out by your collar. Do you understand?"

But I couldn't nod or answer. The best I managed was a small sound that huffed out.

The light changed and a ceiling appeared overhead.

"Sepher?"

"What's going on?" Male voices. Some of the many hangers on.

"Are you—?"

His arms around me went solid. "Out of my way." The walls rattled.

"It got too cold," someone whispered.

"Looks half dead," another muttered.

"Sepher, you shouldn't concern yourself with the creature. Let me take it away and put it out of its misery."

A snarl shredded the air. The prince's hold shifted and one arm shot out. I didn't see what he did, but there was a spray of something warm—unbearably warm—on my skin, and red spattered my dress. Something thudded to the floor, and the hand that came back around my waist was slick.

"Anyone else so much as thinks about touching her and they'll join him."

They fell silent and the sense of other people around us faded.

"Fetch a healer," he tossed over his shoulder before turning to me. "Nearly there, Zita." The purring, growly quality of his voice snagged on the Z of my name, making it buzz from him into me. "We're going to get you warmed up."

I couldn't answer, only get lost in the red of his hair and the way it gleamed differently in the warmer fae light indoors.

It turned the red towards auburn and made the lighter stripes a pale, pale gold.

I wasn't aware of anything else until the sense of movement stopped and he lay me down on something soft. A whimper escaped me as that terrible, beautiful heat left my side.

"One moment." His voice soothed me over the rustle of fabric. Then a weight dipped the bed beside me and that glorious blaze returned, even hotter this time.

I made a sound that was half sigh, half moan as it consumed me, flaming flesh wrapping around my shoulders and hips.

"Your feet are like ice."

I couldn't even feel him touch them. Still numb, and the world grew more and more hazy the longer I lay on this fluffy cloud with the dawn sky skimming overhead.

"You still there, Zita?" Fingers tilted my head, traced my jaw, the touch so gentle it stole my breath.

The best I could manage was a slow blink up at the gorgeous face looking back at me.

His golden eyes were like the edge of a flame. Or the disc of the sun as it emerged from the horizon, turning night into day, burning away the darkness.

"It would be easier if I could wrap around you." He pushed the hair from my face. "Curl up, sharp one."

Sharp. Not sweet. Like he knew me.

He helped me obey, bending my stiff limbs until I was a little ball of ice in the middle of his huge bed.

That dimly registered. I was in his bed. Not just on a blanket at its foot.

I must be delirious or dreaming.

Not only because of that, but because when I opened my

eyes from my next slow blink, a wall of fur greeted me. Rich auburn stripes fading into creamy white.

And soft. Oh, gods, so soft!

It wrapped around me, a huge creature with paws the size of dinner plates. No sign of any claws.

What an odd dream.

A purr rumbled from the great chest at my back, vibrating into me, soothing the pain of the creeping warmth, lulling me into a deeper dream.

I let my eyes drift shut and the world went dark.

21

Such strange dreams studded my pained sleep. Huge creatures. Ice beasts. And something made of auburn flame that tore them apart and kept me safe.

I woke, stiff and warm, cocooned in furs and a dry, dusty scent that seemed faintly familiar. The freshness of outside overlaid it, and a deeper, musky note ran beneath.

And, my word, wriggling my toes had never felt so good. With a little sigh, I burrowed deeper into the furs.

They purred and pulled closer.

Wait. *What?*

A gasp tore through me as I tried to sit up, but what I'd thought was a heavy blanket draped over me turned out to be a huge leg.

A huge, striped, furry leg. A sabrecat's foreleg.

I stared. I blinked. I bit my lip, which hurt.

So this wasn't another dream.

And those stripes... I knew those stripes.

Just like when I looked up, I knew the yellow eyes that looked back.

Sepher. The prince. He wasn't a beast man this time, but a sabrecat, with long canines that curved past his chin and gave the species its name.

His ribs contracted as he let out a long breath. Eyes shutting, he butted me with his head, a gesture I'd seen sabrecats do with their riders but had never experienced directly. It could've crushed me—he was longer than I was tall and thick with muscle. But he controlled his strength, and it was a firm bump, like a slap on the back.

You're awake. The voice in my mind was his, and it sounded relieved. *The healers said you would wake eventually, but I was starting to wonder.* He canted his head. *Lazy creature.* Yet his foreleg pulled me closer and his purr deepened into a thunderous rumble.

I stared up at him, mind still stuttering over the fact of a huge fucking sabrecat wrapped around me.

I'd known he could shift into an animal. And I'd worked out it was likely a sabrecat. But I'd expected something more monstrous and frightening, like the beast man shape he'd taken in the forest. Not something so beautiful. Not *this*.

Predatory and yet gentle.

Beastly and yet regal.

Monstrous, and yet I was not afraid.

As my brain slotted the pieces together and ceased to be quite so occupied by the fact of what he was, I turned to my own state.

Warm. That was a good start. I could move everything, as much as the leg draped over me allowed. That was also good. And aside from the what-the-fuckery of the prince's form, my brain seemed to be able to follow a line of thought and shape it into something coherent.

I checked my fingers—all present and correct—and lifted my feet, managing to catch a glimpse of them past the prince's leg. Toes all there.

You nearly died. There was something accusing in his tone. *But I warmed you up, and the healers were able to save your limbs.*

I'd been that close then. My heart gave a heavy, solid beat as if to confirm I was still alive. But I ran my hands over my arms and chest, just to be sure. That was when I realised I was naked. "Where are my clothes?"

The healers cut them off you. They wanted to see you properly, check for any more frostbite. You should've told me you were so cold. His leg squeezed around me, and his claws unsheathed, just grazing my belly.

I scoffed, which pressed my stomach into those claws. Not enough to break the skin, but it spiked warning through me. Controlling my breaths, I glared up at him. "So you nearly killing me is *my* fault?"

How am I supposed to know humans die when it gets a bit chilly?

"There was snow on the ground and the whole lake was frozen. What part of that suggests it's just 'a bit chilly'?"

His shoulders moved in what might've been a shrug. Thankfully, he'd retracted his claws. *I don't really feel the cold.*

"Clearly," I huffed. "Can you *change*? I can't take you seriously enough to argue with you when you're a cat."

You mean you take me seriously when I'm a fae? He bared his teeth, eyes glinting with wicked glee.

Then the bone and muscle around me shifted. Fur retreated, leaving striped skin. Long sabre teeth retracted to

SLAYING THE SHIFTER PRINCE

elongated canines. And he shrank down from a huge sabrecat to a giant of a man.

Not human. No, you could never mistake him for human. But not quite so monstrous.

Yet still very much naked. And still curled around me, his hot flesh on my back, his arm around my waist, something bulging against my backside.

I cleared my throat and pulled away. "Well, *more* seriously. You're still ridiculous, but it's all relative."

He chuckled as he sat up, the sound bright, his expression open and relaxed instead of closed and cruel. "That might be the nicest thing you've said to me yet." His smile was preening as he rose from the bed. His tail formed an arc behind him, not swishing with agitation for a change.

I tried not to follow its line up to his bare behind. I wasn't entirely successful. "I told you that you were handsome, didn't I?"

"Yes, but you didn't mean that." He threw a glance over his shoulder as he stopped at the side table. "Or at least, you didn't *want* to mean it." Another preening smile.

Pulling the blankets around myself, I declined to respond. Arrogant arse.

He returned to bed with a plate of fruit and pastries. "You need to eat."

My limbs *did* feel heavy and my stomach ached with emptiness. The lack of energy gnawed at me, like the days when I practiced on the hoop and silks so intently, I forgot to eat.

I took an apple and a cinnamon pastry, and accepted a steaming cup of spiced tea when he offered it.

Something about this prickled at the back of my neck. Something... *off*. But I couldn't place quite what it was, and exhaustion blurred the edges of my thoughts, like spilt water lapping at ink.

He caught my cup before it spilt, and I jerked up from my long blink. I must've dropped off.

"I think you're done with that." He disappeared the cup and plate with a flick of his tail, and the fae lights faded. "Lie down."

I was too tired to argue.

A moment later, the blazing heat of his body—his *fae* body, not the sabrecat one—curved around me, chest to my back, legs hooking around mine.

"Now, sleep." His voice rumbled into me and tickled the back of my neck, sending a shiver down my spine. He made a soft sound and wrapped his arm around my waist, squeezing me closer.

I wanted to sleep.

And yet, I lay there, too aware of his hot skin, thinking about how well his large form engulfed me. An altogether different kind of heat gathered between my legs.

What the hells was wrong with me?

I'd almost died and now I was lying naked with the fae who'd killed my sister, *feeling things* about his body and how it fit with mine.

Wild fucking Hunt, I was sick. Twisted. Royally fucked.

Except...

I hadn't been fucked. Not for a long while. *That* was the problem. Since arriving here, I'd had no chance to blow off any steam. Eric might've betrayed me, but he'd been good for something.

All I needed was a little time to myself to work away my body's needs. That would stop these troubling feelings.

22

It was still dark when I woke. And Sepher's arm was no long around me, his chest no longer against my back. My thoughts before I fell asleep must've inspired my dreams, because a dull throb echoed in my centre. I didn't need to feel between my legs to know I was wet.

I held my breath and listened for his.

Long and slow. Deep in sleep.

Swallowing, I eased over on the huge mattress, opening up a little space between us.

Alone time.

With a smile, I closed my eyes and let my hands trail over my body. Light, smooth caresses lit my nerves as I cupped my breasts and tweaked the nipples. Heat shot to my core like a beacon, calling for my hands to follow.

Not yet. Not yet. No need to rush.

If I teased myself, it would make the touch, when it eventually came, that much sweeter.

I kept my breaths deep and quiet as I worked myself up.

My strokes strayed lower and lower across my belly, like a lover who threatened to deliver but kept turning back at the last minute.

I thought of Eric, conjuring his dark hair and eyes and the way they'd look up at me as he kissed his way down my body.

But when I met his imaginary gaze, the betrayal shot through me, bitter and sour—far from the flavour I sought.

When I squeezed my eyes shut, a different face looked back. Cruel and arrogant, handsome and wicked, hungry for my humiliation.

The betrayal was replaced with anger, hot and bright, searing my veins. But my anger at him was sweet. It fuelled my desire instead of tainting it, and I let my fingers finally trail down to my waiting wetness.

I had to bite my lip against making a sound, and my imagined version of the prince smirked at the fact. He and I slid along the edges of my folds, still teasing, still threatening, not quite allowing what I wanted.

It fluttered along my nerves, like a bird against its bars.

I bit harder on my lip, trying to control my heaving breaths.

Sepher was right. I was twisted.

But as long as it purged me of need for a little while, it didn't matter. No one had to know but me.

With that thought, I let my questing fingers slip along my centre, from clit to slit and back again, before dipping inside. My toes pointed, every muscle pulling tight, as I imagined that touch was a long lap of his tongue as I lay on the dining table. He told me I was delicious, just like he'd said about my blood and my fear, then ducked his head for another taste.

"Stop." His deep voice rumbled through the mattress.

I froze. My held breath burned. I swallowed and slowly exhaled. "Stop what?"

"I know what you're doing, pet. Touching yourself. Taking pleasure."

I eased my hand away as though that would make my denial more believable.

"If you are deserving of pleasure, I will give it to you."

My pussy tightened at the promise in his tone. Fucking twisted part of my anatomy.

There was movement from his side of the bed, and I held still, waiting for his touch, waiting for him to deliver on that promise. Goosebumps chased across my skin, despite the warmth of the blankets.

"And since you almost died because of your own stubbornness, you don't deserve any rewards. They are only given for good behaviour."

I exhaled my disappointment and dared a glance in his direction. In the darkness, his eyes glinted as he lay on his side, facing me. The scant light gathered in those eyes, reflecting in their depths, like a wild animal on the road at night.

"Now, go to sleep."

"Fine," I huffed. I rolled over, back to him, and kept still. A few minutes later, I checked over my shoulder. The reflection of his eyes was gone.

In perfect silence, I slid my hand back into place and circled my clit with two fingertips. My suspended pleasure roared back to life, bright and glorious, and maybe fuelled a little by the prince's promise.

If you are deserving of pleasure, I will give it to you.

He wanted me. Despite himself, he wanted me, his enemy,

the woman who'd tried to kill him. The little human who'd come close to managing it.

"I can hear you."

I stilled and bit my lip. What the fuck? *How?*

"Your elevated heart rate. The faster breaths that you think you're keeping so quiet." A glimmer of amusement rippled through his murmured words. "Those slick little sounds where you're so wet."

I clenched my teeth against a groan. To hear him say that sent another pulse of need through me, and although my hand had stilled, I couldn't help but press a little harder with my fingers. That bit more pressure against my clit was a delicious tease, so near release, my body strained closer to it, closer.

"Tell me, Zita, while you fuck yourself with your fingers, are you picturing me having you on the dining table?"

My name. Good gods, my name on his lips, the way he purred through the *Z* sound. If he'd allowed me another stroke, I'd have come apart on that sound. But I held still and swallowed, refusing to admit he'd guessed right.

"I asked you a question."

"No," I bit out.

"Liar," he chuckled. "Now, take your hands from between your legs before I tie them up."

I went rigid with frustration as I obeyed. My anger won its battle with my desire and set my skin alight with a different fire. Teeth gritted, I folded my arms. Another time, when I was away from him.

"And don't think you can do it in the shower, either. I'll smell your arousal, and when I do, I'll come and help you with it." I could hear the smirk arching through his tone. "I know a sick little part of you wants that, but I also know you're too stubborn to give in to it."

He scoffed, and I screwed my eyes tight, hating—*loathing* him for being right.

"Now, sleep."

23

The next day, Sepher carried me to Celestine's rooms, grumbling about having to go to a meeting with his father's representative. "I'd rather keep you close, but at least with Celestine, you can sleep whenever you need it." Still, he scowled and squeezed me when she called for us to enter.

He'd dressed me in another gorgeous gown, with sturdier shoes and a fur-lined cloak this time. Even though we were indoors, he wasn't taking any chances, it seemed.

I'd told him I could walk just fine, but apparently he wasn't taking any chances with that, either.

"Is she all right?" Celestine bustled over at once, her slender hand smoothing hair from my face. "How're you feeling, Zita?"

At her touch, Sepher's arms tightened around me.

"I'm fine." I smiled at Celestine and tried to pull from the prince's hold.

He didn't set me down. "She needs to regain her strength.

146

Make sure you feed her well today. Fruit and vegetables, nuts and some meat too. And plenty of water."

He sounded like a doctor. I laughed.

He did not.

Mouth flat, he took me to the settee and set me down so gently, it set off that odd feeling of at the back of my neck again. He knelt at my side, eyebrows drawn together. "Behave." Fingertips and claws traced the edge of my cheek. "Look after yourself—better still, let Celestine look after you. No going outside. Stay by the fire." He held my chin, golden eyes roving across my face, down to my lips.

Was he going to kiss me?

I wouldn't pull away—no backing down—but still.

With a firm nod, he was gone.

And I had no idea what to make of... whatever that was.

Eyes narrowed thoughtfully, Celestine watched me for a moment, then glanced back at the door he'd closed in his wake. "Well." With a shrug, she turned and set about bustling and fussing over me, bringing blankets and platters of food, a glass of water, and a steaming cup of coffee.

I ate and drank and chatted with her, but all the while that odd sensation crept along the back of my neck.

Wrongness. That's what it was.

An overwhelming sense of wrongness.

Sepher. The prince. His Princely Prickishness was being nice to me. And I meant *nice*. This wasn't just desire making him hold me close or caress me and do things that might be misconstrued as nice. This was...

Weird.

"What's the frown for?" Celestine asked as she topped up our cups from the pot. Its pale blue glaze matched the soft shade in her eyes. "You seem preoccupied this morning."

I chewed my lip. Would asking be displaying weakness? Asking him, certainly, but maybe I was safe to ask her. "It's *him*." I nodded towards the door he'd disappeared through an hour ago. "He's... being *nice*."

Her level attention remained on me a beat longer, then she straightened, eyes widening. "Oh, that was it? I thought you were going to say more." She chuckled, a frown furrowing her brow. "I'm not sure I understand your confusion. Sepher can be nice. On occasion."

"But to *me*?" I scooped up my cup, sighing at its warmth soaking into my fingers. "No, that isn't normal. After everything, why is he suddenly being nice to me?"

She canted her head, a flicker of tension around her eyes as she watched me. "He has his reasons."

"Which I'm guessing you know. Tell me."

Her gaze shuttered as she poured cream into her coffee. "I'm not going to speak for Sepher. As much as I like you, my loyalty lies with him."

"Loyalty? To *him*?" I snorted. "You've seen how he treats people, right?"

She arched one delicate eyebrow. "'People' or just you?"

"He hurt one of his *people* when he was bringing me in from the cold. Badly, I think."

"Killed him, actually." She shrugged and took a sip. "But I hear the man threatened you, so..." She gestured as if to say that justified all.

He'd killed a man simply for *speaking*. Not just any man— a member of his court.

Hungering for revenge for so long had turned me into something monstrous, because the thought didn't horrify me as much as it should've. Yes, there was a slight twist of shock in my belly that he'd taken a life so casually.

148

But that twist tightened into a grasping fist that gathered up the intensity of Sepher's reaction and held it close. The fact he'd killed for me, the woman who'd tried to kill him and still meant to.

I'd spent a decade obsessed with him, and now that obsession was reflected back on me.

The intoxication of it flowed through my veins, warm and delicious.

Yet obsession didn't require niceness. He could've kept me at the end of the bed. He could've ordered me to crawl here. He didn't need to stroke my cheek so softly or leave such thorough instructions for looking after me.

I clenched my jaw and met Celestine's gaze. "So he killed a man for a few words." I wrinkled my nose like I was as disgusted by the fact as I should've been. "He's an evil monster."

She huffed a laugh, but the amusement on her face was cold, edged with frost like my shoes had been. "Sepher is my brother in all but blood. Speaking ill of him is speaking ill of my judgement and of someone I love." Her cup clicked against the saucer as she placed it on the table. "You'd do well to remember that."

Despite her frailty, there was steel at Celestine's core.

I held her gaze as long as I could, looking for some sign that she'd been intimidated or tricked into defending him.

But no. None. And I'd seen no hint of it before.

Somehow, Sepher had inspired genuine loyalty in Celestine. The others I could understand—a lot of the folk here came because they weren't welcome elsewhere in Elfhame because of their inhuman appearance. They stayed for the good time that came from living under a prince's roof.

But Celestine?

She would've been welcomed in the capital city. She wasn't forced to live here. And she seemed level-headed. Clever. Kind... albeit with an odd fae perspective on what constituted kindness.

Yet she was as loyal to Sepher as he was to her... as I'd been to my sister. When he said she was a sister to him, it wasn't one-sided.

I sipped my tea, shaken by the depth of feeling I'd heard in her voice... and the answering depth of feeling in my own heart.

SEPHER STAYED HOLED up in his meeting all day, and I slept in Celestine's rooms. I say "slept"—it was a light, fitful sleep, prickled with the constant anticipation of the prince arriving to take me back to his suite.

He never came.

In the morning, she let me use her shower and lent me a gown from her wardrobe. It fastened with ties, so it didn't matter that we were different sizes. Well, width-wise, anyway —its hem pooled around my feet, comically long.

Yet I struggled to laugh at the fact.

As we ate breakfast, I kept smoothing the light silk and glancing at the door. Would he like this dress? Pale blue, fading into pink at the hem with glittering motes of gold. It was like the rising sun catching in drifting dust or pollen.

The knock at the door had me bolting upright, heart hitching.

When Sepher entered, it was with no crown and shadows under his eyes. But they fixed on me at once as he strode to the breakfast table. "You look well, pet." He scooped a pastry off the platter and flashed Celestine a smile before popping it in his mouth whole. I wasn't sure if he even chewed before he swallowed and brushed a crumb off his lip. "Thank you for looking after her." He squeezed her shoulder. "Though I'm not sure about the dress." He toed the hem and arched one eyebrow.

The criticism spiked in me, especially when she'd done him (and me) a favour. I scowled up at him and let my coffee cup clatter on the saucer. "Well, you didn't leave anything else for me to wear, did you?"

Instead of scowling right back or smirking, he raised his eyebrows and chuckled.

I wasn't sure which was worse—an angry Sepher or an amused one.

No. I did. The amused one. Definitely.

I'd grown used to the angry prince, the cruel prince. I knew how to handle him. I gained sustenance from him. His irritation kept me going through any challenge he threw at me.

But this?

"Now, now." He patted my shoulder, like he was patronising a small child. "It's sweet that you're jumping to Celestine's defence, but let's not leap to getting pissed off at each other today, hmm?" He canted his head, hand staying on my shoulder, thumb stroking the back of my neck.

The hairs there rose.

"Especially not when I have a little treat lined up for you. Come." With a self-satisfied smile, he mussed Celestine's hair and stole another pastry before stalking out.

I swapped a look with Celestine, silently asking if she knew what was going on.

Shaking her head, she shrugged.

His voice drifted back through the doors. "Come on, pet."

I hurried after, but the unsettling question had latched onto my shoulders.

What would the Prince of Monsters consider a "little treat"?

24

His thighs cradled my hips, solid and warm. One arm was wrapped around my middle, keeping me against him. I'd foolishly let slip that I'd never ridden a stag before, and apparently the prince also wasn't taking any chances with this.

"I'm sure I can stay on, even if you let go."

"I'm sure you can." His breath brushed my ear, and when I looked over my shoulder, he was smirking at the path ahead.

"So, you can loosen your grip, then." I wriggled, and the stag's ears flicked.

"I can. But I won't." The arm around me tightened.

Insufferable man.

I gritted my teeth and glared at the path ahead.

We passed the ruined temple and cut through the trees, skirting the lake. The snow and ice had melted, and the day was warm and bright, like spring had come early.

Maybe he was going to let me go and chase me back to the

house. It felt like a wise move to keep an eye on the route and try to remember it.

Although, when he'd returned to his rooms, he'd re-dressed me in an outfit more sturdy and warm than the one he'd given me the day of the hunt. My robe-like gown was a thick, cream velvet edged with heavy gold lace and beads. A fur-lined cloak clad my shoulders. Soft leather boots covered my calves, ending just above my knees. Their softest leather fitted closely, elegant and sleek.

Plus he'd given me perfume—the lilac and juniper one he gave me most days, as though there was something about the scent he particularly liked. So maybe this wasn't a hunt.

Before we left, he'd placed the pale gold diadem on my head and clasped its matching bracelets around my wrists. He'd polished the pale blue stone with his sleeve, before standing back and inspecting me. Then, with an exhale, he'd smiled.

The look had done strange things to my chest and stomach.

Catching sight of myself in the mirror had tightened them even more. I looked like a princess from a fairy tale. But princesses never got revenge—they never sought it and they certainly weren't powerful enough to enact it.

Idiots. They should've used their looks to their advantage, not just to ensnare hapless prince charmings.

I scowled ahead, rubbing my eyes, which had grown suddenly gritty. Strange. I didn't remember feeling even remotely sleepy.

A moment later, I jolted upright, eyelids flicking open.

The landscape around us had changed. No forest. No lake. The stag picked its way down a grassy slope and ahead...

Sunlight glittered on an endless expanse of rich blue

water. Froth-tipped waves chased across its surface, finishing their journey by lapping against a beach of white sand. Gulls wheeled overhead, their harsh cries drifting on the breeze.

"We're here."

He left the stag to nip at the tough grass and tossed a bag over his shoulder, before scooping me up and striding to the beach.

I wriggled in his hold, but was forced to put one arm around the back of his neck—otherwise it would've just hung there awkwardly. "I'm not ill anymore. I *can* walk."

"Yes, but I don't want to hang around waiting for your little legs to catch up." He grinned, canines showing.

Down in the cove, the beach was surprisingly warm. Rocky headlands on either side sheltered it from the worst of the wind, and there wasn't a single cloud in the sky. I'd thought him picking out a light chemise to go beneath the velvet gown was part of his new desire to keep me warm. Maybe it was so I could strip down to it and not boil to death.

With a flick of his wrist, a large blanket fluttered from the bag to the sand, followed by a scatter of cushions and a picnic basket. Except, the bag was just a small satchel—the large basket couldn't fit in there, never mind with the cushions too.

He flashed a grin when he caught me staring and wiggled his fingers. Fae magic. Of course. The normal rules didn't apply in Elfhame... especially when you were one of its princes.

I eyed him as I sat. "Do you have *extra* magic or something, because you're a prince?"

He stretched himself along the blanket, looking every inch of his great size. Somehow, being here under the open sky and not contained by the proportions of anything as mundane as walls or a chair, he seemed both larger and freer. "Different fae have different amounts and kinds of magic."

His shoulders bobbed as he closed his eyes and tilted his face to the sun. It gilded his skin, caressing his features like a lover. "It's generally hereditary, but great power isn't confined to the royal families."

I arched an eyebrow. This had to be the most he'd said to me without making a joke or ordering me to do something for his own amusement. I waited for him to tell me to serve him food from the basket.

But he seemed content to lie on the blanket, fingers interlaced behind his head, a peaceful smile on his face.

I waited. Eventually, I had to peel off the velvet gown. It wrapped around me, like a dressing robe, so it was easy to remove. He'd definitely planned this. The light sea breeze breathed through my chemise, cooling the sweat that had gathered on my skin.

I fiddled with the gown's hem, frowning at Sepher. Still, no instructions came.

"What are we doing?"

One yellow eye opened and turned to me. "Well, *I'm* relaxing. But you appear to be..." His eyebrows screwed together, and he opened the other eye as if he needed to get a better look at me. "I'm not sure *what* that is. Your jaw is horribly clenched, though."

"Because I'm waiting to find out what you brought me here for." I huffed and re-folded the gown, careful to keep it away from the sand. "I'm waiting for something to *do*."

He scoffed, white teeth flashing. "This *is* the thing." He gestured at the beach, the blanket, claws catching the light.

"What? Just... sitting here?"

"Good gods, woman." It was his turn to huff as he sat up.

"First you ruin sex, now you ruin a day at the beach." Eyes closed, he drew a long breath and exhaled. "We're here to relax. Both of us. I know some of my court have perhaps taken my instruction on how they should behave with you to heart. And... perhaps I'm partially responsible for that." His expression darkened. "So I'm not keen to let you out of my sight, or Celestine's, at the palace. Or to let my guard down, where you're concerned. But here, we're away from all that." He shrugged and lay back down. "Enjoy it."

I frowned at him, not a scowl this time, but that screwed up face I pulled when utterly baffled by this fae prince. If I didn't know better, I'd have said he was regretting ordering his court to treat me like a pet. And I'd have said he was concerned for my safety.

But both those things were impossible.

As was his command to *enjoy it*.

Every day for ten years, I'd worked. Exercise first thing in the morning. Fuelling my body with breakfast, followed by travelling between towns and cities. Setting up for performances. Rehearsing. Treating my hair and skin to ensure it looked its best.

Since arriving here, I'd kept up my workouts and fuelling, and I'd treated Sepher's instructions as a new kind of work. Assessing what response would best piss him off had become a job in itself.

But this?

What the fuck was I supposed to do with this?

One golden eye flicked open. With a sigh, he closed it again. "Lie down, Zita."

I pursed my lips at him. I wasn't about to let him tell me to... *Urgh.*

Malicious compliance.

Defiance would only please him and get me punished.

Fine. I gathered a selection of cushions and lay back against them. They were soft and cupped around me, almost an embrace.

"There, that wasn't so hard, was it?" He flashed me a grin before going back to his relaxation.

My fingers tapped on my belly. "Now what?"

"Feel the sun." He didn't look at me this time, just basked in the warm light. "Listen to the sea. Enjoy their gifts."

"I noticed it's unusually sunny for this time of year."

"I *am* a prince of Dawn Court. The sun always smiles on us."

I grunted and snuggled deeper into the cushions. It *was* a nice feeling, a bit like the cloudy softness of his bed. "Where was the sun when my toes nearly froze off?"

"Well, perhaps not *always*. Now, hush."

I managed about five minutes, picking at the trim on the cushions. It was unbearable lying there doing nothing. Too still. Wasted time.

Beside me, the prince's chest rose and fell slowly. So relaxed, he'd fallen asleep. Tiredness did shadow his eyes today—he must've been kept up late in meetings. Or had he taken the opportunity of my absence to call Anya or someone else to his bedroom? I'd ruined sex, apparently, but with me away, maybe he'd found it enjoyable once more.

That thought scraping through me, I sat up and took in our surroundings. We had the wide, white beach to ourselves. Towards the headlands on either side, it became rocky, and light glinted on rock pools. Out to sea, no sail interrupted the horizon's perfect line, just as no cloud marked the clear sky. The path up the grassy valley was narrow but well-trodden, disappearing inland over the brow of a hill.

Whatever had happened while I'd been asleep on his stag —I suspected some kind of magic—we'd left his lands. His ruined estate was far from the sea. If I crept up there and over the hill, I could run. I only needed to head south and I'd reach the Queen's Wall that separated Elfhame from Albion. I'd be free.

I had warm clothes and food if I stole his bag. Hells, I could even take his stag. How hard could it be to ride?

"You're welcome to run, if you want me to hunt you again."

25

He said it without anything other than his lips moving. Eyes closed. Chest still rising and falling slowly. "I won't be as gentle when I catch you this time."

"I don't recall you being especially gentle last time."

"Oh, that was gentle. Trust me." He grinned, and it was an odd comfort, because it hinted at the cruel prince I'd grown used to. "Maybe I'll sit on my throne and bend you over my knee and spank you. I could make you count the strikes and thank me for every one."

My mouth went dry. Fear mingled with the warm comfort of his cruelty, tightening deep inside me. With much effort, I swallowed and lifted my chin, like I wasn't afraid. "What if I want you to spank me?"

His eyebrows squeezed together as he caught his lip between his teeth. "You play a dangerous game, little bird. You shouldn't tempt me like that or I'll need to think up new and unusual punishments for you. Ones you won't enjoy."

My heart sped at the challenge. I would smile and take it all. And the smile would be genuine, because I'd know it was breaking his enjoyment of his toy. "Don't be so sure, *Your Highness.*"

His eyes flicked open. I *never* called him that. Truth be told, I'd only done it to set him off-balance, and it was a joy to watch him frown, trying to work me out.

He jerked to a sitting position and shoved his hand into the picnic basket.

The smell of food wafting from inside stirred my appetite, even though it only felt like a couple of hours since I'd eaten breakfast. Though the sun was almost at its height. How long had I slept for on the ride?

We ate in silence. Not only was the bag enchanted to fit so much inside, but the basket had to be magical, too. The food was fresh and hot, like it came straight from the oven. I savoured slices of herbed lamb and little spheres of potato that had been breaded and fried, so they crunched as I bit into them.

Fucking fae and their incredible food. It was something I'd miss in the Underworld after his guards or friends killed me.

He lay on the blanket after eating, like a sabrecat sated after a kill. But his breaths didn't settle to that slow rhythm of sleep, and a short while later he stood and tugged off his shirt. "I'm going for a swim. You're welcome to join me, if you know how." He shucked off his trousers and stretched every inch of his naked body.

I didn't even try to keep my gaze off him this time.

It might've been impossible.

The sunlight burnished the gold of his skin. The stripes on his arms and side flexed as his muscles stretched and bunched and created all kinds of interesting shadows. The deep *V* over his hips pointed my attention down to the trimmed auburn hair at the base of his dick. Even soft, it hung much further down his muscled thighs than any other cock I'd seen. The stripes didn't continue around it, but it was a deeper shade of gold than the rest of him.

I was an awful person.

I was going straight to a pit of punishment in the Underworld.

Because for a second—the briefest, worst, most delicious second—I wondered what it would feel like. Smooth? Or would the skin be velvet soft, catching a little on my grip? Would I be able to tease moisture from his tip and spread it over the crown with my palm, allowing my touch to slide over him with ease? What sound would he make as I did that?

It was only that I wanted to conquer him. Unman him. Bring him to his knees, admitting that he wanted me, the pathetic little human who'd tried to cut his throat.

I dug my nails into my palms, not looking up at his face to check exactly how smug his smile was. "Of course I can swim."

Standing, I peeled off my chemise. I still didn't deign to look, but I could feel him watching me. I removed my jewellery and unbuckled my collar—the saltwater would ruin the leather. The blazing sun caressed my bare skin as I pushed down my undergarments and stood before it and its prince naked.

Normally, in his room, I slept in my underwear. The only exception was when the healers had cut away my clothes— they'd been attentive and taken them all. But the way his gaze slid down me said he hadn't taken advantage of their work to look. His eyes widened a little at my bare pussy.

With my skimpy performance clothes, anything but the

thinnest strip of hair would be visible, and having none at all always surprised the patrons at my intimate performances. When I'd removed that last strip, their gifts had increased in value *significantly*. Celestine had provided me with fae chemicals that removed it painlessly—another thing they'd improved over our barbaric practice of ripping it out.

And now, seeing his attention captivated for a long moment, I was thankful she had.

I would have him on his knees soon. And with a stroke of luck, I'd have found my iron dagger by then, too. I'd pair listening to his confession of infatuation with taking his life.

I promise, Zinnia. All of this is for you.

The thought crept over my shoulders like a lover's lie.

With a long breath, the prince turned and strode to the sea. "You're a lot less inhibited than most humans," he said as I caught up.

"You've seen the outfits I perform in, right?"

"Are they really that scandalous for your kind?" He raised an eyebrow, mouth twisting.

I chuckled as we reached the edge of the surf. "I'm afraid so. It's allowed on stage, but anywhere else, I'd be kicked out for showing too much skin."

"A pity. Humans are such prigs." He strode in, the water lapping at his calves, his thighs, his waist.

"Not all of us." I gasped at the sea's chill as I dipped my toes in. "Performers are... we're different from other folk."

He ducked so the water covered his shoulders and now turned to me, head cocking. "Your treacherous friend offered an 'intimate performance.' Was that an empty offer just to get me alone, or does your troupe regularly offer that *service* to patrons?"

Teeth gritted, I pulled my foot from the water. Did he not

remember seeing us in his capital city a decade ago? Zinnia had given him and his friends a private performance after the main show, right before he'd killed her. I didn't know if she'd fucked any of them, but she would've touched and flirted with them. I'd spied on one of those performances once. It wasn't the kind of thing you forgot.

Yet he had. A wave of red-hot anger engulfed me, making me forget the chilly water.

It required a deep breath before I could reply. "I've given a lot of private performances. It's earned me plenty of extra money and gifts over the years."

His gaze skimmed over me, making my rage burn hotter. "I bet it has. And yet..." With a heavy sigh, he rose, leaving the waves lapping around his waist. "You still fuck about on the edge of the water." He stalked closer, wet skin glistening in the sun.

I stared, caught by the sight and my confusion at what his last comment had to do with anything.

I stared too long, because a moment later, he had me over his shoulder, hand on my backside.

"What are you doing?" I kicked and wriggled for a second before I reminded myself—compliance.

Just as I mastered myself, the prince heaved me off his shoulder and cold water closed over me. I cried out, bubbles spilling from my mouth, salt slipping over my tongue. A second later, I kicked at the sandy sea floor and broke the surface, just in time to see him rising from the water with a cry of pleasure.

"You fucking bastard."

He stood just out of arm's reach, smirking as he smoothed his wet hair back. "Well, you weren't going to jump in your-self. It was torturous to watch."

164

The waves reached his chest, but I had to tread water at this depth. I glared at him as I did so. "You're torturous to be around."

"Good. Then I'm doing something right." He smiled brightly and ducked into the water until it covered his shoulders.

"Deeply unpleasant," I muttered.

"Thank you." As he sculled through the water, he flashed a smile like I'd given him the highest possible praise.

"It isn't a compliment."

"Oh, but it is." He went very still, easy expression pulling into something intent. "I don't strive to be pleasant. I don't try to please others. I can't play their game of blending in." His claws cut through the water. "And why should I? Why should I file my edges for their consumption? I'm not here for them to eat; I'm here to live my life." He lifted his chin, eyes locked on me. "And, little bird, the same goes for you."

My breath caught as I flinched.

"Your friend who betrayed you—he feared your anger, your justified rage. It made you too spiky and salty for him to swallow down whole, when he wanted something smooth and sweet."

I was naked, but now I felt it even more—like his words had flayed the flesh from my bones.

"But rage isn't sweet. And people shouldn't be." The corner of his mouth twitched. "I like your salt and your sharpness—your unyielding stone that takes everything and still stands."

He liked something about me—*and was admitting it.* Saltwater splashed into my gaping mouth.

With a blink, he shook his head as though waking. Taking a few strokes into deeper water, he ended our conversation.

And what an odd conversation it had been.

As I puzzled over it, he swam around and dived, always throwing a glance my way when he surfaced. After a few minutes, the water seemed less chilly. Maybe my body was just shutting down again, like it had in the snow. I threw him a reproachful look when he next came into view.

Eyebrows clenched, he swam over. "You're not enjoying yourself, are you?"

"Whatever gave you that impression?"

"What did you do before you became mine?"

I frowned. "What do you mean? You know I was a performer."

"No, I mean other than that. For fun."

Fun? I blinked at him and shook my head. What was he getting at?

"Hobbies?" He raised his eyebrows, prompting. "Entertainment?"

The longer I remained quiet, the more intense his gaze grew, until I had to look away, watching my fingers skim over the water's surface.

"I just..." No, there was no *just* to it. "I worked. Hard. I'm sure you wouldn't understand." I gave him a mocking smile. "Between rehearsals, performances, helping with equipment, and travelling from place to place, I was too busy for fun. I spent all my time working and dreaming about revenge. And I drew. See? I have a hobby. I filled dozens of sketchbooks over the years."

His lips flattened, the expression out of place on a face that was usually lit with amusement or cruelty. "What a sad life." But he didn't say it in a teasing tone.

He said it with *sincerity*.

The shock of that—the horror of it kept me quiet.

"I applaud the revenge, of course." His mouth twisted, closer to the expression I'd come to expect from him. "But I've seen your sketchbooks. That wasn't a hobby. That wasn't fun. It was *obsession*."

My movements went jerky as I kept my head above water. He'd looked at my sketchbooks? He'd opened up my chest and gone through my things? How dare he? That was mine —private.

"So, work and revenge? That's really it?" He canted his head. "When did you laugh? When did you give a smile that wasn't for your audience? When did you find pleasure in your life and the world around you?"

With the cut of every word, my breaths became a little deeper, a little harder. I sculled away from him.

The furrow of his brow deepened as he searched my gaze. "It's all so... *small*. And yet, you don't even see that, do you?"

What, did he expect me to agree with him? He didn't understand. He was a prince. What the hells did he know about what was required to live in the real world and earn money?

My feet found sandy ground, and I kept backing away, needing to put distance between myself and the cruellest words he could ever give me. If I stayed, I might try to claw him to death with my bare hands, and we all knew how that would go.

"You're someone who should have a big life, Zita. Huge. Not the stunted thing you've been nursing."

I opened and closed my mouth, but no witty retort came. I spun and splashed to shore, blood blazing. "Fuck you."

The words tore my throat because they meant that in this battle, I'd lost.

26

I barely spoke to him the rest of the afternoon. Just cutting, curt comments. His pity had sliced me wide open, letting the stinging saltwater seep in.

Maybe it was even worse that he didn't seem irritated by my quiet, but *thoughtful*. After the swim, he insisted on drying me with a thick, fluffy towel, watching me with this little crease between his eyebrows the whole while.

I was going to murder him.

Not even for revenge, just to stop that look.

By the time we returned to the palace, with another mysterious snooze on the ride, it was dinnertime. Instead of eating with the others, we sat at a round table in the private dining room off his bedroom. He finished first and disappeared through the door.

With him gone, I could breathe. I slumped over the table, gripping its edge.

I hated him.

Good fucking gods. I hated him even more when he was nice than when he was cruel.

Or maybe they were one and the same. Maybe he was trying this change of tack to keep me on the back foot or because he'd worked out it would hurt more. He had got a rise out of me, after all. Telling him to fuck off was not part of malicious compliance.

I shoved another forkful of food into my mouth and forced myself to chew and swallow, even though it felt drier than the sand from the beach. I needed fuel if I was going to survive long enough to destroy him.

When I finally looked up from my empty plate, I found him leaning in the doorway, arms folded, watching me.

I refused to ask out loud, but the question bubbled inside. Why was he staring?

Jaw clenched, I held his gaze and returned that challenge with one of my own.

One corner of his mouth rose, lazy. "I ran you a bath. Thought you'd want to get that salt off your skin and hair."

I touched the braid I'd tied to keep the straggly lengths from my face. Crisp instead of soft and smooth. I grimaced.

He stood back, heavy gaze on me. "Come."

But before we reached the bathroom, something new in the bedroom caught my attention. The low coffee table before the fire was covered in...

I slowed and peered closer.

Pencils, ink, pens, charcoal. A stack of new sketchbooks. Tubes of paint. Jars and brushes.

Almost as much as my body craved the silks and my hoop, my fingers itched to hold a pencil.

He'd never shown any interest in painting.

"What's that?"

He paused in the doorway and shrugged. "Your sketches were good. I thought you might wish to continue. Especially now you have your principal subject actually present." He gave a preening smile, all dazzling and handsome.

I gave the art supplies a long look. Was this in response to my lack of hobby? Was he trying to keep me entertained? Was he trying to do something *nice* for me?

It unfurled in me, like a wing stretching, ready for flight.

And I hated it.

At least when he was horrible, I could loathe him and lose myself in that.

Not this. Whatever *this* was.

He disappeared into the bathroom and, arms folded, I followed.

The room was dimly lit—no fae lights bobbed through the air, but a whole host of candles covered every surface. Their guttering, golden light blanketed everything with warmth, casting soft shadows. The woody scent of sandalwood and lavender drifted through the steam. A low stool stood at the end of the bath.

"I didn't think fae used candles."

He circled to the other side of the bath and turned to me. Where earlier, he had been a sun god, bathed in that brightness, now he was a creature of dawn, edged with soft light and shadows, equally dark and bright and utterly beautiful.

It stole my breath.

"I heard humans prefer them. Thought it might make you more comfortable while you bathe." He gestured to the bath, the glinting darkness of his eyes heavy.

How... thoughtful.

He could be as thoughtful, as kind, as *nice* as he liked, but that wouldn't change the fact he'd killed my sister. I clung to that thought, dug my nails into it like it was the only thing that would stop me from falling over some horrible precipice.

I untied the velvet gown, achingly conscious of his scrutiny as I pulled each bow. When I shrugged it off, it was a relief—its thickness was too much in the steamy air. The thin chemise clung to me, already growing damp, and I had to peel it off. I started on the first buckle of my collar.

"Leave it on."

The low murmur chased goosebumps across my skin. It tightened my belly. I couldn't say why, only that my body hummed on alert, vulnerability whispering over my skin, followed by something else. Something I shouldn't be feeling.

No. I wasn't feeling anything. It was only my body and its needs. After all, I was standing here naked in front of an attractive man, and I hadn't been allowed to seek gratification for over a month.

That was all. Nothing—*nothing* more.

In silence, I stepped into the bath, and in silence, he watched.

The temperature was perfect. Hot, close to uncomfortable. The iridescent gleam of scented oils danced across the water's surface as I lowered myself in, inch by unbearable inch. I paused to arch back and duck my hair under the surface. Once I was fully seated, I couldn't help sighing.

"Is that good, little bird?" His touch trailed the edge of the bath as he circled to the opposite end and sank onto the stool.

"You heard the sound I just made. You know it is."

His smile wasn't cruel and brutal or wide and dazzling. This one was small and pleased, a quieter, more private kind of pleasure. "Well, you've been a good pet. You deserve a little treat."

I almost thanked him, but there was something in his eyes that said he wasn't finished.

"You've earned a bigger reward, in fact." He dipped one fingertip in the water, sending ripples towards me. His gaze followed their progress until it landed on me. From the hot water lapping at my breasts, up to my collarbones, my collared throat, and finally my too-warm face, he consumed me with just a look.

"Touch yourself."

I stilled. There was only the rise and fall of his chest, the drifting steam, and the flickering candle flames.

I needed it. My body throbbed, just from the way his gaze had passed over me. But he wasn't going to let me claim on this reward later in bed, and he showed no sign of moving from his seat and leaving me alone.

"I said, touch yourself." His voice was soft and gravelly, dark like the dim room. "Start with those sweet tits, Zita, like you did in my bed."

Despite the bath's heat, my goosebumps returned.

If I didn't do this now, who knew when I'd get another chance? And the longer I walked around with all this desire bottled up, the more I would find myself wondering how his cock felt. The more I thought those things, the closer I'd get to exploding and acting upon them in a moment of pent-up insanity.

Slowly, slowly, I pulled my hands up my ribcage. Each breath lifted my breasts from the water, leaving them slick and wet, glistening with moisture, slightly chilled by the cooler air.

He watched my progress, every angle of him intent upon me. A hunting cat stalking his prey.

At last, I cupped my breasts, letting the nipples peek between my fingers.

Between parted lips, he let out a long breath. He gave a nod so faint, he might not have realised he was doing it.

When I squeezed, catching my nipples between my fingers, it lifted me and made him bite his lip.

"That's good, pet. Does it feel nice?"

I slid my fingertips over the tight peaks, my touch slick from the oil coating the water's surface. Heat throbbed through me, pooling between my legs. Even in the bathwater, I could tell my own wetness gathered there. "Yes." Pleasure tore my voice, leaving it low and husky. I let my hand trail lower.

"I didn't tell you to stop. You need to obey your master."

I gritted my teeth, but he only smiled.

"Trust me, little bird."

I arched one eyebrow, and he gave a dark chuckle.

"In this, at least. It will be worth it. I promise. Will you obey?"

Delaying the gratification would be better. I knew it. And I hated that he did, too. Much as it pained me, I nodded. "I will."

"Good girl. Now, keep going."

So I kept teasing my nipples, breaths growing rawer, harder, faster under the prince's gaze.

When I'd performed, the audience's attention had given me the tiniest mote of pleasure. I'd been too deadened for anything more. But this—his close attention sharpened to a fine point grazing over me as his claws and canines had... it matched the pleasure of any touch.

"That's it. I think you're ready now, don't you? I'm sure you're perfectly wet and aching."

I was. My centre throbbed, needy and wanting. Every muscle tightened. Each nerve focused on the apex of my legs, wondering why it was being so horribly neglected.

It was a battle to slide my hand down my belly slowly, rather than delve between my thighs. But with each inch I travelled, the prince leant an inch closer. When I opened my legs, pressing them into the sides of the bath, he eased off the stool and knelt at the foot of the bath, transfixed.

His gaze touched me first, burning and bright. The clear water, with no bubbles, let him see everything. He pressed against the bath's rim—the only way he could've got any closer would've been by getting in.

I paused, a terrible smile tugging on my mouth at seeing him so absorbed, and then I let my middle finger slide down my centre.

Shockwaves consumed me, arching my back. The teasing had done its job—I was slick and just that one touch had me trembling, though I never normally found so much pleasure so quickly. I didn't want to dwell on what else had turned me on.

Not when it was staring at me with such shameless desire.

That in itself was pleasing. So often the people who asked for private performances had a kind of apology about them. They wanted me, wanted sex or titillation, but also hated themselves for it. Their shame ruined my pleasure, like I too should be ashamed for sharing my body.

I was not.

But the prince's look carried none of that. I wasn't sure shame entered his vocabulary. Much as he despised me, he wanted me, and his hate only made his want burn hotter.

It made me smile as I ran my finger along that same course again before slipping it inside. A soft sound escaped me at the fleeting entry. Not fullness, though. That was one of the things touching myself couldn't grant—that stretching fullness, the sensation of being filled so completely, I couldn't take any more. The image of his cock came to mind. I certainly couldn't take more than that, but I'd savour the challenge of it.

Skin burning, I huffed a breath that was almost a laugh, and the prince's gaze flicked to my face.

"What's so funny, pet?"

Not that I was imagining him fucking me. I wouldn't admit that while my finger circled my clit and dipped inside over and over.

"The fact I've spoiled your plans. You thought I'd be too embarrassed to do this. That this would be the thing to break me. But look." I spread my folds and lifted my hips, and of course, he couldn't help but look.

He exhaled with a smile. Not the look of a man who'd lost. "Oh, my dear Zita, you have it all wrong. I told you this was your reward and I meant it. I want you to come, and I want to see how you please yourself, what you like. I want to hear the sounds you make. I want to see your body falling apart. I want to know the exact creases that form between your eyebrows as they peak together." He plucked the neglected sponge from the bathwater and squeezed it out as he moved to my side. "Show me."

I frowned up at him, breaths ragged as I drew tighter.

He only swept the sponge over my breasts. Its slight roughness chafed my nipples, making them tighter, harder, crashing through my nerves.

I bit my lip against making a sound. I wouldn't give him the pleasure of knowing he'd added to mine.

"I think you need another finger, love, don't you?" Eyes

hooded, he gave a lazy smile, his gaze passing from my tits as he lathed them with attention, to the hand between my legs.

I added another finger, using the tips of both to circle my clit, before slipping them inside.

It was like the moment when the music in one of my performances sped and I twisted faster, harder, looking to the audience like I was spinning out of control. But, of course, I was always in control of the hoop, of my body.

Except now, I wasn't so sure.

Not when I was winding tighter and tighter. Not when I couldn't escape the golden gaze taking me in with such intensity, it was like another caress. Not when his ministrations with the sponge were slow and firm, hinting at an experienced touch while also denying the heat of his skin.

I was in control. I *was*. His obsession was mine. I was the one holding him here, captivated.

I spun at dizzying speed now, the music building to a crescendo. My skin burned. My breaths rasped. A whimper edged each one.

The throbbing between my legs was a decimating drum beat that crashed through my veins, my nerves, my entire being. My cry echoed off the tiled walls as I came.

He smiled.

"That's it, pet. Enough, now."

Aftershocks still bursting through me, I frowned up at him. Only one orgasm? I didn't deserve any more reward than that, apparently. Jaw clenched, I pulled my hand away and placed it on the bath's rim.

Long breaths. I needed to pull myself back down to earth if I wasn't going to be allowed to come again.

Still, a deep, hot ache remained inside, demanding more.

"So angry." He chuckled and smoothed the hair from

my forehead. His claws grazed over my scalp as he buried his fingers in my hair. "I wonder if I can soothe that temper."

The sponge discarded, he pressed his other hand between my breasts, and I twitched at the skin-to-skin contact I'd been denied as he'd washed me. His touch, beautifully burning, skimmed over my stomach. The muscles there pulled taut as he got closer to my apex.

"Open for me." His tail slid around the back of my knee, guiding my left leg up over the edge of the bath.

On the other side, I hooked my right leg over to match, heart pounding in glorious and horrified anticipation.

His hand stilled and his eyes flicked to mine. "Tell me to stop, Zita. Tell me you don't want this."

This was just a challenge. Beating him at the game we played.

"No. Touch me, Sepher. Reward your pet." I gave him a sharp smile that spelled out how I would take anything he gave and I would not back down. This was just part of that, just—

His silken touch glided between my folds, and all my excuses fluttered away like a flock of startled birds.

As good as touching myself felt, this was better. Sweet fuck, so, so much better.

I hated it. Loved it. Wanted it. Wanted to run from it. Needed it.

I'd never felt this when any of my patrons had touched me. Or when Eric fucked me.

That had always been straightforward. Physical. Flesh upon flesh.

This was horrible and wonderful and complicated and a fucking mess that I was breaking over.

He stroked my clit with firm pressure, that private smile back on his mouth, a few inches above mine.

I bit my lip harder, resisting the sounds building in my chest even though I knew it was a losing battle.

"Don't fight this, little bird." His gaze roved over me as one canine flashed in a lopsided grin. One finger thrust inside, and I lost my battle, back arching, cry echoing. His pupils blew wide.

"Why are you doing this?" I could understand it if he fucked me or made me suck his dick. But he was still fully clothed and showed no sign of taking his pleasure—at least not yet.

"Because you can come harder than that." With the next thrust, he added another finger, the thickness closer to that stretching fullness I'd craved.

Each breath ripped me in two, but I managed to huff out, "Not just this... all of it... Today... Being nice to me."

His lips pressed together and a small frown furrowed his brow. "When you collapsed in the snow..." He exhaled, shoulders sinking, the creases between his brows deepening. "I thought you were going to die. And I realised I didn't want that."

He maintained that two-fingered thrust, using his thumb to circle my clit, making the pleasure thunder in my ears. It was a wonder I could still hear him.

"So now I'm looking after you, like a responsible master." His hand fisted in my hair, pulling my head back, pulling me even more taut.

I clung to the edge of the bath like I was clinging to sanity. "I'm not going to come for you."

I gritted my teeth and glared at him, trying to picture the corpulent, diseased patron who'd once tried to force me over dinner. But Sepher crashed into the fantasy, ripping out the man's throat before fucking me on the table, painting me with food and blood, then licking it off.

"I'll never come for you."

But, fuck, I was close.

"It's adorable that you think you have a choice. You forget —you belong to me. All of you."

He bent to me, then, and his lips claimed mine as he added a third finger inside me.

Fuck. It was so much. Too much. A sweet ache that slid into and stretched and pushed my limits, as his tongue swept into my mouth, stating that it was *his* with more eloquence than any words.

My climax batted itself against the bars of my control.

No. No. No. I couldn't. I wouldn't.

But I was kissing him back, moaning into his mouth, letting him devour my sounds, my breath, my last shred of sanity.

And something in me swelled and grew, a torturously slow spreading of pure joy. It soared along my nerves like a caged bird finally given flight.

He yanked my hair, and the world exploded. My scream crashed through the bathroom, equal parts climaxing pleasure and shame and anger that he was making me come so fucking hard it didn't just come from my body but my very soul.

And some horrible, awful part of me loved it.

27

Once was not enough.

He mastered me again and again... Until I lost count and one orgasm rolled into the next, the edges blurring and boiling with hate and desire. Until tears streamed down my cheeks, and it only took the slightest touch to send me crashing over the edge again.

I didn't know I could come so much or so hard. Nothing had ever felt so incredible and so awful at once.

"Please," I whimpered as he nuzzled into my throat, canines grazing my jugular.

Just that light touch felt like a dagger being dragged through my flesh, my body was so sensitised. His fingers in me and on me had blurred into a seething mass of sensation and pleasure that I couldn't handle. I managed to pull one leg off the rim of the bath, but the other he held firm with his tail.

He pulled back, a slow grin widening on his face as he met my gaze. "What, love? Please what?"

"Please stop."

I sobbed when he did.

I'd expected him to keep going, to keep torturing me, now he'd found a new way to do it and I was at his mercy.

But he stopped.

"*There.*" He said it like he was standing over a job well done. Slowly, slowly, he slid his fingers from me, and I sagged against the side of the bath.

The world was hazy as arms came around me. They didn't tease or torture, just lifted me and wrapped a huge, fluffy towel around my limp body.

I must've slipped into a kind of dozing unconsciousness as he carried me, because the next thing I was aware of was him lowering me onto the bed.

Now he was going to fuck me. When I couldn't enjoy it. Yes, that was just the kind of thing he would do. Maybe he'd try to shame me by coming on my face or something like that. I didn't have the strength to stop him... but he'd stopped when I'd asked, so maybe he wouldn't fuck me if I told him no.

But rather than peeling the towel away, he wrapped it tighter around me, circled his arms around that, and sat against the headboard with me in his lap. A faint hum like a purr rumbled from his chest into my trembling body. It soothed me, easing my breaths, stopping my shaking. He stroked my hair and my cheeks, my closed eyelids.

His touch wasn't too much now. It coaxed me back from the brink. I didn't even know when I'd stopped crying, but he smoothed the tears from my skin and kissed my brow.

Inside, the ache of wanting was nothing but a memory. The ache of too much also faded, and in its place, my body hummed in contentment. I could feel my pulse at my throat, my heart in my chest. I was acutely aware of the softness of the towel, the bright sparks of thought flashing through my mind.

Something deep and smooth settled in me. A kind of peace.

Because I was alive. And I'd never felt it so keenly.

That was what he'd brought out in me from the start. Fearing he was about to execute me was the most alive I'd ever felt until that point. His challenge, his punishments, the gauntlet he threw at my feet—they'd only made me feel it even more.

Hating him. Fearing him. Refusing to back down from him. All of it had shot through me with the raw intensity of a decade of lost emotions. A decade of living death. A decade of grief denied. A decade where I'd lived on obsession and nothing else.

And now I felt.

Fuck, how I felt.

It burned. It tore. It cradled and consumed. It was bright fire and even brighter ice. It hurt and pleased and froze me and drove me.

And he, the fae who had murdered my sister, had unlocked it all.

"I hate you." I didn't know how long had passed since we'd reached the bed, but I had enough control over my body again to speak. I did it now, glaring up at him with all the vicious intensity I'd nursed.

My peace evaporated on my heaving breaths. "I fucking hate you."

His eyebrows clenched together, and he narrowed his eyes, as though he was trying to work out what he was looking at. "I'm only trying to look after you. Why does that bother you so much?"

"Why?" I laughed and fought against his hold and the tightly wrapped towel.

He'd forgotten. How many humans had he killed that he could so easily dismiss the memory?

I would make him remember.

"Because you killed my sister, you piece of shit."

The creases between his eyebrows deepened like he was confused.

Confused because he didn't remember. Didn't care. Didn't give a flying fuck about Zinnia, about the life he'd taken or about the one he'd left ruined.

I flailed my way free from the towel, lungs searing as I rolled to my knees, facing him, not caring that I was naked.

"Ten years ago. Luminis." Tears burned my eyes, spittle flecked my words. "The Gilded Suns performed for Dawn Court, then Zinnia the Delectable gave you and your friends a private performance."

The creases had faded, and now his eyebrows inched up. Oh, yes, it was all coming back to him now.

Now he fucking remembered.

"You must not have enjoyed her much—or maybe too much—because you left her in the alleyway outside. You'd crushed the life from her throat and left her lying there like a broken toy." The trembling was back now, but for a vastly different reason. Rage seized my muscles, even though they were weak from all he'd done to me in the bath. "You thought you'd got away with it. Of course you did—you're a fucking prince. Untouchable. Above the law."

I laughed, bitter and biting, teeth bared. More monstrous than human, like his beast man form. "But I saw. I saw you." I pointed at him, like I did when I unleashed my curses.

183

My hand shook. My heart thundered. My throat scorched with each word.

The slumbering magic in me stirred, like smoke curling from the embers of a fire thought extinguished.

If only I could curse him all over again. If only I could point and unleash myself again. I'd only been eighteen; I didn't have the imagination I had now.

Now I'd curse him much more thoroughly.

But I'd been innocent. I'd been in a hurry, hiding behind the troupe's discarded packing crates. The best I'd been able to do was curse him to be unable to hide his monstrous truth.

And I could only curse a person once.

I'd screwed up my opportunity. Just like I'd screwed up my revenge.

He sat there, jaw slack, eyes unblinking.

"I saw you, Your Royal Fucking Highness, standing over her, ducking down to take a lock of hair like the sick bastard you are. That is why I came here. That is why I tried to kill you. That is why I hate you and I will not stop hating you until my last breath." I rose on my knees and looked down at him. "I will find my iron dagger, and I will have my revenge or I will die trying."

His chest rose and fell once, like he was waking up from death. "You were there." Another breath, this one deeper. "That night. *You were there.*"

"Well done, idiot. I just told you that." I sneered, the tight feeling welcome after his touch had made me so slack. "I saw you. Your tail. Your claws glinting in the streetlights. Your yellow eyes as you looked over your shoulder."

Back then, he'd walked through his capital city with his claws and tail hidden and those slitted pupils shifted to appear normal. He'd just looked like any other fae. Acceptable for Luminis. Acceptable for the royal family.

But with his friends at that private performance, he'd relaxed and dropped the façade. He'd stood over my sister, obviously a shapechanger. I'd learned enough on our annual visits to Elfhame to understand they were considered little better than animals.

Having one in Dawn's royal family was a shameful secret. A thing best kept hidden.

With my curse, I took that from him. I spilled the truth.

I curse you, prince of Elfhame, to never hide what you are.

I got him exiled.

But it was not enough. Only death would be enough.

"I thought you saw me at first." I shook my head, seeing that moment when he'd turned and the light had hit his face, glinting in his unmistakable yellow eyes. "You looked right at me in my hiding place. I swore you'd seen me. But then you ran."

"You." He sat up, eyes wide, pupils narrowing to paper-thin slits. "*You.*"

He burst from the headboard. I didn't get the chance to move before his hand was around my throat and I was on my back.

"You're the witch who cursed me," he snarled as he crushed me into the bed. His claws pricked my flesh, so close to ripping out my jugular.

I smiled. He knew now, and it was beautiful.

Not only was he obsessed with the human who'd tried to kill him, but he was infatuated with the witch who'd cursed him. He'd tasted her blood, told her she was delicious. He'd cared for her when she'd been sick. He'd feared for her life.

And he'd fucked her with his fingers, drinking up the sight of her pleasure.

"All this time, *you were her*." His muscles heaved. His face shifted, nose getting wider and flatter. He grew over me, making the bed groan. "I swore I'd kill you."

"Go on, then." I hadn't cut his throat, but his obsession was a close second place in my quest for vengeance. I could make do with that.

With a roar, he tore away from me.

The room shook with his bellows as he raged through it. Tables splintered. Stuffing flew through the air from the shredded settee. Vases and bowls shattered.

I barely sat up in time to see him bound onto the balcony and over the balustrade. His striped form disappeared into the night as feathers from torn-up cushions drifted around me.

Panting, I touched my throat. No blood. And I was alive.

Maybe the gods were real, because that was a fucking miracle.

28

The next morning, I woke sitting against the headboard with the towel wrapped around me.

He hadn't returned.

I removed the chair I'd wedged under the handle of the balcony doors. It wouldn't have stopped him getting in, but it would've given me a little warning time. Pulling on a dressing robe, I padded out.

My mouth went dry. Every hair on my body rose.

The ruined temple that had stood on the path to the lake stood no more. There was only rubble. The shredded remains of shrubs littered the lawn. And amongst them lay low brown mounds flecked with white and crimson.

It took me a moment to understand they weren't branches sticking out from some of those mounds, but antlers. White bone. Crimson blood.

A dozen deer. All torn open.

No prizes for guessing who'd killed them.

Or *what*.

There wasn't a single grain of doubt in my mind.

I pulled the robe tighter, hugging myself.

"Your recollection of that night is flawed."

I whirled with a low cry and found the prince's large form tucked into the balcony's back corner. He wore fresh clothes. His hair was a smooth sheet of rosy copper, as though freshly brushed, though he didn't wear his crown. That still sat in his room where he'd taken it off before dinner last night.

A blueish tinge underlined his yellow eyes as he surveyed the field of devastation.

Fear squeezed my lungs. Last night's ferocious joy had fled with the moon.

His shoulders heaved on a long exhale, and his gaze landed on me. "Then again, should I be surprised that a human got things so fucking wrong?" With each word, he stalked closer.

I backed away, barely registering what he said. The small of my back hit the balustrade.

He towered over me. This morning he stood in his fae form, but he seemed larger, as though the rising sun infused him, a prince of Dawn Court, with its power. His lip curled, showing the long canines that he'd used to caress me and could just as easily use to kill me.

His advance didn't stop, as relentless as a new day or the turning seasons—or death.

I craned back over the balustrade as his toes met mine.

Flame flecked his yellow eyes. A ring of burnt orange, like late summer flowers, edged the irises. His pupils slitted down to their thinnest.

I couldn't look away.

I'd heard of creatures whose eyes mesmerised their prey. Legends. Myths. But maybe it was true, because his held me frozen even as he raised his hand, unhurried, like he knew I wouldn't—couldn't try to escape.

His fingers closed around my throat.

"You want to know what really happened that night?" He squeezed, pressing the collar into my skin.

Sweat slid down my spine. I couldn't have answered if I wanted to. Just breathing was work enough. A feather tighter and I wouldn't be able to do that.

He ducked closer, nose wrinkling an inch from mine. "You stupid girl." His voice hissed with savage intensity. "You cursed me, but the person who killed your sister is still walking around enjoying life."

No. That wasn't true. Some fae trick that twisted words and meaning to allow him to lie without speaking an untrue word.

Even cursed, he was still enjoying his life, wasn't he? There was the lie.

"I walked out into that alleyway and I found her there. Already dead. Though I checked." His grip tightened, cutting off my air supply, as if to illustrate that she hadn't been breathing, either.

My pulse throbbed in my temples. The world went suddenly very bright, very sharp, like it was made of razor blades and lit by a thousand suns.

He found her.

No. I managed to shake my head the barest amount. No. That wasn't possible. That wasn't what I saw. That wasn't...

Grey splotches invaded my field of view, growing with the same pulsing beat of my heart.

No.

His eyes widened, just a touch, and he loosened his grip

until I could suck in air that tasted of him. Musk and new growth; the fresh breeze on a summer day.

It was only once I caught my breath that he bent closer, nose almost touching mine. "I didn't kill your sister. But..." He smiled slowly, and it was the cruellest smile of all. It glinted in his eyes like a freshly honed blade. "Maybe I'll kill you. If you're dead, surely that will break the curse."

My brain scrambled over his words, searching for meaning in the rubble he'd left my mind, my beliefs, my *life*. Already I was shaking my head, though I didn't fully understand why. Not yet.

Fae couldn't outright lie. He hadn't killed her.

I'd been wrong.

All this time.

All this plotting.

All my plans.

Ruins. Just like this place.

I'd learned the hoop and the silks, blistering my hands, enduring countless scrapes and bruises. All so I could take Zinnia's spot in the show and keep a place in the Gilded Suns rather than being kicked out. I'd forged my body into something that could endure night after night, that could excel in its performances, so when word reached the prince, pushed towards him by my own manipulations and whispers, he wouldn't be able to help himself but ask us to perform. Eventually. It had taken years—*years*.

I'd even grown my hair like hers, done my makeup like hers, worn outfits like hers—all so it would be like *she* was the one getting her revenge.

And here I stood, his hand around my throat, the aching ghost of his fingers still between my legs, the shattered fragments of failed vengeance cutting my soul to pieces.

And he...

My mind finally clambered over all that and reached the last part of what he'd said.

He was going to kill me.

My head was still shaking.

"It won't," I croaked past his grip. "Killing me won't lift the curse."

I had no idea if that was true or not. But it was the lie I needed to save my life.

The skin around his eyes tightened as he considered me for a long while.

"You would say that. A lying human and her lying little mouth." He sneered, stretching me further and further back over the balustrade. If he let go now, I would fall head-first.

My muscles strained, drawn out. I clung to the handrail like that might save me. I doubted it would.

Even if he didn't drop me, he had only to sink his claws into my flesh as he had the fae who'd threatened to put me out of my misery.

"But if that is true and I kill you now, I'll never be able to make you lift the curse." He fixed me with a glare before sweeping away inside, leaving me to stumble from the balustrade.

His voice drifted through the open door. "Clean yourself up and get dressed, witch. You've got a hell of a day ahead of you."

29

He wasn't lying.

His kindness had crashed to an end with his beast form crashing through that ruin.

Today's outfit was a skimpy dress so short it barely covered my arse and no underwear. He tossed my blanket on the floor, so I guessed my time on the bed was over. He even had me kneel as I served him and his friends at breakfast.

After that, he worked in his study. He made me sit on the floor and write over and over again, "I am a stupid human. I will lift Prince Sepher's curse."

My fingers ached at the rub of the pen, the repeated movement. My shoulders and back burned from hunching over the floor. I wasn't allowed to use a table. Furniture was not for pets, as he reminded me.

"Is that all you've done?" He snatched the pages from me and rifled through. "You weren't even trying." He tossed them into the fire, which sputtered and sparked pink and orange.

I glared up at him, jaw clenched. After asking who'd killed

my sister, which he'd refused to answer, I'd gone back to my silence. This time, though, it was less to punish him and more because... what the hells was I supposed to say?

I wasn't going to apologise. Even if he hadn't been the one to kill Zinnia, he'd never raised the alarm or handed over the names of his friends who'd been there that night. He'd played a part in denying her justice.

He probably knew who'd killed her. Yet, he hadn't told me.

So, no. No apologies for him.

But every moment, my mind churned over it all, from the unhelpful "You were wrong" to the unanswered "Who did it?"

It was easier to manage those thoughts with my mouth shut.

A tight smile on his face, the prince swept down and grabbed my collar. My head snapped back as he yanked me to my feet. "You're lucky it's not *you* I'm throwing on the fire."

For a second he held me there, teeth bared, face an inch from mine, his glare savage, inhuman. Then he shifted his grip to the back of my collar and shoved me ahead of him.

"Maybe I should get you a lead. Though"—he yanked, cutting off my breath for a moment—"I do like keeping you close like this. A little reminder of who your life belongs to."

Him. And it hadn't even got me any closer to Zinnia's killer.

At least when I'd been so sure he'd done it, being his pet kept me near him. I was ready to strike the moment I had access to a weapon that would end his accursed life.

Now?

Now, I had nothing. I'd never been further from avenging my sister.

Head hanging, I walked ahead and went wherever he steered.

I wasn't surprised when we arrived in the dining room, though I hadn't realised it was lunchtime already. The morning had disappeared in ink and my cycling thoughts.

Celestine's brow furrowed as her gaze landed on me and the collar biting into my throat. She cocked her head at Sepher in question.

Instead of responding, he marched me to one end of the table and shoved me to the floor. "You made it look too easy this morning, my precious pet." His smile didn't meet his eyes as he pulled a pouch from his pocket. "So, *so* precious that I'm going to pave your path with gold. Well..." He shrugged and upended the pouch. Dozens—hundreds of clear gems rained upon the floor, catching the light and refracting it into rainbow flashes. "Pave it with *diamonds.*"

They glinted, all different sizes, throwing tiny motes of light across the floor.

I swallowed when I saw they'd all landed with the large, flat facet on the floor—the one that would face outward on a ring. That left the sharp back pointing upward.

Oh, great.

The prince's steps crunched over the diamonds like they were nothing more than gravel, and he sprawled into his seat, legs spread. Glare fixed on me, he gestured to the sparkling floor. "Kneel and come to your master."

I didn't see who the sharp intake of breath came from, but I'd have placed my money on Celestine.

An odd mixture of quiet murmurs and the rustle of fae leaning forward to get a better view spread across the table.

I'd caught my breath from being marched here with the collar pulled tight, so, with all the grace I could muster, I rose to my knees. The nearest sprinkle of stones was six inches away. For now, I only had to deal with the unyielding marble of the floor... and the equally unyielding gaze of the prince as he sat back, waiting.

I slid my knee forward, pushing the stones out of the way.

Roark huffed, thumping the table. "She's cheating. Look, she's—"

"I'm well aware of what she's doing." Sepher spoke calmly and raised his chin. "Hands and knees, little bird. Lift with each step. Or I'll make you do it all afternoon."

Teeth gritted, I smiled sweetly at him. Maybe life would be easier to withstand now His Princely Prickishness was back. Even though he hadn't killed Zinnia, I still had plenty of reasons to hate him.

Plenty.

I sank forward as cool air inched up my thighs in the tiny slip of a dress. Chances were, someone would catch a glimpse under the hem as I crawled. He'd planned this extra dimension to my humiliation. Well, fuck him, I didn't care.

My right hand I slotted into a space between gems, but there was no such gap for my left. With deep breaths, I eased my weight onto my palms.

The diamonds stabbed into my flesh.

It took a few more long breaths, but I could take it.

Swallowing, I lifted one leg and one arm and took my first step forward. A larger stone caught under my knee and no matter how much I tried to wiggle it out of the way before I lowered my weight, it wouldn't budge.

No option but to move forward.

It was only a diamond, relatively small, but it felt like kneeling on a dagger's tip.

The prince shifted in his seat, coming away from its back as he leant a little closer, as though eager to catch every hint of my pain.

I ground my teeth together against the sound clawing at my throat to be let out.

I will not give him the satisfaction.

I seized on that as I took my next step, a mental chant to keep me focused.

I will not. I will not. I will not.

My eyes burned as shards spiked through my knees and palms, streaking through every nerve like a dozen lightning strikes.

With my next step, a horrible realisation crept up my spine. The larger diamond in my knee didn't drop away as I lifted it—it was stuck in my skin. My breath came a little quicker in grotesque anticipation.

I will not. I will not. I will not.

When I placed my knee on the floor and shifted my weight to it, the diamond dug deeper.

I clung to my chant and forged onward.

On my fifth step, the one that carried that large stone forward again and drove it deeper into my poor knee, a hissing noise puffed out between my gritted teeth.

The prince smiled and sat back. But his eyes didn't shine with pleasure at my pain—not like they had as he'd drunk up my endless climaxes last night.

I kept going. There was nothing else I could do. Asking for mercy would get me nowhere and I would not give him that triumph.

Each step screamed in my bones until I reached his feet, trembling, my hands, knees, and shins bloody. Breaths sawed through me, and it took a few of them before I could raise my head and meet his gaze.

But he didn't look triumphant, even as he smirked and pushed his foot closer.

"Kiss my boots."

"Sepher." That was Celestine's voice cutting through the peculiar quiet of dozens of people watching with baited breath. "Do you—?"

He silenced her with a flick of his tail. "My boots," he bit out.

It couldn't be worse than the crawl or knowing I'd done all this for nothing. I bent. I kissed. I made sure to smear a little of my blood on the shiny leather as I gripped his ankle.

"Acceptable. Now, sit here." He pointed to his thigh.

When I stood, a nauseating chill washed over me. The straightening of the joints found new ways for the pain to travel along my nerves, and it pulsed in my whole body.

I sat on his thigh. The warm hand that came around my waist pushed back the chill, but it wasn't a thing meant for comfort, just for claiming.

When he brushed away the diamonds embedded in my skin, a shudder swept through me. His grip on my waist flexed, perhaps an involuntary movement to stop me falling off his lap.

Then, as if nothing had happened, he tucked in to his lunch.

Although everything inside me had changed, a cataclysmic shifting of reality, I kept up my stubborn sexualising of each bite he fed me. I licked the pad of his thumb, letting his claw graze my lip, sucking sauce from his fingers.

At this point, stubbornness was all I had. And it was a small flare of victory to see the hunger in his eyes that had nothing to do with food.

They were dim points of comfort, like the prick of his claws at my waist.

I'd failed and I needed to start again. Only now I had no idea who'd killed Zinnia and I was trapped as the prince's pet.

He brought a glass to my lips. Clutching his shirt to keep my balance, I gulped down the berry wine with its deep, dark flavour that matched its purple-black colour.

"I understand now, little witch. You think this is a game. Perhaps even one you can win."

Goosebumps chased over my skin at his hot breath in my ear.

He pulled the glass away and replaced it on the table, not making me drink the whole thing this time. Still, it softened the world, warming my insides.

"You think you can out-dare me, that I won't rise to the challenge." He pulled my jaw until I faced him, then trailed a claw down my throat, clicking over the collar's jewels. "Do I look like a man who should be dared?"

My chest heaved as his touch grazed over it.

I'd been wrong, and now I was lost. Out at sea with no sign of shore and no north star to guide me.

All this time, he'd been my north star. My guiding point.

And now he was only a lie away from killing me.

The fuzziness in my brain wouldn't budge. I had no plan. I didn't know what to do next in my life.

I had only now.

And my stubbornness.

I lifted my chin and gave him a look that dared to challenge, that dared to *dare*.

I wouldn't be afraid of him.

I would not.

The corner of his mouth twitched like he fought a smile. His claw snagged on the light silk of my dress as it traced over my hip to my thigh. He passed the hem, skin searing as he squeezed. "What if I repeated last night's attentions but they all got to watch?" He nodded towards the rest of the table, but his hooded eyes never left mine.

I gritted my teeth, because heat flared inside me even though this was a threat of punishment.

It was because I was sick. It was because he'd made me come so hard last night and my body remembered the pleasure his touch could bring, and stupidly didn't understand how this would be different.

It was because some part of me, some deep, dark primal instinct, wanted the awful things he offered, the punishment, the cruelty, the pain. It thrived off that, freed by it, breathed to life by him.

Now it knew he wasn't my sister's killer, it could be louder, hungrier, unashamed to want our enemy.

But he was still my jailer. He was still cruel and grotesque. He still loved to punish me.

Yet that part of me didn't understand or care.

It had my muscles tightening as his fingers dipped between my legs, tracing little circles on my inner thigh that came higher with each pass.

At the next seat, I heard Roark put down his cutlery and make a soft sound of interest.

Sepher nuzzled into the crook between my neck and shoulder, his touch fire. "Would you like it if they saw you come apart on my hand? Would you mewl for more as you did last night?"

My breath hitched as he skimmed my edges, sending my heart rate into riotous thunder.

With a soft laugh, he pulled away. "Tomorrow, I will make a public example of my pet," he announced to the table.

They fell still and silent, forks in mid-air, glasses halfway to open mouths.

A wicked smile showed his top canines.

Several at the table leant forward, smiles almost matching his, Roark's the widest. Others replaced their glasses and forks, tension underlying their flat expressions. Celestine and Anya exchanged glances. Essa's brow furrowed. Cadan's lips pursed, but he quickly hid it behind a sip of wine.

Inside me, the threat quivered, anticipation and fear waking. Was he going to hunt me again? The delicate hairs on my arms rose at the memory of being pinned to the tree.

"But first, I'm going to make a private example of her." His smile vanished. "Leave us."

30

"Over the table." His voice crept through the silent room as the abandoned plates disappeared.

I took my time rising from his lap, stomach tight. With no one else here, this suddenly felt much more dangerous. Maybe that was what loosened my tongue.

"Why are you punishing me, Sepher? Haven't I obeyed?" I spread my hands, showing the tiny diamond cuts. "Everything you've asked, I've done."

He bared his teeth, claws digging into the chair's arms. "Yes, but your obedience is malicious, little bird. And you know it. Now, bend over the table."

Around the tight ball of my stomach, anticipation fluttered. What was he going to do if and when I obeyed? I held his gaze a long while, trying to read something in its golden depths.

He raised one shoulder, the gesture deceptively casual. "*Or* you could lift the curse. Your choice."

Except it wasn't, because I couldn't. I'd only placed a few

in my life, but I'd never managed to lift any. Even the one time I'd truly wished I could.

If I told him, he would kill me. I was only worth keeping alive if he believed I could give him back the life and body he'd once had.

So I gave him a sharp smile, like I did have a choice and still chose spite, and bent over the table.

My heart thundered as I pressed into the unyielding surface. It was a wonder it didn't reverberate through the wood and make the candlesticks and glasses clatter.

Sepher's hand slid up the small of my back, lifting my dress, and cool air wafted over my backside. I held my breath, waiting for him to slam into me. That felt like where this was going.

The deep darkness in me quivered with want. It saw its mirror in him, an answering darkness in his cruelty. Mine called to his, wanting to circle it, dance with it, join it in sweat and hate and lust and all those white-hot feelings that screamed life.

I waited.

And waited.

Just as my lungs began to burn, a slap rang across my arse, jolting me into the table, making the held breath burst from my lips in a low cry.

My bare skin stung, and his hand lingered there a moment, fingers flexing, the warmth mingling sweetly with the hurt. When I sighed at that and sagged into the table, he withdrew his touch.

He struck twice more. Hard enough to sting, but not hard enough to cause damage. I wasn't sure if he intended it for my pleasure, or if he wanted to hurt but feared injuring me after my brush with death. He didn't seem to quite understand the limits of a human body compared to a fae one, so perhaps it made him more cautious than he'd otherwise be.

Both times, he stroked the same spot he'd smacked and sent my pussy throbbing. The sweet touch after the sharp pain.

"Hmm." His hand left me, and I braced for the next strike. "You like that too much, witch. No, a different punishment for you, I think."

I heard the way he smiled around the words. Even with my back to him, I could see the exact curve of his lips, the way his teeth showed, the way the canines dimpled his lower lip as he said "witch." In several weeks, I'd learned him well.

There was a whisper of touch over my spine, flooding me with goosebumps, then the tearing of cloth ripped the silence. He spread the tattered edges of my dress, exposing my back.

I refused to look over my shoulder. I couldn't let him see the part of me that had come to crave whatever he had to give, the darkness in me that saw the darkness in him. Even worse, I didn't want him to see how it snaked around my fear, nursing it, suckling life from it, relishing in the chill that raced through me.

The lightest touch traced over the hairs at the nape of my neck, right above my collar. "These give you away, pet. All set on end, and your scent." He bent over me, his hair tickling my shoulders, breaths hot upon my neck. "I already told you how sweet your fear was, but mingled with your arousal... Fuck. It's intoxicating." A dark chuckle breathed over my skin as he rose and his hand came into view, pulling a candle from its holder. "What happened to make you such a sick little bird, I wonder?"

I squeezed my eyes shut, shame burning my cheeks. Of course, he didn't need to see my darkness or my fear—he could scent them on the air, like a predator scented prey or freshwater or a female in heat.

An instant later, something blazing hot patted onto my back. I gasped, eyes flying open, shame forgotten. "What—?"

I bit down on my tongue to keep in the rest of the sentence. Asking what he was doing was weakness. The shock of the sudden heat had driven the gasp into me and that single word out, but I was back in control now.

"You know what this is." His voice was a low murmur, purring through the stillness.

He dotted a trail of heat over my back, and it took me a second to understand.

Candle wax.

And now I was expecting it, it wasn't as hot as I'd first thought. That first drip had felt like actual fire, but this now was uncomfortably hot, yet not unbearable, a lot like the bath temperature I preferred.

I panted through the points of pain, the sudden scorch. The hairs on my arms rose.

As he worked across my back and shoulders, I became singularly aware of everything. The brush of his trousers on the back of my legs. The cool air on my exposed skin. The dim throb of my backside.

The time between drips opened up like a held breath, making each moment exquisitely sharp. It honed my attention, so when he reached over and his foot came between mine, it was as overwhelming as if he'd spread my legs and placed himself between them.

He painted me and I flinched, unable to help myself. The torn edges of my dress whispered over my skin with each involuntary movement.

This moment was everything, like each drop was an anchor point to now.

There was no past.

There was no future.

No plans. No plots.

No failure. No victory.

Only sensation. Only his touch. Only the deep, dark aftertaste of berry wine. Only the bright gold of candlesticks and vases of fiery summer flowers, even though it was deep autumn. Only the afternoon light shafting through the windows and bouncing off the chandeliers. Only the warm, musky scent of him curling over me, mingling with the steady sound of his breaths.

The heat melted away all else.

His claws scraped over me, tugging away the solidified wax, pulling a soft whimper from my throat. The soft caress as he smoothed my hot flesh scored through my very existence.

"Your skin is so pink, Zita." The drips started afresh, making me jolt, working their way down my spine. "Tell me to stop. Take back your curse."

But I didn't want him to stop.

Not just for stubbornness, but for the thrill of it. I lived in the anticipation of the next drop and where it would land. I was the pain and the soothing that came after as he rubbed away the wax. I didn't have space in my mind to think about curses or death or princes.

I was entirely here. Entirely now. Entirely alive.

That was why I turned over.

His eyes flashed wide as I met his gaze, now on my back. I held it as I peeled the remains of my dress away and wriggled it over my hips to the floor. He watched its progress, pupils wide and so dark I could've drowned in them.

Bare before him, I nodded once.

His broad chest rose in a long, long breath.

The instant it lowered, it was like he made a decision. He tilted the candle, letting a drop of wax fall on my belly. At the same time, he reached out with his other hand and grabbed a bottle of oil from the table. The fae drizzled it over salad leaves, but now he poured its gold-green stream over my nipples.

Its sudden coolness caught my breath, a delicious contrast with the hot wax still stippling my stomach.

With a swipe of his thumb, he coated the oil over one nipple, then the other, shooting pleasure to my centre with those all-too-brief touches.

"It makes the wax easier to remove." One side of his mouth rose. "But it doesn't dull the heat."

His gaze pierced me as he moved the candle over my breast and slowly, slowly tilted it.

A single drop of wax fell.

I cried out, arched, my mind momentarily a blank at the searing pain. It faded quickly, leaving me breathless.

He watched me with hooded eyes, his intensity scorching my nerves. He waited for my breathing to almost return to normal before he delivered another spot of wax.

My nails scratched over the table, searching for purchase, for some sense of reality in this waking dream.

There was none.

Reality had left us.

"That's it, little bird, you can take it." A roughness had taken over his voice, leaving it gravelly. He smiled, part cruel, part private pleasure. "I knew you could."

It seemed he'd forgotten about lifting curses and punishment, too.

We were no longer a cruel prince and the witch who'd cursed him.

We were something else entirely.

Both master and possession. Both hate and want. Both driving and driven.

With each drop of wax, he stole my breath and his grew heavier. He stood between my legs, a telltale bulge in his trousers. He pinned my waist, claws prickling me in glorious spikes of sensation.

Finally, when my chest was coated, he discarded the candle and stood back, as though admiring his creation. My breasts felt contained, like I wore clothing too tight.

With a smile, he used a firm sweep of his thumbs to crumble the shell away.

Compared to the solidified wax, his skin was warm and living. I couldn't help arching, biting my lip as I watched him massage it away.

His eyebrows peaked together as his gaze shifted from mine to his touch and back again. "Fuck." It came out of him as he worked my nipples, circling their tight tips long after the wax was gone, then, "Zita."

He said it like it was a curse.

Like it was a prayer.

Like it was loved and loathed and something he couldn't live without, a bitter medicine he needed to survive.

Then his mouth closed over the peak of my breast. Hot and wet, a thundering of sensation. He ran the length of his tongue over me. Its roughness was harsh, so near painful it had me crying out. He sucked and lapped my nipple again, drawing every muscle in me taut as though I held a pose for an adoring audience.

He was my only audience, and he consumed me with his gaze as much as with his mouth.

Somehow, my hands were in his hair, holding him against me. I pulled off his crown and traced my nails over his scalp. He moaned onto me, the vibration shooting pleasure to my pussy, which was wet and wanting.

I lost myself in watching him and feeling him as he switched to my other breast, laving it as he held my waist. The need in me rose and rose, an overwhelming storm cloud rolling in from an angry sea.

When he worked his way down my belly, kissing and licking and nipping, I lost my mind entirely. He passed my belly button and looked up. "Tell me to stop."

My chest was tight with anticipation, breaths fast. I shook my head. "Never."

Glaring at me with flushed cheeks and mussed hair, he said with vicious intensity, "Fuck."

Then the prince kneeled.

There was nothing gentle in the way he gripped my thighs and spread them wide, but I didn't want gentle. His claws pierced my skin, pricked my awareness, sending shards of pain through me at the exact moment his rough tongue ran my length.

The world behind my eyelids exploded as I came. Pleasure and pain combined in a terrible thunderstorm that buffeted me like I was a sparrow caught in its unbending will.

I throbbed and trembled, coming back to earth to find Sepher smirking up at me, even more insufferable than ever.

"Already?" He arched one eyebrow, framed by my bloodied thighs, where a dozen tiny scratches lit my skin. "Was one touch from my tongue all it took to break the stubborn little beast?"

I tried to tell him to go fuck himself, but I hadn't yet mastered my body.

"Let's see how many more times I can break you."

He bent to me with another long lick that lifted me somewhere sparkling. Its roughness speared me as he circled my clit and ran along my slit.

It was more than just touch. It reached into me and pulled out every broken, messy part and put it on display, as I turned into a seething, writhing mass coated in blood and sweat and sin.

He fucked me with his tongue, its length shocking as it swept into me. I came upon it, crying out as he consumed my essence and a low rumble spilled from him into me like distant thunder.

Not pulling away, he released one thigh and held up two blood-tipped fingers.

"I fucking hate you," I managed to push out between ragged breaths.

It was true, in a manner. But not in the same way it had been true when I'd first arrived.

I hated him.

I hated that I wanted him.

I hated that I couldn't bring myself to tell him to stop.

I hated that I didn't even want to try.

And I hated that as he reached for the oil, it filled me with as much anticipation as trepidation, fluttering low in my belly like another building climax.

"What are you...?"

The tip of his tail came into view and he coated it in oil.

"Where are you putting that?" My voice came out in a hoarse whisper.

At last, he pulled away and met my gaze. His eyes glinted

with wicked intent as he licked up my inner thigh, cutting through the thin rivulets of blood.

"You're mine, Zita." Again, that slight purr of his voice over my name. It made my breath hitch as his tail dipped out of sight.

Both hands back in place, he lifted my legs, high and wide, splaying me utterly. His chest heaved as he paused and took in the sight, that private smile curving his lips. "Such an exquisite creature," he murmured so softly, I wasn't sure he intended to say it out loud.

A slick touch slid along the crevice of my arse cheeks, sending my heart racing harder, faster in a race it could never win. The throb echoed in every part of my body, an insistent demand.

He paused at my hole, circling it.

"You're mine," he said again and took another lick of my blood as if to illustrate. "I'll fuck you however I see fit. Unless"—he raised his eyebrows and the touch at my arse ceased—"you want to tell me to stop?"

I could barely swallow, my mouth had gone so dry. Speech was out of the question. I shook my head.

"Good girl."

His tail slid inside me, just a little, but it drew my back in a tight arch and a soft moan from my lips. He withdrew entirely, probed a little deeper, then repeated the process again, watching me all the while.

A new kind of pleasure unfurled in me. Darker. Deeper. I couldn't say whether it was because he touched me somewhere new or because of the sharp point of his attention aimed at me.

"There, see. You take your punishment so well, Zita." With a smirk, he lowered to me.

Tongue and tail, he fucked me.

I stood no chance.

It wasn't the fullness I craved, but with him inside both parts of me, it came closer. Besides, the flex of his tongue pressing upon the front wall of my pussy hit a spot that was better than fullness.

Every breath whimpering, I tilted into his invasion, welcoming it, wanting it, falling apart upon it.

He split me into a hundred pieces, a thousand, a million, each of them a blazing sun that seared away all else.

I was a quivering, panting wreck when he stood, licking his lips, his tail still inside me.

"That's three, but I don't want to pull you apart as much as I did last night." He stood over me, looking down his nose, every inch the arrogant, cruel prince.

I hated that this was the face he wore when he'd just done this to me. He hadn't lost himself as I had. He hadn't forgotten his hate as he'd soared to a blinding peak as I had.

"Is that it?" I scoffed. "Is that the best you've got?" I hooked my heels around his hips before he could back away. "You're not even going to fuck me? You coward."

He froze.

The eyes that locked on mine weren't as cool and detached as the ones that had just looked down on me.

They were golden flame. Hatred. Rage. Desire that couldn't help trailing over my oil-slicked breasts.

"Go on. Prove that you own me." I unfastened the top button of his trousers.

He didn't stop me.

I kept unbuttoning.

His nostrils flared as his chest heaved. That muscle in his jaw ticked.

I drank it all up until I had his length free. I took my time, closing my hand around it.

Smooth soft skin. I had my answer. The end was already slick with his own moisture, which I palmed and spread down his length, adding my other hand.

He shuddered. "Fuck you."

"Promises, promises."

He gripped my wrists, tight as a vice. "You want me, Zita? Fine." He held my hands in place and thrust into them, the tip of his cock nudging my stomach, painting me with his sticky residue. When I tilted my hips, its base slid along my clit and his tail thrust into my arse in time, seizing my breath. "But you'll have me *my* way."

His cheeks flushed as his hips rolled into the space between my legs. I couldn't help watching his thick shaft thrust into my hands, wanting it inside me. That and his tail? I wasn't sure I could take both, but, fuck, I would try.

Eyebrows clenched together, he fucked my hands and glared at me.

I grinned right back, body gripped by feral delight as I watched him fall away piece by piece.

The prince.

The beast.

The master.

The cursed man who'd vowed vengeance.

The loyalty.

The cruelty.

The last thing that remained was his hatred flashing and snarling at me in the depths of his golden eyes.

But at last that too fell away, as he dropped forward, hand landing by my head. He bowed down to the hold I had upon him, and my pleasure rose up to meet it. It was a cruel, petty kind of pleasure compared to what he'd already given me, but I'd take it.

I tightened my grip, and he shuddered, eyes squeezing shut like he didn't want me to see there was nothing left in them.

With a bellow he surged onto my belly. That victory together with the bunching of his tail in my arse threw me over the precipice once more with a beautiful, perverse certainty.

He was mine.

31

After, he stood back, chest heaving, eyes widening for an instant as though he only now realised what he'd done. He pulled from me, taking a step back, and tucked himself away.

"There's healing salve in our room. Put that on yourself."

I eased upright, body sore from being so beautifully used. He hadn't come inside me, but I'd made him lose control for that moment. I grabbed a napkin and wiped away the evidence of it.

Retrieving my tattered dress from the floor, he wrinkled his nose at me. But it was a ghost of his usual glare, like that had died and its shade was all that remained. "I suggest you hurry there. The scent of your blood and arousal will call to the others."

My heart rate had been slowing, but that thought sent it spiking again. If Roark found me...

I pulled my tattered dress up my legs—he'd only split it down to the waist—and the surviving strap over my shoulder.

He watched with a smirk as I held it over my chest and left.

Striding through the corridors—I would *not* run—I held the image of him in my mind. There was something brittle about his smirk. If I'd fucked him, I think I might've broken it entirely—broken *him* entirely.

But I couldn't dawdle and ponder that. I felt eyes upon me, though I saw no sign of Roark or any other members of the Court of Monsters.

It was only once I reached my prince's bedroom that I slammed the door and allowed myself to stop.

And that was when I realised.

He'd called it *our* room.

THAT EVENING, I stood on a stool in one of the many sitting rooms, holding up a decanter of wine. If its base dipped any lower than the crown of my head, I had to drink the lot. My arms burned, but I kept them aloft.

Around me, my prince's inner circle drank and chatted and ignored me. Most of them, anyway.

Sepher sat with a glass of honeyed whisky, watching me even as he had a low conversation with Anya. The slightest weakness, and he'd make sure I completed my punishment.

Jaw clenched, I held his gaze.

We hadn't addressed what had happened in the dining room. Or the fact he'd said "our room." The more time that passed, the more I thought it was just a meaningless slip of the tongue.

As for our relationship, if it could be called that...

It was a mess. Not even a beautiful one.

He seemed more angry at me than ever—there'd been no smiles as we'd dressed for this evening. It wasn't even the kind of anger that pleased me. For some reason, it tangled in my gut, like I'd let someone who didn't know what they were doing pack away my silks after a performance.

I didn't even have a plan to cling to, a relentless call to revenge.

I had nothing.

It had been easy to forget that for a moment with his burning wax and then his burning touch. But now the full weight of it added to the decanter's heft, tugging on my arms.

My next step was to find out who *had* killed my sister. There would be no new plan until then.

Just because it wasn't Sepher didn't mean the real killer was out of reach. They might even be here. Maybe Celestine knew.

"Oh, pet," Roark called, a mocking lilt in his voice. "My glass needs filling." He waggled the empty vessel, leering at me.

Trying to hide my exhale of relief, I stepped off the stool and lowered my arms. My elbows and shoulders strained, aching from holding the same position for so long.

"Lord Roark." I gave him my smarmiest smirk as I bowed and filled his glass.

"Lord Roark? Oh, I like that." He grabbed my collar before I could straighten and tugged me closer. "Maybe I'll make you scream it when Sepher grows tired of you. He will soon. And he likes to share his toys once he's done with them."

Was that what he'd done with my sister? Had his fun, then let his friends have theirs?

It was such a well-worn path, my mind instantly leapt to

those questions. Except Sepher hadn't killed her. It was embarrassing the number of times I'd been forced to remind myself of that fact today.

Turned out, rewriting a belief held for a decade wasn't easily done.

Despite Roark's solid black eyes, I could see the moment his attention slid from my face and his gaze skimmed over my see-through gown.

But his distraction gave me an opportunity.

Still smiling sweetly, I poured more wine into his glass... and didn't stop. It spilled over, splashing into his lap, making him jump and spill yet more of his drink.

"You little bitch!" He yanked my collar, jolting my head back as I stumbled into him.

"Roark." Sepher's voice cut through the chatter and clink of glasses. "Kindly refrain from damaging my property." He said it with a mocking lilt, making a few of his friends laugh.

Not Roark, though. Eyes narrowed, he hissed and released me.

When I straightened, I found Sepher's eyes on us. He smiled, but it was a stiff, gritted thing. He sat up when I met his gaze, chin rising. "Breaking her is my job. Back to your post, little bird."

I returned to the stool and took a deep breath before raising the decanter again. My muscles complained at returning to the same position, but I treated it like training or another exercise routine—this one for endurance.

Enduring the pain, but also enduring the prince and his return to cruelty.

"I don't think she needs breaking, Seph." Celestine canted her head at him, one side of her mouth curling. But there was something fragile about her expression, as though it wasn't as casual as she was trying to make out. "She's so well-behaved. I think you've... trained her perfectly."

Eyes narrowing, he made a low sound, then returned to his quiet conversation with Anya.

I tried to ignore how close she sat to him, the little touches she gave his arm as they chatted and she laughed. And I especially tried to ignore the way it twisted in me, like I'd spun on my silks too many times and their lengths had snarled up.

His gaze was now firmly upon her and not me.

And I wasn't sure I liked the idea of sharing his attention. Not that I *wanted* it, more than I enjoyed that he was a slave to it. A slave to me.

"... Told me to ready the hounds for tomorrow." I caught the tail end of Cadan's sentence as he murmured to Celestine.

Her eyes widened and darted to me, then Sepher.

Hounds. Tomorrow. When he'd promised to make a public example of me.

The hairs on the back of my neck sprung to attention. Another hunt. This time, with the huge hunting dogs he kept in the stable yard. I'd only seen them from a distance, but their backs had to reach my shoulders, and their eyes glinted with a kind of sharp, instinctive intelligence.

"Sepher?" Celestine straightened, fixing him with a frown. "Is this true?"

With a deep sigh, he sat up from where he'd bowed his head with Anya's. "What?"

"You can't hunt Zita with your dogs. They'll rip her apart."

Black eyes glinting, Roark leant forward.

Cadan nodded. "It was one thing when we chased her— we were in control. But your hounds—"

"Cadan." Sepher's teeth flashed. "I only let Celestine speak to me like that because she's my sister. You are not." He stared the other fae down, and something thick rolled through the air, lifting goosebumps on my arms.

Eventually, Cadan looked away and took a gulp of his wine.

Sepher nodded as though satisfied he'd asserted himself and raised an eyebrow at Celestine. "I don't tell you how to treat your pets. Leave me to manage mine as I see fit."

She pressed her lips together, then parted them and sucked in a breath to speak.

"Celestine." His eyebrows clashed together. "You remember she tried to kill me, don't you?"

"Of course I do. It's just—"

"It wasn't her first time."

A beat of silence rang through the room as every head snapped his way.

As though sensing the attention upon him, he spread his hands and gave a bitter smile. "She's the witch who cursed me."

Anya and several others gasped. Celestine's dawn eyes went round, flicking to me as though seeking confirmation.

Sepher huffed into his whisky glass before taking a long sip. "And frankly, I'm offended you think I'd do something as basic as hunting her with my hounds. I have something much more imaginative planned for my bird. I'm going to make her *soar.*" He shot me a vicious smile before downing the rest of his drink and standing.

I couldn't help flinching, not when his voice was so heavy with threatening promise. Soar? Was he going to throw me off one of the palace's turrets?

He tossed his head. "You people bore me. You"—his eyes narrowed on me—"especially. Celestine, since you like her so much, you can look after her for the night."

219

He swept to the door and paused, framed by the light from the hallway. "No one hurt her. You'll be glad of it when you see what I have planned for tomorrow." Throwing a devilish grin over his shoulder, he disappeared.

My heart drummed against my ribs. Not a hunt. Not the hounds. Then, what? Something he didn't want me injured for.

As the chatter slowly resumed, the questions chased through me and I churned over possibilities. None of them matched the threat he'd left hanging.

It was a small comfort that Anya didn't follow him out. He was *mine*.

Celestine remained quiet and pale. Not long after Sepher disappeared, she declared she was retiring for the night and beckoned for me to join her.

Her usually elegant pace was clipped and stiff as she led me to her rooms. Her silence scraped on me, so unusual when she liked to accompany everything with a stream of chatter.

When we reached her rooms, she closed the door and leant against it with a long exhale. She shook her head as she turned to me. "How the hells are you still alive?"

I took a step back, her words ringing a discordant chime through my bones. "What do you mean?"

"You're the one who cursed him." A laugh laced her words. "He's spent a decade talking about what he was going to do to the witch who got him exiled. All the ways he would make her suffer, planning exactly how he would kill her. And yet, here you are."

The best laid plans of men and monsters.

"That makes two of us." I laughed.

It began as a trickle, but the more I laughed, the more ridiculous the situation looked.

220

I'd spent a decade plotting how to kill him.

He'd spent that same time planning how to kill me.

And neither of us were dead.

Eyes round, Celestine watched me bend double and grip my thighs as laughter ripped through me.

I wasn't sure when the last time was that I gave anything more than a chuckle, only faintly amused. But now, tears gathered at the corners of my eyes and my stomach hurt with the full belly laugh that echoed around the room.

Eventually, it subsided, leaving my cheeks aching. I swiped the tears from my face, chuckling at the mere fact of their existence.

"Are you...? Have you lost your mind?" Celestine kept very still, eyeing me. "I wouldn't blame you if you had."

"Not today." I cleared my throat and pushed the hair back from my face. "But I do need a drink."

She nodded slowly and went to the decanter on the side table. "Me too."

We curled up on twin armchairs before the fire and cradled our glasses. Staring into the flames, I drew a long breath and nodded. A sense of calm flooded my veins, as though my outburst had burned a space for it to enter me.

"Let me tell you a tale of two sisters..."

32

We stayed up late, and I told Celestine all about Zinnia and our life *before*. How we'd been orphans making a meagre living by begging and doing odd jobs for locals. How my accident had forced us out of town, a price upon my head. I kept the details of it vague, just saying that my awakening gift had harmed another girl. Drinking helped cover the bitter guilt that threatened to choke me.

I explained how Zinnia had filed down my teeth to help disguise us, and how, eventually, the Gilded Suns had taken us in. Zinnia, because they saw she was beautiful and had a natural skill for performance. Me, only because we were a package deal. I helped out backstage, but really it was a job anyone could've done.

For years, I helped her. I mended her costumes and did her makeup. We worked together on choreography and ideas for how to make her performances bigger, better, more dramatic and seductive. I had an idea of what she did after the shows—

the private performances—and as I grew older, so too I grew in understanding.

In all that time, I never used my gift. Not after the accident. I kept my finger from pointing at anyone in case I unleashed another curse.

But it was a bubbling cauldron inside me, with a lid fixed on too tightly.

Then, the night she died, I pointed at the man I found standing over her, and I let it all go. So much magic, so much hurt and hate, it had fired into him, strong enough to affect even a fae.

But it had given me no relief.

And not only had I lost my sister, but my reason to be with the Gilded Suns. Without Zinnia, they had no use for me.

I begged the owner to give me a month. A month, and I'd take her place in the show or they could leave me in the next town.

So I threw myself into learning to do what I'd always watched her do. I used her cosmetics to shine my hair and make myself pretty. I wore her costumes. I took the first letters of her name and named myself Zita.

So easily I stepped into her place in the world once it was left empty.

And so easily, the audience lapped me up. None of them realised I wasn't the woman from the posters—so many had been printed, we had to keep using the same design for several months after she'd gone.

After a while, I think the rest of the troupe forgot that I wasn't her. Like maybe I could undo it and we could all pretend I'd been the one to die that night.

Eric most of all.

He'd always watched Zinnia from the wings, lips parted, attention rapt, and I'd always watched him.

Then, once I'd taken her place on stage, I'd also taken her place in his gaze. But when I finally won him, it hadn't felt the same.

Nothing had.

Because without her, it was all grey.

That was when I'd realised my only cure was revenge.

I plotted and planned. Eric joined me sometimes, throwing in ideas, laughing when I came up with particularly good ones.

That should've been my warning.

He'd never taken it seriously. He'd never believed I'd actually go through with it.

That was why he'd betrayed me in the end.

Celestine listened and topped up our glasses, eyes widening at some points, narrowing at others. By the end, tears spilled from them.

"What was done to your sister..." She shook her head and dashed her cheeks. "That was awful. And you..." She pressed her lips together and stared at me a long time before going on. "You did all that work alone and still didn't get justice for her... or for you."

I nearly spilt my drink as I jolted at those last words. "For me?" I scoffed, though salt coated my throat. This was the first time I'd told our story and my newly unlocked emotions hadn't let me get through it without tears of my own.

Her delicate brow furrowed as she canted her head. "You were both wronged. Your childhood—left alone with only each other. The way you had to deal with your wakening magic alone—no one to guide you. And then..." A muscle in her jaw feathered, a softer twin to the one in Sepher's. "The way the Gilded Suns took advantage of you both."

"Advantage? I never did anything I didn't want—"

"Tell me, Zita, what cut did they take from your 'private performances?'"

"Only a quarter. Though I'm not sure—"

"*Only*. They sold you off to anyone with enough coin and they took a cut. They knew you were desperate. They knew you had no one after your sister died, and they filled their pockets by putting you on their posters and promising a more intimate experience for those who could afford it. Tell me what part of that is 'only.' They used you for their own ends." Despite her outburst, there was no sign of anger in her face. There was only a softness in her eyes, a downward turn of her mouth, and all the horrible hallmarks of pity.

I hadn't told her all this for pity. I didn't want it. Didn't need it.

It was supposed to be me opening up to someone I thought was becoming a friend—or something close to it. She might know who'd killed Zinnia and this would show her why she should tell me.

"I don't want... This isn't about me." I gritted my teeth in the face of her *pity*.

"Your life isn't about you?"

No.

The answer rang in my mind, but I bit my tongue before it could betray me. My life *wasn't* about me. It was about Zinnia and trying to repay how she'd always looked after me by looking after this one thing for her.

Justice.

Revenge.

Call it what you like, but I needed to get it for her.

"I mean this. *This*." I cut the edge of my hand into the arm of the chair. "You've been friends with Sepher all this time. You must know about that night. And now you understand why it matters. Who killed her?"

With a sigh, she lowered her head. "I don't know."

"Liar," I breathed, fogging my glass. The outrage of it seared my muscles, making me spring to my feet. "*Liar*. You must know." I pointed at her, gift bubbling in my veins.

But she didn't return my anger in kind. She looked up at me, sorrow gleaming in her eyes as she shook her head. "I'm sorry, Zita. I don't know. And you know I can't lie about that."

Of course she couldn't. She was a fucking fae.

I tucked my finger back in before I could speak a curse. Each breath tore through me, and I had to turn my back on her before she could see the temptation fizzing under my skin.

I was angry at her for her questions, for her pity, for her inability to help, but that didn't mean she deserved my curse.

"I want to sleep now." I bit out the words, glaring into the fire.

"That sounds wise," she said softly.

I heard the quiet noises of her putting away the decanter and gathering blankets for me.

For me. It tangled inside and circled my throat. Care. Kindness. Friendship. That was what she offered me again and again, and I deserved none of it.

"Goodnight, Zita." Her voice came from the other side of the room, by her bedroom door. "If you want to talk more, you know where I am. Any time."

It burned in my eyes, pressing on their backs.

When I turned to apologise, she'd already gone.

33

The next day I reached the stage's wings and understood why Sepher didn't want me injured. Out on the stage hung a set of silks, ready for me to perform. I couldn't spot any telltale glimmer of broken glass or diamonds on the stage to cut my bare feet. There was no sign of the hounds.

He'd probably mentioned those to Cadan to toy with me.

Arsehole.

In the wings, a box awaited me, with a note on top.

Wear this.

And inside?

Nothing.

My punishment was to perform naked in front of—I peered out through a crack in the curtain—yes, in front of his entire court.

Arsehole. Bastard. Prick.

Eyes squeezing shut, I clenched my fists and took deep breaths. "I will not back down."

I shrugged off the dress Celestine had lent me this morning. I'd apologised over breakfast and she'd waved it off. Things had felt something like normal between us, though I thought I detected a hint of stiffness to her. Maybe it was because of this.

Cool air whispering across my skin, I stretched backstage, keeping half my attention on the audience. Just as they grew unsettled, I spoke the word that dimmed the fae lights and stepped out onto the stage.

Even though they were fae, when I reached the spotlight wearing precisely nothing, they drew a collective gasp.

Except for Sepher.

He sat at the front, on that throne as he had the first night I'd come here. His teeth showed in the dim light.

Celestine bent to his ear for a hissed conversation. He shook his head, jaw tightening. Celestine shot me a look before erupting from her seat and walking out.

Sweet of her to stand up for me. But I didn't need it.

Shoulders back, arms spread, I presented myself to my audience, left and right, using every angle of the thrust stage. My heart pounded in anticipation of performing. It had been so long.

He thought I'd back down from this. That I'd hate it enough to lift his curse.

Even if I could remove my curses, this wouldn't have made me do it.

I shot him a smirk before mounting the silks.

From somewhere drifted strange dark music, unlike anything I'd ever heard. It raised the hairs on my arms. It reverberated in my bones, ancient and haunting.

I rode that music and took to the air, like it was an air current and I was a bird.

Twisting, spinning, spiralling. The silk in my hands, soft but strong. The pull of gravity that I refused to bend to. The curves and angles of my body that looked effortless and yet were the result of years of training and practice and the strength of my muscles.

I felt it all more keenly than I ever had before.

And I understood.

At last, I understood what Zinnia had spoken of and why Sepher called me "little bird."

Because I *flew*.

It was free. It was beautiful.

It was joyous.

I couldn't keep the smile from my face. Not the calculated, coy one that seduced the audience, but a pure reaction to the soaring feeling in my chest. Warm and bright, I was alive.

The fact of my nudity was nothing compared to the breathless feel of escaping land. I laughed at the creatures below, stuck on the ground. I let the dark music creep over me, command me, like we were dance partners and he led.

I played in the air, flew through it, made love to it.

And as I climbed higher and higher up the silks, I locked eyes with Sepher.

Lips parted, he stared. His expression was so wide open, I understood it in an instant. Wonder.

Then he blinked.

And as he blinked, I remembered.

Why I was here. Why I wore no clothes. All that he'd done to me. All that had happened between us.

He must've remembered, too, because his mouth snapped

CLARE SAGER

shut and his expression closed as his eyebrows clashed together.

Oh, my poor prince, you thought you could break me.

Foolish, foolish boy.

I smiled, sharper than the diamonds he'd made me crawl over, then I turned that smile from him to the dozens and dozens in the audience.

I didn't know this music, but I could feel it building to a crescendo, and I knew exactly the move to end with. The perfect bit of payback for my prickish prince.

Legs wrapped in the silks, I stretched forwards, like I was flying towards them. Then, smooth as water, I spilled down the silks, spinning end over end. I locked on to Sepher's golden eyes to stop me growing dizzy.

All the air sucked from the theatre as they wondered whether I was going to stop in time. Being fae, they no doubt hoped I wouldn't, pondering what my frail, human body would look like broken upon the stage.

But of course I did.

Legs spread. Arms wide. Smile its widest. I stopped at the exact moment the music reached its crashing peak, like a thunderstorm breaking upon the shore.

Breath surged through me as I held that pose and the attention of an entire audience, all staring at my exposed pussy.

I graced my prince with a triumphant smile.

I will never back down.

The applause deafened me. A wave of pure sound and adulation. It washed over me, lifted me, so it was like I was flying once more.

Good gods, was this what the other performers felt on stage every night? Was this what I'd been missing?

230

Still in the silks, I bowed, taking perverse pleasure in Sepher's smouldering stare. He did not clap. His claws were embedded in the arms of his throne.

I had won.

Jaw rippling, he rose.

The applause sputtered out.

Very quietly, eyes locked on mine, he said, "Get out."

34

I held my pose, refusing to cover myself even though my muscles strained.

He'd wanted me to perform naked, and that was exactly what I'd done.

Once the theatre was empty, he prowled onto the stage, gaze locked on me as it had when he'd hunted me.

"You did this deliberately." He flicked a glance over my body. Every muscle of his flexed, like he fought to contain a deep and terrible rage.

It only made me smile more.

"I simply did as you commanded."

He exhaled with a growl, closing the distance between us. He gripped my cheeks and tilted my face up to his. "You..." His jaw ticked as though he didn't know how to finish the sentence.

"You made me perform naked, Sepher. And that's what I did. You got exactly what you wanted."

"Infuriating... Stubborn... Fucking witch. I'm going to..." Tight, fast breaths ripped in and out of him as he glared at me.

I took delight in his flared nostrils, in the rigid grip pressing into my cheeks, in the wide, wide expanse of his pupils. It stoked my joy and anger in equal measure.

"You thought you could break me, Sepher. Well, bad fucking luck. You chose the wrong woman." As much as I could in his hold, I raised my chin.

Then he was kissing me.

Hard. Harsh. Brutal. A clash of lips and teeth and tongues. More a battle for dominance than anything romantic. His grip slid down my throat, but I wouldn't have moved even if he'd let me go.

Not when this battle was a beat in my bones, a song in my soul.

I bit his lip, hard enough to taste the iron of his blood, and he bit right back, making me whimper in pained delight.

He tasted me, tore me, lighting me up with the glory of hate.

At some point, he released my throat, and I took the opportunity to push up into him, hungry for more of this mutual devastation.

Too absorbed in the kiss, I didn't realise he was doing something else with his hands until he pulled away an inch, a feral grin showing his canines. His chest heaved as he looked at my wrists and knees and the knots he'd tied there.

I tugged. They didn't budge.

"You fucking—"

Then his stupid, smirking mouth was back on mine.

I took it, opened to it, whimpered into it as he slid a hand between us and swiped his fingers down my centre.

"Already so wet," he murmured against my lips. "I think

you enjoyed that performance too much, little bird. So twisted. I love it." He laughed and fisted his other hand in my hair, using that to arch my body back.

"Do you think I'm ashamed? Did you expect me to back down?" I laughed right back as he kissed and bit his way down my throat and over my shoulder.

He tugged on the collar as though to remind me of it, but otherwise gave no reply and instead occupied his mouth with my tits.

Between that and his stroking fingers, my heart raced and my breaths panted, faster and harder with each moment.

"Poor prince," I huffed, only able to look up at the chaotic jumble of catwalks above, thanks to his unyielding grip. "Can't even beat a pathetic little human into submission."

Mouth still wrapped around my nipple, he hummed something that was part groan, part amusement. The vibration sizzled through my veins, spearing pleasure at my centre.

He yanked my hair so I was looking at him. "There is nothing pathetic about you, you treacherous witch." His nose wrinkled in a snarl as he slammed a finger into me.

My cry was lost in the theatre's open space as he thrust once, twice, added another finger, and rubbed his thumb over my clit and, so quickly, made me come apart.

I raced into the nothingness of it, blasting into smithereens of glimmering awareness.

Even as I floated back down, I hated that it was so easy for him. I hated that my hate for him boiled over into desire. I hated him and loved it.

"Did you come so easily for your human friend, Zita?" He sneered, a perverse joy slithering through his eyes, like molten gold pouring through their depths. "Or is it only me who can break you apart so quickly?"

"Asking about my former lovers? Careful, prince, you're beginning to sound obsessed."

He flinched, eyes widening for a moment, unguarded. Then he bared his teeth and growled, "Fuck you."

I grinned back, high on the victory of making him use such a weak come back. He knew what I'd said was true. And being fae, he couldn't deny it.

"Fuck me?" I arched an eyebrow. "You keep saying that and yet..."

If my wrists hadn't been bound, I'd have torn his clothes off by now. In their place, I clawed at the silk, wishing it was his throat, his hair, his shirt.

Tied up, I was helpless to pull myself onto him, but that didn't mean I couldn't manipulate him to do what my burning flesh demanded.

With an innocent smile, I batted my lashes. "It's a shame you're too much of a coward to follow through, isn't it?"

His grip on my hair flexed, jerking my head back. "Coward, am I? That's the second time you've called me that." His voice rumbled into me, low and dark and vicious. "I'm going to make you regret them both."

He tore his fingers from me, and I couldn't help the sound I made at their absence.

"Get on with it, then."

"Impatient witch." He whipped his belt out of his trousers and pulled it taut, eyeing me thoughtfully.

My breath hitched, fear snaking along the gaps between my desire. He wouldn't.

He sniffed the air, then chuckled darkly, before tossing the belt to one side. "That was worth it just to see the look on your face. But the scent..." He shook his head as he unbuttoned his trousers.

"You prick."

He scoffed as his dick sprung free, already hard, its tip glistening with moisture. "That's what you asked for." Grabbing my hips, he pulled me closer. My position in the silks gave me no power to resist.

And I didn't want to.

I wanted him to succumb. Even though he had full power over his body and everything in this whole situation, I wanted him to have control and *still* find himself unable to resist.

He ran his length along me and I made a soft sound at the same instant he let out a shuddering breath. "Tell me no, Zita." His voice came out ragged and raw as he held my gaze and placed his blunt tip at my entrance. "Tell me to stop this."

I pulled myself more upright in the silks—about the only movement I could manage with my knees and wrists bound. "Never."

The sound he made was animal, part growl, part roar, and entirely feral. "Just remember, you asked for this, pet." He thrust into me with one brutal snap of his hips.

It decimated me in one brilliant, shining moment.

I had never been alive until now. Even all those moments with him where I'd hated and raged and *felt* so keenly... they were nothing—*nothing* to this.

Dim stars compared to the blazing sun.

He pulled me onto him, standing there fully seated in me, smirking when I could open my eyes again. "I love how easily you're undone by me."

"I hate it." It was a lie and wasn't. But I kept my teeth gritted at the end as he pulled me off his cock, like I was an object to be manoeuvred and used, helpless.

"Yes," he huffed out as he drove me back onto him with a speed that made me see stars. "You really looked like you hated that. You're so fucking wet, Zita. You can't hide the truth from me." He spoke with breathless, vicious pleasure. "You love this." He punctuated each word with a thrust, filling me exactly as I wanted, right at my limit.

"Are you telling me..." I caught my breath around his relentless rhythm. "You didn't watch my whole performance with your cock this hard?"

"Your performance was filthy, and you know it."

He kissed me again, squeezing my backside. One of his fingers slid into the crevice between my cheeks, circling my hole. Everything he did poured pleasure into me, rapidly approaching the brim.

When he pulled away a fraction of an inch, his golden cheeks were flushed and sweat slicked his chest. "If you'd carried on a moment longer, I'd have leapt onto the stage," he rasped against my lips. "I'd have fucked you like this in front of them all. But this—you are mine. The sight of you coming apart is mine only. The feel of you doing it on my dick as you fight yourself—wanting it and not. Fuck, Zita. It's all mine."

I wanted to deny it, tell him he was wrong. But maybe it was something in the air of Elfhame that prevented lying, because I just couldn't push the words from my lips.

Not when pleasure rose and rose with his inexorable drive into me, his cock skimming over my clit over and over.

"And yet," I managed, somewhere between a huff and a moan, "you're the one fucking the witch who cursed you. The witch you swore to kill." I flashed my teeth at him, wishing they were still sharp as they'd once been. "What is it, Sepher? Do you think if you paint my insides with your come, it'll lift the curse?" I tried to laugh, but it became a staccato series of cries driven out by his thrusts.

He growled, reverberating in my chest and open thighs, in

the grip on my arse, and most intensely of all, in my pussy. My rapture overflowed in a breathless moan, followed a moment later by his, pulsing inside me with even hotter pleasure.

The aftermath was a silence broken only by our panting. His massive body surged with each breath as he held me on him. He needn't have bothered—I hung limp in the silks, little shocks running through my muscles, out of my control.

At last, his great hand cupped my cheek and lifted my head. When I met his gaze, the look he gave me reminded me of the day he'd lifted me out of the snow.

"I'm all right."

He gave a faint nod, then pulled from me with a wet sound and a soft grunt. Without a word, he untied me, lowering my feet to the ground. My knees shook, but I clung to the silks to keep myself steady.

What was that? It felt like an explosion of hate and anger, weeks of frustration, and now...

Now something altogether different hung in the air. Something I couldn't quite place.

"Get your clothes on." He jerked his chin towards the wings.

I obeyed, his come slicking my thighs as I moved. It should've disgusted me. Usually, the stuff did. But this was evidence of his need for me, the want he'd tried to mask behind punishment. It was a mark that said I was his property... but also that he was mine.

When I emerged, fully clothed, it was with my back straight and a strange kind of serenity.

The effect was slightly spoiled when he scooped me up and strode from the theatre.

But, for once, I didn't have the energy to argue.

35

In silence, he carried me through the palace. He didn't look at me, keeping his head high, but his jaw tensed and flexed like he had something he wanted to say but thought better of it. Eventually, he deposited me in the bathroom before disappearing into his bedroom. I went to the toilet and showered away the sweat and sex, still bathed in my strange serenity.

When I emerged, wrapped in a thick robe, he was sitting before the fire shirtless, a tumbler in hand, another on the low coffee table. He frowned into the pinkish flames before looking up at me. "Come here." There was no harsh command or dare in his tone, just a rumbling softness.

I took the glass from the table and approached him slowly, in case this was a trap.

But it was too late for that, wasn't it?

We were both trapped. Had both walked in, each thinking we were the one in control, when really neither of us were.

Maybe the universe had spun us together for its own amusement.

I still didn't believe in any gods, but if I did, I'd have said they were laughing at us both.

So, when he patted his lap, I sat in it.

He let out a long breath, gathering me against him. His heat, his hand coming around my waist like I was something precious he wanted to keep close—I liked it. I tucked my legs up and splayed my hand over the broad expanse of his chest.

"We can't keep on like this," he murmured at last. "We'll destroy each other."

"I thought you wanted to destroy me."

"So did I." His eyebrows squeezed together before he nuzzled into my neck, breaths fanning hot over my skin. "I don't want to want you, but you smell so delicious." He ran the bridge of his nose along my jaw, lifting it. Such sweetness after such harshness whispered over my nerves. When his eyes met mine, they were softer, too. "The way you look pleases me."

"Say it." I lifted my chin more, peering down my nose at him. "Say what you really think about how I look."

He exhaled, shoulders sinking, and lowered his glass to the floor. Now free, he used his fingertips to sketch my cheekbones, my jaw, the line of my brow, his sheathed claws just tickling my skin. "You're beautiful, Zita. Human, and yet perfect." The corner of his mouth twitched, but even that was softer than his usual smirks. "Despite these blunt ears and teeth." He touched the rounded edges of my ears and brushed my lips as he spoke, sending a shiver down my spine.

A shiver that warned of danger, yes, but a danger of a different kind.

This softness, this sweetness... part of me craved those as much as I craved his savagery, but they were no use to me. At least his cruelty had unlocked something inside me.

But maybe he was right.

Maybe keeping on like this would destroy us. I certainly couldn't afford to stay locked in battle with him—not when my sister's murderer still walked free.

"What if there was another way?"

His eyebrows flickered.

"What if we could both get what we wanted?"

Slowly, slowly, like he knew there was a catch, he narrowed his eyes. "What would that look like, exactly?"

I gave him a half-smile and took a sip of honeyed whisky, sweet and smoky. "Well, you'd carry me around less, for one."

He made a low sound and caught my ankle. "You don't like being carried around?"

"It's... unnecessary. I have perfectly good legs."

His lips curled as his palm slid up my calf. "Yes, you do."

"I meant from a functional standpoint."

"They're a little slow." He scowled and traced a spiral on the side of my knee. "You take so long to walk anywhere."

I chuckled and found my hand skimming up over his broad shoulder, like it wanted to explore now it wasn't tied up. "Just because they're half the length of yours doesn't mean they're defective." I shook my head. "Look, we're getting off track. I just mean... you could treat me more like a person and less like a pet."

He pouted and worked his way up my thigh, pulling me against him. "I don't see how that gets us what we want. Besides, you make a good pet." He grazed his nose along mine. The nearness of him, completely dominating my field of view, was overwhelming. "I like having you close. It makes hating you easier."

I scoffed and lifted my chin so my words whispered over his lips. "Believe me, the feeling's mutual."

His eyes sank shut as though he enjoyed the brush of my breath. A low rumble came from his chest, humming into me.

"But we can still hate each other and work together."

Eyes snapping open, he arched an eyebrow and pulled an inch away. "Work together? You, work *with* me?"

"You don't know who killed my sister, but you know who was there that night, don't you?"

He inclined his head once, cautiously.

"Then help me catch her killer, and I'll lift your curse."

His expression didn't budge, but his pupils gave him away, contracting. I'd piqued his interest. "Why do you want them?"

"I want justice."

"Liar." His canines showed like I'd amused him.

"Fine." I exhaled the pretty lie and let my true desire show, all sharp and seething. "I want to kill him like he killed her. I want to end him. I want revenge."

His pupils blew wide as his lips parted. "Oh, now *that's* more like it. Yes." He shifted me higher up his lap until I was over his hardening cock. "Determination. Viciousness. A thirst for vengeance even after all these years."

He said these things like they were parts of me a poet might name in a sonnet cataloguing my beauty. Eyes like a doe's. Shining hair. Creamy skin. All that bullshit.

Eric had called me stubborn, like it was a bad thing. He had frowned and gone distant when I'd let slip my secret desires to make the prince suffer. He hadn't taken my need for revenge seriously, and when he finally had, he'd betrayed me for it.

But Sepher looked upon me now like they were as much things of beauty as my thick hair and full lips.

To be seen like that lit a fire in me, one I'd thought burnt out in the theatre.

Smiling, he bent closer. "Do you have any idea how much that turns me on?"

I rolled my arse over him and was rewarded with a twitch of his dick and a groan so soft, I felt it more than heard it. "I have an inkling."

He plucked my glass away and deposited it with his before twisting me so I was straddling him, the robe rucked up around my waist. "You'd make a fine queen, Zita. I could be your throne."

Some part of me must've liked that idea, because my fingers were already on the waistband of his trousers. I had to seize control of myself to stop them from pulling him free.

I could fuck him again. It didn't matter. It didn't mean anything. Sex never did.

But I had something important to do first.

"Do we have a deal, Sepher?"

His pupils flickered as I said his name. "There's a little fae in you, I think."

"I hope there's about to be more than a little fae in me." I smirked. "But first, our bargain. Help me find my sister's killer, and once I have my revenge, I'll remove your curse." The lie twisted in me, something dark and dirty—a shame I'd never felt before, but that I imagined was like the shame other people felt over sex.

"You have a deal." He pulled me against him, not caring that I was getting the front of his trousers wet where he pressed my pussy against his hardness. "It is so. Now say the words and get on with fucking me, witch."

My pulse soared both at hearing him saying the words of power that sealed our bargain and at the exquisite friction.

I freed his dick and lifted myself to its tip. "As my prince commands." Groaning, I lowered onto him with a promise I knew I would have to break: "It is so."

36

The next day, our work began.

He cleared his private dining table and covered it with pens, pencils, and paper. My sketchbooks also appeared, stacked amongst the supplies, and my chest sat on the floor.

"I thought you might need them to refer back to," he said with a shrug, when I asked about the sketchbooks.

At once, I rummaged in the chest for my locket and fastened it around my neck. I squeezed it, absorbing the familiarity of its smooth oval shape.

He watched me with an odd look, then had me work at one end of the table, writing a list of everything I remembered of that night. Everything—from watching the audience arrive to cradling Zinnia's body after he'd fled the scene. If I focused on the outer details rather than the inner experience, I could write it without tears.

Meanwhile, he set to work on a list of the friends who'd

accompanied him to the private performance and any details he knew.

We worked in companionable silence until I looked up and found him watching me. The skin around his eyes tensed in calculation.

Was I wrong? Was he the killer, after all, and this was all part of some greater ploy to punish me with hope? Fae were skilled at manipulation and all the little ways to deceive without lying. He might've slipped something sneaky into his phrasing.

Or was he really helping me?

"Have you finished?" I peered at the sheet of paper before him, and my shoulders sank at the long list of names. Over a dozen.

"I've seen every part of you, and yet I've found no sign of magic written upon your body." His gaze trailed down me, like he could undress me with his eyes alone.

I gripped my pen, otherwise I might've obeyed that unspoken instruction.

He canted his head. "Where's your fae mark?"

"Gone." I pushed up my top lip, displaying my blunt canines. "These were sharp like yours, but Zinnia filed them down so no one would realise what I was."

His face dropped. The gold of his skin went ashen. Not tearing his attention from me, he rose. In an uncharacteristic display of clumsiness, he knocked the table as he stepped out from behind it, and that shook me even more than his look of horror.

As soon as he was within arm's reach, he lifted my chin. His eyes gleamed as his gaze followed his fingertips, questing over my jaw and lips. I opened my mouth when he pressed. I let him run his thumb over my blunted teeth.

With a long exhale, he shook his head and sank to his knees. "You call me a monster, and yet humans made you do that. It's despicable. Your teeth." His eyebrows pinched together. "*Your beautiful teeth.* They should be a matter of pride. A sign of your power. A warning to fools who might think to cross you." He looked up at me like I was an idol at a shrine. "All the world should see them and know Zita the cursewitch is not a woman to be crossed."

A knot tied in my throat, salty and tight. I'd never been looked at like this. Leered at, yes. Admired for what my body could do and for its appearance, a thousand times.

But never seen like he saw me now.

Framing my face with his hands, he dragged in a breath. "If I ever find the people who made you feel like you needed to hide, I will tear them apart and hang their remains outside their houses. A reminder of what happens to those who wrong you." The softness of his voice was a lie, almost masking the full depth of fury shaking each word.

That fury cracked me like his cruelty never had. His face blurred as the pressure behind my eyes built beyond bearing. I tried to hold it back. I tried to hold my breath and not let it show.

But the tears spilled.

He acted like I was the one who'd been wronged. He acted like *I* deserved vengeance. He acted like I wasn't just some*thing* precious, but some*one* precious.

Arms coming around me, he nuzzled away my tears and murmured comforting nonsense sounds. I clutched his shirt, too shaken and broken to pull away.

After a short while, he said, "No tears, love."

When I looked up, I found myself on the floor with him, gathered in his lap.

He wore a fierce frown, but for once, his ferocity wasn't aimed at me. "Yours isn't a sad story; I won't let it be. Not anymore. Yours is a story of revenge and living. Of obliterating those who wronged you. Of making the world *see you* whether it wants to or not."

I stared up at him, no more of that horrible pressure on my eyes. What the hells was I supposed to say to that?

"And, besides,"—the corner of his mouth lifted—"I have something that will cheer you up."

"THAT NIGHT, you saw me take something from your sister's body. But it wasn't a lock of hair." He frowned at the box he placed on the table before me. "It was this." He opened it, revealing a brass disc large enough to cover his palm.

Craning forward, I peered closer. Cutout sections in the top layer revealed a regular series of lines below, showing the paths of planets and stars. An arm a lot like a compass needle stretched across its full width. An astrolabe. I'd seen other fae with them during our visits to Elfhame. They carried these or orreries like human gentlemen carried pocket watches.

But Zinnia? I shook my head. "That wasn't hers."

"I know." He pulled it from the box and held it out to me. "It's fae-worked. I..." He exhaled, shoulders and gaze falling. "I took it because I knew it would incriminate one of my friends."

I shot him a look pointed enough to kill.

"I won't apologise, Zita." Though the way his eyebrows pulled together *looked* contrite, and he deposited the astrolabe on the table like he couldn't stand touching it. "I didn't know you then. My loyalty was to my friends. Little did I know how many of them wouldn't be so loyal to me."

At my confused expression, he grabbed the list he'd written, not caring that he crinkled the paper. "Most of these are still in Luminis. I haven't seen some of them in ten years." Nose wrinkling, he shook his head. "They still look 'normal,' so they can remain there, living their lives without comments about *what* they are, rather than *who* they are." The muscles and tendons of his neck corded.

No wonder he'd sworn to kill me. I'd robbed him of that.

Where once it had been a matter of pride, now it scraped over my nerves.

I swallowed, then said something I never thought I'd say to him: "I'm sorry."

The skin around his eyes twitched tight. "Don't be. You thought I'd killed her, and... I suppose you were right to leap to that conclusion. You did what you thought you should. It probably served me right for taking the evidence. No, just like I won't apologise to you for doing what I thought was right at the time, you shouldn't apologise to me. They are the ones who owe me. They were meant to be my friends."

I looked at the names. "Roark?" I raised my eyebrows. "How was he able to wander around the city looking like that?"

Sepher grinned. "We smuggled him in. Nightfall might leave Dusk Court in charge, but it does bring the benefit of darkness, and darkness can hide a multitude of sins."

Like Roark's horns and grey skin.

He'd made no secret of his desire to have and hurt me. Was that what he'd done to Zinnia? My heart lurched, and I rubbed my chest like that would help contain it.

"Zita?"

"Do you think he did it?"

Sepher blinked. "No. But then again, I don't think any of my friends would, yet we know one of them did. So perhaps this is one of those vanishingly rare occasions where I'm wrong." The corner of his mouth twitched, but I couldn't summon an answering smirk even if it was at his expense.

Another question bubbled in my gut. "That night... At the performance or after... or ever, really... Did you and Zinnia...?"

I must've fucked people who'd fucked her. After all, we played the same circuit of Albion and Elfhame year after year. We looked so alike that someone who'd paid to have private time with her would undoubtedly have requested me, too.

That wasn't what made me queasy. It was the idea of *Sepher* with her. The thought that the things he'd done with me were an echo of what he'd done with her. That I was a dim reflection of what he truly wanted.

"Me and...?" His eyes widened. "No. I didn't do anything with your sister. She performed for us. She touched us over our clothes as she danced, but nothing more than that. Not with me." He raised his eyebrows. "To be clear, no kissing. No sex. I'm not hiding a lie between my words to keep anything from you, like my kind enjoy doing."

My breath out was shaky, soothing the tightness in my stomach. "Good." I kept the word clipped, like this was just business.

"So..." I finally picked up the astrolabe. The cool metal bit through me with the knowledge that it had once belonged to the killer. "We just have to work out who this belongs to and then we know who did it."

I turned it over. No engraved initials. Of course, it couldn't be that easy. But there was the small stamped shape of a bird. I peered closer. A gull, perhaps?

Sepher's huge hand wrapped around my shoulder. "That's the maker's mark. They make dozens of these every year and have done for centuries. It's a dead end, I'm afraid."

I frowned up at him, jaw clenched. "Then why bother showing me?"

He squeezed, claws fully sheathed, so they didn't prick my skin for a change. "The maker might not be able to point us to the guilty party, but it may still help us yet. Between that and the list, we have our killer cornered. Patience, little witch. Patience."

37

Despite the fact Sepher let me walk, I scowled my way through the corridors. I wanted to continue going through the love letter I'd found with Zinnia's belongings, as well as my old sketchbooks and the scrawled notes and drawings inside. There had to be something I'd overlooked, some little clue. Maybe I'd seen the astrolabe on the killer that night and hadn't realised its relevance.

But, no, a week into our plotting and Sepher had arranged, of all fucking things, a *party*.

"You can glare at me all you like." He placed a hand on the small of my back, bringing me a little closer to his side. "But you're not going to want to miss this."

I gritted my teeth to keep from replying.

Roark. Loy. Celestine. Mayrie. Cadan. Tavin. Thurl...

The list went on and I recited it like a prayer. One of those names belonged to my sister's killer. One of them was the person whose blood I'd thirsted for all these years.

Celestine. It seemed impossible that it could be her, and yet her name was amongst the others. Zinnia had been strangled, the killer's grip hard enough to leave marks. Celestine was frail, but she was still fae. Did she have the strength to do that?

That question followed me through the winding corridors and out into the gardens.

The party was in full swing when we arrived, though much smaller than I'd expected, with fewer than fifteen people on the lake's shore and bathing in its shallows. They all turned and raised their glasses at our arrival, and Sepher milked the moment perfectly, one arm slung around my shoulders, chin raised, a smug smirk on his lips.

He waved them off. "Get back to it, you degenerates."

As he scooped up drinks for us both, several of the folk slapped him on the back and greeted him. Though their broad smiles were perhaps a little stiff. His expression was as easy, as arrogant as ever, but I noted his tail's slow swish from side to side.

Who were these people? I only knew a handful from the Court of Monsters. Celestine, Roark, Cadan, and a few others. The rest were new faces who eyed me with interest as we passed.

Sepher didn't bother to introduce me. I supposed he wanted to keep up the appearance of pet and master in public. I hadn't included that in my bargain. A foolish mistake.

Eventually, he sank into the throne under the domed structure overlooking the lake—the same one he'd occupied the day I'd collapsed in the snow. A drink in each hand, he spread his arms and nodded at his lap, the instruction unmistakable.

"I can't believe you've dragged me out here for this," I muttered as I sat on his knee.

"I told you to have patience, little bird." He handed me a glass of deep orange liquid. It smelled of sour citrus and something sweet and tropical that I'd only ever had at the tables of my richest patrons. "You'll be able to spread your wings and capture your prey soon."

Lips pursed, I gave him a hard look. My time would be better spent inside, working on the clues we had, not playing his pet at a party.

But I took a sip of whatever this drink was and couldn't help the sound that came from my throat at its taste. Summer and sunshine. Our day at the beach. Sweet and sharp, zinging on my tongue. All that from a single mouthful.

He grinned like he took pleasure from my pleasure. "It's good, isn't it?"

I huffed. "I suppose it is."

He chuckled softly, and pulled me up his lap. "Well done for admitting it. Now, listen closely..." He spoke in my ear, little more than a breath, and I leant in until his lips brushed my skin. "Roark, Celestine, Cadan—you know all of them. And those three over there." He nodded to a group lying on the bank playing cards. They lived here at the palace full-time, so I'd encountered them at a number of parties and meals.

I canted my head, not understanding why he was pointing these people out to me when I already knew them.

"There, with the indigo hair, that's Mayrie."

Playing in the water was perhaps the most beautiful woman I'd ever seen. Deep blue hair pooled around her on the lake's surface, and her skin held a pale turquoise tinge.

"Her mother was a selkie, so as pretty as she looks, she has a sharper side."

Dark, dark eyes snapped to us as she caught us looking, and her mouth spread in a wide grin full entirely of sharp teeth.

"You see what I mean?" Sepher raised his drink in greeting. "Then, over there, you see the brothers, Tavin and Thurl."

Two fae men lay sunbathing, their naked bodies perfect, deep bronze skin flawless. Apart from the pointed ears poking out from their charcoal-black hair, they might've been human. Albeit, I'd never seen humans quite so handsome.

Sepher's tail curled around my calf. "They still live in Luminis." A gritted edge entered his voice, and when I tore myself from them, I found him staring, jaw and brow tight.

He saw in them what he had once been. They still lived the life he'd once had.

I ran my fingertips through the silky thickness of his hair. "More fool Luminis." His gaze shot to mine. "They're missing out."

He raised an eyebrow in question.

"Well, they're very... boring, aren't they? Why look like a pretty human with pointed ears when you could be so much *more*?" I grazed my fingers over his claws and flexed my calf, where his muscular tail wrapped around it. Sliding one hand under his open-fronted shirt, I traced the stripes that wrapped around his sides. "One of them couldn't fuck my arse with their tail, could they?"

His pupils blew wide. "They couldn't," he said with a growl, tail tightening as it slid up my leg. "Maybe I should do that again tonight to remind you."

Goosebumps flooded my skin, but I went on, "They would never have warmed me as quickly as you did when I was freezing to death. And none of them are nearly as perfectly princely and prickish and arrogant as you are." Yet I found

255

myself smiling as I said it all, not hating those features of his nearly as much as I had two months ago.

It seemed he didn't take it as an insult, either—at least not entirely—because his muscles solidified around and under me as he straightened in his throne. "Clever girl." He planted an impulsive kiss on my lips, shooting a sweet kind of pleasure through me. "But are you clever enough to work out why I've brought them all here?" He cocked his head in challenge.

I narrowed my eyes at him before turning and surveying the people he'd pointed out.

Outsiders who weren't members of his court and still lived in Luminis, suggesting they were people he'd been closer to in the past when he'd lived there, too.

And their names. Mayrie. Tavin. Thurl. I *knew* those names.

A buzzing began under my skin, and I had to gulp down another mouthful of my drink before I could speak. "Let me guess. Loy is also here. And so are all the others on your list."

"That's my cunning little witch." He squeezed me close and nuzzled into my neck. "Sun and Stars, I love it when I can see the cogs whirring in your mind. I'd never realised plotting could be so damn hot."

But the warmth coiling through me was thicker and deeper than just the physical. "You did all this to gather them here?"

"I did it all for you. They're staying for a month. I pitched it as a reunion. 'Like old times,' my invitation said." He rolled his eyes, then swept a small, tight glare over the assembled fae. "They all came running at the promise of a few weeks living off the royal coffers. Fucking parasites."

It was hard to breathe, never mind reply. The warmth in my chest took up too much space. I wanted to thank him, though, so I did it with a kiss, winning a surprised exhale from him.

I teased the roof of his mouth and traced the points of his teeth. I nibbled his lip and drank up the deep groan that followed. It was a sweeter kiss than any of our others, and he opened to it, letting me probe and explore, rather than gripping me and battling for dominance.

It tore me in a way none of our other kisses had, like some thin membrane in me broke on the lazy sweep of his tongue against mine.

When I pulled away, breathless and too hot, he gave me a wide-eyed look. "What was that for?"

But speech was still beyond me, so I just shrugged and turned to survey the dozen suspects spread before me.

My sister's killer was in reach.

38

That evening, he gathered the same group in a large, circular room of the palace. An unbroken glass dome shielded us from the night, but it was too cloudy for any stars. Shadows pooled between the room's pillars, little pockets of darkness the fae lights couldn't reach.

Platters of food far more lavish than usual appeared at a gesture from Sepher, and once we were done, the dirty plates cleared themselves away just as quickly. A show for our guests. Even though he no longer lived in Luminis, he was still a prince of Elfhame, and he still held power.

I suspected it was as much a reminder for him as it was for them.

I did it all for you.

There was that, too. He'd gone to a lot of effort to organise this at such short notice, and that fact wasn't lost on me. It spread inside, some part of me wanting to be comforted and pleased by it, another part twisting away like it was a bramble I might get caught on.

After dinner, a blood-red baize cloth appeared on the table with a deck of cards and an odd set of chips unlike any I'd seen before. All pale green jade and all the same shape—I couldn't see any way to differentiate between their values.

Despite the strangeness of the chips, as the fae divided them up and dealt the cards, chatting and laughing, it all felt very familiar.

I sat on the arm of Sepher's chair and glanced at his cards. A decent hand, but not guaranteed victory.

Around the table, the players' eyes shuttered as they read what they'd been dealt and tried to smother any reaction.

My jaw tightened. One of these was my sister's killer. Although it was only poker, not anything important, the thought of that person winning made the contents of my stomach curdle. I couldn't let them have even a moment's victory. Not after they'd had ten years of freedom and fucking cheer.

Muscles buzzing with the outrage of it, I rose.

Sepher caught my ankle with his tail. "Where are you going, pet?"

I bent close to him, movements smooth and graceful despite the terrible tightness of my body. "You like to win, don't you?" I whispered.

"I never lose." His smile was slow, like he truly believed that.

Victory was great, but it required work.

"If I touch their right shoulder, they're bluffing. If I touch their left, they have a better hand than yours and will need bullying into folding. If I rub my nose, you should fold and save yourself for the next hand. Got it?"

It was a technique I'd used with Eric for years, simple but

effective. Especially as so few people took a pretty, scantily clad woman seriously.

His eyes narrowed. "I know how to play poker, Zita."

"I'm sure you do. But"—I ducked close, the tip of my nose brushing his—"I can't stand the thought of her killer winning tonight. I need you to dominate the game. Because if you don't, I'm going to find your sword and cut them all down."

He bit his lip but couldn't hold back his widening smile. "So bloodthirsty. How didn't I see what you were the instant you first appeared on my stage?" He shook his head and his tail loosened from my leg. "Very well. Let's begin our ignoble quest with a little financial revenge."

I jerked away from him as though our quiet conversation had been an argument and circled the table.

They placed their first round of bets, each declaring what they were gambling—a sum of money, an item of jewellery, their prized stag. The words appeared on the chip as they tossed it in. Several folded, but Roark raised the bets, marking him as the person Sepher needed to beat.

When the first set of community cards hit the table, I touched the back of Roark's chair. He arched an eyebrow, laying his hand flat. "Spying for Sepher, are we, *pet*?" The way he said it was sharp and glittering, like his eyes, with none of Sepher's warmth.

But his breathing sped as he took me in, and I had no doubt he was remembering my performance from a week ago.

I chuckled and bent closer, hanging on his chair, careful not to touch his shoulders. "Why would I be helping him? You've seen what he's done to me. And now you know what I did to him, too." I smiled and canted my head, running a finger along one of his horns as I shot Sepher a glance. "It's much more fun to frustrate him by touching his friends."

Sure enough, a muscle in my prince's jaw twitched as he watched us over his cards. It was a wonder his eyes didn't burn a line through Roark's horns, he stared so hard at the path my fingers took over their rough surface.

Roark snorted and murmured, "He *does* look pissed off. You play a dangerous game, human." But he didn't bother to disguise his leer as I angled towards him, the tight bodice of my gown barely containing my tits.

Still, he didn't lift his cards from the table.

"Besides"—I shrugged and continued my path from his horn down the edge of his hairline—"I'm all the way over here. I won't be going back over there to whisper in his ear like some little snitch." I wrinkled my nose as if the idea disgusted me. "But if you don't want my attentions..." I straightened and turned to Cadan in the next seat.

"Wait." He took the bait, grabbing my wrist. "Stay a while." He gave a cutting grin, gaze flicking from me to Sepher and back again. "I've never seen him look at me with envy before," he said softly. "I like it." He raised his cards as I draped myself on the arm of his chair.

I didn't look straight away. That would be too obvious. Instead, I returned to his hairline and slid strands of his hair between my fingers. It was surprisingly silky. I wasn't sure what I'd been expecting, but not that. Yet his skin was cold and unyielding under my fingertips, as though he were made of stone.

I smirked over at Sepher, like I really was just trying to make him jealous, and that was when I glanced at Roark's cards. A two and a seven. On the table sat a king, a three, and a five. Roark had nothing.

Internally, I laughed as I leant on his right shoulder as though for balance.

On my other side, Cadan held his cards close to his chest.

I braced my feet on the arm of his chair. His gaze slid to my legs, stretched between his seat and Roark's, and as he licked his lips, his hand fell forward. A little further and I'd be able to see.

"Are you enjoying having some of your friends from Luminis here, Cadan?"

He jolted upright, eyes darting to mine as though he hadn't realised he was staring. "I'm usually in Luminis, save for this extended trip to see Sepher." He smiled at my prince, who didn't return the gesture as betting continued around the table. "So I see most of them frequently." He shrugged, and his hand moved that half inch I needed.

But if I looked down at them, he'd see what I was doing.

Shifting, I arched my back like I was just seeking a better position, but it had the effect I truly desired, making his gaze sweep down my taut body. Only for a moment, but long enough that I got a glimpse of his cards.

A flush—or the makings of one. We had to wait and see what the last two cards held. A good hand, if luck smiled his way, better than Sepher's three of a kind, if—*if* another diamond hit the table.

"Of course," I giggled, and nudged his elbow with my toes, "a handsome fae like you can live in the capital full-time. I forget." Behind me, Roark grunted, but my attention was all on Cadan and sliding my foot up his left arm to his shoulder.

His chest rose and fell a little deeper. He was too absorbed with following my path up his shirt sleeve to realise I'd sent a signal to Sepher.

A cold touch came around my waist, and I only had time to gasp before Roark pulled me onto his lap. He grinned wickedly, like he enjoyed my reaction. When he glanced up, I understood he also fed off Sepher's.

The table's attention slid to us. Perhaps they were wondering whether the prince would let Roark manhandle his pet like this.

If he wanted to keep up the pretence that we weren't working together, he would. If the killer realised we were laying a trap to uncover their identity, it would spook them and our chance would be lost.

Roark squeezed me, narrowing his eyes. "Why doesn't he just order you off us?" He spoke loud enough that the rest of the table could hear.

Opposite, silence, but the muscle in Sepher's jaw was going crazy. It was a wonder he hadn't broken the glass in his hand, his knuckles were so white. He needed a reminder. I may not be his pet anymore, but they all had to believe I was.

So I laughed and tossed my head as I cosied up to Roark. "Because that would be admitting defeat."

I kept my attention on the grey-skinned fae I was sitting on, but I could *feel* my prince's eyes drilling into me.

"Defeat?" Roark arched an eyebrow. "How do you reckon that? I don't see how a little thing like you could defeat one of us."

"No, not in a fight, I admit. I'm so small compared to you." I looked up at him from beneath my lashes, selling my slight stature in an attempt to make him feel even larger. It was a technique I'd used with patrons who tipped better when they were made to feel *so* big and strong.

"But there are other kinds of defeat." I shook my head and clicked my tongue like he should know better, before swinging to my feet and over to Thurl on his other side. I smirked at Sepher as I bent over the black-haired fae and stole a raspberry from his drink, caressing his right shoulder. "If he told me to get off you, he'd have to admit *why* he wanted it."

Thurl lifted his chin, eyes narrowing. "And why is that?"

I flashed him a grin and patted his cheek. "I'm so glad you asked." Straightening, I turned to the group, who all stared at me now, their cards forgotten. "His defeat would be admitting that he's obsessed with the witch who cursed him."

Their eyes widened. Several smirked. A couple chuckled and bent together in hushed conversation. Celestine raised an eyebrow at me as though wondering what game I was playing. No doubt she'd ask next time we were alone.

But when I met Sepher's gaze, it wasn't smouldering with hate. It wasn't clenched up tight at me touching his friends, as it had been moments ago.

No. It was something else entirely. Something bright and wondering. Something I had never seen before in an audience or even from Eric. Something that I wanted, but that also made me want to squirm in discomfort.

I hated that its name eluded me. Even more than that, I hated that I grasped for it so desperately.

39

Winning was as much of an aphrodisiac for Sepher as it was for me, because he didn't wait until we reached his rooms to work his way under my clothes. In the ruined courtyard with the open dome, he bent me over the mossy rubble. One hand on the nape of my neck, he pulled up my dress before sinking his fingers between my legs. My gasps drifted through the chilly space and up into the night sky.

"Tell me what you'll do to the killer when you find out who did it, Zita," he purred into my ear as he circled my slit. One finger rested on my back entrance.

My fingertips sank into the damp moss. "I'll kill him." I couldn't help picturing a man as the murderer, even though Celestine and Mayrie were both potential suspects.

"No." His touch stilled, suspending my pleasure. "More. Give me details. Tell me *exactly* what you want to do to him once he's at your mercy, my wicked little witch."

My heart raced, pumping heat to my skin despite the cold

air caressing it. "I'll make him kneel." I could see it, a man on his knees before me, his features indistinct.

"Good." He plunged into me, making me whimper into the darkness. "What else?"

"I'll stand over him." My voice was breathless and raw as he worked me. "I'll look down on him and remind him of what he did."

"Yes. That's it. And if I gave you back your iron blade, what would you do with that?"

The thought of it sliced through me with bright, hot light like the kind Sepher was driving me towards. "Iron burns your kind, doesn't it?"

"It does." His grip on my nape loosened just long enough for him to shift it to my hair. He pulled, arching me back, the tension in those muscles heightening the tension building in my pussy as his fingers drove into it. "It scorches horribly. They'd suffer at just its touch."

"Then I'll caress him with it. His throat, his chest, his face, all the places he might've touched her." My eyes burned, but the pleasure in me burned hotter.

"So vicious, love. So, so vicious." He gave a chuckle as dark as the empty courtyard and removed his fingers. I made a sound of complaint, which only made him chuckle more. "Patience, my cruel queen." He smeared my wetness over my back entrance before returning to the pumping rhythm in my pussy and the circling sweep over my clit. He pressed another digit over my arse, not quite entering. "Then what, my little villainess?"

My breaths twitched in pleasured anticipation. As my chest, my throat, and low, low in my belly grew too tight, like he was pulling every part of me taut with the fist in my hair. "I'll say her name as I cut his throat, so she's the last thing he hears. And I'll taste his blood, bathe in it, and at last, I'll have peace and so will she."

"Good girl." With those words, he sank into my backside, and it was too much.

The arching pull, his touch invading and circling me in three places, and the words said with such fierce pride. Too much to bear. Too much to contain. I fell apart on his fingers, crying out into the darkness, lost in it.

He turned me and gathered me close while I panted through the aftershocks. Overhead, the clouds had lifted, revealing a scattering of stars as though they were the pieces he'd broken me into.

He grinned and kissed me. "Or maybe I should've said bad girl." He bit his lip and ground against me, spiking fresh pleasure through my nervous system. "But I do so like it when you're bad."

"Show me how much." I tugged at his trousers, rubbing the outline of his stiffness through the fabric.

"Oh, I'm going to." But instead of letting me free him, he swung me over his shoulder. "And it kills me to wait, but after that, I need to fuck you every way I know how, and that's going to take some time. I don't want your little toes getting cold." His claw grazed the sole of my foot, wrenching a shriek from me that dissolved into a groan as he slid a finger into my pussy.

"Sepher. Shit. What are you doing to me?"

"Enjoying you." He laughed as he carried me through the corridors, finger-fucking me all the way.

By the time we reached his rooms, I was trembling on the verge of another release, but every time I came close, he stilled his hand.

"What the hells?" My voice shook with frustration and something close to rage when he threw me on the bed.

"Patience." He laughed as he kissed me and sliced his claws through my gown. He parted its tattered edges and took me in like he had all the time in the world and hadn't just stopped me from climaxing.

"You wear my patience very thin."

"Mm-hmm." He nodded as he peeled off his shirt. "Maybe now you understand just how deliciously infuriating *you* are." He shucked off his trousers, and my mouth went dry at the sight of his cock standing proud.

"Oh, I understand." I smiled up at him and crawled across the bed. "Maybe I can make you understand how cruel it is to stop what you've started."

His eyes widened as he realised what I was about to do. With a flash of my teeth, I wrapped my hand around his length. He went very still as I held his gaze and bent down.

I ran my tongue over his broad head, tasted the salty bead of moisture there, lived for his sharp intake of breath.

He watched as I lapped again, and this time I tongued the small slit at his tip, catching a little more of his salted slickness. The heady taste filled me, gathering more heat between my legs.

Then I sucked him into my mouth. I tried to take it all. And failed.

Even when I loosened my throat, I had to use my hand to help cover him.

"Fuck," he muttered. "Yes, Zita." His hand fisted in my hair. When I met his gaze, I found his pupils blown wide, only a thin rim of gold remaining as he stared at me with my mouth around his cock.

I pulled back, pumping with my hand as I swirled my

tongue over his head. He twitched with a groan, and when I swallowed him down again, his hips surged forward to meet me. That was it. That was what I wanted—him fucking my mouth, my prince greedy for me.

"That man," he rasped, chest heaving. "The one who betrayed you. Who is he to you?"

He wanted to talk about Eric now? I grazed my teeth over his underside and frowned up at him as we kept up our rhythm.

"Did you do this with him?"

Yes and no. I pulled off him and licked again. "Sometimes."

The hand in my hair tightened as I took the tip between my lips and ran my tongue around the ridge between his head and shaft.

His darkened eyes narrowed. "Did he make you come like I do?"

I sucked the end, flicking my tongue over it, and shook my head.

"Good." He said it with a feral intensity that should've warned me of what was about to come.

He ripped from my mouth and grabbed my hips. With one swift movement, he had me bent over the bed. "He wrote to me."

His hand splayed across the small of my back, pinning me so I could only grip the sheets and look back over my shoulder.

"Asked about your fate." He squeezed my arse, opening me to his inspection.

Like his gaze was a touch, it heated me, made me even wetter, and I arched my back for him. A wicked grin curled his lips as his nose wrinkled in something like a snarl.

My heart thundered in response, recognising the need in him and the anger, wanting them both.

"He asked if you'd ever be freed." With a roll of his hips, he ran his cock along my slick folds. They'd been without touch for too many minutes, and I couldn't help moaning at the pressure. "He thought"—his grip on my hips tightened, pulling me up to meet his thrust—"if he gave back my money, he could have you back."

The thought seized my throat, seized my pleasure, filling me with dread.

He pulled away, eyebrows clenched together, the lines of his neck corded. "He'll never have you back, Zita. You're mine." He speared me, hard, fast, deep, as much with that final word, *mine,* as with his cock.

I cried out, one shout merging into the next as he slammed into me again, again, again. It was like a raging thunder storm with crack after crack of lightning licking through me, lighting me up, threatening to blot out the rest of reality.

His tail snaked around my ankle, as though he needed to hold me with everything he had to *show* I was his.

He didn't need to hold me with anything. I feared he'd already somehow made it true.

I sank into that thought, into his rolling rhythm, the fullness, and the press of his thumb into my arse.

I *was* his. And I let him possess me.

I let him break me.

My cries reverberated into the bed as the earlier crescendo he'd denied me rose and joined this new one in sweet-sharp obliteration.

40

He fucked me on the bed. Into the bed. Over it. Up against the headboard. Over the dressing table. Splayed on the coffee table. With my back to the bedpost and the wall. And hanging upside down, my ankles over his shoulders, held up only by his hands around my hips.

I lost track of how many times I climaxed and the times he flooded into me. Apparently, fae men weren't subject to the same limitations as human ones in that respect.

As I came, hanging from his grip, all the blood flooded to my head in a dizzying orgasm unlike anything else I'd ever experienced. At the same time, he gushed into me once more with a hoarse cry.

I wasn't sure which way was up or down. What was me or what was him. Where I was. Who I was. What was right or wrong or why that even mattered.

I just *was*. Sated. Full. Sticky and slick. Every muscle melted. Every hard edge knocked off.

He cleaned me, the soft cool touch of a damp cloth at once soothing and almost too much to bear. Then he made me go to the toilet and carried me to bed.

With that peace, though, my brain buzzed, like the clearing out of everything gave it clarity.

Eric had written to Sepher asking "to have me back." Like I was his to begin with.

I didn't want to dwell on what I'd realised as Sepher had slid into me—who I *did* belong to.

But even more than that, I didn't want to go back.

I had never belonged to Eric, yet he didn't see that.

From there unfurled more truths, like a bird in the nest slowly spreading its wings for the first time, testing just how far they reached.

Eric had never been in love with me, just the *idea* of me. He wanted the version of me I sold on the stage—sweet and flir-tatious, innocent but not *too* innocent, curious enough to follow through on that flirtation.

A good girl with a naughty side.

But I wasn't sure I *was* a good girl.

I was sharp and spiked, not sweet and gentle. A woman with muscles and teeth, not a girl with soft flesh and smiles.

Zinnia had been those things.

But not me.

I shifted in Sepher's arms, frowning.

"You're not sleepy, are you?" His voice rumbled through the darkness.

"Yes and no." I traced a circle around his nipple, that small movement manageable in my body's liquid state. "I think I need a little while for my brain to switch off."

"Hmm." He nodded and a single dim fae light drifted into being, golden and warm. "We could... talk, then?"

"About?"

He slid his fingers through my hair. "Tell me about your sister."

"Why?"

He sucked in a long breath, brow slightly furrowed. "I lost my sister before I even got to know her. Sometimes it feels like there's something missing. When something good happens or I want to laugh at someone else's misfortune, I find myself looking to my side to share it with..." His shoulders rose. "But there's no one there. Or, at least, there wasn't." His gaze shifted to mine.

An understanding passed between us then.

Some of it I could name. We'd grown accustomed to each other. Comfortable with each other, in an odd way. Maybe we'd even come to like each other. We filled gaps in each other's lives.

But some of it was not only unspoken, but unspeakable. There weren't words for the fullness in me. I couldn't name the feelings I saw in the flashing reflection of his eyes.

Maybe it was just as well I lacked the words. Because as mind blowing as the sex was, this was only a temporary thing. I had a fae murderer to kill, and I didn't expect to survive the attempt.

This was just meant to be fun until then—giving in to our mutual obsession.

"You told me about her death." The knot of his throat bobbed as he swallowed. "Now tell me about *her*."

With a deep breath, I grabbed the locket from my nightstand. I flicked it open, called the fae light closer, and showed him the tiny drawing I'd made of the two of us together. "That's her."

His eyebrows rose as he craned closer. "All those sketches

in your book... I thought they were you, but... they're all her."
He traced the edge of the locket. "You look so young, here."

"Sixteen." Cheeks still rounded, eyes bright, a girl compared to my sister, and much shorter. Those with fae magic were often taller, stronger, faster than most humans. I had a little of the strength and agility, but only stood at five feet tall. "She towered over me in comparison," I murmured, thinking of all the times I had to look up at her. "Five foot six. When they saw her on stage, people always thought she was taller, though."

He nodded slowly. "I remember her. I didn't realise she was so small, either. Though I don't remember seeing you back then."

"I worked backstage. You wouldn't have seen me, and even if you had, you wouldn't have noticed me then."

"I wouldn't be so sure."

When I looked up from the locket, he was giving me an odd look, intent, like he saw me—truly *saw* me where Eric had not.

I cleared my throat and tore my gaze from him, not liking the intimacy of his long eye contact. "Although I have a fae gift, she was truly gifted. She took to the silks and hoop so quickly, it impressed the manager and she became top of the bill rather than just another dancer in the chorus." I scoffed, tilting the locket into the light. "Her skill and strength—it was beautiful, incredible. Better than my magic. I mean... I can only curse people. It automatically makes anyone who knows about it wary. It can't do any good in the world. It's a curse, not a gift."

He shifted, making a low sound, but I didn't look up, too lost in the past contained in that locket.

"I have to be so careful about what I say in anger. I accidentally cursed someone when my power first woke." I shook my head, the chill of that memory working its way over my shoulders.

His arm around me tightened, and his touch slid to my neck. With a soft click, he unfastened one buckle of my collar. "And what about before that? What about your parents?"

"I don't remember them. Zinnia was seven years older than me. She basically raised me."

"Zinnia." His voice purred over the buzz of the Z as it did when he said my name. He unfastened the next buckle as he gave a soft laugh. "Your parents must've liked Z names."

"My name isn't actually Zita."

"What?" His chest tensed under my cheek. "But it suits you so well." He toyed with the last buckle. "What did you parents name you?"

I didn't have to worry about True Names—humans weren't born with them as fae were. But it still felt like a step further to tell him. Like I'd be handing over some final part of me.

So I scoffed. "And have you teasing me about it for weeks? No. Not happening."

"Hmph." He pouted as he unfastened the final buckle of my collar and pulled it away.

I sighed at the touch of air, followed by his fingers as he massaged the skin there.

As he worked my neck and shoulders, he asked for more details of my life with Zinnia, and I told him how I'd helped her prepare and choreograph. How I'd washed her hair and smeared special masques onto her face to keep her looking perfect for her performances. He listened in silence, absorbed with the details of our every day life as it had once been.

When I'd talked myself out, he made a soft, thoughtful sound. "Even then, you lived your life for her."

My heart lurched. "She deserved it. She'd given up so much to look after me, to keep me safe. She didn't—"

"Calm yourself, little witch. Don't curse me again." He smirked and stroked my hair. "I'm not criticising your sister, just making an observation. She sounds like a remarkable woman. You were overshadowed by her, scuttling around behind the scenes." His smile softened. "I know something about being overshadowed."

I raised an eyebrow. "You? Who overshadows almost seven feet of solid fae with blazing red hair and *stripes*?"

His deep laugh rumbled into me, into the darkness, all the more enjoyable because I'd caused it. "Before *someone* cursed me, I only had stripes when I lost my focus. I reverted to this" —he lifted a finger and pushed out a single claw as his tail curled around me under the sheets—"to my true form in private. My parents banned me from doing it at all, but what can I say? I was always the rebel son." He flashed his teeth, but something soured his earlier amusement. "No, even when I could hide what I was, I always came second to my brother in every possible way."

Frowning, I splayed my hand over his chest, like there was some way I could absorb that bitterness and leave him only smiling. My sister had never placed anyone above me. And the parents of the Lightning Siblings had never shown any favouritism or placed one above the other, apart from in their pyramid.

For the second time, I said those two words to him: "I'm sorry."

"Mm." He ran a finger from the nape of my neck down my spine. "The golden son of Dawn Court. The firstborn heir. The perfect Day Prince." He snorted, lines between his brows. "He's the worst of them all. When we were younger, before I grew taller than him, he was so cruel to me. Little things while our teachers' backs were turned. A pinch or the rap of a ruler."

The way his glower darkened, I knew it got worse. It twisted in me, ratcheting my jaw tight.

"When he got away with that, it escalated. I think he wanted to see just how much he could get away with. What is the line for a future king?" His voice had softened, like he wasn't entirely sure he wanted to say these things out loud.

I stroked his chest and squeezed closer to remind him I was here.

"He broke my tail, slammed it in a door repeatedly." It squeezed my thighs, pulling me closer. "It almost came off—it was a wonder the healers could repair the bones at all. When he saw it, he said they shouldn't have bothered, practically admitted he'd done it deliberately. 'Cut out the animal in him.' That was what he told our parents they should do." He frowned into the darkness, gaze distant. "They looked away. I think they agreed with him, but didn't have the stomach to admit it."

My eyes burned for him. My veins bubbled at his brother and his parents. How dare they? Their own son?

I managed to swallow and finally speak. "Oh, Sepher." I slid on top of him and pressed a kiss to his lips. "I'm so sorry. They should never have done that—*thought* that. You are..." I pressed my forehead to his and closed my eyes until they stopped burning quite so much. "I love your tail. Even your claws. And your stripes... They're beautiful. They remind me of streams down a mountainside after a heavy rainfall." I slid my fingers along them. "They're paths converging and splitting, leading to such interesting places. I want to follow them all."

He opened to me when I kissed him, held me close, his touch gentle.

It was his softness I hated the most, because where all the punishment and the brutal, beautiful sex had failed, this was the thing that broke me.

And I gave back in kind.

41

"I've been thinking," he announced as we ate breakfast at what had become our work table.

"I feel like I should be worried." I arched an eyebrow. "You thinking usually leads to you doing something unpleasant to me."

He smirked. "You didn't think it that unpleasant last night, judging by the way you screamed my name."

"I'd say that was more of a shout than a scream."

He shrugged. "Semantics. The point is, I made you come *a lot*, and I didn't hear a word of complaint. And all those different ways I fucked you were because I'd thought about it while you draped yourself over our guests. So is my thinking really so bad?"

It *had* led to some quite interesting ways to spend the time. I took a long gulp of fruit juice—that fruity, tropical one we sometimes mixed with spirits. "Maybe not." I tried to keep my shrug nonchalant.

His smirk said I failed. "On this occasion, I was thinking

about our ignoble quest." He pushed his plate aside and leant forward. "There was nothing wrong with your plan to use performance to get close to me—quite elegant, actually. It's just you had the wrong man."

Or the right one.

The thought rang in my mind, clear and horribly bright.

Shit.

Shit!

Because the feeling in me... it wasn't just not hate. It was... the opposite side of that coin.

I was falling in love with him.

And it had to stop.

Because although my plan no longer involved killing a prince and getting killed by his guards, I still knew getting revenge for Zinnia was the last thing I would ever do.

I had no future. Therefore, we had no future.

Breathing deeply through those thoughts, I lost track of what he was saying.

"You said a piece of her hair had been cut, right?"

I blinked up at him. I didn't trust my voice, so I nodded.

"That suggests obsession. A wish to possess. If we can immerse the killer in that night, in the woman they were so infatuated with, they won't be able to help but act."

My fears evaporated as something brighter buzzed through me. "Act? What are you thinking?"

"You give a grand performance. Like that night, but... *more.* You look very much like her, though..." He smiled, gaze trailing over my face. "Your chin is different, your eyes sharper. But I don't think they'll remember that over the decade gap. They'll see *her.*"

My pulse throbbed in my throat. "A performance to lure him out?"

"Exactly. After, we'll make it seem like you're alone, vulnerable. You'll extract a confession from him. Using the astrolabe, perhaps—when he sees it, he'll react, and you'll be able to get him to admit it was his."

"*Seem* like I'm alone?"

"I'll be nearby. Far enough that he can't detect me right away, but when you have him talking, he'll be distracted and I can come closer."

I gritted my teeth. "I don't want you killing him."

"I won't. I'm just there as your right hand. You need him held down: I am your shackles. He so much as thinks about hurting you: I will keep you safe." He swallowed. "I don't want you hurt in this, Zita."

It was... almost sweet of him. Maybe even sweeter, because it was futile. I knew in my bones this would be the end of me. I knew I was going to slice the killer's throat while he crushed the life from mine like he had hers. And I didn't mind.

But I didn't have the heart to tell Sepher that.

OVER THE FOLLOWING WEEKS, we plotted and planned for my great show on our guests' last night. Costume and set design. Music and choreography. Right down to the food and drink we'd serve that evening. We left no element to chance. Sepher's attention to detail impressed me, though perhaps I should've expected it when he chose my outfits and accessories so well.

He ordered servants to set up the theatre to my exact specifications and came up with the idea for me to perform in a glowing hoop. It was something fae could make, but it wasn't what Zinnia had used that night. When I resisted, he pointed out it would all be part of making the night *more*. I had to admit, maybe he was right. And the glowing hoop would certainly pull every scrap of attention to me.

Doing this for Zinnia was more important even than my own stubbornness.

Between the preparation, we entertained our guests every night. I resented the time more and more with each day that passed. I could be rehearsing. I could be mapping the theatre's jumbled catwalks. I could be practising the conversation I'd have with the killer when he found me alone after the performance.

Instead, I simpered and served drinks and laughed at their stupid jokes. But the times I caught Sepher's gaze and we shared secret smiles—they soothed my irritation. All this time I'd spent planning revenge alone, I'd never realised quite how good it could feel to have a partner.

Even though each day brought us closer to my performance and my revenge, part of me was sad. Sad that I didn't have this sooner. Sad that I only got to enjoy it for a matter of weeks. Sad that letting it go would be the price I paid for vengeance.

But everything had a cost.

After the evening's entertainments, I slipped away to the theatre to rehearse. Until, that is, he came and found me, which usually resulted in him seducing me, then carrying me to bed or carrying, then seducing. Whatever the order, the outcome was the same. I lay in the dark playing out in my mind the moment I would finally—*finally* have revenge until utter exhaustion sank its claws into me.

This night, a couple of days before my show, was no different. They'd played poker again, Sepher and I had cheated again, and together we'd won. He collected me from the theatre—practically had to drag me off the glowing hoop. Now it had been delivered, I could wholeheartedly admit he was right. It was incredible, like the sun or moon had been brought indoors and I got to perform with it.

Tonight, he didn't fondle me as he carried me to our rooms. He stalked in silence, the shoulder I was draped over tense, his grip on my thigh tight. Something was wrong, but I didn't dare ask while we were in a corridor where anyone might hear.

By the time he closed the door and set me down before the fire, I couldn't take it any longer.

"What's the matter?"

He held my shoulders and my gaze for a long while.

"Sepher? What is it? What's wrong? If it's something to do with the plan, we can work out a solution. We can—"

"It isn't the plan. Let's forget about that for tonight. This is..." His fingers flexed as his brow furrowed. "This is about us."

42

G oosebumps crept over my skin. There wasn't meant to be an "us." Shouldn't be. Not in any sane world.

He stroked my cheek, gaze roving over my face. "Zita, you have taken everything I've given you, every cruelty, every punishment, and you've transformed it. Such brilliant stubbornness." The corner of his mouth rose. "Such brutal beauty. Such exquisite suffering."

My chest echoed with the thunderous beat of my heart. This felt... It was like I stood on the highest catwalk of a theatre, teetering on its edge, with no safety net below. I was about to fall and I suspected he would be the one to push me.

"When you arrived, I found your stubbornness fascinating." His teeth flashed in the briefest grin as his knuckles grazed my jaw. "Normally when I find something fascinating, it's because I want to fuck it or break it—or both. And since you can't fuck stubbornness..." He scoffed and shrugged. "Well, I had to break you, didn't I?" His amusement faded as his eyebrows squeezed together slowly, like he was pained. "But when I thought I'd broken it, broken you... I realised I loved it. I wanted it."

I slipped closer to that edge. Every frantic beat of my pulse roared *danger*.

But for some reason, my foolish feet wouldn't run.

His gaze pierced me, not with its hardness, but with the fact it *saw*. "You know I never apologise. I did what I believed was right at the time. But this is the closest I can do."

Not taking his eyes off me, he lowered to his knees. Like a steel bar being bent slowly, he craned his neck back and bared his throat to me.

Mouth dry, I could only stare. At the pulse leaping. At the slow rise and fall as he swallowed. At the proud line of his jaw lifted to give me the most vulnerable part of him.

Sabrecats did this to their pride leaders, their riders, and their mates in a show of trust—of surrender.

Long moments passed before he frowned. "Don't you understand? I submit to you. *You've broken me.*" His eyes widened as though trying to prompt me to respond. "I don't even want revenge against the witch who cursed me. I only want you."

What did I say to that? That I wanted him too, but he wasn't the *only* thing I wanted? Revenge had to come higher up that list. I'd worked for it for too long. It was the only way I could come close to paying a debt long owed.

"If not words, then give me your actions." His voice shook, raw, like I'd hurt him. "I lay myself before you. Do whatever you wish to me. Whatever revenge. Whatever cruelty. I am yours to punish and command."

Beneath the bewilderment, something snaked through me. Something that whispered he was right. He *had* hurt me.

He'd frightened me. He'd humiliated and degraded me, and although I'd risen to every occasion, he had deliberately done those things in front of his court to punish me.

He deserved to be punished in return.

Maybe he wouldn't obey. Maybe this was a test or a trick.

There was only one way to find out.

I worked my tongue around my mouth as I lifted my chin. "Kiss my shoes."

He bent and pressed two firm kisses to the silk slippers I wore.

The prince—His Princely Prickishness, my Prince of Monsters, the man who'd paraded me around as his pet, kissed *my* shoes.

I took a deeper breath and lifted my foot. "And the soles."

Golden eyes on mine, he cupped my heel and bent again, kissing the dusty underside of my shoe. He betrayed no hint of hesitation or dismay at doing it, which made that slithering thing in me coil tight and hiss its irritation.

"You hurt me," I told him between gritted teeth.

He nodded.

Just nodded.

That simple acknowledgement angered me more than any denial or excuse. And the way his eyebrows crept together in contrition irritated me even more.

I slapped him, the sound ringing through the room.

It swung his head to one side, and when his gaze returned to me, he nodded again. "Thank you, love."

I didn't *want* him to thank me; I wanted him to beg me to stop. I wanted him to end this. Because I couldn't—or wouldn't. I wasn't sure which.

"You collared me in front of your entire court." I swept the same hand in a back-handed strike that stung my knuckles and whipped his head the other way. The red mark it left bloomed in me, loved and loathed.

When he straightened, he looked up at me with something close to adoration. "Thank you, love."

I didn't want fucking adoration. Didn't deserve it.

Hate.

Hate was easier to give, easier to take, easier to withstand, and easier to understand.

This? I didn't know what this was. What he was doing to me, what he was asking me to do to him, or why he wanted it.

It had to be a trap. Eventually, I was going to overstep a line he'd drawn in his mind and he would surge up and stop me and then he'd turn the punishment on me. It was all part of some fiendish plan. Maybe this entire plot to bring the list of suspects here and capture the killer was an elaborate scheme he'd concocted in order to truly, painfully, punish me. A punishment for trying to kill him and for cursing him.

Fine. I'd push him to that line. I needed to know what he was really up to, because the wrongness of all this crawled up my spine, setting every instinct on edge.

He kneeled up, waiting.

I placed a foot on his shoulder and shoved him down on his heels. "Take off your clothes."

"Yes, love." He obeyed, revealing his golden body.

"Bend over that table, hands behind your back."

"Yes, love." Again, he obeyed, no hesitation.

I slapped his arse as hard as I could, leaving a red imprint of my hand on his striped skin.

His tail jolted straight with the impact, but he only thanked me.

I did it again and again, hitting the same spot. He had to stop me at some point. Soon? Now?

I didn't like marking him like this. It had to hurt.

"Thank you, love."

When I looked up from the bloom on his arse, I found him watching me in the dressing table mirror. He inclined his head, prompting me to continue.

The slithering darkness in me rose, gripping my throat. "What is this, Sepher?" I choked out. "What are you doing?"

His gaze lowered like he was an obedient servant. "I told you. I am yours to punish and to command."

"Liar."

"I cannot lie."

I spun from him, hands fisting. "Oh, you lot fucking can." My laugh shook as I looked for something that would *make* him admit the truth.

His belt lay on the coffee table with the rest of his clothes. I snatched it, hand trembling as I turned and showed it to him in the mirror. "There's something else beneath your sweet story about submitting to me. There's always something else with your kind. Some secret twisting between your words. The lie unsaid. *Tell me.*"

He inclined his head again. "Give it to me, love. I can take it. Whatever you have to give, I accept."

"You fucking..." I shook my head and looped the belt, keeping the buckle and end in my hand. Deep breaths. I didn't want to do this in anger. It was just to get him to back down. When my trembling subsided, I held up the belt again and gave him a chance to tell me to stop.

He didn't.

I struck it across his backside. Not hard, but over the same point I'd smacked him.

His tail twitched, but he kept his hands clasped behind his back. "Thank you, love."

"Stop saying that."

"What would you prefer I call you? Mistress? Queen?"

"Stop thanking me."

He shook his head, smiling in the mirror. It wasn't a smirk or a cruel grin. Just a smile. A soft one, a regretful one. "I can't do that. Please continue."

So he'd be obedient, but only when he chose?

I gritted my teeth and cracked the belt across his arse again. This time the slithering thing in me took over, pulling my muscles harder and faster than before, and I left a red welt on his golden skin.

The sight of it burned, like I was the one who'd been struck. A sickly cold rolled over me in horrible contrast with the heat of my anger.

"Thank you, love."

I hit him again. Another red welt. Again. Another.

Each one I hated. Each one he thanked me for.

Sickness and rage battled inside me, each riling the other up higher and higher until I was drowning in the horror of them. His backside was a series of streaks, such a bright red they almost glowed.

I hated them. They were an outrage upon his perfect body.

I hated myself for inflicting them. And I hated myself for hating it.

But in the midst of all this hate—a feeling that I'd indulged in all the time I'd been here—I couldn't bring myself to hate *him*.

Hate wasn't the worst of all feelings. It was guilt. It made me long to return to my former numbness. Anything to escape it.

Shaking, I flung the belt to the floor.

I didn't want to hurt him.

I had once, but not anymore.

"Tell me." My voice came out breathless, pathetic, and I hated myself even more for it. I dragged him off the table.

He didn't fight me—he was strong enough to resist easily, but he let me fling him to the floor, and he knelt before me once more. He looked up at me, cheeks flushed, eyes glassy, sweat on his brow.

I'd hurt him. I'd really hurt him. And he'd never once asked me to stop.

"Tell me the truth, Sepher," I shouted, voice cracking on his name. "Tell me why you're letting me do this."

"Because..." His teeth showed as he spoke, blood on them from my backhanded strike. "I love you."

My heart didn't skip in my chest. My stomach didn't flutter like butterflies on a summer afternoon. My skin didn't warm with happiness.

No.

My heart crashed into my ribs with the same shock as the first drip of hot wax on my back. My stomach swooped just as I'd swooped on the silks while performing naked for his court. My skin burned the way it had in my too-hot bath as he'd kissed me the first time.

Because love wasn't like that. The reality was far messier, dirtier, bloodier. It edged close to hate, had that same feral intensity. It had teeth as well as heart. It could hurt as easily as it could soothe.

It clawed me because I didn't want it.

"You can't." I shook my head.

"Cute that my little human thinks she can tell me what I can and can't do." He grinned up at me, the bloody tinge on his teeth a pretty shade of pink. "I assure you, I can and I do."

He drew a long breath, shoulders squaring. "Why do you

think I lost my fucking mind when I thought you were dying? Why do you think I lost every shred of dignity when I found out you were the one who'd cursed me? I didn't want to shift that night, and I certainly didn't want to kill those deer, but I was unhinged. I lost grip of who I was, and it took every last ounce of energy to get away so I didn't hurt you." He really did look sorry, gaze lowered. Even his scoff sounded regretful. "I'm sure that's very comforting. 'I could've killed you, but I didn't. You're welcome.' But it is true. All of it."

I stood there, stunned.

His eyebrows peaked as he looked up at me, waiting for a response.

I had none.

"I realised when I saw you collapsed in the snow. I couldn't stand the thought of you dying because somehow, in some horribly hilarious twist of fate, I'd fallen in love with you. Then, when I realised who you were, I was enraged that I'd come to care for you too much to follow through on my vow to kill you."

I'd have called him a liar again. But there was no way another version of reality could slither between his words. No way in the world.

It was the truth.

"Say something."

Waking from my stupor, I shook my head. "I don't... I can't... I can't say it back."

"I know." He shrugged with a smile. Not the cocky one or the cruel one, but our private one. "I didn't expect you to. But after everything I've done, I needed to give this to you. To surrender myself to you." He touched his chest, looking up at me with such sincerity it stole my breath. "Do you accept?"

I wasn't sure what it meant to accept. Frankly, I didn't

want to poke too deeply into that. If this was an apology for all his cruelty, then I accepted that. I nodded.

His arms came around my hips, drawing me to him. Eyes closed, he rested his cheek against my belly and gave a long exhale. "Good. *Good.*"

I found myself stroking his hair and the edges of his ears, making him shudder since they were so sensitive.

Eventually, he looked up at me with a crooked grin. "Do you think you could put some of that salve on my arse?"

I laughed, the tension draining out with the sound. I ducked and kissed his brow, tasting the salt from his sweat. "I will do that for you."

"Thank you, love."

43

The next day went like the others, but there was a new softness between us. His, because he was insane and in love with me. Mine, because of a lingering sense of guilt over what I'd done to him.

Even if it could be argued he'd done worse, apparently, despite my love of winning, in this I wasn't keeping score.

I exercised. I rehearsed. I ate lunch on his lap with our guests, letting him feed me like I was still his pet. The way he watched me—how had I not seen how he felt? It seemed so painfully obvious now, knotting my stomach.

I spent the afternoon and evening trying not to think about it as I pored over our plans. Locked away in our rooms while he had dinner with the others, I drew the layout of the stage again and mentally walked around it. When I couldn't bring myself to do that any longer, I settled into my routine of writing their names over and over again in my sketchbook. There was something meditative in the whisper of pencil on paper.

Roark. Loy. Celestine.

I still didn't think it could be Celestine, but the possibility was a thorn in my heart.

Mayrie. Cadan. Tavin. Thurl...

Although I tried not to think about Sepher's confession, my pencil had other ideas. I found myself sketching his eyes in the margins of the page—the way they'd looked up at me as he'd knelt at my feet. The pain in them.

The love in them.

Like I'd summoned him, the door opened, and he entered wearing a smug grin. "I have to say, I can't believe you're actually staying here and not trying to get to the theatre to practise."

I gave him a sidelong look. "It's called malicious compliance."

He scoffed and sauntered over, tail held high. "I've been thinking..."

I groaned and closed my sketchbook before he could see its contents. "Didn't I warn you about that?"

"Like I said the other day—rebel son." He raised his hands as if helpless to change it. "Besides, this is something that would benefit you. I was talking to Celestine, and it sounds like one of Luminis's healers could regrow your teeth. Not guaranteed, but if they come and have a look, they'll be able to tell us whether it's possible."

A nice idea, but... I shrugged, flicking through my sketch-book. Another look at the stage layout—check I hadn't missed anything.

"Or... don't you want them back? I thought you'd like the idea of being able to face my kind with sharp teeth of your own."

"I just don't see the point."

He narrowed his eyes, giving a cautious smile. "Was that an intentional pun?"

"No. I just..." With a sigh, I closed the sketchbook again. "Do you not understand?"

"Not until you explain, no." He sank into the seat opposite and folded his arms.

I wasn't going to get rid of him until I gave an explanation. Fine.

"I know you'll be there, and you think you'll be able to keep me safe, but I've spent a decade—"

"Yes, yes, I know. You've spent a decade planning your perfect revenge, and I fucked that up by not being the one deserving of it. You've said this a hundred times, Zita."

"Then, *Sepher*, you should know by now that I never expected to survive taking you down. And I don't expect to survive this." I hugged the sketchbook to my chest. "I can feel it in my bones."

"*Huh.*" His head cocked. "And here I was thinking you'd spent all this time thinking about vengeance and still didn't understand it comes at a cost."

"A cost? Yours against me didn't."

"My backside would beg to differ." He winced as he shifted in his seat, and I tried to ignore my pang of guilt. "But no"— he shook his head—"I didn't have the revenge I swore against the witch who cursed me. I've given it up."

A sudden attack of conscience?

That wasn't something I expected from the man I loved.

No. Not that. I didn't—couldn't. Yes, he'd allowed me to escape the deadening cage I'd lived in for so long. But that wasn't because I loved him... rather... maybe I felt something for him because he'd freed me.

But that still wasn't... it wasn't the thing I'd worked for so long. It wasn't the thing I owed Zinnia—the thing I'd promised her.

And now he was trying to get me to give up on that because he wanted me to himself.

The edges of the sketchbook bit into my fingers. "You're just like Eric."

He flinched in a way he hadn't when I'd whipped him with his belt. He flinched like I'd torn him open and raked claws over his very soul.

It lurched in my throat, but I didn't let it stop me.

"You don't want me to have what I need. Here you are trying to come between me and my revenge, just like he did. I warn you now, Sepher, stay out of my way. I won't let anything stop me. Not even you. No matter how much I..." I bit back the words before they could leak out. I didn't feel them. I didn't even know why my tongue tried to sneak them out.

"How much you what?" He said it softly, little more than a breath.

I swallowed back what my tongue had tried to trip me up with and formulated something safer. "No matter what I feel about you. No matter how good a partnership we are." The acrobat and the fae prince. Who'd've thought?

But I couldn't wallow in the warmth of that. I needed to know. "Will you stand in my way? Tell me now."

He exhaled, sinking back in his chair, frown deepening. "No. I won't stand in the way of our plan, if that's what you truly wish to do, even knowing there will be a price. I want to see her killer bleed."

"Good." I said it with finality. That was the end of this nonsense about me not carrying out my plan.

Standing, he gave me a half smile. "Now come to bed or you'll be too tired for your performance tomorrow."

I dropped my sketchbook on the chair and stretched. "I was going to go and have one last rehearsal."

He sauntered over and slid his fingers into my hair. His finger-tips whispering over my scalp dragged a low exhale from me. "You can do that in the morning. I've locked the door. Not to stop your revenge, but because you need a good night's sleep for it."

The massage eased the tension that had been building in my head all afternoon and evening as I'd focused so hard. I groaned, pushing into his touch, letting myself notice his musky, outside scent. "You're good at this."

"Of course I am." My eyes were closed, but I could hear the smug smile in his voice. "I'm good at everything."

I grumbled but had to admit I hadn't found anything he was bad at. Not yet, anyway. "If you want me to sleep, you're going to need to fuck me until I'm tired."

"I was going to do it to distract you, but that works, too." He swept me into his arms and carried me into the bathroom, unlacing the back of my dress.

I frowned at the bedroom door. "In here?"

"I want you in the shower." He tugged down my bodice, making me gasp as cool air reached my nipples, tightening them. His low sound of approval purred into me, and he bent and flicked his tongue over one aching peak. "I want your whole body drenched, just like your pussy gets so drenched for me." He gave a wide, wicked smile, claws clicking on the rubies of my collar. "Do you object, pet?"

I was already tugging off his shirt as I answered, "No, my prince."

"Good girl."

AFTER, he took me to bed, and I sank into his arms, deliciously sated and tired out, despite all tomorrow would bring. Aside from our argument earlier, this might be the closest thing to a perfect last night on earth. I'd take it.

For a long while, he traced circles on my back. "I have something for you," he said at last, reaching for his night-stand. From the drawer came the glint of metal.

But this wasn't a pretty bracelet or another diadem.

Hilt first, he handed me a blade.

My Prince of Monsters, the man I'd tried to kill, sat here naked, giving me a weapon.

I frowned from it to him. "What's this?"

"A dagger? I expected you to be familiar with the concept already, since you were holding one the first time we met."

I scowled at him.

He grinned right back, the full length of his canines show-ing. "I had your iron blade reworked to something that suited you better. That old thing was so ugly. After all our hard work to ensure everything tomorrow looks perfect, I couldn't have it ruin your moment."

His attention fluttered in my chest, bright and winged, stealing my breath for a second.

Sure enough, the dagger's pale gold-coloured hilt and light blue stone matched the bracelets he'd given me.

I twisted my wrist, testing its weight. That too had been improved, rebalanced, so when it slashed through the air, it sang.

At last, I had a weapon that could kill him. But...

I believed him. He hadn't killed my sister or conspired with anyone else. And I no longer wanted him dead at my feet.

He'd given himself to me last night. He loved me. The fool. The sweet, wicked fool.

Still, it didn't hurt to play with him a little. I looked past the dark iron of the blade reforged to my prince. "And you give this to me now when you're so vulnerable. Aren't you afraid I'll cut off your cock?"

"My cock? Ha! No, you enjoy it too much." He lifted his chin, preening and arrogant.

Then again, I wasn't sure it counted as arrogance when it was so deserved.

He gave me a sheath and watched as I put the dagger inside, his amusement fading. "What if our plan doesn't work? What will you do?"

I swallowed and tucked the knife away, taking my time. The full weight of my lie hit me. He was living in its illusion, thinking he'd be free of his monstrous appearance, able to mix freely with other fae back in Luminis. And he had to really believe I'd survive if he wasn't asking me to lift the curse ahead of the performance.

"You mean, whether I'll lift your curse?"

"Oh, that? No. I mean... It's a good plan, but what if it doesn't draw out the killer? What will you do?"

My jaw tightened to the point of pain as I stared at the sheathed dagger on my nightstand. "I'll get him... or her. Even if I have to kill them all."

When I looked up, I found him staring at me, wide-eyed, mouth open.

"Oh, don't judge me," I snapped, hating how the look raked me. "You killed someone for saying he'd put me out of my misery."

He shook his head, eyebrows clenching together. "I'm not judging you, little bird. It's..." His throat rose and fell slowly. "I can't protect you from them all. There are too many. They'll kill you if you try to take them all on. And I can't..." The muscle in his jaw ticked.

"Then so be it. With a little luck, I'll take the killer down before they get me."

"But I want... I want you here. With me. After all that." His hands bunched the sheets.

I tried to keep my breathing even, but the look he gave me seared my lungs like the frigid air on a winter's day.

He wanted more than I had left.

"Sepher..." His name was sweet on my lips, but bitterness edged my tongue. "This thing between us has no future. Because *I* have no future. Only revenge."

He pressed his lips together. "But you could. Why not try? You could have years yet. We could—"

"I told you. This is going to kill me. I know it. And I don't care if it does."

He sucked in a breath.

And I realised it wasn't entirely true. Not in the way it had been the night I first performed for him. Then, I truly hadn't cared. I'd almost welcomed death. Part of me still did. But another part of me regretted that tonight was my last night. In the past few months, I felt more alive than I had in years.

"You don't mean that." He shook his head like that would persuade me.

"I do." My eyes burned. My breaths shook with too much feeling to contain. I hated him for unlocking it in me. Because this was worse than being deadened. This feeling scouring my nerves and throat was worse than the guilt from marring his beautiful body. It was worse than my hate, worse than desire for a man I shouldn't want, worse than *anything*.

It was the thing that had chased feeling from me.

A truth too horrible to let myself dwell on, so I'd always stayed adjacent to it, blaming someone else.

But it was the reason I deserved to die right alongside my sister's killer.

I'd stayed so absorbed, first with hating him, then with planning this, I'd managed to evade it. But now it came for me, consuming and jagged.

His nostrils flared as his expression hardened. "Why?"

"I am a curse, Sepher." I pulled my knees close, and I didn't need to see the flickering frown on his face to know he didn't understand.

I had to make him understand, even if that meant showing him the very worst of me.

44

"They came for me the night my magic woke. No pitchforks or torches, but they carried lanterns through the streets, searching for the witch." Goosebumps flooded my skin just as they had that night. "It didn't matter that I was a little girl, because I'd..." I swallowed down the salt in my throat as it threatened to choke me. "I'd cursed a little girl."

I couldn't bear to look at him, but I could feel his gaze prickling me as he listened in silence.

I shook my head. "Didn't realise I *could* curse anyone, but I did. She laughed at me for my ragged clothes and pushed me over when she found out I had no parents. So I pointed at her and said, 'May you get boils.' And she did. So many. So, so many. They erupted on her face, covered her eyelids, lined her mouth. When they broke out on her eyeballs, I screamed. And that was when everyone turned and saw what I'd done." The image of her was seared into my mind. I never drew it, because I didn't have to.

I hugged myself tighter, like I could hug the little girl I'd cursed. "Did you know that if you get boils in your throat, you can't breathe and you die?"

Pale, Sepher shook his head.

"Me neither." I sank against my knees, letting my gaze slip away. "That was what happened that evening. I was ten. She was eleven and dead, thanks to my 'gift.'" I laughed at the irony of that name for magic. "So, of course, they came to find the witch, and they carried iron. That was why we ran. That was why Zinnia filed down my teeth to hide what I was. That was how we ended up in the Gilded Suns."

On the periphery of my vision, he moved, perhaps coming closer, but I pulled away. "What does this have to do with you having a death wish?"

"Don't you understand?" My voice rose, rasping in my throat as my fingers bit into my legs. "If we hadn't joined them... If we hadn't gone to Elfhame with them... If she hadn't given that private performance..."

A hundred *ifs* that chewed on me day by day, but chief amongst them was one.

"If *I* hadn't let that curse loose, she would never have been killed in that alleyway."

All this time, I'd searched for vengeance and I'd never expected to survive it.

Because deep down, I knew they were one and the same. I didn't deserve to survive it, because it was as much my fault as it was the person who'd killed her.

There it was.

The thought I'd been running from all these years.

I'd escaped into sketchbooks and plans, into the air as I performed, into my obsession with *him*. I'd used my vanity to soothe the wound where it had worked its way into my body like a splinter of glass. But hair treatments and skin lotions couldn't patch over this wound.

Nothing could.

Because it was my fault.

I was the one who truly deserved to suffer to give my sister justice.

"You blame yourself," he murmured into the quiet that yawned in the wake of my story.

He sat there very still, but it was the stillness of a hunter poised rather than any state of relaxation. It was the stillness that had made me wary a couple of months ago—the kind that could lash out.

A laugh came out with my next breath.

I'd been punishing myself for a decade. No wonder part of me craved his punishment.

Oh, I'd found myself a perfect partner, hadn't I?

"Come here." His tail patted the space between his legs.

I frowned at him, because... he didn't look horrified. Or disgusted. He didn't glare at me like he thought I was some awful creature for killing another child.

Maybe his handsome face was a trap. It wasn't the first time I'd thought that. It wasn't the first time I'd fallen for it.

This time, I did so willingly and crawled across the mattress to him.

Even before he touched me, his blazing heat reached my skin, eradicating my goosebumps. His outdoors scent curled down my throat, thick and heady, comforting and familiar. I loved these things. I loved the way they reminded me of lying in the sun with Zinnia on the hottest day of the year. How we'd withstand it as long as we could before running down the bank to the river.

And I loved the way he wrapped around me, arms, legs, and tail, even though I didn't deserve it.

He nuzzled into my neck. "A million things took your sister to that alleyway, Zita," he murmured against my skin. "But even if there had only been one, even if you were the sole reason she was there, it still wouldn't be your fault."

I jerked back, but he held tight. "But I—"

"Do not speak when your prince is explaining, love. Especially not when it's something you need to hear." He pulled away just enough to press his forehead to mine, our noses brushing. "Your sister contributed to her being there that night. Do you blame her for what happened?"

He might as well have gripped my throat. I tried to gasp but couldn't. It was like my lungs had forgotten how to work.

"Was it her fault? Did she deserve it?"

My heart hadn't forgotten anything, though. It rammed against my ribcage, not caring that it broke a little more with each strike.

"Did she get what was coming to her? Was she asking for it?"

"No." The word cracked from me, a shard of scintillating pain that pushed tears to my eyes. "*No.*"

I felt his frown against my brow as it darkened his eyes. I tried to pull away from it, because I had a horrible feeling about where it was leading. And I wasn't sure that, even after all these years, it was somewhere I was prepared to follow.

He gripped my hair, clamping me in place. "If you wouldn't blame her, an adult, why the hells would you blame yourself when you were a child—a fucking child, Zita?"

I opened my mouth to answer.

But I couldn't.

To blame Zinnia for what had been done to her was monstrous. Unthinkable.

To blame the little girl I'd cursed for what I'd done to her was equally unfathomable.

But to blame the little girl I'd once been for an accident—a terrible, terrible accident...

She looked up at me. Brown hair dull and tangled. Small for her age and skinny, in tattered clothes. She lived for those rare days when we got to play—like the one by the riverside. The rest of her time was spent begging or running messages for tiny copper coins.

She never meant to curse that little girl. She hadn't known that was a thing she could do, never mind that it would lead her and Zinnia along a path that ended in one of Elfhame's dark alleys.

How could she?

He caught my tears with his thumbs. "Do you see, now? Do you see how monumentally untrue the story you've been telling yourself all these years is? Do you see the lie in it?"

I did. Good fucking gods, I did.

He couldn't keep up with my tears. They covered my cheeks and chin. They dripped onto his chest. They burned my eyes and salted my tongue.

But there was something cleansing in salt and fire.

When I managed to nod, he pulled me close and squeezed so tight it was like he could make us one through sheer force of will.

"There is only one person to blame for what happened that night. And tomorrow, you will find him, and you will kill him."

It was the most comforting thing he could've said. I sank

into it, letting his arms claim me, letting him hold the truth of it around my body while I fought to believe it.

After a long while, once the fae lights had dimmed to just one, I shook my head at him. "I don't know why I told you all that."

His teeth gleamed in the darkness. "I do." And he looked terribly smug about it.

I thought perhaps I did too. Why else would I tell someone a story I'd never spoken to a single soul—admit a weight I'd never dared utter out loud?

Yet, I couldn't force my tongue to form the words.

Instead, I scowled at him and said the next best thing. "I hate you."

He smiled, amused and pleased, and wrapped his tail around my leg. "I know. I hate you, too."

And that made me far happier than Eric telling me he loved me ever had.

45

Somehow, the following day both disappeared in a blur and dragged. I lived in an odd, buzzing state, unable to sit still, until I found myself dressed to perform, waiting behind the curtains.

Roark. Loy. Celestine. Mayrie. Cadan. Tavin. Thurl...

An oval table stood on the stage, and one by one, the fae took seats around it.

I rubbed my throat. No collar tonight. We'd decided its bright colour would risk jarring the killer out of their memory of Zinnia. Sepher had removed it and slipped it into his pocket, and now I felt naked without its familiar press on my throat.

Even in the dim light backstage, my gown glimmered as I moved. I'd already stretched, and I'd rehearsed this morning. All that remained for me to do was wait. Still, I couldn't help shifting from foot to foot and fidgeting with the bow tying my wrap skirt in place.

At last they were all seated, Sepher at the far end of the

table, a gap remaining closest to me. They helped themselves to drinks and fell quiet, waiting. My pulse leapt, fluttering in every part of my body, like I contained an entire flock of birds wanting to be free.

When the music began and the lights lowered, I ran out. My skirt spread behind me like a pair of glittering wings. It swirled as I somersaulted onto the table, and I was rewarded with a collective gasp from my audience.

Smiling, I prowled a circuit before them and slowly untied my skirt. They watched, not a single one able to look away or even blink, glasses forgotten on the table.

Sepher's gaze was a claw point on my skin. When I whirled the skirt off, I let it pool in his lap, a gesture others might read as confirmation that I was his possession. But for me, it meant trust. I swallowed when my eyes met his, because this was one of the precious and finite number of times that remained for us.

Their gold sparked for me, molten and warm. His wide pupils drank me up, adding my essence to their depths, which already brimmed with determination and desire and pride and, of all things, love.

He loved me.

Maybe I was even deserving of that love.

It pressed on the back of my eyes, but the time for giving in to that had passed with the dawn.

I inclined my head, and his magic whispered over my skin as I spread my arms. The music softened to something awed, and from above appeared a blazing ring.

It was like I'd summoned the sun itself.

A chorus of soft sounds came from my audience—my suspects, as I reminded myself. The thrill of performance ran through me where before I hadn't fully felt it. But this was not just *a* show, it was *the* show, and I had to outdo myself—even outdo Zinnia.

With the beat, I snapped my hand to the hoop and let it lift me. My weight was a warm hum in my muscles, a sweet stretch like lying in bed with Sepher after making love.

The higher I went, the faster the music's rhythm grew, a slow build that thrummed with anticipation. I held still, taut beneath the glowing hoop.

I could feel their breaths held beneath me and the energy they contained. I fed off it, waiting, waiting, waiting, until...

A single thunderous drum beat, then silence.

Every light cut out, save for my hoop.

The music crashed into life and so did I.

I flowed up into the hoop, defying gravity. A one-armed handstand within its circle, held for a burning beat, then I swung through it.

Legs spread, arms wide, holding on with fingers, elbows, knees, balanced on the small of my back, the nip of my waist, I let every fluttering thing inside me free.

I soared, I stretched, I ached and flexed. I turned with the music and against it, like we duelled over control of my body, just as Sepher and I had duelled over control of who and what we were.

We had both lost that battle.

And, in doing so, had both won.

Every smile that tore through me at the sheer and glorious pleasure of this dance I gave to him. I let him see the different kind of ferocity in me, the one that said what my tongue had refused to last night.

I danced for Zinnia, but tonight, I also danced for him.

The music soared, and I spun with the hoop. Feet on its lower curve, I went faster, faster, faster, the world a beautiful blur of dark and light, until it crashed into a roaring finale.

Just as Sepher's magic stilled the hoop, I slid my toes off and let myself drop.

Gasps joined the music.

For a breathless moment, I fell.

Then, with the final booming note, I landed. Back arched over the hoop's curve, arms spread, toes pointed, I looked like I'd been beautifully broken upon its lower edge.

Thunderous silence rang through the theatre.

I held the pose and Sepher's gaze. His chest heaved like he was the one who'd just given the performance of his life. His claws were buried in the arm of his chair. For the briefest second, his lip trembled.

Arching my neck fractionally more, I bared my throat to him. His gaze flicked there, and I hoped he understood what it meant.

I lay here, hanging from my hoop, still and splayed, surrendered to him, just as he'd surrendered to me.

His dark brows clenched together.

He knew.

Applause shattered the moment.

I'd forgotten to expect that. I'd forgotten about my audience. About my purpose for the night.

I was his and had been for a short but brilliant while.

Eyelids fluttering, I sucked in a deep breath and woke myself from the spell.

Revenge. I'd promised Zinnia.

I slid backwards from the hoop and snapped my legs down, landing lightly on the table, my back to Sepher. I needed to remember myself and what this night was about, and that would be easier when I wasn't looking at him.

Bowing, I soaked up the applause and surveyed my suspects. Celestine gave an enthusiastic nod, eyes bright. She didn't look obsessed, just like a friend who'd enjoyed my performance and was proud of me.

Roark's gaze trailed over me, enjoying the arch of my back when I straightened and the way it thrust out my tits and arse. Maybe? He did love to look at me.

But then, most of the other fae watched me similarly as I turned and took each of them in, bowing over and over.

Cadan, though. When I reached him, he just stared, eyes round, lips parted, like he'd seen a ghost. The ghost of my sister? Or was it just that he liked me and that was why he'd tried to be kind with the salve?

I couldn't dwell on him, though, not without looking suspicious.

So, smiling, I turned to give my final bow.

And it was to my prince. He'd earned it. He deserved it. For every defiance, for every instant of malicious compliance. For every time he'd broken me apart. For every cruelty and harsh word. For trying to kill him and for cursing him. For everything he'd given me, good and bad, and for everything I'd refused to give him.

This was the perfect goodbye.

He lifted his chin as though he sensed it too, and his nostrils flared as he scented the air, like he could inhale me one last time. The flicker of a frown crossed his brow, and he glanced to the side as though he expected to find someone else there. But with a small shake of his head, he returned the full weight of his attention to me.

Stiffly, he rose. "That was quite a performance, little bird." He smiled, and on the surface it looked broad and cocky, but beneath that brittle layer was something soft and tremulous.

"We should give you some time to recover. Come"—he gestured to his friends, but his gaze remained on me—"let's leave her and see if we can find something strong to drink. And maybe, for some of you, someone interesting to fuck."

A ripple of laughter followed them out of the theatre as they chattered about my performance.

While I tied my skirt around my waist, Sepher paused at the door, taking up most of its space with his large form. I etched it in my mind—the width of his shoulders, the narrowness of his hips, the mane of his hair, and the thickness of his thighs.

I didn't need to commit to memory the glint of his eyes in the dim light, the way they held me for a short moment that felt closer to eternity.

They were already carved into my soul.

46

Once I was alone, I sank into Sepher's chair. It was still warm, and I soaked that up as I checked under the table. The dagger and astrolabe were on the hidden ledge where I'd left them, ready for the killer to be lured here by the chance to see me alone.

I dragged in one deep breath after another, muscles jittery and spring-loaded, despite how hard I'd worked them. Would this work? What if they didn't come?

Wondering, straining to listen, I poured myself a drink in Sepher's glass and waited.

And waited.

And waited.

I'd finished the drink and was picking at the splinters he'd left in the chair's arms when the back of my neck prickled. Eyes on me.

I took another steadying breath and poured more honeyed whisky before throwing a glance over my shoulder, like it was a casual gesture.

The gleam of silver hair, light in the theatre's gloom. So human-like, but tall and beautiful, he approached. He watched me, eyes wide and unblinking, like I was a ghost.

"Cadan." I gave him a friendly smile, but my voice shook as I said his name.

The name of my sister's killer.

I stood and grabbed the empty glass from his place at the table, tilting it in offering. In my left hand, the iron dagger was a reassuring weight, hidden in the folds of my skirt. If he tried to grab me and kill me as he had my sister, he wouldn't find me so helpless.

Cadan tilted his head, a small frown between his eyebrows. "How long were you with the Gilded Suns?"

I chuckled like that was a strange question. He couldn't know this was a trap, that I was expecting him and knew exactly what he was and what he'd done. Not until he was too close to escape.

And, part of me piped up, not until I knew for sure he was the killer. I'd got it wrong once before.

A shudder streaked through me at the thought. If I'd been successful that first night, Sepher would be dead. I'd have ended his life before getting the chance to know him. I'd have never felt all the things he'd opened me to. I'd have gone to my grave while the true killer walked free.

No. I needed to be sure.

Pouring Cadan a drink, even though he hadn't answered, I shrugged. "I was with them for a long time."

"Did you know...?" He shook his head and exhaled a breathy laugh. "But of course you did. You look just like her. Even the names... Zinnia... Zita. You're her sister, aren't you?"

Rage surged through me as he said her name. How fucking *dare* he?

I turned and offered him the whisky. Its golden surface rippled in my trembling hand.

He'd done it.

What he'd said so far was proof enough.

The bastard even had the audacity to look sad about it. Tears gleamed in his damned eyes.

My gift sizzled in my veins, begging me to point and curse him. But he was still too far away. If I revealed my hand now, he would escape. And cursed wasn't as good as dead.

Patience, little witch. Patience. The memory of Sepher's voice eased through me.

A low, slow breath. "This is yours, isn't it?" I revealed the astrolabe.

His eyes widened in recognition.

The dagger's leather-wrapped hilt creaked in my grip.

"Where did you find that?" His eyebrows peaked together as he shook his head.

When I didn't answer, he looked up at me, and I cocked my head to remind him my question came first.

"It isn't mine, no. I gave it to Zinnia the night she..." He swallowed. "When I asked her to stay with me, to try for a real relationship rather than only seeing each other for a few nights a year."

Pieces slid together in my mind, like the shards of a vase I was trying to rebuild. She always disappeared after shows while we were in Elfhame. I'd assumed it was for private performances. The love letter that had been with her belongings—it could've been from him.

I lifted my chin, muscles coiling in readiness. "And she said no, so you killed her."

His eyes widened, shooting from the astrolabe to me. "What? No, I... She said..." Half a step closer he came, setting my nerves on a knife-edge. He downed the whisky and bared his teeth like it cut through his own nerves. "No. She said she needed to think and talk to her sister about it, because it wasn't her decision alone. I confess, I might've scared her off a little with the shock—I don't think she was expecting me to ask. She hurried out, and I wish..."

He screwed his eyes shut, an odd move for a man who was about to commit murder, but maybe this was how he planned to lull me. I shifted my stance, ready to lunge for him or roll back onto the table.

"Sun and Stars, I wish I hadn't let her go. If I'd just kept her with me..." He hung his head. "But I didn't. I wanted to give her the space she needed. Then the next morning, I heard..." His voice grew thick with grief, like mine had when I'd spoken to Sepher. "I didn't kill Zinnia. I... I loved her."

47

The words cut through me like claws or teeth or Sepher's sword at my neck.

The world narrowed to the image of his bowed head, the fall of his pale hair, the sorrowful beauty of his grief.

I didn't kill Zinnia.

I couldn't...

I couldn't *anything*. This wasn't possible.

Liar, the rage in me hissed.

But... just as Sepher couldn't lie about not killing her, neither could Cadan.

Where my muscles had coiled, now that energy fizzed and sparked, making me shake. "Get out," I whispered.

His gaze shot up to mine, then to the dagger in my hand.

"Get out!"

Eyes wide, he stumbled back a few steps, then turned and ran.

My lungs seared with each terrible breath. Each breath that went on and on and on, because I wasn't dead, because I hadn't trapped my sister's killer, I hadn't got revenge, I hadn't...

I'd failed again.

The astrolabe wasn't even the killer's—it had been *hers*. Briefly. Just for that night. But hers.

If Cadan wasn't the one, who fucking was? *Who?*

I sank against the table, vision blurring with stupid tears of frustration.

"Zita?" Sepher's voice.

"It wasn't—"

"I know. I heard it all. That's the only reason I let him leave." His hands closed around my shoulders. "I'm... I'm sorry."

I frowned up at him. "I thought you didn't apologise."

"This..." He sighed, eyebrows pulling together like my pain was his. "This and you are the exception. To a lot of things." The corner of his mouth tugged, but everything about his expression was edged with sadness and frustration.

"This whole night... all this planning... for nothing." The astrolabe's edges bit into my fingers.

He stroked the hair from my face with just the tips of his claws. "We'll make a new plan. I'll extend their invitation. Or we'll outright ask each of them in turn. Screw subtlety. I'll make them tell us. They won't be able to lie."

So patient. So rational. But I wasn't in a rational place. I was drowning in disappointment and hurt and anger, and my lingering grief was a distant tidal wave closing in, ready to finish the job.

Much as I'd accepted death as an inevitable outcome of my vengeance, I wasn't ready to let anything drag me under until I'd taken the one who'd taken her.

Shaking my head, I twisted away. "I need..." I tossed the

astrolabe on the table, but my fingers wouldn't give up the dagger. "I need some time."

He stood back, hands fisted at his sides. "We can go back to our—"

"Time alone." It came out far harsher than I'd intended, but he didn't flinch.

After everything we'd done to each other, of course he didn't.

"Zinnia and I"—I softened my voice—"we would go up on the catwalks to chat. It's hard to get privacy in a performance troupe, but we found it there. It's where I do my best thinking."

For a moment, he stood there, stiff and frowning. At last he exhaled. "Fine. But keep that on you." He nodded at the dagger. "I want you armed. Just in case."

I raised an eyebrow. "You didn't arm me when you left me to walk back to our room from the dining room, your come on my belly." I couldn't let him get away with that.

"You really think I left you to walk through the halls in tattered clothes stinking of sex?" He shook his head, the furrow in his brow deepening. "I followed at a distance. I watched you the whole way back."

Through my haze of disappointment, it hit me. Even amongst the hurt, there had been care. After I'd nearly died in the snow, his punishments had shifted to things that didn't truly endanger me. There had been no more hunts where his friends might get hold of me. There had been no hounds. It had all been *different* after that.

I rubbed my head, not able to process this alongside Cadan's revelation about Zinnia.

"We'll talk in the morning," Sepher murmured, "find a way that doesn't involve you killing them all." The sardonic twist of his mouth lit the smallest flame of happiness inside me.

I nodded and headed backstage. Before I ducked behind the curtains to the steep staircase leading up to the catwalks, I paused and watched him stalk away along the theatre's aisle. His squared shoulders spelled out his tension. My pushing him away had hurt him, but he'd still given me space.

Yet hurting him hurt me.

"Sepher." I said it softly, but even before he stopped and turned, I knew his shapechanger hearing would pick it up. "It's Marigold."

With a small frown, he cocked his head in question.

"My name. It's Marigold."

He didn't laugh. He didn't mock or tease me about how sweet a name it was. He simply stood there a long while before giving a soft smile and nodding like it made sense.

Then he was gone.

I climbed to the old theatre's jumbled catwalks and circled right around to the central walkway. From here, I could see the entire stage. The astrolabe. The empty glasses. The discarded chairs. It was like seeing the whole table in poker, along with every hand.

But right now, I only knew what Sepher and Cadan held. And the game was about to end.

My eyes blurred again at the unfairness of it all. Zinnia deserved better than this. I'd worked so hard, and I was so sure it would lure the killer out. It had been enough to bring Cadan to me, hadn't it? Why not—?

The scuff of a shoe on wood snagged my thoughts.

At the end of the walkway, silhouetted against the dim light, stood a figure.

48

A man. Not as big as Sepher. No horns like Roark. Was it Cadan? Had he come back to talk about Zinnia? Had he somehow hidden a lie and really was her killer?

Questions clamoured in my throat as the figure approached, his stride light and assured on the narrow walkway. He was familiar, of course. I knew all the fae who lived here, now, and I'd spent a month studying the suspects.

Up here, I was in a precarious position—he blocked the only way off this catwalk. One of the other walkways might be close enough to jump to, but they hadn't all been repaired in Sepher's refurbishment. Some rattled and shook under the weight of a single step.

I rose, pushing a smile to my face, hiding the dagger in the folds of my skirt. "Hello?"

He didn't answer, just continued that well-balanced stride closer.

Wait. I knew that stride, the lithe muscles of his arms and shoulders. I'd known them a long, long while.

"Eric?"

Dark hair gleaming, he stepped into the light with a smile I couldn't help returning. "I watched your performance from up here." He shook his head. "You were incredible. The best I've ever seen."

"What the hells are you doing here?" A laugh of disbelief edged my words.

His brow furrowed as he took another step closer, almost within arm's reach. But something stopped me from going forward and hugging him. "The fae wouldn't give you back, so I've come to take you."

Like his letter. "What if I don't want to leave?"

The lines on his brow deepened as he came closer and snorted. "What? Why the hells would you want to stay here with him?"

My jaw ratcheted tighter at his assumption, and my brain threw at me the image of the last time I'd seen him. "And why the hells would I want to leave with you when you betrayed me?"

He sucked in a breath, eyebrows shooting up before they clashed together. He bent in, looming over me. "I admit that was hasty. I handed you over because... because of how you reacted... or *didn't*. I told you I loved you, Zita, and you... you..." He shook his head, gaze raking over me. "You're just like her. Blank." He bared his teeth, the small canines all wrong. "There's something wrong with you."

Something in his tone made me back away when he advanced, but my mind caught on how odd his teeth looked compared to the fae ones I'd grown used to.

"You were both broken, unfeeling wretches."

"Both?" I held the rail, not for balance, but to feel for one of the upright supports. It would warn me I was reaching the end of the catwalk. I didn't dare look away from the strange intensity in his eyes.

"I tried, Zita. I *tried* to make you feel, to make you feel *me*. But..." His chest heaved. "You reacted just like she did. She didn't care that I loved her, either."

I missed a step. He closed in as I exhaled her name. "Zinnia."

"Of course fucking Zinnia." His smile was tight as the words burst from him, flecked with spittle. "I thought handing you over to him would feel good. And if there was any lingering guilt, the money would soothe that, right?"

For a second, I thought the music had started again, but it was my pulse drumming in my ears. My breaths sped, shallow. My feet moved back of their own accord—they understood something the rest of me didn't yet.

"But," he went on, "it didn't feel as good as my hand around her throat. It didn't feel as good as knowing I was the last person she saw, the last voice she heard, the last man who had her."

No. *No.*

He was... he was angry and trying to scare me into coming with him. This wasn't—

He held something up to the light—the ring he always wore, a sovereign with a flower etched in its flat surface. It glinted gold as he turned it. Behind the sovereign design, tucked in the back where it would be hidden against his skin as he wore it...

The rhythm in my ears built—louder, faster, like a performance coming to its crescendo.

A carefully braided lock of chestnut hair.

The world spun. I clung to the handrail, because without it, I would fall.

When I met his dark gaze, it held no denial. "You..." I shook my head, brain faltering over the impossibility of this. The treachery of it.

I'd cried in his arms that night and many after. I'd given him my virginity, thinking it might soothe me, thinking he wanted me, thinking if nothing else, it was payment for his kindness. I'd shared my plans for revenge with him as they'd built and come together year by year. I hadn't loved him—I couldn't in my deadened state—but it had been the closest I could manage, and I'd called him my friend.

But he'd... he'd been the one behind it. He'd taken my sister. He'd taken my virginity—a stranger in my bed, in my underwear. He'd listened to my grief and anger and hurt and my plans, and he'd taken them all.

No wonder he never liked hearing about my violent fantasies about what I'd do to the killer. No wonder he cringed away from my righteous wrath.

It should've been aimed at him.

Well. Now it was.

I sprang forward, pulse surging, dagger glinting.

As agile as he was on the trapeze, he bent away, evading me even on this narrow catwalk. His grip closed on my wrist as Sepher's had.

Not this time.

I twisted, lashing out with a kick at the same instant. He couldn't dodge that and keep hold of me. I pulled free.

Despite our fitness, we were both panting within seconds. I lunged and slashed, but he was always just out of reach. My burning need wasn't enough to give me immediate victory.

He caught me across the belly when he swung from an overhead bar I hadn't spotted. Breath bursting out, I fell against the catwalk. The only thing I saw was him arcing through the air, feet-first, aiming for my head.

No time for thought, I let instinct throw me off the catwalk.

For a stomach-plummeting moment, I fell.

But my grip closed on one of the upright supports, and my fall became a swing down and around, bringing me to the walkway just behind him.

Barely reaching my feet, I swiped at his exposed back. Some instinct must've warned him, though, because he rolled out of reach.

Our fight might've been beautiful to an observer. We spun and swung from the catwalk's scaffolding. I flipped away from his punch so it only grazed my cheek. He leapt to another walkway, and I followed, dagger clenched between my teeth. I couldn't work magic with the iron blade touching my skin, but I didn't need magic to cut his fucking throat.

Still, the touch made my gut turn, and I landed heavily.

It was the chance he needed.

In a blur, I hit the timber, a weight upon me. The impact jolted my bones, pushing a grunt from my throat.

The dagger fell.

Somehow—some-fucking-how my hand snapped up and caught it by the blade before it dropped to the stage thirty feet below.

Teeth bared, Eric clambered up me. "Your sister was a treacherous fucking bitch, as well."

"Shut your unworthy mouth." I fumbled with the dagger, righting my grip so it was on the hilt. "You don't get to speak about her."

As he rose above me, I slashed.

A grip closed on my wrist.

No. Not again.

The dread cold of defeat welled up in me like water flooding a sinking ship.

I twisted, but his grip tightened. He had my body pinned, too.

But not my other hand.

I dropped the dagger.

Eric didn't stay idle, though. With a grunt, he slid us sideways.

Just as I caught the knife in my right hand, the edge of the narrow walkway bit into my back. It grated down my spine, my backside, and then, once more, I was falling.

49

F uck.
     I jerked to a stop, legs looping around the first thing they could.

As I caught my breath, caught in the miraculous shock of still being alive, I took in how it had happened. My thighs were wrapped around Eric's chest, and he dangled off the walkway, knees hooked around one of the uprights.

We hung there, staring at each other, our panting and the faint squeak of the catwalk's fixings the only sound. For a performance like this, there should've been crashing drums—something dramatic. Not pathetic quiet.

He still held my left wrist, but my right was free and that hand held the dagger.

He twitched like he realised it at the same moment. "You can't kill me. You'll fall." He nodded down to the stage below. "You know at this height, that means death."

We both knew that. We'd attended the funerals of performers and stagehands who'd learned it the hard way.

I held the dagger to his throat.

He stared at me, eyes widening. "You wouldn't."

"Wouldn't I?" I smiled at his shock and fear. "You know I'd give anything to make my sister's murderer pay. Haven't I been telling you that for long enough?"

One inch, and I'd cut his throat. One inch, and his blood would spill over my hand. One inch, and I'd get to taste it.

Then his legs would go slack, and he'd fall, and I'd fall right with him.

We swung gently on the rickety walkway, and I caught a dizzying glimpse of the stage's boards below, so distant, so small.

One inch, and I'd never again see Sepher. One inch, and I'd never again make that muscle in his jaw twitch. One inch, and I'd never get to tell him the words I'd been too cowardly to say out loud.

I'd miss him, but...

Heart pounding like it was begging for life, I halved that inch so my blade touched Eric's vulnerable flesh.

Between my thighs and around my wrist, he went rigid.

Yet I still hesitated.

There had been no hesitation when I tried to kill Sepher.

"Zita!"

With a gasp, I turned.

On the next walkway, reaching out, part man, part beast, it was him.

Seeing him, feeling how it made my heart soar, I understood.

I hadn't hesitated over killing him, because back then I'd had nothing to lose.

But now... Now I had plenty.

"Take my hand." He stretched across the gap, his beast

man form large enough to almost bridge it. If I reached out with my right hand, I would be able to take his.

But that would mean dropping the dagger.

It would mean giving Eric the chance to escape.

I gritted my teeth. "He's the one, Sepher. He killed her."

"I heard."

"I thought you wanted to see him bleed, too."

"I do." His eyebrows squeezed together. "But I don't want to see you bleed for it."

Traitor. It seized my throat. How could he?

His fingers flexed. "Please take my hand, little bird. I'm afraid you cannot fly."

"'Little bird,'" Eric scoffed. "You let this *thing* speak to you like that?"

With a snarl, I pressed the blade to his skin, silencing him. A bead of blood pooled against the iron's edge. The blood I'd wanted all these years, and it had been right before me the whole time.

I shook, muscles screaming, the worst part of me lusting for the thing it had pursued for so long.

"Zita, ignore him. Look at me."

It wasn't even malicious compliance when I obeyed. It was just that I couldn't deny him. I wanted to look at him, even in this shape.

My beautiful, beastly Prince of Monsters watched me with eyebrows knotted together, like he could will me to take his hand with a look.

"I want you to live. I want *you*. As simple as that. As selfish as that." He scoffed. "I am not a good man. I want to possess you and be possessed by you. I want all the best and worst of what that means. I've killed for you before with no remorse, and I will do it again." His golden eyes drilled into the very depths of me, like he could see that I wasn't as horrified by that thought as I should've been.

"But..." There was too much in me, too much clamouring in my chest to say anything more than that. Between my legs, Eric shifted, and I squeezed my thighs tighter. He wasn't going to wriggle free.

"I know you can't lift my curse."

That snapped my attention from Eric. He knew?

But he didn't look angry about the fact I'd lied. The corner of his mouth hinted at a smile. "I've been reading about curse-witches, and every record says their curses are permanent." He shrugged. "But I don't care. I've accepted what I am. I've accepted what happened. I've let go of revenge, not because it was the right thing, but because the cost was too great."

That phrase again. What was the cost of his revenge? What was the price he'd refused to pay?

The question must've shown in the tight lines of my face, because he raised his eyebrows. "Because if I'd taken the revenge I'd promised and killed you, I'd have lost the woman I loved."

It curled through my veins and muscles, chiselled through my bones.

He loved me, and he'd let that trump vengeance.

"Don't die for this, Zita. You've already lost the past ten years to it. I don't want you to lose everything else, too."

There it was, the horrible, choking truth. I hadn't just spent the past decade in a deadened state, I'd spent it as a ghost.

I'd played the part of Zinnia. I'd grown my hair to look like hers. I'd modelled my shows on hers. I'd smiled sweetly at patrons like she had, fucked them like she had, taken their money like she had. Everything—*everything* I'd done for her, like her, so consumed by her death that I'd completely forgotten to live.

That was what he'd meant on the beach.

You're someone who should have a big life, Zita. Huge. Not the stunted thing you've been nursing.

That was why it had shaken me.

He'd been right.

I could see that now I had a life that was bigger than before. One with him, yes, but also with friends like Celestine, Anya, and Essa. Maybe Cadan could become a friend in time —we had Zinnia in common.

Pressure built behind my eyes.

Because even worse, Eric had continued just like before. Performing, laughing with his friends, fucking me. Enjoying life.

While I had nothing to show for my adult years, just this moment. This night. This knife in my hand.

And once I cut his throat, I'd have nothing.

The pressure grew unbearable, threatening to spill over. I shook my head. "I can't just give up. I still haven't given her justice."

"What he did to your sister was awful and it never should've happened. But it did. You can't change it. You can't bring her back. But you can stop yourself from being lost to it forever. You've given ten years to revenge. Your sister's shade will be happy with that. But ten years is enough."

Was it, though? Was anything enough? My throat closed around my harsh breaths.

Sepher nodded gently, his fingers flexing in the air before me. "*Enough.* You've given enough. Now give the rest of your life to living... with me."

The rest of my life? I frowned at the blade, checked it was still at Eric's throat, then up at Sepher.

His eyebrows rose and one canine flashed in a crooked grin. "You dangling above a stage with your dagger at someone's throat—not how I'd planned to do it, but considering how we met, it makes sense." He drew a deep breath, the stripes at his sides shifting and stretching. "Selfishly, I don't want you to die, Zita, because I want to keep you around... not as my pet, but as my wife."

50

The world went still. Eric might've said something, but I couldn't hear him over my pulse and Sepher's words, which were just as vital.

He wanted...?

"You are sharp and sour. Focused and as stubborn as an aurochs. I don't think I could budge you unless you wanted to be budged. And I wouldn't have it any other way." His long, curved fangs gleamed as he smiled. "Because I love all this about you. I love the way you cut me. I love how you challenge me. I love the bite of your razor-edged tongue, the viciousness of your wit. Believe me, it kills me to ask you to let him go for now, because I am hungry to see your righteous rage in all its bloodthirsty glory."

That pressure was back in my eyes, but for an entirely different reason.

He saw me.

Sun and fucking Stars, he saw me.

And he loved me for it all.

He didn't try to blunt my sharpness or soften my edges. He wanted those edges, held them close so he could feel their cut, licked them like beloved razor blades.

"I may be a prince, but you are my queen. And I will kneel before you a hundred times if it gets you to agree to live and let me be your husband."

No wonder he'd flinched when I'd said he was like Eric: he wasn't like him. Not at all. Because he saw me, all of me, and he wanted that. He wanted to save that person so he could spend his life with her—with me. With who I really was, not my stage persona or a version of me he'd conjured in his mind, not with my sister's ghost.

With *me*.

There was only one answer I could give.

The knife clattered to the stage below, ringing in the silent theatre.

But I wasn't done. Not yet.

Hand now free, I embraced the sizzling power in my veins, called to it, beckoned like I was seducing it.

I smiled at Eric, and I pointed.

"May you get the justice you deserve."

My gift buzzed in the air like a swarm of angry bees. Every hair on Eric's head stood on end. Goosebumps pricked his forearm as his grip on my wrist faltered.

A curse wasn't death, but it would have to do.

For now.

I took Sepher's hand. At once, his hold was sure, and I let my thighs loosen from Eric's chest. As I swung across the gap, Sepher lifted me with ease, and I ended up in his arms.

His shoulders sank as he breathed a sigh of relief. "Zita."

I clung to him, inhaling his musk and fresh air scent, even

as I watched Eric right himself and run away into the theatre's shadows.

"It's only temporary," Sepher growled, as though he could feel how Eric's escape grated on my bones. "We know who it was now. He only got away with it for so long because no one knew." He cupped my cheek. "You cursed him with justice. He can't escape that."

"I hope you're right." But even as I said that, the heat of him burned through me, and I knew I'd made the right decision. I was alive, and I'd be able to bask in that heat for a long while. There'd still be time for revenge—I didn't need to let it consume me.

He answered with a slow smirk. "I know I am."

I rolled my eyes. "Of course you do."

He nuzzled me, sniffing over and over like he could inhale not just my scent, but me. "At the end of your performance, I could smell another human. I thought it was just the lingering scent of the Gilded Suns on your equipment." A low growl laced his sigh. "I should've known."

That moment when he'd sniffed the air. It made sense now.

"You couldn't have known." I touched my nose to his, enjoying the simple pleasure of his proximity. "Did you mean all that just now, or was it just to get me to take your hand?"

"Every word. No lies. No twisting of the truth. I love every part of you, Zita, good and bad... especially the bad." He flashed a wicked grin, one hand fisting in my hair. "I'd get down on my knees now if this walkway wasn't so damn small. But..." Grunting, he shrugged and tightened his hold around my waist.

With no more warning than that, he leapt. I jerked, not at the sensation of falling, but the fact that stopping it was in someone else's control. Yet I wasn't as afraid as I should've been.

He caught the rail from another catwalk, which shuddered and groaned under the weight of his beastly form. Then he swung us to another, and another, until he leapt the final distance to the stage. Above, the old walkways screeched and pinged from their fixings.

But before me, my prince kneeled.

As scaffolding crashed to the stage, he held my hips and my gaze with complete intensity, as though he knew the falling debris wouldn't dare strike us. "Zita, Marigold, my wicked witch, my little bird of prey, my queen. Will you let me be your husband?"

I lifted my chin, like I really was a queen. "Ask me with your claws."

He unsheathed them just enough to prick through my clothes, and I relished the vitality of their points threatening to pierce my skin. He murmured, "Will you, love?"

Instead of answering, I lowered to my knees and cupped his beastly face. "When I told you I hated you, I didn't mean that—not entirely. And when I told you my name... I meant more than that."

"I know. You were saying you loved me, too."

I scoffed that he'd known what I couldn't say. "I do. I love you." I kissed him, briefly but deeply. "And if you knew that, then you also know my answer."

His smile was lopsided, foolish, his eyes hooded, like my kiss had left him in a daze. But his hand snaked into my hair and gripped it, tilting my head back. "Say it."

"I will be the curse you cannot shake, Sepher. I will marry you and only leave you once our bones are dust and the world has ceased to care who we were."

He stayed still for a long, long time, like he was trying to sear the moment into his mind like a brand. At last he exhaled, eyes sinking shut. "So perfect. I knew I'd break you in the end." He grinned, nuzzling his nose to mine. "I just didn't realise that you would break me, too."

I laughed as I squeezed him closer, loving the solid reality of his huge body.

I was alive and ready to start truly living.

5I

Frustratingly, one of my first tasks in "living" involved waving Sepher off the next morning. He needed to travel to Luminis and pave the way for an official visit where we'd enter the city as an engaged couple.

When I'd accepted his proposal, his royalty was still an abstract idea. However, as I crunched across the gravel drive, arm-in-arm with Celestine, thinking about the need for a parade, it struck me like a very solid brick.

She grinned, delicate canines flashing. "So, should I start calling you 'princess' now, or should I wait until you're actually married?"

I shot her a scowl. "You just call Sepher by his name."

"Yes, but that's because he's basically my brother." She shrugged as we entered the beautifully crumbling palace.

I bit my lip as we wound through corridors I now knew almost as well as I knew Sepher's stripes.

When we reached her rooms, she cocked her head and frowned, holding my shoulders so I couldn't sit. "What's wrong? You're not having second thoughts, are you? I was only teasing."

"No. I..." I swallowed down the thickness in my throat that had built on our walk. "I think that, given a little time, you could be something like a sister to me."

Slowly, like the sun rising, her eyes widened and brimmed with tears. "A sister? I know yours was taken from you, so I'm truly honoured the thought has even crossed your mind."

"You're honest with me like she was. You know I'm not sweet. You've tasted my sharpness, but you're still here."

"Of course I am." With a tremulous smile, she threw her arms around me. "That's what family does. Whether we're bound by blood or by choice, we remain."

THE CROWD ROARED, louder than any audience I'd performed for. It hit me even harder, larger, more overpowering than any brick. Sepher was a prince. Second in line to Dawn's throne. And I was going to become his bride.

Insanity.

As was the fact I rode a stag through the streets of Luminis, a future princess, not just a performer. I drank up the way they looked at me, the admiring glances.

But amongst the cheers, there were frowns and curious stares, and folk spoke behind their hands to one another.

At my side, astride a huge stag, looking resplendent in hunter green and his gold crown, Sepher smiled and waved like he hadn't noticed.

I knew he had.

"Should I strangle one of them with my tail?" he gritted

out between his smile. "Give them something to really stare at?"

I laughed like he'd told me a charming joke and not a ghoulish one. "I think the Prince of Monsters riding with his human bride-to-be is quite enough of a spectacle for one day."

"It is." He turned his attention from the crowd and his smile softened to something sincere. "And I don't think even a little casual murdering would be enough to overshadow you."

Warmed by his molten gold gaze, I steered closer as we turned onto a wide thoroughfare lined by shimmering iridescent buildings. Despite their beauty, the thought that he might be hurt by these strangers slithered in me. "Are you...? I'm sure their stares are only curious."

He shrugged and touched my thigh. "I don't give a solitary fuck what they think of me. I'm a shapechanger. That is the magic the gods gifted me with. They may look down on me, and my father might prefer I stay away from his court, rather than tainting it with the embarrassment of my existence. But screw them. I accept myself, thanks to you."

I sucked in a soft breath. "But I forced you like this. I made you—"

"You made me live like this for ten years. You made me accept my magic. And when you returned to my life, you accepted and loved and wanted me, whatever my form." He lifted his chin and smiled. "If that's not a gift, I don't know what is."

My chest tightened, but I still managed to say, "You are beautiful in every form, Sepher."

If anything, he only sat taller, and I knew that if he'd been in his feline form, he'd have wanted me to scratch under his chin at this moment.

It probably wouldn't have projected quite the right appearance for a prince of Elfhame returning to the capital.

He grazed the silk of my gown, not quite snagging it. "These claws are as much a part of me as my heart, as cold as that may sometimes be."

"You? Cold-hearted?" I snorted.

"Not for you. Never for you." He squeezed, and his claws pierced my dress.

"Sepher!" I scowled, but he just chuckled and spread his hands as though helpless.

"I was only going to tear it off you later, anyway."

I didn't let the heat of that promise soften my glare. "Yes, but now I'm going to be presented to your parents with holes in my dress."

Instead of replying, he pressed his lips together as though fighting a smirk and looked away.

But when we entered the glittering palace, perched atop its volcanic peak at the centre of the city, he didn't lead me along its wide corridors to a throne room.

He took me down.

52

The staircases grew narrower and darker as we descended. Some were hewn from rock and made for much taller people than I. He helped me down those.

"Where are we going?"

Pupils wide in the gloom, he surveyed the corridor ahead. "You'll see."

Down, down, down, we went, until at last we reached a large door that looked like it had been carved from the black rock of the volcano. "Some benefits of royalty," he explained when it ground open at his touch.

Deeper darkness gathered beyond, but at the end awaited a flickering lantern.

Dread crept down my spine, digging its talons into my vertebrae. "I thought I was being presented to your parents."

"After. First, I have something to present to *you*. A wedding gift."

I wasn't sure I wanted to see what waited in the lantern-light, but he offered me his hand and I took it, drawing comfort from his hot skin.

On either side of the corridor stood doors with barred windows and hatches just large enough to fit a tray through.

This was a dungeon.

The realisation twisted my stomach. If he'd brought me here to be punished, I had to give it to him for playing a very long game indeed. But, no, I didn't believe that. I trusted him.

As though sensing my discomfort, his fingers tightened around mine and he kissed my knuckles. "It's almost time."

When we reached the edge of the lamplight, the corridor opened out into a room lined with pillars carved of the same black rock. At the centre, two masked guards held a stooped man. Their gleaming armour looked something like leather but not quite, and on their chests they wore the insignia of Dawn Court—a blazing sun emerging from a dark horizon.

Covered in grime and blood, their prisoner clearly hadn't arrived in the dungeons this morning. Yet beneath the dirt and his tattered clothes, his arms and legs were still well-muscled. They hadn't imprisoned him long enough for that to wither.

I frowned from the guards to Sepher. "I don't—"

The prisoner's head snapped up at the sound of my voice.

A single dark eye stared at me, wide and bloodshot. A bloody bandage covered the other, and bruising puffed up that side of his face. I still knew him, though.

I would know him anywhere.

"Eric."

The air sucked from my lungs. My fingers spasmed against Sepher's. It was a month since I'd seen him, but the rage flooding my veins was just as hot as it had been on the theatre's catwalks.

Sepher disentangled himself from me and went to a low table between two pillars that I hadn't spotted as we'd entered. "Since he's your wedding gift, I considered tying a bow around his neck, but Celestine insisted it was in poor taste." His smile was edged as he turned from the table, holding a sword as long as I was tall. "So I put one on this instead."

Sure enough, a black satin bow gleamed around the sword's hilt. It might've been merry if not for the colour or the dark lick of magic that cut through the air.

"After all, I'm really giving you the gift of justice." He held the sword out for me to inspect.

A black snake and a silver one coiled together to form its crossguard and hilt. Tiny silver stars inlaid the black snake's body, while dark voids studded the silver snake with constellations. Dark, decimating magic poured off it in waves.

I frowned up at him. "I don't understand."

"I didn't give you the entire truth when I said I was here informing my parents of our engagement." He twisted his mouth. "I did do that, but first I hunted him down. I wasn't sure how long it would take to find him, so I didn't want to tell you and get your hopes up." His eyes narrowed. "I have a feeling you're going to forgive me, though."

My mouth was dry. My heart thudded, resonating through my whole body, like I was a drum being struck in a slow, consuming beat.

"He confessed, so his life is yours, just as yours was mine, once upon a time." The corner of his mouth twitched.

I glanced at Eric, who bowed his head as though afraid of being seen looking at me.

"I may have helped with the questioning." Sepher's upper lip curled as he watched Eric, the gold in his eyes keen like it had been forged into a blade. "You have the same choice I did. Execution"—he lifted the sword—"or he belongs to you for the rest of his days or until you choose to set him free."

I'd made my choice a long time ago, but I frowned at the wicked sharp edge of the sword. "I can't lift that."

"It's enchanted. Even the smallest, weakest child can wield it if it's being used in service of justice. If you want it, take it." He presented it to me, bowing.

The guards shifted, as though surprised to see their prince bow to anyone.

I closed my fingers around the hilt. The two serpents flexed like they were alive, and I almost dropped it in shock, but they pressed *into* my grip as though welcoming it.

Just as Sepher had promised, I lifted the sword and found it as light and balanced as the iron dagger he'd reforged for me.

The sword's magic pulsed in wave after wave, overwhelming. But second by second the beat of my heart aligned with its rhythm, pounding in my ears, my veins, under my feet, like the floor trembled with it.

It was like lying on Sepher's chest after making love, listening to his heart. It was like learning to lie with him in the sun. It was like throwing myself into a song's crescendo.

It was right.

"No, no." Eye wide, Eric shook his head as I approached.

I wondered if they'd taken the other one as part of his questioning. I would ask Sepher later.

"Please. Zita. No. You don't want to do this. Don't."

The guards held him still, without difficulty.

"Please," he whimpered. "Zinnia would have wanted you to spare me."

346

"On your knees." My voice wasn't my own. Two more joined it, light and dark, echoing through the chamber.

The guards let go and, begging all the way, Eric obeyed as though he couldn't help it.

I was aware of Sepher on the edge of my vision, but for this moment, all my attention was on Eric. And I knew—*knew* my prince wouldn't try to stop me from claiming vengeance.

"Ten years ago, you took a life. You thought you got away with it. But now your life is forfeit. Bend over."

He bent to my will, squealing like he'd forgotten how to speak.

"Zinnia may have wanted me to spare you. But I am not her. She is gone. You took her, and now I take you."

I lifted the sword.

I let it fall.

There wasn't even a moment of resistance, just a dull thud as Eric's head hit the floor, followed a second later by his body slumping.

It was a clean death. Quicker, smoother, kinder than he deserved. But as I stared at his blood pooling on the floor, lapping at my shoes, I was glad.

Driven by something deep inside, I swiped my fingers along the flat of the blade and licked away the crimson.

Copper and iron and salt.

It didn't bring me peace—I'd already claimed that for myself in my new life—but it was cleansing.

And, perhaps, most of all, it was a relief.

The obsession that had suffocated me for so long ebbed away with the sword's magic, as the blade grew heavier in my hand. I took a deep, deep breath, deeper than any I had drawn in years, and surrendered the sword to Sepher.

It was done.

EPILOGUE

I paused at the door that led from the bathroom, a little zing of nervousness darting through my veins.

Technically, I wasn't his pet anymore, so I didn't need his permission, but still. Sometimes I liked to ask for it or challenge it or outright disobey him. It always led us to such *interesting* places.

I touched the blunt ends of my freshly cut hair. It hung an inch above my shoulders in thick, choppy waves. In the mirror, with my newly regrown teeth, it looked good. It looked... like me. Or at least the person I was becoming, rather than the sister I'd mimicked.

Despite the change between us and my continuing thrill at disobeying him, I wanted Sepher to like this.

Still, if he didn't, it wasn't the end of the world.

I thought I'd gone through that the night I found him standing over Zinnia. But that wasn't the end. It wasn't even the beginning. It just was another doorway I'd stepped through. And that corridor had stretched on and on and on, twisting and turning like a maze I thought I'd never escape.

But I had.

And now I was here with a life and an identity of my own to build, a *me* to get to know.

It wasn't going to be easy. But when had anything in life been easy?

Sepher and I had got through the worst of each other. We'd got through the whispers and stares of Luminis, and the stiff welcome from his parents a few weeks ago. Together, we could get through anything.

Thinking of that, unable to control my smile, I stepped into our bedroom.

From the armchair before the fireplace, Sepher's gaze snapped to me at once.

The closeness of his attention still had the power to make my heart skip a soaring beat.

As he took me in, his eyes went so wide, they were in danger of falling out. "You cut your hair."

"Ten out of ten for observation." I smirked at him. "What do you think?" I fussed it, enjoying how much lighter it felt.

"Hmm." His eyes narrowed as he put down his drink. "Come here. Let me get a closer look."

Something inside me said *danger*, a delicious thrill that sent my pulse racing. "I thought it would be better for the beach tomorrow," I said with a shrug, like I wasn't aware of the trap he was laying for me.

"You know I'm going to fuck you in the sand."

The rawness of his words pulled my muscles tight. "I'm counting on it."

"Good."

I took my time approaching, not technically disobeying his

instruction, but edging towards rebellion, pushing his patience, tempting his punishment.

I paused at the table and stroked the ink and watercolour picture I was working on. As part of discovering myself, I was diving into the art supplies he'd bought me, and this was an initial study of Zinnia. I was pleased at how I'd managed to capture the complex shades in her hair and the sweet light in her eyes.

Sepher had promised that when I produced a painting I wanted to display, he would make a prominent space for it in the palace. Somewhere we'd see it every day and remember.

"Little bird," he growled. "You wouldn't be disobeying my instruction, would you?"

For a moment longer, I smiled at my sister's face, at the way the colour made her look more alive than she ever had in my pencil or charcoal sketches. Then, I turned to Sepher with wide, innocent eyes, and clutched my chest. "Disobey? Me? I wouldn't dare."

I couldn't bite back my grin as I closed the distance between us.

"Malicious compliance," he muttered, shaking his head.

"I'm perfectly well-behaved, I'll have you know." I stopped just outside arm's reach and gave him a twirl. "Well?"

"I need to check something." Eyes hooded, he beckoned me closer.

My pulse sped even faster as I slid into his lap.

"There's a good girl." His claws grazed up the back of my neck, chasing goosebumps over my shoulders. He took a fist of my hair. "Ah, yes, I can still do this." His teeth flashed in a teasing smile. "I wouldn't have liked it if I couldn't get a good handful of it, but this is perfect." The mocking edge to his expression faded, and he ran his nose along mine. "It looks very... *you*. So, of course, I love it."

I arched in his hold, loving the attention almost as much as his words.

He'd watched me like a hunter, but the predator in him *saw* me. He'd seen when I hadn't been living. He'd seen what I hadn't yet understood. And now, maybe he saw a little more of the woman I was discovering inside.

I kissed him for it. Deep, slow, sweet, and sharp. I pressed my tongue to his canines, savouring the speck of pain as I let him taste a little of my blood. With light strokes of my fingertips, I teased his ears and ate up the rumbling groan it dragged from him.

"But," he said against my lips, gripping my hair so I couldn't continue our kiss, "I don't recall giving you permission to cut your hair."

"Oops," I breathed. "I probably need punishing for that, don't I? Should I wear my collar?"

His smile was the private one that tangled my insides. "*Only* your collar."

A thrill ran through me, right to my centre. I might've been his pet once, with no choice in the matter, but sometimes it was fun to choose to play that part for an evening.

That probably said something about me and the pleasure I derived from defiance and pain. It definitely said something about my prince—my beloved monster. There were layers upon layers I could dig down to, beyond what I'd already uncovered about him and myself.

And I was excited to have the chance to get to know both of those people better.

Killing had been a good revenge, but living happily would be an even better one.

THE END

Read on for a note from the author plus a preview of
Slaying the Frost King by Candace Robinson and Elle
Beaumont—the next book in
Mortal Enemies to Monster Lovers!

AUTHOR'S NOTE

Thanks so much for picking up *Slaying the Shifter Prince*! I hope you enjoyed Zita and Sepher's twisted little tale.

This was an interesting one to write. If you've read my other books, you'll know this is a bit of a departure for me. Morally grey enemies-to-lovers, yep, I'm into that, but a villainous hero? And the punishments he deals out to Zita? That was definitely new territory.

And I fucking loved it! It was so much fun to write their antagonism and Zita's sheer grit and determination to (say it with me) **not. Back. Down.**

If you enjoyed this book, it would make a huge difference to me and other readers if you would leave a review on Amazon and/or Goodreads. Reviews help others decide to take a chance on a book and that will give you more people to squee with about Zita and Sepher.

And if you're going to miss them, don't worry! You haven't seen the last of these two. They have their HEA, but they still have a part to play in the Sabreverse.

All my books are set in the same world, with characters cropping up in other books/series. You might want to start my Shadows of the Tenebris Court series, which begins with *A Kiss of Iron*. Not to give any spoilers for books two and three, but... if you'd like more of Zita and Sepher, this is a good place to start...

If you'd like to keep in touch and be the first to know about new releases, pretty character art, and any other book news, join my newsletter (I give out some free books and other good stuff to thank people for joining) or follow me on Instagram.

Thank you again for joining me in Zita and Sepher's story and, always, happy reading! <3

All the best,

Clare, February 2023
  x

SLAYING THE FROST KING

PREVIEW

CANDACE ROBINSON & ELLE BEAUMONT

I

MOROZKO

Snow fell onto the cobblestones in the castle's courtyard, painting the picture of serenity—or at least it would have—had it not been for the writhing body beneath Morozko's boot.

Whimpers escaped from the mortal, and he clawed at the ice, chipping away his nails in a futile attempt to escape the king.

The wind in the mountains whipped through Morozko's hair, catching on his nose. "Stop moving. You're sullying the ground with your blood." Morozko frowned, motioning to the flecks of red soaking through the snowdrifts. Soon enough, the mortal would cease moving—he was, after all, a treasonous wretch.

Not only had he been milling around the castle, which was forbidden unless summoned, but he—and the entire village of Vinti—had chosen not to hold a ceremony that had taken place for centuries. It was not only Morozko's honor at stake but so much more. Certainly, the villagers thought it wise to continue celebrating but somehow forgot the most significant part of the ceremony: the animal sacrifice.

Oh, but Vinti believed themselves clever by dancing around their bonfire, drinking, and partaking in food meant to celebrate the animal's spilled blood. They not only slighted and mocked him but Frosteria as well.

The Frost King would remedy that.

How fortunate Morozko was to send an emissary to witness it all, and said emissary was accompanied by the captain of the royal guard, Andras.

Andras had done well by capturing the flailing man, bringing the mortal to Morozko for him to question and, if he felt so inclined, torture.

Morozko increased the pressure of his boot, and the human's life spilled further from a gash on his side. The flesh peeled away, revealing muscle and bone. "I—I told the captain," the male coughed, "it was the chieftain's decision to pass on the sacrifice. Not all of us wanted to displease you so. But we lost a lot of our livestock in the past storm." His body convulsed. "Please, sire, please. We only thought—"

"That is just it, mortal. You didn't think at all. None of you did. You could have easily cast one of your own on the slab instead of an animal and have been done with it." Removing his foot from the man, Morozko turned away and stepped toward the captain of the guard. The frost demon's crimson hair danced in the wind, and Andras didn't so much as blink as Morozko pulled the captain's sword free.

"But Vinti couldn't even do that. The village will pay, starting with you." Morozko narrowed his eyes as fury rose within.

All Morozko had asked once they had slain his mother was to hold a ceremony—a ritual—where they would sacrifice an animal on an altar, allowing the blood to saturate the ground, and speak the words she demanded of them. *Let this blood sate you. Let this blood please you. It is freely given in remembrance of your life.* Leave it to Maranna to want praise even in death. He snorted.

Morozko's mother had been a cruel and unfair ruler, which was why she was overthrown and murdered by the mortals. If it hadn't been for her foresight to hide Morozko in an ice cavern, he likely would have been slain, too. But his guards took pity on him, protected him, and assured the masses Morozko was different, and in some ways, he was.

The mortal slapped his hand at the ground, pulling himself to his feet, and swayed. "Have mercy, Your Majesty, I beg of you."

Morozko looked into the eyes of the captain, who watched the futile attempt to escape. He shrugged one shoulder and sucked in his bottom lip, then spun on his heel, throwing the sword. It flew hilt over tip until it met its mark in the villager's back with a sickening squelch. The man fell to the ice at once, twitching until he moved no more.

"A pity your blood is a waste and couldn't save someone else." Alas, his body wasn't on an altar, nor were the sacrificial words spoken. Morozko's lip curled in disgust as he turned away. "Sever his hand. Make sure Vinti receives their gift of *gratitude,* with the explicit instructions that they're to hold a ceremony in a week's time. Oh... and clean up this damn mess." When Morozko stepped away from the captain, strands of his white hair fell into his view. Crimson marred his pristine tresses. He scowled, wiping at his face, which also had flecks of blood. What a mess the mortal had made. Sighing, he walked toward the entrance of the castle, and two guards opened the massive ebony doors.

"Missives have arrived and are in your study, Your Majesty." Ulva, one of his servants, bobbed a quick curtsy before disappearing down the long, winding hallway.

Letters from peasants in the villages, or perhaps noblemen trying to pawn their daughter off on him, swearing her hair was a fine shade of gold. He was not in want of a wife, but a plaything. He was always in need of one of *those*.

Morozko's boots fell heavily on the marble flooring, echoing off the walls. Even the promise of a warm body against his wasn't enough to distract him. The foolish mortals didn't have any knowledge as to *why* the sacrifices needed to continue.

He frowned. His steward, Xezu, was nowhere in sight. There were matters to address, a *celebration* to prepare for. Where was he?

Not having the mortal in his reach gave him time to consider the refusal. More than his pride was at stake. Unrest lapped at Morozko's patience, akin to a dam readying to burst. The mortals did not know what they'd done. Their world as they knew it could crumble with just this one minor misstep.

He gritted his teeth, scanning the foyer and the grand staircase. Xezu was still nowhere to be found. "Where is that mortal?" he growled, flinging his cape back lest it tangle in front of him.

Morozko didn't want to think of his mother or the curse she'd laid on the land. The queen had protected him from outside evils, but that didn't mean he was safe from *her*. There was a definite lack of maternal instinct.

Morozko never knew his father. In fact, his father hadn't lived long past Morozko's conception because Maranna had driven a blade of ice through his heart. It was something she'd gloated about.

To Maranna, her son was another subject, another pawn that was of use to her. A means to continue her line and ensure her rule.

Her death hadn't struck him in the heart, but it *had* made his blood boil because the humans had thought to rise against their superiors—their prince.

"Xezu!" he bellowed for his steward.

The middle-aged human male rounded a corner. His long, dark hair was neatly braided and fell over his shoulder as he bowed at the waist. Soft lines crinkled the corners of his eyes, but his sun-kissed face was otherwise smooth. "Your Majesty."

The steward of Frosteria sullied his hands, so Morozko didn't have to, but that didn't mean the king wouldn't. The proof of that was in his hair and on his fingers. But Xezu was his second in-command and when the king needed him, the mortal did whatever was asked of him.

"Unfortunately, the mortals have thought themselves clever and didn't perform the ritual." He sauntered toward Xezu, sneering. "And you know what that means." A flicker of surprise—and possibly fear—entered his steward's gaze. Morozko was anything but gleeful, but he didn't want to show the uptick of panic within. Of how the *others* would knock at the seal that his darling mother loosened. Morozko could almost hear the claws scraping at the magical seal, the high-pitched keening...

"But that means..."

His steward knew the truth. Once a villager himself, Xezu was oblivious to the reason behind it. Now, in Morozko's service, he knew and feared the dire consequences. Rightfully so.

"Precisely. Therefore, they will be forced to sacrifice one of their own. We don't want to ruffle mother dearest's feathers, dead or not. Her curse is alive and well." Morozko reached forward, his fingers taking hold of the popped collar on Xezu's leather uniform. "We will not risk being overrun by my mother's creatures, do you understand?" He gave a tug on the fabric, then smiled mirthlessly.

Xezu bowed his head. "Y-yes, Your Majesty."

Morozko started to walk away, then turned his head. "Find Andras before he leaves. Make certain Vinti puts their all into this ritual. They're to make it bolder. The bonfire, the feast, the music... They're to decorate their entire village." He paused, his smile widening into one of wicked delight. "This time, their sacrifice will be one of their own. And I will decide who it shall be because *I* will be there to ensure they're holding up their end of this age-old bargain." He'd take the one that would hurt the village most. The one the village sought to protect because he wanted the cut to sting.

Xezu blinked. "You mean to go there yourself?"

"Indeed. I don't trust them now, and if I'm not present, who is to say they won't try to spite me again?"

His steward seemed to understand the reasoning and nodded. "Very well. I will relay this to Andras, Your Majesty."

He'd better.

For now, a hot bath was a top priority.

The white marble flooring gave way to a black staircase. The balusters looked like willow branches, and their gnarled limbs twisted around one another, jutting toward the railing.

Morozko ascended the stairs and unbuttoned his doublet. By the time he reached his chamber, he'd slid the article of clothing off and tossed it.

A grand bed sat in the middle of the room, and four black walnut posts held up a silken canopy of white. The far wall was mostly a window that looked over the mountain range, and on most days, mist or snow clouds cloaked their massive forms. But on clear days, the sharp contours of the mountains and the snow-covered valleys were visible. And at night, the vibrant blue, green, and purple hues danced like a banner in the wind.

Sauntering into his washroom, he filled the bath. Steaming water hit the porcelain, and the heat rushed into his face. He removed the rest of his clothing, then stepped in, groaning as the heat lapped at his ankles and calves.

The warmth ate away at the tension in his form but did nothing to quell the fury bubbling within. Mortals always thought they knew better with their novel ideas and new ways to accomplish tasks. When in truth, the old ways were there for a reason...

"You wretched fools." Morozko swiped at the water, glowering as he cupped a handful and poured it over his head. "And yet, I'd be the one you'd blame after all that I've done for Frosteria."

After all the protection he offered.

The peace.

Now it was *they* who threatened to disrupt it. And the blame would rest on his head, like a crown of daggers.

No. He wouldn't allow it. The mortals would pay.

2

EIRAH

Mortality in a world of immortals was but a weakness. Even the animals outside Eirah's homeland lived forever. Frosteria, in a sense, was never meant for humans. The biting cold was endless, and only a fire in one's home provided true warmth. However, living for eternity could also be one's curse, especially in an existence destined for loneliness.

The harsh wind blew, sending shivers through Eirah. She drew her fur cloak tighter around her body. "Perhaps immortality would be lovely at this moment, then I could walk outside bare if I so chose," she murmured to herself. "I mean, not that I would. But there would at least be the opportunity."

Eirah's teeth chattered as she stared through the darkness, up into the branches of the snow-covered trees where the moon's light shone. As on most nights, she couldn't get a wink of sleep, so she'd ventured out from her cozy cottage to the edge of the forest behind her home.

"Where are you, Adair?" Eirah whispered toward the familiar branch where he usually rested. Over the years, owls came and went, except for one who had continued to return since she was a child.

The beat of wings sounded, followed by a loud hoot piercing through the wind. A wide smile crossed her heart-shaped face as she peered up toward the stars. Bright ivory stood out against the night, and she took a step closer to the tree as the owl's talons cradled his familiar branch.

"Ah, there you are, sweet prince." She beamed, no longer thinking about the freezing weather.

Adair cocked his snowy-white head at her and released another hoot before hopping to a lower limb.

As always, Eirah lifted her arm and motioned at it. "Come on, it's the same as resting on a branch, only softer."

The owl watched her silently, his eyes glowing a brilliant orange. He inched nearer, and she took another step toward him—the closest they had ever been to one another—when a high-pitched squeak radiated in the distance.

The owl jerked up his head and darted off into the distance to snatch up his nightly meal. "Perhaps tomorrow we'll meet again." She sighed.

Some demons in Frosteria had animals that were their familiars. Humans didn't have that luxury—an owl she endlessly tried to provoke to land on her arm was the closest she would ever get.

Eirah glanced once more at the stars painting the obsidian sky. The moon rested above, seeming to watch over them, its shape the thinnest of slits on this night. If only the stars were made from ice and she held magic, then she would have created a frozen rope from water, latching onto one of their forms. She would have pulled it down to her hands and gifted the star to her father. Perhaps then he would smile, knowing her mother's soul may not have been eternal here but possibly somewhere else.

She wondered if she achieved such things, would a star's flesh be soft or hard? Would its temperature be cold or warm? And once in her hand, did the way it shone mean it would pulse like a heart?

"Enough with the nonsense, Eirah. So many foolish questions that will never be answered. And stop talking to yourself —the villagers already look at you strangely enough." Unless they wanted to purchase items from her and her father. Even then, she felt their heavy stares as they studied some of her more grim music boxes and marionettes. Those were for herself and herself alone.

"Bah!" She threw her hands up in the air and whirled around. "I don't give a damn what anyone thinks."

The snow sloshed beneath her boots as she headed back toward her cottage. After she closed the door behind her, a rush of heat pricked her frozen hands. A new log rested in the fireplace, flames eating away at its wooden layers. Her father —Fedir—glanced up at her from the desk in the corner of the room, his spectacles sitting low on his nose while he worked on attaching an arm to a marionette. Ever since she could remember, the sitting room had been littered with parts for toys and music boxes. Her father used to make weapons before Eirah was born, but when her mother became with child, his craft had turned to toymaking for both mortals and demons.

"Couldn't sleep?" she asked, removing her cloak and hanging it on the wall hook.

"No, but it seems you couldn't, either." He smiled, patting the stool beside him. Under the room's low light, the wrinkles beside his gray eyes seemed to have deepened these past few months. Even his chestnut hair held more streaks of gray.

Eirah warmed her hands by the fire for a moment, regaining the feeling in them before sinking down on the wooden stool. Her father hadn't slept well ever since Eirah's mother passed away from a cough that had turned fatal. Eirah had only been five years old then, but she'd taken over assisting her father after that. She'd thought he would marry again, and Eirah wouldn't have minded, yet he remained content with his toy-making and daughter.

At twenty, Eirah didn't know when, or if, she would ever leave home. But for now, she had her marionettes, music boxes, and wind-up toys. Before starting on one of her creations, she quickly pulled her dark hair into a braid, then wound up one of her unfinished boxes and opened it. She watched as the dancer spun in a circle, elegantly holding out her hands while wearing a gown of blue ice and matching flowers in her hair.

The music drifted around her, its melody a little too crackly. She needed to work on that, but before she could think more about it, the music stopped.

Damn. If she *did* have magic, she knew precisely what she would have done with it, created a dancer of *real* ice, and let her rotate for eternity without the song ever having to end. There would be no constant need to keep winding the box, and the mechanics wouldn't need constant tweaking.

"Are you going to paint her face?" her father asked, his gaze meeting hers.

She studied the smooth brown face of the dancer, the onyx

curls falling to her waist. "No, I like that no one knows what she's thinking or feeling."

"Gloomy thoughts, daughter."

"Ah, Papa, but they are the best thoughts for creating, aren't they?" She laughed, adjusting a piece of metal at the bottom of the box. She wound it up once more, letting the soft tinkling fill the room, this time the melody perfect.

"You're so much like your mother. And me—but the second part might be a terrible thing." He chuckled. "How about I make us some tea since our heads want to stay busy?"

"Peppermint, please." Eirah scooped up one of the incomplete marionettes for a customer. This one did desire a face. Lifting a brush, she dipped it into pink paint to make the marionette cheeks.

For the remainder of the night, Eirah concentrated on painting, carving, and drinking tea until the sun rose through the window, lighting up the room. Her mind hadn't rested once, taking her from one project to another, leaving some unfinished, some completed, even sparing a bit of time to make a deceased marionette wearing a wedding gown of all black. Too "macabre."

Her stomach rumbled, and she glanced down. "Oh, you troublesome thing, always getting in the way of work."

"Would you like me to start breakfast?" her father asked, using a needle to move around a minuscule piece of metal on a toy sleigh.

"No, it's my turn." With a yawn, Eirah stood from the stool and padded toward the kitchen when a knock pounded at the door.

"Tell the customer we don't allow them here this early." Her father frowned.

Eirah rolled her eyes. "Now, now, we can't run them off."

Even though she would have rather snatched a piece of fruit first, she brushed her palms down the front of her deep sapphire dress before opening the door.

Desmond, the village chieftain's son, stood on the porch, his thin lips pursed. "Good morning, Eirah." He pushed a few dark braids behind his ear, his mahogany eyes appearing as unenthusiastic as his expression. "There's to be a village meeting."

She arched a brow. "When?" Eirah's stomach now roiled with unease instead of hunger. It was much too soon for the monthly meeting, seeing as how they'd just had one the week prior.

"Now. It involves the king." His fingers fidgeted with the edges of his cloak.

Morozko... Even thinking his name unsettled her, and she'd never once met the Frost King. "What is it?"

"Father hasn't told me, but I know it isn't going to be pretty. Hurry. I need to finish rounding up the other villagers." With that, he turned on his pristine booted heel, adjusting his fur cloak, and trudged to the cottage next door. Desmond knew something, but she could tell the chieftain had most likely told him not to say anything. She'd grown up with Desmond—they were the same age, yet they'd never been close as he was too focused on carrying on his father's legacy.

When she turned to grab an apple, her father was already fastening his cloak. "It must be important if it involves the king. We'll have to eat later."

"Grabbing an apple first won't hurt anyone," she mumbled.

"You can have two when we return." He tossed Eirah her cloak.

"More like three." She grinned and wrapped the thick

369

fabric around her shoulders as they walked out into the snow. No one lingered in front of their homes as they all headed toward the center of the village. Most of the people had already gathered around the dais, where the chieftain stood in front of his carved throne, chatting with one of the elders. His thick gray fur cloak was bundled around him, and his onyx braids were drawn back with a leather strap.

Someone stepped beside Eirah, and she glanced over to find her friend toying with the lace of her cloak. "His Righteousness demands we come here," Saren said in a low voice. "Why doesn't the king come himself?"

"Perhaps because he's an arrogant prick." Eirah rolled her eyes. "Most likely too busy relaxing in a bath while sipping on a goblet filled with blood."

Saren pressed a fist to her mouth to muffle her laughter. "Indeed." They'd been friends since they could walk, even though everyone in the village noticed Saren—her long, golden hair, and eyes the color of the sky. She shone like sunshine and twinkled like the stars. Eirah had always preferred the shadows, but even shadows needed the sun sometimes.

The chieftain cleared his throat, taking a scroll from inside his cloak. "The Frost King is quite disappointed in us. In a week's time, there is to be a village celebration. There, he will choose a maiden sacrifice, then we will return once more to providing him with an annual animal sacrifice. If we deny his request, the entire village will end in bloodshed."

Gasps echoed throughout the crowd. Eirah's eyes widened, the cold, dry air stinging her flesh. How could that self-righteous bastard do this? Couldn't he see that the village had stopped sacrificing their animals because there was no reason to? If they sacrificed more, there wouldn't be enough to feed their bellies.

Vinti had held the ceremony ever since Morozko was crowned king—a pointless ritual with no true purpose except to please him.

"A maiden, you say?" one of the young men spoke up.

Eirah rolled her eyes at the fool, who must have been proud to be a man, safe.

"Only... one of his choosing." The chieftain glanced toward his son. "And if we don't allow him this, he will decimate the village for disrespecting him. To prove his point, he sent Jonah's hand after he was found near the king's palace. Jonah knew it was forbidden to go there unless summoned."

The crowd gasped, and Eirah's throat grew dry... he'd given a *hand* as a threat. Even though Jonah was a fool and shouldn't have been there, he didn't deserve to have his hand removed from his dead body and sent to the village. A chill crawled through Eirah, not for herself, but for someone very dear to her. If the king was to choose a sacrifice, then he would most likely choose the most beautiful girl in the village... *Saren*. Beside her, Saren paled.

"At the celebration," Eirah whispered to her friend, "keep your head down and wear the ugliest dress you own. Untidy your hair as though birds slept through the night in it."

"You do the same," Saren whispered back. "I don't want to lose anyone here, but especially you."

That was incredibly sweet of her friend to say, but Eirah didn't need to work on doing that at the celebration. She always looked unkempt, and the Frost King, in all his arrogance, would never choose her.

This was precisely why immortality was a curse. It created a blasé male who had nothing better to do than end an innocent's life because mortals chose not to be at his beck and call any longer. He and his wounded ego wouldn't even allow someone to choose to sacrifice themselves if they so wished.

The bastard.

Continue Eirah and Morozko's story in *Slaying the Frost King*.

COLLECT THE ENTIRE MORTAL ENEMIES TO MONSTER LOVERS SERIES!

Read these scorching hot romances in any order for monstrous romance, morally grey leads, and guaranteed happily-ever-afters!

ACKNOWLEDGMENTS

As always, I have so many people to thank for helping in various ways with this book.

First, my awesome Mortal Enemies to Monster Lovers authors—Carissa, Candace, Elle, Jess, and Helen. Thank you all for making the project so much fun! I've had a blast working with you and I'm thrilled to see all these wonderful books finally coming out. <3

As always, to my author wives—Carissa (again), Lasairiona, and Tracie. Thanks particularly for listening to my worries and enabling my fictional villainy on this one!

Alyssa and Andrew, Andra, Clare, Laura, and Meg. Thank you so much for your beta reading and editorial feedback, and especially for all the *squee*s and emojis! This was a departure from my usual, and it helped so much to see your enthusiasm for Zita and Sepher's story.

Natalie Bernard—for making INCREDIBLE cover art not just for my book but for the entire series. Thank you for being such an absolute pleasure to work with and producing such stunning results.

Saint Jupit3r Graphics—for designing the GORGEOUS under dust jacket covers for the series. I'm totally blown away by them and so excited to share them with the world. Thank you!

YOU! Yes, you. Thank you for reading this, for sharing on

social media, for reviewing, for telling your friends, for the messages and comments—for ALL of it. You let me keep doing this. <3

And last but never ever least—thank you to Russ. I was about to call you my partner in crime, but I just spotted I did that in my last one of these... but it's *true*! Still, I'll thank you for something different this time. Thank you for being my social secretary and making sure I still see actual people. XD All my love, always.

ALSO BY CLARE SAGER –
SET IN THE SABREVERSE

SHADOWS OF THE TENEBRIS COURT

Gut-wrenching romance full of deceit, desire, and dark secrets.

Book 1 – *A Kiss of Iron*

Book 2 – *A Touch of Poison* – Coming 2023, pre-order now.

BOUND BY A FAE BARGAIN

Steamy fantasy romances featuring unwitting humans who make bargains with clever fae. Each book features a different couple, though the characters are linked.

Stolen Threadwitch Bride

These Gentle Wolves

BENEATH BLACK SAILS

An enemies-to-lovers tale of piracy, magic, and betrayal.
Featuring Kat's sister Vice. Complete series.

ABOUT THE AUTHOR

Clare Sager writes fantasy stories with adventure, intrigue, darkness, and a heaping spoonful of steamy romance. Her favourite tropes include enemies-to-lovers, forced proximity, and tricky fae bargains that just might be more trouble than they're worth.

She lives in Nottingham, Robin Hood country, so it's no surprise she writes about characters who don't always play by the rules.

When she's not living in a fantasy world, she's sketching, lifting weights at the gym, or spending time with her husband and two troublesome cats. She loves stationery, coffee, and cocktails.

You can find her online home at www.claresager.com or connect with her on social media at the links below or by email at clare@claresager.com.

instagram.com/claresager

tiktok.com/@claresager

bookbub.com/authors/clare-sager

facebook.com/claresagerauthor

amazon.com/author/claresager

twitter.com/ClareSAuthor